Invisible Car Dealer

Peter de Lissovoy

Also by Peter de Lissovoy:

Feelgood: a trip in time and out

The Great Pool Jump, editor and co-author

The Angels of Zimbabwe

Wisconsin

Copyright © 2017 Peter de Lissovoy
All rights reserved.
ISBN: 978-0-9844139-5-9
Library of Congress Control Number: 2017904258

YouArePerfectPress, Lancaster, NH

If I say, Surely the darkness shall cover me;
even the night shall be light about me.

—Psalm 139

Invisible Car Dealer

I'm a car dealer, not the kind you think though—not the distinguished-looking gentleman with the golfer's tan who smiles you to the like-new Porsches under the lights and flags.

I look on as the cars migrate from place to place, like wild geese, as they find their way to you by a means something like Julie's "karma," I'm sure.

Freedom is everything to me now, how about you? At the moment I'm sitting by a blue lake far north of San Francisco, in Washington State, or Oregon, possibly Canada, somewhere or other like that, taking it easy, surrounded by water, green woods, and a few cars. The fishing's not too bad, and the weather is perfect, even when it rains. I've made my break with the world, or at least you have to give me credit for trying.

On a still day I can see my growing collection of antiques reflected on the shining waters. In front of my cabin I already have several rare old American beauties. The natives are friendly, and they're helping me with my research. They don't mind a bit that I'm going to restore them and make a mint back in L.A. They don't believe it for a minute. They think I'm a fool. They may sense that I am hiding out, too.

Other than hunting for cars, and fishing (for fish), there's not a hell of a lot to do around here. I don't believe there's a tennis court or a movie theater within a hundred miles. I live like a monk in a junkyard in the woods. But I won't be here forever, or I hope not. I enjoy what the day brings, and this country—the silvery air!—is so nice. The cloudy days have a pearly luster. There are a lot of Indians around here, something new to me, at the same time nothing new, these are the dispossessed otherwise we would not be here. I mean we "whites" call these people "the Indians," because Columbus thought he had arrived in India, so I've read somewhere, he thought he was in "the Indies," in his head. Talk about adding insult to injury, not even knowing who we were about to wipe out. A case of mistaken identity, for sure. Not only am I going to rob and murder you, but get your name and location wrong. Of course he and the ones to come were under no illusion *why* they were on these shores. *That* was crystal clear. No wonder they turn looks of blank hostility on me at the edge of town, when I'm on one of my outings. Well, sadly, it's human nature, from beginning to end.

Naturally, I notice the "Indians." By the way, by now, having been up here a while, I do know what nation, or tribe, these "Indians" belong to, of course, even if I know nothing about them, but like Columbus I am going to keep calling them the "Indians" since I am trying to keep my exact location quiet as you will understand if you keep reading this story. Anyway, who am I to try to improve on history—although soon enough I was going to try. At this, my heart stops, as I think of Julie, who would have found everything to love up here, starting with the "Indians," all the free time to hang out and pow-wow with them. Julie never calls them "the Indians." I feel like driving down to Berkeley and begging her to come up to stay with me and keep me company. No way she would, though. She's a woman of principle, I'll give her that. She's put her body on the line, in front of troop-carriers, for the Cause. She cut a fence once and snuck onto the nuclear reservation, for some reason best known to her. She was glad to go to jail for a hundred days. She's sold flowers on Telegraph Ave, gone hungry, been a pretty pan-handler, rather than sell out. So it's nothing, I guess, to deny me a little comfort, for the sake of a dead man.

This lake must be smack up to a reservation, the original, non-nuclear kind, that is. Strange how the same word is used for storing Indians and fissionable material. Julie would know what to make of that. No matter how cold they are with me, the Indians would be friendly to her, and she'd have half the nation in the cabin with us, feeding them off my car-buying funds, pouring my whiskey down their throats, and feeling solidarity forever. I can picture It easily—we'd all get drunk and go on the warpath together. Down with the white man! I'd get into the spirit myself under Julie's spell.

The more I am away from her, the more I think not only of her, but like her. I see the scene through her eyes. I think of her too much, it's true. Yes, some days it feels like the end of the trail for me, too. Trapped by too much freedom! I do have a lot of time on my hands. I don't know how much more freedom I can take. I try to keep my mind off Julie—if only I could. Maybe she's forgotten about me. Women have such capacious storage rooms in their hearts, they just shift things around a little, slip you behind or next to someone or something else, put you in mothballs, there's always room for more, we're all one big happy family in their minds. But I have my freedom.

I've bought too many cars. I stand on my doorstep and count more than a dozen. I glance out my cabin window and see cars rumbling through the forest like bears, peering up at me like giant trouts from the deep. Their headlights streak the night sky like falling stars. I'm about to go broke buying relics from these farmers. At first I loved this country up here, and still do, with its buying opportunities, but I can't afford to stay up here and buy more cars. I buy them to keep from thinking about buying them. In the city at least you can get rid of them again. What with the cars themselves and the extra chassis and bits and pieces I've purchased for my restorations, my edge of the lake is beginning to look like a wrecker's yard, almost like Dahomey's, down in Richmond. I can't stop buying old cars, and I can't leave here yet either.

It's nothing but a misunderstanding, but what a misunderstanding. A tragedy all around. A case of mistaken identity, of which the world abounds. I have to use all my self-control every moment to keep from just abandoning everything, all my gear, all my rusty cars, everything including my senses, giving up and jumping in my '69 Jag cherried-out XKE convertible, putting the pedal to the metal, and heading south (or perhaps west, I won't say, as I'm sure you can understand) to California once more.

Nothing more oppressive than all this peace and quiet. Too much of a good thing. But in a rush, I understand again what I have to understand. I calm myself. I jump in the motorboat and run out on the lake for some relaxing fishing. First though, right in the

3

Invisible Car Dealer

middle, I cut the motor, and dive in and swim around, soaking in the water's cold energy like my own wished-for lucidity. Hey, it's beautiful, and the sun is dancing on the waves so pleasantly today for a change. I haul myself back aboard with considerable effort and make for the far shore and one of the good fishing spots I know. Now my soul enters into the zen of the casting and waiting, and all the tension begins to ease.

Ah well, just enjoy. Once I happen to turn my head and look to my left at a protruding finger of shoreline. A man, yes, I see he's an Indian, rises up from behind some bushes and stares at me. He stretches out his arm. For God's sake, he's got a rifle! My hand jumps a foot toward the motor as my fishing rod clatters to the bottom of the boat. Hell, there's no point starting the motor. It's too late. If he's going to shoot . . . nothing happens. Talk about paranoid, Jesus. Well, for good reason, or *a reason*. I berate myself anyway. I'm going to lose it soon. It shows the state my nerves are in. The guy finally quits staring at me and stoops again. He must have been stretching his legs, his cramped fingers. He goes back to what he was doing. I see he's picking berries.

Yesterday a couple of boys came by wondering if I had a rightside exhaust manifold for a '79 Ford V-8. I took them out behind the place, and showed them my '55 Chevy, my '67 El Dorado, my '54 Ford Victoria with the glass roof! Classics! Not a wrecking yard! Are the local people beginning to talk? But they got the picture and realized maybe they could sell me something. They managed to drag me to three or four far-flung locations first in town and then on some farms to look at piles of scrap metal they imagined were still cars and had begun to have greenback delusions about. And that's all they were, junkheaps, a waste of my time, if such a thing were still possible. I would never have bought anything, but I took the precaution of bringing not one dollar with me. I have no intention of buying anything more, unless of course it's something special. I won't have any money left with which to clean up these rough diamonds later.

And I almost bought something from these guys. What a close call. Looked at in a certain light those rust piles of theirs were promising. Thank God I left my cash in the stove, what little is left of it. We went back to town and I bought them a beer instead—on my tab. The bartender is a nice guy, something more than an

4

acquaintance by now. He was the first person I met up here, and I found my cabin through him. And two of my cars. I hope he is named Packy, as that's what I call him. He believes in my restoration project. Everyone has faith in cars. As good Americans. I believe it's in the Constitution. So my credit is still good with Packy, at least for another month when I can't pay rent. They're all beginning to know me at Packy's bar, the guy with all the cars in front of his cabin. I'm becoming a character. I'm wearing thin.

I steered the conversation away from cars toward something else as soon as I could. After a beer, I found I wanted to buy something worse than ever—*anything*. I wasn't listening to what was being said, but instead doing mental calculations. I realized I was scaring myself for nothing. I could afford to buy half a dozen more cars, depending. After all, I'm up here, I might as well make the most of it. The old-timers used to park their vehicles behind the barn and let them rot. If only they'd had the foresight to put them on blocks and throw an old tarp or something over them.

The boys in Packy's were bitching about the Indians. You'd think by now there would be very little left to blame the Indians for, wouldn't you? Not so, everybody around here still hates and blames them—just for still breathing, I guess. Not enough tourists around this summer? It's the Indians' fault one way or another. Taxes too high? Welfare for the forest niggers. The fishing lousy? That's clearly the Indians' fault, since they gill-net the lakes and rivers in the spring, their treaty right. Time to tear up a few more treaties, a waste of good paper, why did our forefathers bother? I have to keep my mouth from hanging open that at this late date the Indians are still a problem for somebody (other than me, I mean). They're to blame for everything, or at least quite a few things, to hear the clientele of Packy's cry about it. If anybody could blame an Indian for his problems, I guess I could. Sometimes, on these long afternoons, I'm tempted to tell my story.

"Hey, think about it, we did to them what the Germans did to the Jews, didn't we? Only worse. We about really finished the job. Did you know that Hitler read up on American history when he was trying to figure out what to do with the Eastern Europeans and the Jews? That's how he thought up his plans. From reading American history as regarding the Indians. That's a true fact. I read it in a book. Maybe they deserve a few lousy fish, for Christ sake!"

They scowled in their beer at that. They were thinking, all right, even if that is possible, which it isn't, it's going too far, and what does it have to do with anything, or me, anyway? And they were right. They had their real problems, unlike mine. (I don't mean to make light of my sins, or crimes, if that's what it is, I was in dire straits, but like most people, my friends in Packy's had come by their problems in an honest and straightforward manner, whereas I had somehow gone out of my way to acquire mine, I don't know just how, but it feels that way.) Strange how with Julie I always felt like a foaming out the mouth conservative, and with these guys I am a bleeding hearted liberal.

But on the subject of the Indians. I disagreed with both sides in their cultural argument, with Julie and her and her friends' idea that the European settlers had disrupted a Garden of Eden on the American plains, and also with the average American citizenry's thoughtless acceptance of the status quo (now that events had caused me to confront it) resulting from sanctimonious Manifest Destiny we had been taught, brainwashed I'd say, without ever once considering the monstrous, dismal, and bloodthirsty deeds. I was somewhere in the uncharted middle of this dispute, as it turned out, the unexplored depths of it, a vague philosophical terrain wider than the Plains themselves. I was about to get lost in it, wandering frozen and numb, a new pioneer on a disappearing trail. This is what happens to you apparently when some untoward incident causes you to take a hard look through the cocoon of culture that always surrounds us. A dreamscape unravels. Was this someday going to happen to more white people than me? That's debatable. In the tavern they were having their doubts about me, even thinking how they would get me back for my comments, and I added loudly, *"We stole all their land, man!"*

"Stole, hell," shouted somebody. "Stole nothin', *fought for it,* an' won!"

Packy, the bartender, saved things. "Stole it *fair an' square,* ha ha ha ha!"

Fair and square! Good old Packy. He filled my glass with another draft, the guy with all the cars in his front yard, and I raised it to him, and everybody, and we all laughed good-naturedly, or evil-temperedly.

Invisible Car Dealer

Julie and I had a special spot on a hillcrest a ways northeast of town from which there was a view of the Bay. We'd start out on the highway toward Moraga-Orinda, then curve up into the hills on back roads. Some of the climb was slow going, with sharp hairpin turns, and the driver had to pay attention. Once parked on the edge of a sheer drop, there was the bright shock of the lighted grids of the cities, the graceful pearls of the freeways and bridges. We always seemed to go there at night. The first moment held the same awe, no matter how many times we'd seen it before, even if we'd been arguing on the way up.

Julie was hip. She saw what should be. She lived God only knew how, usually by attaching herself (she had some sort of degree) to a social welfare agency, clinic, or outreach program, of which there were always plenty in a town like Berkeley. She always had some scheme or other going to milk the poor government. But she was no bureaucrat, she never could knuckle under to somebody else's ideas, and her independent spirit got her into trouble. She was always coming up with a better approach to the question of dental care for the children of unwed mothers, or how to charm unwed dentists who only aspired to move to the Berkeley Hills into volunteering some attention to the teeth of "street mothers," or whatever. She saw it as her duty to be creative and helpful, and couldn't understand how others could just plod along in a straight and selfish line. I tried to explain to her just how numerous such others are, and that there was no point clashing with such a majority, but she couldn't dig it. She needed to help people, she said. That was another difference between us, a failing of mine, according to her, I didn't "need people," whatever that meant, since half the time she was fighting with them. So anyway her career was pretty rocky in spite of her best intentions. Her hole card was her utter serenity if her principles got her in trouble, or even fired. She was one of those dignified people who are always resigning in protest from something. If she had to go out on her lonesome, it was okay with her. She meant it, and could handle the fallout, even selling beads and trinkets on Telegraph Avenue to the tourists like an Indian till she found a new job.

I worked nine-to-five, or more often nine-to-nine, selling cars for a Pontiac dealer in Oakland. I had been doing it for two years, and despised it more and more each day, perhaps because I didn't "need people." I've noticed that the most successful salesmen are the gregarious ones, the kind who need people a whole lot, who just wolf people down, bones and all. I hated the red tape and rigmarole in the legitimate car business, the worries about inventory, interest rates, the Japanese competition, the fickle customers most of all. Oh God, having to put on the dog and charm the "buying public"! Those long hours I was having to put in for Harmless Harry, the Pontiac dealership's slavedriver of a sales manager, were killing me.

Julie *looked* like she came from Berkeley, from her long blonde hair to her sandals. I looked like, well, downtown Oakland— I can't help it, I like a sharp suit, or I used to at that time. I was just a more or less regular white guy from a small town in Illinois (or somewhere like that), and a lot of Californians are like me, believe it or not. Years after I had migrated out here in search of the normal illusory things people come to California for, and found instead the real California, I finally recovered from shock and developed a taste for Mexican food, partly because Julie made her own tortillas. She well understood the interest and the importance of Spanish culture, and spoke Spanish, the better to minister to the illegal mothers in her charge. I was so white I was a gringo even in California! Listen, I can't emphasize enough to you how average a white person I am, because that is the only way the strange adventure I was in for can be explained to you.

Invisible Car Dealer

To tell the truth, like so many Americans, my pride in the "melting pot" of our society lay chiefly in the pleasant assurance that I personally had never been in it. There were a lot of things I hadn't seen before I moved to California from the suburbs of the Midwest (or somewhere or other like that). For instance, I'd never seen a live Indian, at least as far as I knew, even though I used to go fishing in Wisconsin (or Maine or North Dakota), and there were Indian reservations up there. I guess I was too young to go to the casinos was all, probably. It was ancient history to me. Anyway I knew no better.

This may sound idiotic, but I am so white it had never crossed my mind that there were Indians still walking around among us coping with life like everyone else, after their fashion, I mean normal Joes, like you and me, in contradistinction to glamorous Hollywood movie types. Seriously, have you ever really entertained such an idea? I mean, be honest (if you are an average, honest, extremely white small-town person like me). Well, I hadn't. Probably you have, but I can't help it, I'm just telling you about me. Maybe that seems odd, I mean, now that we have run across the real California instead of the dream. But the truth is, I believe, the further back East you go, but not too far, in the central part of the country anyway, where the white people really congregated and laid waste, you don't have to go too far, a lot of plain old Americans in a state like I come from, Illinois (or somewhere), have never actually seen any live Indians, at least if you're a boy from the suburbs like me. There may be thousands of them still left walking around, and now I know there certainly are, but they must be hiding away pretty well, either according to their personal tastes, or more likely because the government makes them do so, driven underground from ongoing persecutions by the gringos in general spearheaded by the FBI.

Poker, blackjack, slots, and the billiards tournaments on the reservations must be changing this now for the average white player or gambler. Then one day, I'll never forget it, I read in the paper about the standoffs between the Indians out West and the FBI and other federals, and the romance of it, that those people were still fighting, still holding out, in fact shooting it out, well it almost knocked me down, I was so moved and impressed. I'm sorry, there wasn't any question whose side I was on, the Indians',

9

what other side could there be? These were the underdog's underdogs (and I have always been an underdog), and I used to silently cheer for them in front of the big TV at the sports bar I used to hang out at back home whenever a little news came on. Strangely, this did not ameliorate the extreme whiteness of my condition. The realities of American history were still very remote to me back then. I did not think of sharing my sympathies or feelings. I vaguely understood it would have been inappropriate to do so in that particular tavern. But I guess I have always been a rebel at heart, in spite of putting up with my oppressive years at the Pontiac dealership.

The thing that got me watching those protests and armed standoffs out on the plains was that the beleaguered Indians stood for something spiritual and meaningful to them, it was a last ditch effort for them, and what was the FBI doing, I didn't know, if not protecting us whites—from what or whom, some Indians? It seemed absurd and even offensive that whites needed protecting at this date. How cruel could you be? I knew that much even before that fateful night Julie and I drove up to our hilltop with its view in a desperate and dreamy state of mind.

In certain taverns in East Oakland (among other places), it is altogether another story, too, and on many a back road on the West Coast, and elsewhere, I was about to find out. I hate to tell you, and Andrew Jackson, Kit Carson, John Wayne fans and the rest, but the Indian wars might not really be over, even now. But I am getting ahead of my story. You have no idea why I have Indians on the brain so, but if you keep reading you are about to find out. At this point I am just trying to establish my credentials as the most normal white American. That should not be hard for someone like me to do, believe me.

It could have been not just me but anybody that discovered they were white. But you know, these days, white people aren't all that into describing themselves so, and it would be bad taste to do so, as we are all Americans, by now, and at the same time they don't want to be thought of as not hip. This is something I have learned. (Back then it would have all sounded absurd to me, that is, I was about as white as white can be, and these cultural questions were under every radar.) Try telling your neighbor that he or she is a *white* person—get what I mean? They think you are insinuating something. I know what I'm talking about because I was just the same, before that terrible night of Julie's and mine.

What I'm saying is, we have all been in the soup probably, but which pot is the question. We all have our limitations, that much is clearer to me every day. Julie had hers, I had mine. It was the source of our problems, our arguments, our private culture clash, and great sex. (You can easily plug in your own story into mine so far, I'm sure, but you won't feel that way in a moment, if you keep reading about what happened to Julie and me on our hillcrest that night, and yet that is when our story, yours and mine together, truly become one.) In short, there is always enough blame to go around. It's hard to precisely locate the guilty party, if it wasn't Adam himself of course, who blamed Eve. So by no means was it all Julie's fault, I was always first to tell her. (That would always make her laugh bitterly.) If what we had in bed held the manic allure of a desperate drug, or just because of our problems, our differences, in our private sky it was always the heat of the night, as a matter of fact, it was usually the Fourth of July, and the fireworks about to get out of control, and burn somebody. It's a well-known fact too that what hits you in the face came straight from your heart.

In my memory of the night that it happened, the sparkling view from our hill had been more compelling than ever. No smog, twinkling skies and Christmas tree freeways with all the stars and colored lights below seeming to go on in an infinite glitter in all directions as if life on earth and in the heavens were one. Maybe we'd been smoking some of Julie's Colombian. No, I'm sure I'd been drinking. I rarely smoked her stuff. I don't even think we'd been fighting or anything that night, but we were both dissatisfied in general, you know. Julie was unhappy that some community group she was involved with had failed to get funded by the government and might have to disband (de-tribe). She had her money problems too, worse than mine, although on another order since, although she'd half starved once or twice (so she claimed, and I believed her), she still thought money grew on trees. I was thoroughly sick of my job, the grueling hours, complaining customers, and poor commissions, because the country was going through a mild recession, sales were off, damn the country! People weren't buying enough cars, that was the only problem, if they just bought more cars, the good times would roll for everyone, especially guys like yours truly. Damn the Japanese and the Germans! Damn General Motors! Damn the Pontiac dealership, and my sales manager in particular who had knocked a point off our commissions, "Harmless Harry," as we called him, and as he was called, matter of fact, by himself, on his own business cards. That was the name of his used-car lot before he went with the dealership, "Harmless Harry's." He held onto the moniker affectionately. What an asshole, a phenomenal salesman, a lover and needer of people, a cannibal in fact, eat you alive, unconscious cog on the big wheel.

Where a wide shoulder at a curve looked through a sheer break in the wooded slope, our secret spot, about six feet from the edge, we soaked in the awesome and almost meaningful expanse of mankind's pretty signal lights. She smoked a joint. Stars and hisses. "It's like some cellular level, molecular level, isn't it . . . there's level after level—thank God!" she muttered trippily, tossing her head, singing out green smoke, offering me the joint which I didn't take.

"No, it looks like an anthill of army ants where every ant is required by the enforcer ants to strap on like little miner's helmets, with those little headlamps on them."

That made her giggle. I knew that it would, especially when she was stoned. But it was too grim (that was why I'd said it, as the grass makes you see every image so literally). She frowned away my ants.

"You know why it's so beautiful? Because it makes you really see you're obviously part of something larger and wholer, right? And up here we get an intimation of the next level, higher than this hill, and up and up and up, don't you think? It's all a *symbol,* isn't it?"

I almost said, well, send your grant proposal to that level! But the view was starting to take hold of me too, banishing everything morose and petty. The odd reflection came to me that it was the cars down there, the too many cars that everyone complains about, the *cars* that were making this awe-inspiring beauty, all that unstoppable glittering we were gazing down upon, and inspiring this talk of the "next level."

"The fires of the Native Americans," Julie mumbled almost to herself, sort of privately, in the awe-drawl of the marijuana. The *what?* I thought. She had gone off in her thoughts, she did that, God knew where. "If we knew what they knew, we could get out of this mess," she added.

That did it. Which mess did she mean? Not our ill-starred relationship! Perhaps our separate personal dilemmas which were weighing on us tonight, coming to a head up here, a sort of synergistic sum of our singular messes? No, the grander mess, no doubt, "modern life," which she loved to weigh in on, that was what she alluded to. If by any chance even unconsciously it was our chaotic love life she was complaining about, I resented her bringing the Indians or anyone else, especially all of "modern life," into it. I suspected that was just what she was doing.

"In the future," I really couldn't ever follow her sentimental drift, but for diplomatic reasons I elected not to inform her again of something she already knew, "with solar power, *after* solar, *after* wind—we'll cook with the *pure light,*" I said hopefully and facetiously, as I couldn't help it. I was doing my best to get into the spirit and ever failing. But after all the *pure light* might not yet belong exclusively to any faction. She gave me a wildly suspicious look and ignored my remark.

"The thing is, up here, I feel we'll just muddle through somehow, I really do," she said. "I always *do* feel that way," Julie added rapturously. An image came to me of what Julie meant by "we"—it was hardly she and I. An old noble animal, one of those whose fate Julie was deeply concerned about, which I like too as well as the next guy, a panda, or a bear, seemed to waddle near. A giant sea tortoise struggled toward the shore and its traditional nesting grounds, not giving one turtle-shit about *me.*

There was finally an oppressiveness and monotony in the commotion of lights below us that almost did suggest some primal process in a microscope. It was very good to be high above it, at another "level." I saw where along some road a gapers' block of cars made a necklace of lights bunched tight like pearls. *There a traffic jam was shining!* I was glad I was not in that one. I felt that if you could ever just get a little distance, a little height and distance on things, a little freedom from it all, like we had up here but for a moment, everything would be okay. This was the key to the puzzle, it was quite simple, you know, never mind the fires of the Indians. Never mind what we will never know. And now I have my freedom and my distance, and I know.

It must have been a construction or sewer project down there, not a traffic jam, because I saw that some guys smaller than ants were using arc welding equipment, tiny intense sparklers throwing out blue, white, and orange sparks.

"Check it out!" I pointed at the miniature explosions far below.

"Ooh, cool!" she cried, and for a moment we shared joy.

"And think of it, they are fixing some main pipe, some culvert, which results in that beauty," I couldn't help adding, jeopardizing togetherness. But I sincerely felt grateful for the moment. I like the commonplace beauty, the *lowest* level of things, too. Don't I get to be sincere too?

"Do you get it?" I asked in response to her silence.

"No, not when you put it like that," she said, but mildly. We were back on familiar ground. We rested silently and happily enough for a time in the sheer luxury of the whole lovely vision off our cliff, in our separate fashion, our usual fashion, yet together, not tormenting ourselves further over our dispute as to what the vision might be *of*.

Infinitesimal blue and orange sparks disappearing in black deeps. For a second I believed that we would witness something extraordinary, an unprecedented beacon. Our souls flew toward the million lights, valley of flowers, ships on the sea. We made love in a frenzy, right in the small car. Had the brake released, we would have gone over the cliff. Anguish of the gear knob and bucket seats only heightened our delirium. It was the last time, so I'm glad. There was a cloying feverishness, as if all we had left was each other, and it was not a good thing.

There's something so fine about speeding down a winding wooded slope at night (in my Alfa anyway). The still forest comes at you almost blindly, pine and eucalyptus in lonely waves of dark fragrance through the open windows, precise engagements of the gearshift, edgy protests of the brakes, bright engine roar, deep throaty, then high-pitched, downshifting, so lovely, so lonely, the forest floor muffling your passage with its masses of dead leaves.

When the undeniable impact—no, at first, merest insinuation—of life—someone's life—against metal came, I caught her eyes in the mirror in a dream. I saw her instant trouble. I was no more startled than if I'd nicked myself shaving. I hadn't seen a thing. But on the face in the mirror there was the tear of blood. Whatever it was stuck in the wheels, and a violent shuddering from below shook us in our seats, and I knew then.

"Oh!" she cried softly, no more than letting out a breath. And now came the dreadful terror. We lurched over it into the air. Then nothing—we were free. I hit the brakes. For a second we waited, for what I don't know, our senses, I guess. The space in the car between Julie and me was so big, so charged, it was like a black cave in which we could barely see each other. One of the headlights had been smashed, and the lone beam filtered up the road. I stared into the patch of misty silver light as though something else might come at me. The hood had buckled just visibly. Julie breathlessly cried, "He fell right in front of the car!" and I finally accepted the strange, new, and very soon inconsolable reality. She started to follow me, but I pushed her back in the car. There was really no cause for us both to retain the specific image, whatever it was going to be. The regret was already unbearable.

"See if you can find the flashlight. Under the seat I think." I couldn't remember if I had a flashlight in the car, but I believed not. I hoped not. It would keep her busy for a moment.

There was room in my fear and confusion for anger. How could this happen to *me?* How could some idiot choose *my* car to jump or fall in front of? Know what I mean? I'm sure you do. I ran quickly back up the road, and almost stumbled on the dark lump before I saw it. The breath went out of me in a rush. In spite of Julie's cry, and my own resignation, I had still hoped for a deer or a dog. A small figure in a stained windbreaker lay molded to the dim road. I who had never before seen death recognized it unmistakably. The hands and feet reached out at intricate angles, seeming to search like tendrils, as if the body were trying to enter the earth already. He might have been dead for hours, and it seemed to have nothing to do with me.

I picked up an arm. It was limp, and I awkwardly felt for a pulse. I was sure there was none. His hand was sticky and moist. My eyes were still getting used to the starlight. I gazed at the forest. Where could he have come from? Could I have been going that fast? I dropped the hand, which fell with the finality of a stone. Anguish and sorrow shot through me. I turned the head gingerly with my fingertip and saw a very Indian face, even I could tell that, like an image from an old Western, big eagle nose and sunken flat cheekbones. An old Indian man, greasy grey hair hanging down, in a cheap jacket with the logo of some school's sports team on it, the Cougars, incongruous, a kid's jacket. The eyes were fixed and glassy.

As immediate and overwhelming as the shock was, I felt increasingly remote from the scene and had to make an effort to bring myself back and keep confronting it. His face, hair, and clothing were wet with glossy blood seeming to come from all over him, every pore, and something else. The stench of cheap wine was in the air. I smelled my hand. Most of what was all over him was Thunderbird wine. At this moment, the corpse moaned, unless I was hearing things. I jumped about a foot. I gazed again into those dead glazed eyes. He'd never moaned! The woods themselves, the stars, my heart had groaned. It must have been a reflex action of his lips, some last bit of air escaping past his vocal chords. I was hallucinating out of fear amplified by Jack Daniels and all the secondhand smoke she had blown at me up there. For a moment I stood there completely frozen, imagining things, unable to deal with the reality.

Out of the corner of my eye, I saw a soaked and shredded paper sack twenty feet away. I walked over and kicked it, the bottles inside all broken. Green glass of cheap wine bottles glittered out the mouth of the bag. What a deadly sweet smell. The scene explained itself, even resolved itself. I felt my own soul wandering inexorably on its way down highways. I could feel my own blood moving in hot spurts within me, seeking its course, like intoxicating wine going down the gullet. This interlude was an aching alternation of violent sorrow and absurd serenity, dull pain and damnable, strange excitement. I glanced up at the sky, and at the forest around me. I believed I could have told another car coming, yet the curves in the road and the thick tree cover could hide things till the last moment and surprise you.

I walked back to the car, trembling, but able, I hoped, to seem cool. I felt very sorry for what the machine of the universe had just rolled in front of me and done. Julie was sitting there trying to be calm too. In fact she was frozen in shock. She didn't mention whether she'd found the flashlight or not. Perhaps she hadn't even looked. Some of the withdrawn stillness of the forest seemed to have entered her while I'd been away. She faced me with eyes bright, seeming to await my news, some decision. My love for her existed now burning without shadow, under the spotlight of total crisis and death.

I didn't say anything to her, just took off driving fast, thinking that would be all the news I'd ever give Julie. As for that I was in for my usual surprise. As usual I was sadly and completely deceiving myself when it came to Julie. Neither of us spoke for twenty or thirty minutes, till we came down out of the hills to the towns, and nearly to Berkeley. During this time I deluded myself it was because no more needed be said. For once, in this happenstance, she was leaving things to me, I imagined glibly. All this time she had been thinking steadily, and summing things up in her own way, of course, and going to and arriving at her places, so we were miles apart by now.

"Aren't we going to the police?" she said in a distant voice as if she were suddenly waking from a deep sleep and taking her bearings. It was the silence that I had mistaken, as if I were the only one coming to conclusions. For a second I couldn't believe it. She was only saying such a thing now? I realized I was being very stupid when it came to Julie, my usual mode, that hadn't changed anyway. But we might have gone to the police before reaching Berkeley! What could she be thinking? Hiding my tremendous disappointment, I just said, "It would be senseless. What for?"

"Somebody's got to help him!"

"He's beyond help."

"They might help him. Are you sure?"

I didn't say anything.

"You don't know. You can't be sure. We have to report it."

"I'm sure. It's been reported."

"What do you mean?"

"To the Cosmos."

She took that in. I knew that she would. She knew what I meant, must hear that I meant it, and that there was something that she ought to respect, by her own lights, regardless of her qualms.

"You have to come clean about it."

"If I'll ever be clean, I already am, and if not—"

"Others are involved."

"Who? You are, that's all."

"You don't say! Everyone's involved in something like this. If he's really dead! His family. *He might need help!* We have to tell somebody, man!"

"We hit him going over sixty. One nuclear bomb can ruin your whole day, Julie."

"You don't mean you're planning to forget it? To run? You'll regret it your whole life! He's lying back there."

"Why didn't you say something earlier? It happened nearly an hour ago. It's only the bomb, Julie. Let's boycott it. Have a protest. What say? Since when do you like to talk to cops?"

"I like to talk to them when they can help me, for God's sake! When someone may need their help!"

"Julie, this is our lives!"

"That's what I'm thinking about! Our lives!"

For myself I couldn't help picturing my whole life before me, from the little plans I had for tomorrow, to the whole pattern of my larger hopes, especially for my eventual freedom from the car lot, you know? I didn't think I'd regret anything, unless I caved in and took the rap. How would that help that dead Indian now? As for helping him, maybe she should have seen him.

"Julie, your pupils are dilated, your eyes are red, you're stoned on weed, and I'm sure I've drunk more than the legal limit too. You want to go talk to cops?"

She had no answer, at least she said nothing. With a lump in my throat I thought to myself that the poor Indian might be calling on his comrades to even the score and push me off a cliff the next time I drove up that way, he might wish me ill personally, but I was certain he wouldn't blame me for not going to the law, and would have been surprised if I had given myself up. Being an Indian, I mean. He might have understood a white guy being that stupid. But if he wasn't that stupid, he would respect that I wasn't. The very grief and guilt that I felt saw my road ahead clear.

"Hey, I can't bring the guy back to life, that's the only cause for regret from here on out, unless we get the fucking law mixed up in it, cops and lawyers forever, that'll be something to regret," I said in a whisper. I reached out and squeezed her hand, an unequivocal appeal. "Believe me he was gone, Julie, gone. If you don't think I'm sorry about it, I give up trying to understand you, I really do. Maybe you should have seen. No . . . of course I am *sorry.*"

"Oh Christ!" She began to sob. "You were speeding! You're a terrible driver for a car salesman! You're so absent-minded! You were looking over at me when he walked in front of the car. I saw him do it. So what—if it was his fault! I mean I am your witness. He just slipped right out of the forest! I mean he slipped, and fell, I saw it. But you did it. I mean, it happened to *you.*"

She was hip, smoked dope, had visions, like me took the underdog's side, despised everything "commercial," ate healthy food, was a quasi-vegetarian (ate eggs and salmon), believed you are what you eat, believed in the healing power of music, that plants can hear music, that plants have feelings, had taken acid quite a few times, assumed there were higher "levels," was anti-nuke etc., even though she couldn't see that *this was the bomb,* was a sort of a socialist, if she understood that sort of thing, constantly worked for the betterment of humanity, worried about the plight of the farm workers and the quality of the air and the well-being of all God's creatures, practiced sexy yoga, jogged sometimes, had sold flowers from a stand on Telegraph Avenue, and was as righteously agitated, as intensely serene, as mellowly stirred up, and crazily sincere as the most overwrought and laid-back Berkeley-ite there ever was or will be, and just as damned *conventional!*

"Julie, think about *me!* While you are thinking about everyone else, think of *me* for a change!"

"That's who I *am* thinking about. Who the fuck do you think I am thinking about? *You.* And *me—me,* of course—*us!*"

I finally felt the answering pressure of her hand in mine I'd been waiting for.

Yes, I was driving one-handed. I was almost driving no-handed I was imploring her so. A violent emotion racked me, chaotic and dense, into which my whole life seemed to sink like into deep erotic mud, my soul sucked into a blinding red sun. I felt my fingerhold on reality being ripped away by love and love only hitting me a pure jolt.

She wanted me to risk going to jail (and going into debt to lawyers forever) not only for my own good of course, naturally, but so we could continue being together. The feeling was like being kicked in the stomach—and loving it. I was tempted to collapse into her sure arms and let her take over. Which one of us was right, I really didn't know.

All at once, I felt release, granted first by a proud waive of the Indian's spirit, although I was certain he was harboring enmity for me at another "level," but no less by Julie's virtuous, precious love. I knew she meant every word, and I was proud of her, and so grateful to her. I could still smell the blood and the exploded sweetish wine, it was on my hands, feel the dumb thump of life on metal, then the violent commotion in the wheels, hear her first faint cry. It was all as if not even a second ago. But it was fading fast. She was asking what I finally could not give, the sane and sanitary process she asked for was too much. Sitting with her shoulder to shoulder, but worlds apart already, I saw myself speeding away down unmapped roads, into solemn unknown freedoms.

"It was a Native American we hit back there, wasn't it," she said suddenly, softly and soberly.

I hadn't wanted to add that particular information to the volatile mix that was Julie's mind, for obvious reasons, but she must have seen something.

"They won't bother much about an 'Indian,' right?"

That thought had never explicitly crossed my mind just like that and I didn't reply.

"I saw him," she said in an insinuating tone.

The only thing I could think was how unfortunate that she had been the one staring straight ahead at that moment while I must have glanced at her fondly and seen nothing. I should have had my eyes on the road, especially on that winding road. I didn't like where she was going right now.

"We're all guilty of what happened to the 'Indians,' even this one, that's what you're thinking, isn't it! I know *you!*"

No, that was what she was thinking, not what I was thinking. But that was brilliant actually. I had to bite my tongue to keep from telling her so. I hadn't thought it through as far as all that, that was for sure, but now that she mentioned it, yes, the whole white American race, every white infant and white senior citizen, especially the seniors as they were that much closer to the genocide, and even every last immigrant and "illegal alien," too, every Russian Jew and Middle-Eastern refugee from the ends of the earth that's come to these shores yesterday, all are guilty, enjoying the fruits of history, of genocide, guilty as charged, now that she had said it—and so they had all as good as *caused* it, too. Why hadn't I thought of that before? Probably because I had never thought about Indians in my life before (except when she was stoned and brought them up), I mean outside of a movie theater or the TV news.

But now I had thought it. It was a stark sad fact. That sorrowful and bitter U.S. history of ours had turned that Indian into an alcoholic and a non-car owning pedestrian as well, and had culminated in this cross-cultural tragedy.

"You know what, you're right, Julie," I said. Maybe African Americans should be exempted for obvious reasons, but I'm not even sure of that.

"It's not your responsibility because far worse has been done to Native Americans," she went on, developing my defense so brilliantly, "and society or American history is responsible for his walking along the road dead drunk, and even falling down in front of you—but not *you! Everybody* caused this! Not *you,* or me. That's it, that's your reasoning, or excuse, isn't it?"

She kept on in this vein. What was she saying! Only Julie, with her special genius. And I listened. Yes, indeed, she was right. How well she put it! She was frankly and coldly right, never mind the prosecutorial irony with which she delivered her speech. I was amazed and nearly grateful. They all enjoyed the proceeds and the fruits of the wholesale robbery and murder of the Red Man that had driven him into alcoholism and faltering pedestrianism on dark roads, and caused this very accident, it was certain. The finishing touch would have been for me to hand myself over to the cops and the overburdened and unpredictable California court system that had no jurisdiction over genocides, which lets real mass murderers go scot free, and would probably put me away for five years thanks to the lawyers I would have given all my money to. That would have been the true crime, one against good sense.

"I can't bear it! If he were white, would you sneak away like this?" Julie concluded her now less convincing case.

"The thing is, with my luck, something about me, I don't know, they would nail me for it, especially for his being an Indian." What I was thinking bitterly and with horror was that the first Indian I had ever had the opportunity to meet, as it were, or run across—I had run over! I felt evilly singled out, deprived, depraved, and panic came over me in a wave.

At this she sobbed uncontrollably for half a minute or so, overcome and distraught. She finally said no more on the topic, and in fact said no more at all. I gently tried to pick up the thread and spin out her own idea to a positive and useful conclusion.

"Look, isn't the irony of being judged by the authorities for accidentally running over a guy whose entire family and race have been systematically wiped out by our country on purpose as a matter of policy even a little much for you, Julie? I'm just trying not to become a *statistic,* which is what they have planned for every one of us, as you well know, Julie, particularly those of you who take government grants, which they would find out about immediately and that would be the end of that! I mean, you want us to give up to the same forces that mowed down whole villages of the Native Americans in the bloody dawn! Now the two-faced palefaces are going to judge me, or us! I don't want to go to jail, that's all. It would be too stupid. Two wrongs don't make a right."

"No, this is reality, they'll catch you, that's what will happen, and it'll be worse. You think you can get away with it— they'll forget all about it because it's only an Indian! Just wait till they catch you!"

"The prosecutor and the judge'll get sanctimonious and sentimental about it when it serves their interests. It'll look good in the papers. You're right! We can't let ourselves get caught!"

I was just imagining our freedom, if she would join me. I had my head on straight, as much as possible on such a night. I was still in control. Now she'd mentioned it, she had a point and it cheered me up a little. She'd said it, not me. Okay, grim as it sounds, if it helped me escape the hangman, I was for it. Damn it, killing Indians, accidentally or manifestly as it may be, has always been the key to our freedom as Americans, our whole existence, in America. It is the subtext, the beginning of it all, was official policy, half the time it was the main story, for centuries, and such as I could not be even the merest footnote to the slaughter. This is our transparent history, the obvious fact, so horrible and blatant that it's totally invisible to everybody, and to mention it is in bad taste, and actually proof of insanity, or worse, tendentiousness, you know? Of course, by the same token they would *nail me* for it. That was *my* karma! They would just love to make a scapegoat to project their guilt onto out of some piteously powerless ordinary white guy like me. My road ahead could not have seemed cleaner and clearer to me.

Yes, by now I *was* thinking it, she had led me to it. The cops probably would not bother about it too much. Was that my fault? But she wanted me to turn myself in to the same racist system, which would always like to throw one or two hapless white guys on the flames as sacrificial lambs! Freedom is not something you get for playing along. The Indians know that. That was what they were fighting us and scalping us for. They knew it as well as we have ever known it, and far better than we know it now. That's why they fought and went on fighting against insuperable odds, and still hold out. They are in touch with that one beautiful thing, even if dispossessed of all else. That's why they won't give in and be "normal Americans" today. I admired them for it. And they were blamed for burning a few settlements. They needed to burn the whole lot down. Would any of them have turned themselves in to the benighted authorities on my or any account? At this late date they were still holding out and refusing to be square. Noble people. I had no intention of giving myself up any more than they did.

By this time we had been sitting for a quarter of an hour in front of the house in south Berkeley where she rented a couple of rooms. Various of her hippy roommates had been going in and out, and it had been very strange to be going through all this in the middle of the usual nighttime crowd of kids and stoned-out childlike adults, some of whom glanced our way, as if they might approach us and ask me for a loan, which had happened.

"Listen, Julie, naturally you are thinking of the *one specific guy* we had the bad luck to be driving down the road when he decided to fall down in it tonight. All the Indians that were killed in our history are in the abstract by now, ghosts, lost to the pages of dusty history books, but think about it, when we killed them, they were just as specifically irreplaceable individuals and the unique creations of the Great Spirit, beautiful chiefs, handsome maidens, brave warriors, faithful wives, with those cool Indian names. You love to think about the Native Americans usually. Think of all of them for a moment! I'm not getting blamed for it."

Other than groaning faintly in pain she ignored my convincing speech. Into my ear at close range and against a tender spot in my neck her breath warming a vulnerable spot of skin

23

there, she admonished me urgently, "I don't care if he was red, blue, or green. You won't ever be free! You're mistaken. I don't want you to wind up in the middle of nowhere and sink in despair and be on the run forever! I want you to go *through* it! You're *innocent!* Can't we face up to it? That is how you'll get past this and be *free.* I don't want you to regret it or wind up in bad trouble later. Think about it. I saw it all happen. You couldn't possibly have stopped. I'm your witness!"

She might be right. I had another moment of violent indecision, fueled by love, weakness, and desire, and couldn't help cursing softly. She was very often right about things.

"Maybe in the morning? We've already left the scene. It'd be very bad to have to explain that tomorrow, but better than if they get the breath-o-lyzer on me tonight. I'd have to refuse to be tested."

"That's nothing to what you may have to deal with later if you split. I'm afraid it'll wind up haunting you. What if it won't leave you alone? I absolutely can't imagine you thinking you can walk away from this, I know I could never live with it. Even if they never catch you, it will haunt you. It would poison our love from the start."

"We'd be paying off the lawyers forever."

The truth is I have always been much more afraid of lawyers even than of cops.

"Money you're worried about? *Money?* You gotta face it. Isn't this a 'hit and run'? What is worse than that, tell me? If they catch us later it'll be much worse."

"Never happen. Leave it to me."

"The car's all smashed up with blood on it—evidence."

"Tomorrow the car won't exist—molecular level."

She frowned at that. We were touching each other with the tips of our fingers, like blind people reading messages beyond words. All at once she pulled back, seeming to awaken, to come into her own, and through her red eyes, she studied me with a radiant lucidity, as though she finally understood and accepted the truth of what I was saying—at least the truth that I was saying it, which sent a new chill through me bitterer than when she'd been fighting me. I could sense her giving in. I had won the argument, but what had I won?

"Are you sure you know what you're doing?" In my memory now, her voice had the sonorous finality and sadness of a bell tolling unexpectedly.

"Yeah, I'm sure," I said, with a tear in my throat, wondering if I did.

"Why do you have to . . . leave town?" she asked kindly, scrupulously, carefully, and I could only shake my head. She continued gazing at me, with respect and tenderness, so tears welled into my eyes. She kissed me, and whispered, "One thing you can be sure! This night will die with me!"

I watched her run into her house and didn't drive away for several minutes. No longer battling my emotions, but completely submerged in them, I soon found myself in the middle of Oakland freeway traffic, unaware how I got there, fairly heavy traffic, too, although it was late. Nobody was remotely looking at the front end of the Alfa. They were all on their own erotic, drug-related or other missions. I was conscious only in flashes. I was drowning in loneliness, lost love, guilt and raw fear, in short, *freedom*. The poles of the magnet had broken apart at last, and the liberated electricity was blazing over a tormented landscape. Deranged, I missed her more and more.

And then from God knows where, and God alone does know, I believe, a surge of life, a love of life, came up and washed over me, and washed away all the horror and grief if only for one precious pulsebeat, and I came up for a breath of the night air, and all the lights on chrome and enameled motion and sparking hieroglyphs of the freeway, everything was coming into view brand new, flying past me gleaming, dripping with fresh life.

I pressed the accelerator and began to weave through traffic fast. I couldn't wait to get to my apartment, grab a few essential possessions, and go. The traffic seemed a mighty river headed for the sea, and me on my raft. A molten feeling was in the air, as if everything were going to be heated, liquefied and recast into new shapes, and so it has, too.

Julie's image in my soul felt like a wound that would sting forever. At the same time, I was feeling lighter and lighter, till I felt the car was going to take off and fly across Oakland. I even felt like singing, I did sing hoarsely, giddily, in pain, something or other. She was wrong—I did have to leave town. The veil had been pierced and I'd had a glimpse behind the curtain at the stage business, and whatever had been binding me to Oakland, my job, my miserable life here, and our misarranged life together, had been run down like a rabbit in the road. I didn't know who was the dead man, the Indian, or me.

Julie needed a community, and everything she did was constantly to try to forge one—and I didn't know the meaning of the word. The beautiful gesture she made at the end, for which I will always be grateful, was to have proposed that the community could begin with just us two.

But I'll never quite understand, or forgive her, for not coming with me. On the other hand, why the hell should she have? To set out for a life on the run. Nothing is more understandable than her refusal. To imagine otherwise would be the height of egoism, a height which we all scale with the greatest ease, however.

Consciousness was a lonely blues sporting riffs of terror, stark guilt, and weird joy, it was a heavy wheel turning over and over, down into the mud, then up into the sky, the chords changing from sorrow to hope, the wheel spinning faster and faster, which I promised myself was going to catapult me into orbit and land me someplace wonderfully far out of this place and condition. I wandered around my apartment looking for the clothes and tools I wanted to take with me, telling myself that all confusion would end as soon as I was on the road. Somehow I fell down and slept for an hour. I was drawing energy from the devil knew where. It was by now after three in the morning. The night outside my window was solid black. I drank a cup of coffee, made a phone call, and after a while locked up my pad and went outside to stand on the curb and wait for my friend Jack G. As soon as he arrived, I handed him the keys to the Jag, and followed him in the Alfa out to Richmond, to Dahomey's wrecking yard where he worked. It was an eerie ride.

Jack hadn't said a word. Nor had he protested on the phone about the early hour, though it had taken him a few seconds to wake up, and I had heard his wife say something to him. You get a hint of Jack's character in his having understood the urgency at once and hung up the phone without comment. He'd been in Vietnam, and something had clicked in his brain intuitively, exultantly, I might even say, and he'd been on his way. I found a new peak of respect for Jack this morning, to add to the mountain of respect I had for him already, not to speak of my profound gratitude. He greeted me with a patented understated look he had, as much as to clarify beyond words, beyond thought, unworked-out, just ready, he was ready for anything, and the thing about Jack he'd make it stick. I could guess underneath he was slightly alarmed though, or soon would be when he saw the implications of the situation, for more than good friends, we'd had some plans to be business partners. We'd been talking about opening our own car shop together, getting away from our respective bosses and going out on our own. As I drove along behind him, I realized how those plans had always been vague to me, but that he had been counting on them, and I felt bad about it, on top of everything. Strange how another measure of sadness and disappointment could find room beyond nightmare. Layers on layers of grief can come down on you, you know, and there's always room for more. It was something else I'd have to fight through. I would just have to trust him to forgive me for the time being, and keep the faith. But he never showed anything, let alone said anything. That was loyal Jack.

Jack slipped between the corrugated metal gates of the junkyard and chained Dahomey's dog, which had been lunging at the sound of us. I could hear him cooing to the annoying beast. As soon as he swung open the gate, I zipped inside and, spotting a set of welding tanks in the gloom, shot over next to them. I fired up the cutting torch with my cigarette lighter, throwing a blue illumination on the night scene, and set straight to work on the offensive fender of the Alfa, unceremoniously carving through its front-quarters, while Jack pulled the Jag in, locked up again, and went down to Dahomey's shack to come back with a pan of water and two greasy cups into which he'd spooned instant coffee. He lit up his torch and heated the water in the pan in a matter of seconds with it. The trick was not to blow a hole in the bottom of the pan. His flame was too rich, and flakes of carbon wafted into the air like black snow.

Leaving nothing to chance, we chopped up the hood, the front fenders, the twisted bumper, the smashed grille, the radiator, even tie-rods like slicing the tendons of some sacrificial creature so that at last it couldn't fly away and tell its tale.

Dawn began to break after an hour or two of this, and in the silver light we minced everything up very fine, and distributed

27

the small chunks of metal among scrap bins at far corners of the yard. I had Jack's assurance that before the day was done, he would have pulled the engine, trans, running gear, anything and everything he wanted, rear-end, doors, seats, interior, and sent the remains to the crusher, that by tonight all these saleable odds and ends would have been shipped here and there to other yards in Hayward, San Jose, San Francisco, the diced-up scrap to the furnaces, and the Alfa would be a ghost. For his troubles, he could keep whatever he made, at the rock-bottom prices which would move everything at once and in all directions, and after Dahomey's cut, of course. I slipped him three C-notes out front.

He tried to refuse, with his lightning grin that showed he was getting his reward from the fun of the job itself. And he was too, it was no strain. But I wasn't going to let him not take the money on this occasion. Not only was he genuinely glad to help a friend in a pinch, he was glad of an occasion to enjoy feelings of loyalty and generosity, especially with more than a hint of danger, so he was sort of doubly or triply glad and rewarded, never mind money. That was the kind of man he was. He never had asked any questions, and he didn't now. I felt the gratitude tighten up my throat. When he finally took the money, it was only not to hurt my feelings. We drank more coffee, with the sun rising up.

Jack was a strapping, big-hearted guy for whom anything like this was fresh meat. It was better than breakfast. He was a Vietnam vet who was nostalgic for the good old days flying choppers in Nam and running around wild in the jungle and night-life stoned on Thai weed. Normally taciturn, given a chance he would bend your ear off, his voice glowing and his words tripping over each other in their rush to get out, as he spun his cherished tales. The thing that dragged him was the tameness and smallness of civilian life. His sport was car racing, but he didn't have the money to pursue it at the moment. He'd been racing one thing or another around California since he'd gotten his driver's license, and knowing Jack, well before that I'm sure. We had met at Blue's garage, where we were mechanics together, and then later we were at the Pontiac dealer together, where he had been a mechanic when I went to work there and got sideways promoted to salesman. Jack really preferred the relaxed atmosphere of the funky wrecking yard to the rather pristine and claustrophobic conditions at the dealer, which was well for him, since he'd argued with our boss, Harmless Harry, at the dealer, and been fired.

I can't speak too highly about Jack, even though you might say well enough that after the night in question, or the morning rather, I am prejudiced in his favor, a man with elan and excellent instincts. He had that military way about him. If he didn't want to tell you something, well, you couldn't have tortured my secret out of him. Now in my hideout I miss him more than anything, more than Julie in a way, a reminder of how good and clear things could be. What I faced in Jack every time I met up with him was a far better man than I, and somehow the realization never came as an affront or even an admonition, but as pure fellow-feeling and admiration for him.

He liked me, too, I'm not entirely sure why. That is, nobody could have helped liking a spirited kid like Jack, but his liking me was more complex, and may have had more to do with a wistful and unhappy side of him than I knew then. I guess he liked my attitude, saw I knew the score. I liked Jack in the way you can't help liking extreme loyalty and unaffected youth. Not that I was so much older than he, just a few years, but I guess I've always been old for my age. Maybe he liked me because I always listened to his Vietnam stories, with interest and respect, which he poured out and lavished only on people he thought would dig them or if he was drunk. It did make me sad that such a young guy would be so full of memories, that he seemed to think his best days were already behind him. On the other hand, all his war memories seemed to be *good* ones, and in some way he seemed to draw a promise for the future out of them. This struck me as unusual. I know nothing about the War, except from the media, which had given me the idea that Vietnam vets should be universally disgusted or troubled. Not Jack! Far from it. Those had been the days! Standing in farewell in the gaping mouth of Dahomey's junkyard, we didn't speak about the plans we'd had to open our own place. Nobody had to tell Jack they were on hold.

If he was disappointed, he never let on. I explained how I was going to free-lance the cars for a bit, and we arranged that he would be my man if I had a car that needed some work and I was anywhere around Oakland or San Francisco. We avoided the subject of our car shop, and parted on an upbeat note, and with a firm bond between us. You don't jinx a dream by mentioning it. I could imagine what grim thoughts had kept him silent company in connection with our morning's work with the torches, his worries about his own future, when once he'd realized the gravity of my problems. I couldn't have put into words my own feelings by now, but I was sure he knew what I felt about him, and how sorry I was to say so long, and that I meant what I said about keeping in touch. I liked Jack awfully much, for his competency, his good nature, even his obsessive Vietnam reminiscences, which were sometimes chilling, and sometimes touching, everything romanticized and embellished no end I'm sure, admirably so. I had always liked him, but never so much as this morning. How strange it was, that I was leaving town, leaving friends, for the lonely life on the road, the freedom of the road, and at this moment I loved my friends as never before, maybe because I was leaving them!

This was not the case with the owner of the wrecking yard, Dahomey, however, who was another kettle of fish altogether, a roiling black kettle of gumbo. I had a lot of respect for Dahomey, but he was not a man to stir much affection. For some reason, he had taken a dislike to me. Not that that necessarily got in the way of business, because he was all business. I'd done some business with him in the past, which I think he would be glad if I left out of this story, so I will, believe me. Dahomey always impressed me, the success he'd fashioned from thin air, the sheer size of his labyrinthine wrecking yard, the physical stature of the man. He was a black dude who had come up the hard way and then some, and starting from less than nothing become a rich wrecker, not by failing to exert every advantage, however, or to see what was happening under his ample nose. I was anxious to head out before he pulled in this morning, before he smelled me out. I didn't think he would recognize the remains of the Alfa by themselves as anything to do with me, as I had never driven out here in it. But he might put two and two together. Jack could cook up some story later. Dahomey loved Jack, and would let it slide. Better if he did not see anything of me.

So I didn't linger much longer, though I would have if I could've, because I loved Jack's company, and would to this day, though he doesn't care much for me anymore of course. He's no blame for that. Well maybe he does a little bit still. But I've gone where he can't follow. The common peacefulness of Dahomey's junkyard at dawn, the prosaic happy sight of hundreds of car parts strewn about in the aisles, dirty great reassuring piles of them, the first sun dazzling us over the mountains of pleasant greasy wrecks and rusting chassis, and Jack, like a lone survivor on one of those numbered hilltops they'd killed each other for in Vietnam, his hands thrust nonchalantly deep into his pockets, his wistful, loyal grin as he wished me good luck, all made a fleeting anodyne for the difficult events of the past night and the uncertainty of the future.

There was one tie I was going to be very glad to have cut, if I wasn't looking forward to the actual cutting it. I had to go see my boss Harmless Harry, tell him I was quitting, and ask for my check, a request that would evoke the pathos of begging a thrashing shark to regurgitate your swallowed leg. I was due two thousand dollars in commissions, otherwise I would have passed up the pleasure. I was in no position to write off that kind of money, as it was going to form the main part of my capital for dealing cars in my private line, which I had hatched as my plan now, a dream I had had on the back burner of my brain (along with our car shop), suddenly called into action by fate. You know what I mean—what is your escape plan?

Not that I intended to spill any of that to Harry, who would have been jealous, and looked at it that I was going around him. I didn't have any idea what I was going to say to him, all I could do was leave it to the spur of the moment.

It was not long till 8 o'clock, the time when he usually arrived at his office. I was eager to get it over with, but in dread I drove slowly. I was apprehensive about what he would smell, or guess, about me. Though I'd cleaned up as well as I could with mechanic's soap, I had rust and grease under my nails and all over my clothes. I wondered what might show in my eyes. I forced myself to go over it all again, to harden myself up, so Harry wouldn't sense any weakness. I'd killed someone, left him in the road too, I'd just said good-bye to my dear girl, and so-long to my best friend, and I figured if I could handle all that, I could handle an old fart with an orange hairpiece. The thing about Harry, he really did look harmless, an old man shrunk up in a too big suit, with a smarmy half-smile on his face that made him look senile, and that red rug. But he knew all his salesmen's secret fears. He could smell your fear, and he could certainly smell blood, if there were any. He

31

used to like to unsolicitedly reassure the guys their jobs were secure, thus creating doubt, which he knew how to play on. He elicited customers' apprehensions, working their worries to the surface one by one, acknowledging them with apparent transparency. That way he got a good gauge on what he could rip you off for, customers and his salesforce alike. He could read people and he didn't mind if you knew it. Maybe the clientele found it flattering and reassuring, so it seemed. They even somehow got the impression this was an honest as well as caring salesman, a terrible, preposterous misconception about Harry.

There was nothing to do but ask him for what he owed me in a steady voice, as if I hadn't a concern. He never bought it for an instant. At first, he acted like there was no question of a check at all, if I was leaving without notice, then that I was going to have to come back for it another day, in two weeks, which would have been unbearable, and impossible. He sat there like he didn't know what to make of me and wanted me to know it. How could I walk in and tell Harmless Harry I was quitting out of the blue? Too bad for me then. He sat there like a stone wall with a pumpkin on it, like a flounder with a sweet potato for a garnish, with one round opaque eye outraged and the other a narrow cunning slit.

In spite of every intention, I was trembling in front of him as usual. He had all the advantage and he didn't have to know much to know that. He did an ominous thing, nevertheless. It was intended to be a mindblower. He pulled out of his desk drawer his .38 with the pearl handle, and placed it on the desktop in front of him, pointed not quite straight at me, but near enough. Was it offense or defense, it didn't matter. I really thought he'd read my recent history and all my thoughts then. The meaning became clear when he finally told me he would pay me and wrote out and handed me my check. It was for seven hundred dollars, more than a thousand short. I protested, wildly spluttering, but he cut me off.

"How about me?" he said. "How about my trouble—short a salesman with no advance warning? Let's face it. You're not interested in my problem, and I'm not interested in yours. Right? I have my problem—and I see you got yours. That's life. You can't do me like this, just quit. Head on out then, if that's what you're doing."

"Harry, this may have been my check once but there's nothing left of it but the head and the entrails!" All I could do was try humor. He started to smile slyly. He took it as a compliment. He mumbled something about having had to deduct money because of a questionable trade-in for which I had given too much value, some shark nonsense of his, his smile growing big as a sting-ray.

"Harry, this aint even the head of it. The guts and the genitalia all you left me, man. Please!" I wrinkled up my nose serviley, hoping he'd laugh and relent a little.

He liked that and did laugh, relentlessly. It did me no good. He liked to see me wriggling on the hook. He slumped in his chair comfortably, his old rheumy eyes relaxing to slits now he'd done the dirty deed. With a smirk of contempt, but almost warmly, for him, he observed me a while more in case I would provide more amusement for him by actually weeping crocodile tears and begging for mercy. At last, he pulled out one of his old cards and flipped it to me.

HARMLESS HARRY'S

"The cars are like new, and we are true-blue."

It was one of his cards from when he'd had his own place before he'd come to the Pontiac dealer. He told me he was going back in business for himself again soon, and I could work for him any time—"when you come back to town"—with a knowing glance at me that said it all. A new phone number was scrawled on the card. I was thoroughly humiliated, and alarmed. He seemed to sense all my immediate plans and the danger I was in, if not the particulars, and to cast a doubt like certain judgment on my hopes.

The pearl-handled gun lay pointed almost at me. He moved the barrel of it a bit with the tip of his finger, toying with it, making sure it was almost aimed at me, not quite. Harry was always out front with everything, that was his game. He never talked trash. He told you his worst opinions of you at once, he didn't hide anything if he thought he smelled something. If he had you at a disadvantage, he took advantage, that's all, he never held back. He'd understood all he'd needed to know about me at a glance. Some guys in my shoes would have been threatening to kill him. To my credit I did not come to that. With Harry, you actually would have to kill him. Just do it. To make a threat would be laughable, and he would laugh mercilessly in your face—a laugh that said, well, do it then, you miserable phony. He enjoyed your helplessness. So I made no empty threats. Face it, for Harry I was the dead man in the road.

"You'll be back!" crowed Harry after me as I left. He couldn't know why that was unlikely. He had no idea of the shape I was in this time. Not even Harry could have guessed how bad it was. It was even worse than he could have imagined, and that's saying something, considering Harry.

Steeled by my certainty that he was dead wrong about my coming back, anyway, with my paltry check in my hands, better than nothing, I hit the road, headed for L.A. and my newfound liberty. So he had robbed me of a thousand plus. It was going to make it a little harder to gain traction and make my start in the dealing business. It's safe to say nobody has ever robbed me like Harry, but few there are like Harry, and soon it didn't matter. I set to work carefully buying my stock one by one with what little I had and refurbishing it on credit with mechanics of whom I soon made acquaintance. When I thought of it, it was the mightiest blessing not to work for Harmless Harry anymore at the Pontiac dealer, even if he had cheated me royally, even if it had taken a dead man to emancipate me from the car lot. I was guilty, lonely, scared, as haunted as Julie imagined I would be—but free. Finally, nothing has struck me the way evil and good change places at the drop of a hat in this life.

Day by day, I felt the knife edge of freedom as it cut my soul loose, and kept on cutting. I was a new settler on the prairie, alone with wide vistas. I didn't know anyone for miles. It was dangerous and solitary but breathtakingly beautiful and free. I passed through lush valleys with their billboards and cottonwoods, glitter of gold in the L.A. hills, an anachronistic smog coloring the Sunset Blvd plains, constantly on the alert, I don't know for what, if not painted noble Indian warriors defending the blue hilltops. Propelled like an arrow by the darkest of ironies, I found myself at one of Julie's higher levels, or so it seemed to me at first.

Invisible Car Dealer

In the mornings, I drink my coffee high above the city, in this sort of neo-colonial Spanish penthouse my earnings have enabled me to rent. Cars may not fly but they've carried me to this hilltop to which pink high-rises cling. I would have gotten here sooner with that extra $1,300 Harry cheated me out of. Back then a sum like that was almost life and death. But I made it in spite of Harry. Who knows, maybe Harry and the Indian were at one and the same "level." Two sides of the same fateful coin with me squashed between them imprisoned, till I flipped that coin. But I get ahead of myself, such reflections belong to a later period when I have the means and leisure for pointless speculation, in short, freedom of the mind. Today it was all business and all necessity, those redeemers.

Early morning sunlight glinting from my neighbors' windows, playing like quicksilver in the streets of chrome and avocados below, touching the fat wisps of cotton-candy smog hanging above the trees with flamingo incandescence, and at 9:00 a.m. the exotic birds began to sing, a marvelous assortment of them, thanks to Mr. Ramos the manager's affectation. In the mornings and the evenings he plays Audubon recordings through loudspeakers down by the pool, every imaginable waterfowl and marshbird. It's bizarre, outlandish, but he thinks it's the thing to do, and maybe it is, I don't know too much about L.A.

Telephone rings, breaking through all the whooping and singing. It's a car buyer for sure. They'll think I'm in a swamp or a duck blind. I try to remember what sort of a bird I have out there for sale at the moment, perched on the curb. My mind is overtaken by ornithological images at this time of morning as a result of Mr. Ramos's hobby. I hurriedly close a window hoping to muffle the cacophony before picking up the phone. Try as I might I can't remember what I do have for sale—I think I have two—this will give me an excuse to ask which one. If it turns out to be a popular model, I'll be so grateful that my touch hasn't deserted me, once again.

  I had a vintage MG which I had bought from a little old lady, yes the proverbial little old lady, the very one. Stole it from her, as we say in the trade—*fair and square,* ha ha! Now what was an old lady doing with an MG? I didn't ask. (Might have been something else, by the way, I say it was an MG, might have been a Triumph, a Volvo P-1800, or a Mercedes gullwing roadster, but we'll settle on an MG, since it does explain Gretchen somehow.) Somebody had put a fine seven or eight coats of red lacquer on it (I'll call it red), the old lady I guess, and it had a removable red hard-top. The girls stared at it at the stop lights. A car like that promised fun in all the right ways. You would certainly drive along the coast to dinner at a chic restaurant out in the country with a view of the water in a red roadster like that, you would zip along delightfully getting there. A romantic car, yet also respectable, solid, downright chipper and wholesome as all British cars are, from a Morris to a Rolls. They have a reputation for being finicky and breaking down a lot, which perhaps they do. (My Jag certainly let me down in a pinch one terrible night later on.)

  The MG ran beautifully with the exception of a strange flat spot at high r.p.m.'s, and one afternoon I decided to tune it up in my little shop I kept for the purpose of being able to make such adjustments myself. I popped the bonnet and made a quick check of timing, point dwell, tightness of manifold gaskets, valve clearances. I had taken a tennis lesson that morning and still had on my white tennis shirt and shorts, which were soon covered with grease, which gave the absurd duds some character. The problem was in the carburetion, I was sure, and I shut off the engine, and unscrewed the round filter elements.

  That classic MG (or whatever it was) had those little bell-domed carbs operating on pistons with metering-needles that respond to engine vacuum. By working it up and down in its round chamber with my thumb, I noticed that one of the pistons was catching something nearly imperceptibly at the upper range of its play. I tore down the carb, and yes the silver bell had a spot of baked-on carbon inside, and I dropped it in an acid bath. I was in extremely high spirits when a test-run showed I had solved the problem, and by the time I got home to my apartment in the hills I was whistling. It was the perfect mood in which to have met Gretchen, with her quick little girl's flash of a smile. We nearly bumped into each other as she stepped out of the elevator.

"My, you've been working on your car," she put out her hand impulsively toward a huge smudge of black grease, "in your tennis clothes!"

However it had happened, I'd made an impression on her, and I was in the palm of her hand, too, someone who liked grease on a tennis sweater. I had my tennis racket over my shoulder. The truth was I couldn't have cared less about tennis. I had been taking lessons only in order to meet someone like her. Her hair was as blonde as Julie's, but cut as cutely short as Julie's was menacingly long. I had a feeling I was meeting a woman exactly the opposite of Julie in every way, one from the official California culture, not the Berkeley variety, the kind of girl in vacation ads and Hollywood movies about California (not the *noir* kind, the other, happy kind), who didn't come with a lot of strings, thorns hidden in the rose petals, environmental problems, warnings on the label if you read the fine print, on the contrary, a California gold nugget, a drop of nectar. She and that little red MG seemed made for each other. They *looked* like each other (that's why I say it was an MG). When she saw it later she swooned with love. That evening we sped up the coast to a chic restaurant with a view of the water and drank blush wine (I deferred to her choice, I know nothing about wine) while she told me about her family in a suburb with the usual mellifluous Spanish name and her work as an executive secretary at a company which sold both fresh and canned Hawaiian pineapple across America.

She was a real California girl, who loved surfing, skiing, sun bathing, tennis, fast cars—and cocaine, I was soon to find out. Romantic waiters glided silently by refilling our glasses, and cool jazz just one doubtful notch above elevator music played in the background making me perversely wish for Mr. Ramos's screaming bird recordings. The sun sank red-gold as a designer's dream over the edge of the planet, and the waiters came around and lit candles. On our way home to our apartment building, already neighbors and soon to be lovers, the MG moaned lustily in well-tuned crescendos. My afternoon work in my little machine shop had paid off in every way.

It's precisely one's neighbor one is always falling in love with, isn't it, damn it? In any case, the seeds of community, with its ceaseless and irrational demands, soon began to sprout insidiously as weeds. I had left all that behind, with Julie, I had hoped. This time it was supposed to be that other thing, you know what I mean. But no such luck. I didn't recognize the serpent's tooth in Gretchen's Colgate smile at first. Within the aura of a perfect pleasure about that little old lady's red MG in which Gretchen and I tooled around morning, noon, and night, deceiving me and delighting her to pieces, her imitation of a self-confident little swinger that she carried off so well, and apparently believed in herself, persuaded me I had landed in that zone of true freedom and guiltless fun, that blue heaven and sunny stratosphere promised by, and which we all associate with, that something in our head called "California." Instead, as it turned out, Gretchen had certain problems of an emotional nature, to put it mildly. And if that weren't bad enough, she had *friends,* whom I was lulled sufficiently to take as just that, and to sell nice, pretty, rather unusual cars to, in my light-hearted way, as if we were all good guys, sharing a positive view of life. That's how they came on at first, not a cloud in sight, the kind of people who didn't sweat life's little problems, philosophers all, mental hygienists, spiritual winners, new-age Californians of the first water. Like I say, I'm from the Midwest, lately from Oakland (which is only physically and nominally in California). I had a lot to learn.

The first one I met was the biologist from the university, surprisingly enough, since Gretchen had a way of rendezvousing with the coke dealer quite often. She must have just laid in a good supply. The biologist, who worked on his cats at a laboratory in the valley, lived in Hollywood—to be near the action, as he charmingly put it, to let me know right away that I shouldn't mistake him for an egghead who lived the pure life of the mind or any of that nonsense. He needn't have bothered. Gretchen knew him from her tennis club, and they had once been lovers, a fact which the biologist's wife and I were supposed to overlook, according to the Californian view that any jealousies and other bad emotions engendered by such a situation were meant to be transcended, a positive sin against good taste to notice them. This set up evil undercurrents. The biologist used to indulge in a clumsy joke or sexual innuendo now and then, just to put us all at our ease. This drove the biologist's wife and me to make a show of flirting even though we'd barely met, and couldn't care less about each other, and the show perversely began to create desire. Gretchen and the biologist weren't about to get together again, they were just *friends* now, in a disabused and knowing sort of way, and so they used to end up being the ones who were jealous after a doubles match at the club on a Sunday morning, while his wife and I just felt confused.

But this was how it was, and I wanted it more than anything, this light-filled, sexy existence devoid of shadow which we celebrate in "California," but which I had never known in California, certainly not during my arduous days at the Pontiac dealer in Oakland, or on Berkeley nights with Julie, who was always so serious about everything. Now I thought I had it. I was worse than Gretchen, who never really believed in it at all, except in her head, whose body, whose addiction, gave the lie to it. I was even worse than her friend the biologist, who at least was clear about what they were doing in the lab with those poor cats.

"I assume you, like everybody, would like to find a cure for cancer, and that is going to happen as long as researchers like me have total freedom to pursue our lines of research where they lead us, using whatever means are necessary. Certain fringe groups are trying to hold up progress."

"In other words, you want a donation. I can understand where you're coming from," I admitted. "We all want our freedom, it's in the Constitution."

He beamed at that. We were on the same wavelength and even friendly terms, despite his overbearing penchant for crude innuendo directed toward Gretchen. He pulled the Dodgers baseball cap off his head and flung it at me. "I want you to look for that old Chevy for me, okay?"

"We have three cars already," objected his wife presciently but irrelevantly.

"Now we're talking. You can never have too many cars," I said, mistakenly, but now he was talking my language.

"If I buy an old car, that's one less new car on the road," he remarked liberally, winking at Gretchen, then me, but forgetting his wife, and as much as I wanted to sell him a car, I got tired of his game with Gretchen.

"I'll get you one with a cage in the back for your cats."

He looked at me like I had slapped him and he wondered why. I wondered why I had said it myself.

"No animals are hurt, they are anesthetized, kept in humane conditions, and given a good life afterward!" he irately retorted but in a low voice. I was pretty sure he was lying.

He was a fitness buff, an earnest tennis player, a brilliant scientist, and a fanatic on the subject of animal rights. I mean he was *against* them, believe it or not, in California (another Californian who went against the grain, of whom I was meeting more and more), not because he didn't love his own pets, but in the name of progress. So I understood him perfectly. And then came the day when he took a fancy to one of my cars, and we came to an even more perfect understanding.

But I should have seen that all was not as I had imagined it with Gretchen and her friends long before that. I might have gotten a hint of it from all the cocaine I saw her sniff from day one. But those were the days when such drugs still held a certain glamour, and were thought to be daring, sexy, musical, etc., or at least were not viewed as an intolerable threat and affront to society and the main reason we can't compete with the Chinese. Then, the milder drugs at least, a little cocaine, were thought to turn you on, and open you up, they were thought to be aphrodisiacs, and even helpmeets on the path to truth. People like Julie used them, let alone Gretchen. However, now that they have been uncovered as a scourge, and society has gone on a vast witch-hunt against them, concentration camps privately built to house the weed-smokers and coke-sniffers, whose homes, cars, boats, honor, and finally freedom have been taken away from them, deservedly since they don't drink booze and when they're stoned out they indulge in visions about such quixotic enigmas as what did the Native Americans know; now that we've finally understood that all these dopers are not that eager to be retrained to look through microscopes and assemble tiny electronic components in the war against the Chinese and add to our wealth rather than give it away to Indians, but don't want to work at McDonald's either; we'll eliminate them, imprison them all, and we are going to have a wonderful life, filled with California sunshine, what seeps in through the bars. I have to admit to a certain satisfaction to learn that Julie and Gretchen and people like them have finally made the most-wanted list, and are going to pay for it. But as I say, back then, I had no idea such things were as bad as they seemed.

Back at that time, animal rights were a total novelty to me too, let alone somebody who took a reasoned and moderate position *against* them, that was like novelty-squared, you know, and my mouth used to almost hang open when the biologist speculated on the whole astonishing subject. The biologist's conversation used to make my head spin. When the day came that the lawyer joined us one dinner advocating for the *vote* for them, I mean one vote–one cat, sending Gretchen's other friend right up the wall, in spite of the fact they were good friends, I thought I had arrived in a circle of true philosophers, who would appreciate fine automobiles, as they enjoyed exquisite argument in good fun, an unwarranted conclusion, I was soon to find out to my horror.

I had no idea then to what extent people like the biologist would be willing to go in the name of progress. Maybe you've always known about the British Society for the Prevention of Cruelty to Fish, and it's no surprise to you, but I couldn't believe my ears when he informed me. These people go about stealthily along the trout streams of Britain, little old ladies sneaking up on anglers and throwing rocks into the water to disturb the fishing. This Society, or whatever it is (if it really exists) . . . if there is anything truly criminal in this world, surely it is to make a noise while somebody is fishing! I agreed with the biologist on that one, if I was never quite on board with his sacrificial progressive cats. He claimed the British Society had recently opened a chapter in Hollywood, had gone global, and branched out to cats, and that our entire modern way of life with its conveniences was threatened, if his experiments were disrupted. He planned to take certain measures, he insinuated, if he found out which members were stalking him in his lab. He had his ways, he suggested. I should have paid attention! Well, now all I can think is, wait till the Society finds its way to Washington State and Idaho and all the northwoods towns of America. Maybe the Indians and the rednecks will finally get together in the face of the new threat to *fishing itself*, not the merely contentious issue of whose fishing license is more lenient and broad, or more likely the general melee will only grow more intoxicating with a third party of old ladies involved.

The biologist had hardly seemed rabid at first meeting, however, and after tennis while we downed a beer or two and so forth on their patio, his accounts of how super-humane his lab experiments on kittens were, which he claimed he had caught the Society secretly photographing through a vent in preparation for an exaggerated, one-sided expose on television, were enough to bring a lump to one's throat, in the name of progress. He let on he wanted to stalk the whole spike-the-tree crowd and eco-terrorists and administer lethal and untraceable doses of radioactive poison in granola bars, the vehicle of delivery decided on a case by case basis, lacing the tea of the little old ladies in the British Society (or putting rat poison in the cocaine of its Hollywood branch). This was a new trend, it always happens in California first, scientists doing such things. In the name of progress of course. Otherwise, he argued, how would the American people get their necessary cosmetics and smorgasbord of powerful pills? Our freedom, in the deepest sense, depended on his, in his lab. He seemed a vastly enlightened individual, and probably was, a Californian and an American who typically wanted it all. I can't deny him all sympathy just because we later had a disagreement over a car.

His careful allusions to the animals in his labs used to get to Gretchen, leaving her teary eyed and disturbed, though not fully willing to face why, and only out of respect for his drug connections and, I suppose, their past did she sit there and put up with it. And I out of my respect for her. With the images of the suffering cats, behind his righteous stance of a defender of humanity, there was a sense of endless unacknowledged guilt, blank indecipherable foreboding, and apparently inevitable necessary horrors in the interest of progress. I had my own thoughts. My recent background must have come into play half consciously touched upon in some way or another by his diatribes. I mean that night Julie and I ran over that poor man, and reacted to the accident in our different ways, and parted company. Something deep inside me was still asking the Universe, "Why me!" She was right (Julie was always right), it was still haunting me, though I tried not to remember. I had discovered America, quite by accident, like Columbus. In my own light I understood the price that must be paid for progress.

"In America our progress begins with ethnic cleansing the red man. We have to deal with this or be lost in sugar-coated homilies and unable to make any moral distinctions whatsoever."

Most of all, this was my first social life since I had left Oakland, Julie, and the Pontiac dealership, and I was bubbling over to talk and mix it up with new friends. Those were heady days, in my new life, with my new love, at some new "level" where I was making a little money without being a slave about it, and I hadn't had anyone to talk to in quite a while. They all looked at me with some alarm, curiosity, and apparent misgivings. It dawned on me that they would never understand me unless they knew my story. I wondered if I was about to tell my story.

"I don't like the spin you put on it," said the biologist.

"I'm all for progress as much as the next guy."

"The strong win out over the weak, that's nature. Among people, high tech beats low tech. That's why we need progress. A new pandemic could boil out of Africa at any time."

I wasn't ready to tell my story, I was still too close to it. I'm sure gut instinct told me correctly not to tell this guy my story. I kept my mouth shut, said no more, and opted to be thought mildly eccentric on the subject of Indians, rather than tell my story, very wisely I'm sure, as it turned out. His certainty that there will be retribution to pay someday when our civilization collapses because of lack of progress on account of do-gooders and the lawyers doing pro bono lawsuits on behalf of chimpanzees, something all too easy for me to believe once I met another of Gretchen's friends, the lawyer, well, it all cast a pall of science fiction–anguish and even apocalypse over us, to listen to him go on. I returned Gretchen's uneasy stare with a felt longing to get away.

Later I came to understand how totally irrational and self-serving this old friend of Gretchen's was when he wouldn't understand that when you buy a classic antique car it won't have a brand new engine in it, unless you pay extra for one. Progress indeed! Well, in the car-buying public one finds an example par excellence of all the foibles of mankind.

These arcane discussions of ours, about the dangers from the old ladies of the Society for the Protection of Fish, with their weird cat operation details barely hidden under the biologist's apologetics, and his sense of outrage at a universe about to go wrong (for him), if liberals and animal rights advocates got their way, that is (ironically recalling to me, as everything always did in the end, Julie), his funding and grant sources threatened by cat and fish lovers, once Gretchen and I had gone home, only added to the frenzy and delight of our lovemaking, as if there really would be no tomorrow. You might have thought it would have put a damper on us, but we were so glad to be escaped from her friend the mad scientist, even jamming powder up your nose seemed wholesome and sane. She laid it out on her mirror carefully like a cosmetic she dabbed thickly on her soul as we rolled around our bed.

Having gotten more than a hint that the first friend of hers I had met was a crazy zealot disguised as a professor, who plotted annihilating certain liberals with anthrax secreted on exhibits of grim fishing gear, whose conversation roamed insatiably to his ardent and "humane" lab experiments for the good of us all, I might have begun to wonder if her, and our, world was really as I supposed it to be, here in mythical California, light and easy and carefree, but instead on these mornings I was drawn more thoughtlessly and avidly to her charms than ever. I never imagined myself to be in love with Gretchen as I had been with Julie. Julie had cured me for a while of that. Julie and I had had a love, which, after the worshipful acts which had characteristically expressed it, had often left me shaking in my soul. Whatever it had been, it had never been sweet spice and clean fun. After a short courtship it had graduated (or degenerated) into an unstable compound of worried, near-frenetic domestic sharing of our earthly survival concerns with spine-tingling portentous sexual investigations of life's meaning and awe at each other's mere bodily existence which didn't relieve but exacerbated every tension and inexorably spiraled downward into a primal attraction more of the pounding blood than the dear personality, an obsessive blending of souls along with financial and job problems which had left me always more edgy as a love-addict and constantly hungry for more of her. I think the incident that set us asunder, running over that Indian, came as a positive relief from all that crying dark need.

But now I was supposedly free. From her karmic studies Julie had gleaned that there are no accidents, which before had seemed doubtful to me, but I was no longer so sure. And now, from my fatal vantage point on the lake in Washington State, or Idaho, or Canada, or someplace like that, I have decided she was right (at some level). So at first what Gretchen and I were into seemed sane, cheerful, and light-hearted to me, by contrast, or I hoped so.

I was glad that times in bed with Gretchen were all good times, healthy, acrobatic, aerobic, filled with shouts and even laughter, laced with wholesome snorts of white crystal up the nose that the drug dealer (Gregory, whom I was soon to meet) assured us were the equivalent of putting tarragon on your red snapper. But on those sunny Sunday mornings, romping on our bed together, with images of tortured cats and disturbed trout in the name of progress hovering around our heads, I had intimations that I was falling in love with her, that our bond might become stronger, grimmer, heavier, needier—real love, in fact. Something febrile had entered our relationship, I had no idea from where, it really wasn't just the cats and the trout. It wasn't like the old days in the Bay Area, when Julie and I, both so anxious, exhausted, and unsatisfied by our jobs and lives, had clung to each other for dear life, but it was starting to seem like it could become so.

Could it have been pure freedom itself, my new vaulting, overarching, and triumphant freedom, from which I perceived some threat? But such thoughts belong to a later time, the present in fact, when I have curtailed my activities, shortened my reach, quite voluntarily, out of a puzzlement about our Bill of Rights and the Constitution, whether they are always so good for us. On those sunny mornings with Gretchen after tennis with the biologist and his wife, I hadn't a doubt in the world that I could name, except about mankind versus the animal kingdom generally. Yet something ominous was in the air, and this shadow, soul's hunger, scraped-raw feeling must have been the cocaine, I have concluded, which all four of us used to sniff at the biologist's house, and which I used to consume just to keep Gretchen company, once we got home, in the ever huger quantities she preferred, which was making me nervous, and her increasingly silent and moody.

Invisible Car Dealer

There it lay on its round mirror glittering in the sun in which a trace of lavender from the morning smog lingered. Most coke users arrange their poison in narrow lines, called in fact that, *lines,* rather poetically, a poetry of the simple and obvious, of forthright hunger, with the help of a razor blade or a charming letter-opener or some fancy inlaid instrument, so as to add a sense of measure to their hysterical havoc. Gretchen used to just lump hers out in ragged peaks, with a sugar spoon, the hills of the Mohaves, voluptuous, stark, and awe inspiring. And so you can move mountains with a spoon. A consuming clarity, poignancy of the too-sharp senses, a bright tumble in the sheets, dubious laughter and our high, confident chatter, later a ragged let-down, too-much-upper blues, as the repair bills came in. And the mountains grow cold of an evening.

And then in came the dealer, Gregory. He had a way of showing up late Sunday afternoons, as if he had a nose for what we'd been up to. He also kept a calendar and had an idea of when she'd be running out and need a fresh supply. But you wouldn't have guessed his trade, for he never evinced any interest in that, at least not in the first hour, but went straight for the stove. He came in with a bag under his arm, but it was filled with Chinese vegetables, exotic cheeses, sweet herbs. He was a gourmet cook, a chef who had missed his calling, or practiced it strictly for love, honored it in that way, he said, the pure culinary spirit. He fancied himself a sort of nouvelle Oriental cook and tossed together a fantastic brunch (late afternoon for that night liver was time for brunch) for the four of us—he was always accompanied either by his dog, a gigantic Great Dane, who received his helping on a plate the same as ours, or his bodyguard, who ate his plateful without speaking so much as the dog. (Yes, I was attuned to the animal world those Sundays, and even if the bodyguard was professionally silent, it seemed to me that dog with its huge mouth and teeth really talked to me through its growls, barks, and slobberings, and that retribution might be very near.) In this way over brunch came the subtle implication about the cocaine the chef Gregory later sold to Gretchen that it was practically a food too, or a rare spice, nourishing, even wholesome, and very hip. I would have loved to dispute this with him, for though I'm a firm believer in everybody's right to ingest what they will, and digest it how they may, this is not to say that black is white. But his dog had those teeth, and his bodyguard was armed or at least was a karate expert, and Gretchen's dealer had a very negative aura about him. (You could have photographed it with no difficulty—I say that, and I'm sure of it in his case, and I don't even believe in that stuff. He had an evil shadow as big as he was small. It filled the room. He himself was a diminutive dude, very rich on his ill-gotten gains so I understood, although he dressed like a common street hustler, with a leather vest and boots, trying to pass himself off as an average Joe.) So anyway, I kept my opinions to myself, for the time being.

I realized that we lived in two different worlds, he was into herbs and spices, while I was into freedom. I knew that they didn't mix, but guessed wrongly that they could co-exist. I was also trying to figure out if we could share Gretchen, in some helpful sense, I mean, in her best interests. I had begun to glimmer that she would be a handful ere long. He and Gretchen had some kind of past too, I never asked about it, but it was obvious. And his way of dealing with it was to leer at us openly, to be quite suggestive with Gretchen, to kiss her and fondle her, make it clear he could dominate her if he wanted to, since he was her source. I didn't like it, but it's a free country, particularly for the women these days, and if she didn't object, but went along with apparent good spirits, who was I to cavil.

We were all grown-up Californians and liberated, weren't we? It would have been more surprising if she hadn't given him a passionate kiss or two, if only for the sake of appearances, given the situation, the time and place. It would have been un-Californian for her not to have, this is how Californians behaved, I knew. Or so I told myself. Because I didn't want to have to find the stuff for her. And of course she had to have her coke, her snow for her mountaintops, and he was her supplier, her Sherpa guide, for the hopped-up Himalayas or at least Sierras, so I kept my cool. I was afraid if I didn't she might get very upset, this girl whom I had idealized as the soul of cheerfulness and good taste when I'd met her, and who I now sensed might crack in two at any moment, who seemed on the verge of an avalanche of the soul, fended off only by her spiritual leader and main cook, the coke dealer.

Something was wrong here, wrong and evil, more than the obvious. Still, when Gregory asked me to look for a Corvette for him, I did so, fool that I was. I have always respected people's desire for a new car, "new to them," as we say, and admired them for it, so for a time I thought better of him on account of his request, and looked for a car for him and found one, too. I wished to stay on his good side, just on general principles, as he was an intimidating character, but more to the point, I harbored a hope that he might share a reasonable concern, if not a responsibility, toward his friend Gretchen, whom I felt slipping away. But anyway we ate well on Sundays.

I began to spend more and more time with Gretchen, every minute, when she wasn't at her job, or I out looking at a car, or on the street with some buyer. What did we chatter about? Her friends, her parents, her employer the pineapple company, her workmates, problems on the job (which she went to less and less), the goodness of the talented Gregory, she did all the talking, and I used to pretend to give her a little advice, nothing fancy, the odd suggestion about moderation. She was quite a talker after a few hits of the white stuff. She must have made her boss an excellent executive secretary and (as long as she had some in the desk drawer) entertained his guests right up the wall, or had when she had showed up for work regularly.

I never could make head or tail of it, but I always enjoyed the effect that her sprightly commentary had on me, like jittery bright music. I kept resisting the feeling that there might be anything hidden, any crags or pits under that fine sun-shot mesh of gossip of hers. The last thing she would talk about was the elephant in the room, and I didn't either. But now it had come to the point that she wouldn't go out at all, other than to work, and she even missed two or three workdays in a row, hiding in her bed or moping around my place. This transformation, which had been swift and had passed almost unnoticed, seemed uncanny until I came to admit to myself that I was recognizing reality, what had always been there, after my initial infatuation with her. There had been no down to this, only up, no bitter, only sweet, I had hoped and imagined. How blind.

One Saturday we went sailing on a boat belonging to a lawyer she had met at work. It was the first of several Saturdays. I really couldn't understand how she'd met him, because he was a famous consumers' rights advocate, I was given to understand. And she was a food industry girl. Was he recruiting her for a well-paid mole in the canned fruit industry? She needed the money for her habit would be the hook that landed her. Or maybe he was a counterspy, tipping off her boss about a sting in the offing, and Gretchen's charming company was a perk in the countertrade. It must be one or the other, but I hoped it was neither but just happenstance. I was fighting off reality with a will, was actively avoiding seeing the obvious, as usual, until it hit me in the face, because the truth was Gretchen was my best and only friend.

I can't stand sailing, far too quiet, no motor or anything, and I was in a glum and dull mood. I'd better not say anything about this guy (the lawyer and sailor), you'll soon understand why, except that it was a very pretty Mercedes roadster that was the cause of all the trouble. I'll only say that if you could have put seat belts on a sailboat he would have had us all wearing them. He was a control freak with everybody's best interest at heart. He had an instrument he kept looking at which told the wind speed, I think. Everything was under control down to the last knot, and this was supposed to impress us. He kept showing Gretchen this and that, things about sails and ropes and knots and jibs and various nonmotorized things. As you can imagine, I had no reason to like this guy, and every reason not to, starting with his obvious infatuation with her, and hated being dragged along. He was coming on to her right in front of me.

He was crazy about Gretchen, in spite of the fact that he had his own girlfriend, or kept alluding to one, whom he never brought along, and when we all wound up back at Gretchen's place for a drink on those Saturdays, and he found out that the old Mercedes 190 she and I had been riding in lately was for sale, he bought it on the spot, just wrote a check for it—to impress her, I believe. That's the only explanation I can give for his behavior. But it was a lovely old model, with those big, soft curves like blown out of a saxophone that are out of fashion now, but will never be out of fashion, you know, and it had beautiful, lustrous robin's egg blue colorings, so I had no misgivings. In fact, the way he was kissing up to Gretchen, I thought he had an eye for beauty in general, and took it all as a good joke and good times ahead (possibly). When the "transmission fell out of it," or whatever the problem was—those were his words, I didn't stick around long enough to find out precisely—I told Gretchen she shouldn't give it another thought because (a) the transmission was only part of the car, in this case a semi-rare and exquisite 190, nothing like it, and (b) he had bought it just to snow her, and should have taken it to a mechanic if he was worried about every little inconsequential thing about such a classic. He couldn't very well blame me. I hadn't made him a single promise about it, he hadn't given me a chance to, he hadn't even asked me. Now who looked like a fool? But anyway for a rich guy like him what was the big deal about a transmission?

This would have been a good argument, and it did work on Gretchen, but naturally the consumers' rights advocate got a hard-on for me right away, really just because he was jealous of me as he hadn't been able to make any time with Gretchen. What I now gathered at this point was that she had made up to him and accepted his invitation to go sailing in the first place on the orders of her employer. So that was it. The lawyer had been in her office investigating some spoiled pineapple that had poisoned a few thousand consumers, and she'd been supposed to cool him down. But she didn't like him, she loved me, and she'd been so grateful when I had helped her by finding a car for him, hoping this would get rid of him somehow. (But that was silly, it's always the opposite, once you sell someone a car, you are spliced together at the hip for some time, if anybody should know that, it's me. That's why the type of car dealer that has a lot, acres of cars, and banners flying makes you sign off on all that fine print.) So I saw how I had been had from every angle, and gotten caught in the middle of something. If she was being used by her boss, I was in turn used by her, and rather unsuccessfully. Still, I believe in being reasonable, I always have, and this attitude has served me, so I offered to pay for half the lawyer's repair bill. It seemed like the only way out, and maybe even the right thing to do. The generous thing. But what the heck, this wasn't some new Ford or Toyota, but an antique car which was worth something even without a transmission. I mean, the man should have had better taste than even to have mentioned a transmission. It was a gaffe on his part in my view.

The thing was, being in the line of work he was, he knew every agency, board, and commission in the state which could put some heat on me, and he knew every law, regulation and custom that I was possibly violating or at least skating too close to. Since I owned no lot, and rarely had more than one or two cars at a time in my possession, I was acting like I was no dealer in a legal sense, but he informed me how wrong I was, how there were a hundred laws on the books to protect consumers from the likes of me, and I was afoul of every one of them. One fine day he even phoned me to tell me he was going to get me because the old car had no seatbelts, and when the transmission fell out, he had bumped his head, but I wasn't that gullible. I laughed at him as it struck me funny. He put a couple of his investigators on my trail. He used to call me up once a day to spell it all out for me, and I even offered to give him all of his money back. In desperation I offered him his money back and he could keep the car, since it was such a lemon! But by now he had decided I should be punished. He just hadn't decided yet which punishment. His investigators were looking into it.

"Look, don't you think it is more than a little ironic, you are trying to remove every danger from the land, to criminalize the adventure of investing in American auto classics, and put seatbelts on every man, woman, and child in California, whose ancestors committed *genocide,* and seatbelts for even the Indians on the reservation that are left, those we did not completely kill? I mean that is the blackest irony that the few remaining Indians should have to wear seatbelts, whether they want to or not. And after the buffalo have been exterminated you will see to it that we all eat only foods approved by some committee, pineapple or not, depending whether you get Gretchen to sleep with you, and if possible everybody will return to a garden of ultimate safety, after the Indians being wiped out to the last man, and we should never buy another used car in our life, even the most beautiful, adorable old T-bird or Mustang of the heart's desire, in a country which began its civics lessons by teaching the Indians that they all had to be shot dead or at least live in the desert. You talk about safety, and whine about a lousy transmission—what's the equivalent of a transmission on a horse? Would Custer've survived that night if he had the proper permits and been wearing seatbelts? What's left of freedom and romance and the American way anymore?"

He let a silence grow on his end of the phone line in a manner I was getting used to, like I was not only a raving maniac but a fraud, and an idiot to think such things, let alone say them aloud in normal company. I was getting used to it, I was stating the obvious, I was a child, a sophist, trying to weasel my way out of my responsibilities, etc. The strangest thing about professionals, with their credentials proving they know something, is how if you go back to square one, logically, and reveal the basic premise of their whole position, it is not enough that you are wrong, but you must be a holy fool as well.

"Two wrongs don't make a right," he opined in a superior tone after a long moment. "The point is, you don't have a license."

He imagined he had me there. The truth was he wanted me out of the way so he could make his play for Gretchen, that was the two wrongs he wanted only one of. I wondered if I ought not to blow town and let him assume the responsibility of her, which is what it was becoming, an arduous responsibility, and that was what he was all about, bearing responsibilities, to listen to him. That might have been the smart move and the best revenge on him. But how sadly unfair it would have been to Gretchen. I believe her employer really had asked her to get something on the guy. I couldn't leave her. I started to get a little worried and moody just like Gretchen. I was worried about *her*. She had her problems, I didn't know how bad, until one Sunday brunch, at which I was mostly a silent guest, she blurted out the whole story about the lawyer and his vendetta against me to the coke dealer Gregory and begged for his help. She thought I needed help. The kind Gregory might give?

I was feeling pretty grim, preoccupied as I was with the question of why my luck had turned sour, and hadn't been paying much attention, and this absolutely floored me. Gretchen was taking up my case with the drug dealer! I had hardly imagined she would have noticed, since her habit was her sole preoccupation. After that I felt amazed at Gretchen's presumption that I needed anybody's help, least of all her friend the drug dealer's, along with a surge of gratitude that she cared, as well as a really absurd flash of gratitude before-the-fact to the raunchy breakfast cook himself, I don't know for what, certainly not for any help I wanted or supposed he'd give me, but that he stood there at the stove and listened with what passed for a sympathetic expression on his face to my troubles, as she described them, all of which annoyingly revealed to me the pitifulness of my condition. It should have alerted me Gretchen was coming apart at the seams and ready to cry about anything and everything. Naturally this guy had mixed feelings about lawyers, though, too.

The cook looked up from the sauce he was concocting, gave me an eye so cold it didn't look human but more like one of his ingredients, an oyster or squid, and asked me if I wanted the guy "nudged." He didn't like lawyers in general, either, he hinted, particularly the ones he'd paid good money to and gone to jail anyway. I'll never forget that funny movie-script word, *nudged*. Well, we were in Hollywood. I could have laughed but I knew he meant it seriously, or he took himself so seriously (not that he seriously would "nudge" a lawyer, certainly not to help me, but that he seriously meant us to know that he could have if he were insane enough to want to, he had the power to). I had reason to remember it, very soon. Just now I imagined a cliff, the lawyer on the edge of it and then a little nudge. Very nice, okay. I indulged in a moment's reverie. The cook in fact moved something, something from the sea, forward on the counter to the very edge with his knuckles ever so slightly, and we all looked at it about to go over the edge, its tentacles hanging over. The dog itself stood waiting, panting, all big pointed ears, waiting for it to fall over, for my reply.

"We wiped out the Indians and replaced them with lawyers. We should've learned from them, not murdered them."

"What! Guy on the prairie didn't emigrate there, it's where his parents were screwing around. History is one thing, happening to be there for it is another. War party wants to scalp you and—Gretchen. You shouldn't empty your bullets into them?"

Everybody wanted to impress Gretchen endlessly, it seemed, if that was it. There was something about her so obviously impressionable, even malleable. This nudging business was solely for her benefit, surely. I lost my appetite. I knew quite well this guy did not have my best interests at heart, any interests of mine whatsoever, whatever his motives were. It was none of his business, but Gretchen was the best sort of customer, big habit, good job, car dealer friend, otherwise rather lonely, all of which spelled plenty of cold cash and no other connection. He didn't know how broke we both were getting. I told the drug dealer thanks, but no thanks. Not that there was the least danger of him "nudging" an important lawyer, for the likes of me, or Gretchen either, or maybe anybody, it was only a piece of phony gangster stage-business, revoltingly transparent, meant to *scare* me, not help me, if anything. He didn't scare me but he was a drag. In fact, I soon enough realized, he and the lawyer were practically business partners; he was the coke connection and the lawyer was the insurance. They had become a team.

A cold chill started at my forehead and went down my back. What did he want, or would he soon want from me? Was Gretchen that far behind on her bill? I too could be "nudged," that was it. In my case I had to admit it was possible. I had to hold my lips closed tightly to keep from saying something inadvisable, and just plain to keep my jaw from dropping at the transparent threat. So I could be sued, arrested, slapped with a fine, and nudged all on one day, and in fact, soon he and the lawyer were on the same side against me, and I even found out they were doing various business together.

He shrugged, and began to slice up some Chinese vegetables like a machine gun. I thought he had only noticed my existence because of Gretchen, and had put me out of his mind again. But then after a moment, he looked up to ask how my search was going for his Corvette. I was touched that somebody still had faith in me. For a moment it seemed to me I was liked because I could probably find him just that car. That was all it took to restore my faith in life, artist in the trade that I am. As a matter of fact, I had found just the one he was looking for, but in my depression had forgotten all about it. I told him what I had for him, and he bought it that afternoon. I believe it was the rear end that "fell out of it" a week later. Have you ever noticed how people often speak of things "falling out of" their cars? An odd metaphor really, as nothing like that ever happens.

Gretchen got the phone call, and tearfully brought me the news in bed. It was very early one morning and I didn't feel like waking up but could tell I would have to. She knew how badly I was feeling about the lawyer's car already, and now this. I could almost see and hear the lump in her throat. No sooner had she spoken than I heard it all again in greater detail from the guy himself, as soon as I sleepily picked up the phone and reluctantly said hello.

He was hopping mad and wanted to be sure we both got the message. He was "disappointed." He'd been up all night. If it was very early for me, it was very late for him. All his savoir faire and cool were gone and he was a hysterical little bastard, he howled as if his ass were cooking on a skillet, and he intended mine to be there as well. According to him, he had been on his way to Vegas, and it had caused him great inconvenience, and ruined his vacation. With a good-natured laugh I tried to point out to him how much money I had saved him at the blackjack tables but he failed to see the humor. He was worse than the lawyer with his threats. Now that touching moment when Gretchen had begged a favor from him on my behalf, and he had made an offer which I could only refuse, and which he had not had the faintest intention of carrying through, came back to haunt me, as I had suspected It would. He reminded me that not only had he bought a car from me, but he'd been ready to help me once. His last words to me on the phone were that it was not just a car (I couldn't have agreed more, it was a priceless classic Corvette, a treasure), it was a matter of a promise broken and a trust violated. I'm sure that somewhere in his crazy lecture he actually used the word "community," something that he pretended we had had formed, around Gretchen I guess. I nearly choked on my bitter laughter when I put the phone down. In California even drug dealers spoke in such terms with a straight face.

"Gretchen, he said we were part of a *community* together!" I said to her, laughing to keep from crying.

"So?" she said watching me nervously and cagily.

I got the picture. He was providing us a service, i.e. high-grade coke, in the spirit of *neighborliness*—in California, money never enters in. Or rather even money has a sanctimonious and healthy odor, just like sex, and Chinese cooking. The cloak of "community" covers all sins. Now he wanted me to make amends like a real "brother," he said. (That was one word that had always made me want to run the other way fast clear back to Chicago or at least to Oakland and to it I now added "community.") I was soon to find out that his community included the consumers' rights lawyer as well as the biologist with his cats, who both got to know him and each other and became clients of his as a result of their separate altercations with me over cars. Of course they all had an eye on Gretchen. They made a community all right! You see communities need *enemies* above all. To each of Gretchen's friends I had tendered a rare and exalted specimen of world-class automobilia, gorgeous and splendid machines, paradigms of style, all. So they needed some minor mechanical adjustments. If they wanted cars that ran well and that was all, they should buy a Taurus! Together these dudes shared a "community" of the most wretched taste and no class. Such people do not know what a nice car *is*, I swear.

Gretchen put a little hillock of cocaine on her mirror and held it out to me to cheer me up. I indulged, and it dulled the pain for a few minutes. We sat and sniffled for a while enjoying the buzz and our own little faltering community. In a strange voice on a falling note of gloom and trembling despair which I now suddenly heard and really disturbed me, whose real depths at first I couldn't plumb, though I had gazed over the edge down into them dumbly, and now I understood was the status quo and normal tenor of our life together, she told me that the dealer would not be by to cook us breakfast again until I had squared things up with him.

So what, I didn't like his so-called cooking anyhow, I wanted to say. But she ominously meant more than the cooking. I had never heard her take this tone, nor seen such a frown of worry, even raw fear, cross her face. I realized at this moment that my sunny Gretchen was a real cocaine addict, something I should have understood all along. She wanted the stuff dearly. She was dependent on that creepy dude, and the spectral product he peddled, and it was up to me to patch things up as fast as possible with him, and restore our community.

It was one thing to be treated in a high-handed fashion by an attorney, whose business it was to be a prosecutorial asshole, but to be lectured by a dope dealer was a little much. If it hadn't been for Gretchen I would have told him to take a hike—back to Vegas. But I agreed to pick up his repair bill, and his towing bill— the guy had been about thirty miles outside L.A., but he'd had the Corvette towed clear to Vegas! The amount was astronomical, like a category in NASA's budget, nearly as much as the car had cost, pure thievery. But it didn't matter, it was all my fault, for I had trifled with the sacred faith the guy had put in me.

My fault? I should know every detail about these cars, with their ineffable lines and terrifying beauty? After their classic allure and timeless aura there was more to know? Even after I had forked over the money, though, it was clear things would never be the same in our community. I had no idea things had been one way or another in the first place. Apparently those unfortunate brunches had meant a lot to the guy, so he claimed. They did mean something to Gretchen, and now I was going to pay for it. It was up to me to dream up some way to restore our fragile bond, something additional, rare, over and above. He would be waiting for my "spiritual gesture." That was the latest blasphemous terminology in our relationship! What blackmail and baloney all this brotherly love, this community and "spirituality" is, and as far as I was concerned it had reached a peak of mockery. So I very nearly decided not to send him his money either. Let him walk, I thought.

But the coke dealer had poor Gretchen over a barrel, and I had to do something. He could have threatened me physically, but that hardly bothered me, the real threat was to cut off her steady supply. I was on the verge of giving her a stern talking to. The folly of getting hung up on some product that you can't go down to the corner store and buy! Be an alcoholic for God's sake, if you must. But I couldn't say anything. It wouldn't have changed anything or straightened her out but just torn out her heart with a gruesome ripping sound. To have spoken forthrightly might only have torn the shred of our happy friendship that still remained.

Her supplier was a very special somebody to her, and in the case of their sort of relationship beyond the pale of the law it might not have been so far-fetched to talk of an element of faith and community. The consumers' rights advocate had offered us some very high-grade lines on his sailboat and she might have borrowed a taste from him, but he was not speaking to us either, because of me. And, yes, believe it or not (I refused to at first), on a trip he had taken, the biologist's car had developed a little motor problem, too (thrown a rod on the Golden Gate Bridge, so he said, but I doubted that embellishment, I had a hunch he had talked to the lawyer), and he was after my scalp as well, so Gretchen couldn't go to him either unless she got rid of me first, something they all had begun insisting on (after I paid them first), and (as I think looking back on it now) something she amazingly wasn't prepared to do. I am touched deeply thinking on that now. She needed me too then. So much for her friends, they all had their quid pro quos and trade-offs—while all I needed was her love. She needed my love too.

I was deeply upset with myself for having broken my own rule against selling a car to somebody I knew even slightly, since one always got far too much credit if things went well and undeserved blame if they did not, since as we all know, cars are more than a machine, they are a total mystery. Critics of the industry exclaim over accelerators sticking, tires exploding, tie-rods flying off, and this and that little thing. I wouldn't be surprised to see every last car on the road evaporate like buju powder, or cakes of dry ice. It's a miracle one or two of them stay in one piece long enough for me to sell to you. Who made these things anyway? Tinkerers, con-men, snake-oil salesmen, company men, Harmless Harry's, cogs on a monstrous wheel that's going too fast to stop. People drive too fast, and so do you. Slow down, I say.

Where does it all come from anyway? American know-how, product of an unfathomable ragtime too lovely, dire, and profound for you or me to worry about much—imagine something that's a blend of Greek myth, knowledge of explosives, a donkey cart, Marilyn Monroe—and mass murder of a whole race, an ancient and noble one, the natives of America.

That is what mechanics are for, those kind, reliable, professional, and underappreciated souls, to check out cars for prospective buyers, something Gretchen's three friends had forgone to do, since they "didn't trust mechanics" (a sign of their naïveté, paranoia, and malevolence, right there) and preferred buying one from "a brother," God forbid.

I was in an incredulous mood in those days, and took to leaving my apartment and going for long drives around the city all day just to get my mind off things. Sometimes I stopped at a theater and watched whatever movie they happened to be showing, it hardly mattered, anything was more real than my own life seemed to be. What had society come to? Nobody could change a flat tire anymore, or imagine such a consumer-unfriendly happenstance. We are to be protected against everything, even beautiful high-powered antique cars. We are to wear seatbelts if we go two blocks to the convenience store to buy the latest pill to cure our boredom. In order to get some relief and peace of mind from it all we wind up depending on the coke dealer for ever more powerful mind-expanding drugs in an epidemic. You can see the result on the beaches of Venice, and clear down to Baja, in the evenings, matchflames lighting up benighted palefaces, as they lie on their backpacks gazing at the stars twinkling like sheriffs' badges, a

Children's Crusade against "reality." We are so safe, no one knows where we misplaced the romance and excitement. I tried to remind Gretchen's friends that their cars were works of art and pieces of Americana worth putting up with a few hassles for, but they acted like I should have offered them a warranty on excitement and romance. It was a lot to mull over on my drives around town.

One afternoon, on one of my solitary drives, I was astonished to see my little red MG (we are calling it an MG, but I am not in a position any more to be too specific) darting through traffic ahead of me, Gretchen's MG now, and I only imagined it should be darting, according to its character, and that of its owner, or driver, who usually steered with zestful abandon, cutting off people right and left self-absorbedly and good-naturedly. But it was no longer darting, actually, but plodding at a slow deliberate pace, seeming so peculiar for an MG to be doing. For a moment I doubted it was she and my MG at all. But it was, I saw as I drew desperately close.

Gretchen's personality had undergone a terrible change without a steady supply of drugs. She was brittle, nervous, and plain mournful, her color and bounce had vanished, and by now she no longer chattered. She thought every moment about where she would get some "for next time" and kept measuring how much she had left. She had other friends (who fortunately had not bought any cars from me) from whom she could borrow and beg a day or two's ration of drugs, and she was always running off to scrounge some up. She hadn't actually completely run out of them and so day by day she was staving off the profound paranoid depression of a cocaine addict left high and dry. But her peace of mind was gone without the security of a steady source and her dealer coming by every Sunday to cook brunch and drop off a little package. She hadn't begun to hate me and blame me for his absence, but I could sense this coming. She looked at me with grim expectant eyes, letting me know she was waiting for me to do something to fix things. Since the dealer arrogantly had never let me know just what else would restore us to his good graces, and "community," since I had already offered him his money back, on top of the towing bill I'd paid, and he was playing some flaky power game, I really didn't know what to do. Ahead of me in traffic, the MG was weaving lackadaisically, somewhat erratically, as if Gretchen hadn't made up her mind where she was going, and was driving aimlessly.

Invisible Car Dealer

I wasn't sure how desperate she was getting. I was suddenly afraid she was going to take me to southcentral L.A. where on some sad street corner I would have to watch as she purchased dope from a gang punk. Her whole scene was out of my world, and she had closed up, become secretive, I couldn't gauge how far she had descended. As much as our love had been a happy miracle, I was ready for anything from her despair, and felt she would stop at nothing to get drugs.

So at first I was relieved when she took us across town to an exclusive neighborhood in Westwood and parked in front of an expensive home. If you had to buy or borrow drugs, this was definitely a preferable spot to do it. Looking down at her feet, guiltily she skulked up to the doorstep, where to my surprise she turned the handle and walked straight inside. There she remained for an hour, during which time I speculated darkly as to what she was up to. I was so worried and low by now, you can imagine some of my thoughts. Or maybe you can't, which is fine too. For one thing, why wasn't she at her job? She rarely went to work anymore, and maybe she had no job.

When she finally came out again, she looked as if she'd been through the wringer. Her eyes were red, and she hurried dazedly to the car. She didn't look as though she had scored. There was none of that glittery false confidence about her lent by cocaine, on the contrary. This time when she drove off I couldn't bear to follow.

Later that evening when I broke down and confronted her, she told me that she had only been visiting her therapist. For me there was no "only" about it. It gave me a shock of hope, which I doubted though. But a sense of the possible came to me, which I suspected even as I was uplifted. I hadn't known she was seeing a therapist, she had never mentioned it in all of her chatter, and after a moment of surprise, "Then you're trying to get off the habit?" I none too gently inquired, rather doubtfully.

"Not exactly," she at least admitted truthfully, but with a pout. "It's not a goddamn *habit*," she added with an accusatory glare. I wasn't dissuaded from a sudden urge to bore in.

"Oh no? What are you going to a therapist for then?"

"What for? Everybody goes to therapists, don't they? Everybody has a problem sometime. So do you!"

"All right. But what's yours?"

"The personality, like an onion, you peel off layer after layer to get to the real you. You harp on about freedom all the time. I've been going to that therapist for eight years, for my freedom from bad things that happened long ago."

"Onions, right. Eight years! Peeling onions. I know all about that onion. It doesn't take eight years. Give me a break. And you're still monkeying around with drugs!"

"What's that got to do with it? What, you think eight years is a real long time? You don't know much about anything, do you? You don't know what anything takes. It's none of your business anyway. Coke is not the problem. It's not having any that's the fucking problem."

"Why *do* you go to a therapist? Other than to peel onions. I saw your red eyes afterwards."

"To get rid of negative emotions! That this society and all societies and assholes like you give you so you can't enjoy life."

"Coke is positive?"

"It is what it is. I never had to think about it until you and your goddamn phony cars blowing up with my friends in them!"

"What does the therapist say?"

"About you?"

"Not about me, about your cocaine hang-up!"

"He gives me drugs himself."

"What!"

"Other things. Not coke. Like tranquilizers? To take the place?"

"Never mind. You are the biggest fucking square, Gretchen, and you think you are hip. Strange what liberation means to some people. Perversely the desire for freedom somehow leads straight to more onerous dependencies."

"What the fuck! Will you stop pontificating *please.*"

"I hope it's the dark before the dawn."

"What? Couldn't you . . . you get around so much . . . with your cars . . . don't you know anyone? Can't you help me?" She moaned, burying her head in a pillow.

"Gretchen, it is getting dark, girl." I decided to voice my worst suspicions. "Do you go to your job every day when you leave here mornings?"

"So far. Some days. I don't know how much longer I can cope though."

"You've got to go to a hospital. The only way you can get your independence back is to lose it completely for a while and put yourself in the hands of professionals. Sometimes freedom requires nonfreedom, paradoxically, even I can see that. I don't know how you manage to hide this from that therapist."

"I don't want to go to the hospital. I'm not going in any hospital! I don't want to lose my freedom. I just want my life to go on like it was before—before *you* showed up. You have to help me!"

We slept a few sad hours till dawn. Where had been golden abandon now was shadowy defeat, excruciating note of amorphous pain, an unbearable rending. On top of the mound of dirty sheets on her bed, within reach of her hand, lay her phone, symbol of her frantic search for drugs. I felt I had to do one of two things, take her to a hospital, or get her a great big bag of her desire, enough to last a year. She was right, I could have "helped" her. I'm good at finding things, I happen to concentrate on cars. I certainly don't know any dope dealers (other than Gregory), but of course I could have gotten her all the cocaine she needed, if I'd really wanted to. But I hesitated on the edge of that endless slope.

I didn't know about sending her to a hospital against her will. The rumpled filthy bedclothes, an ashtray full of half-smoked butts—she'd used to smoke moderately—the relentless red glow of sunrise beginning to pour through the windows, something grainy, something slimy in it, a dirty dawn, a blood-red stagnant light, Gretchen naked and helpless in the bed, her suntanned skin gone ashen, the phone crowning the disorder, begging an answer, a blind mute cripple holding out its amputated stub to heaven . . .

Mr. Ramos the manager's marshbirds suddenly went off, too early, the recording he played by the pool in the mornings, so loudly, like an out of whack Disneyland exhibit. Did he imagine the tenants found it restful or authentic? A lot of banshees and doomed spirits crying from hell. Gretchen clung to me.

"I want us to be married!" She laughed coyly or slyly, with a loony tremble that made me cold. "Not the way you think, don't worry . . . in a deeper way."

I watched as she bent over to rummage through a dresser drawer, the sight of her skinny bare ass which used to give me a wonderful thrill making my heart overflow with pity. She stood up with some strange paraphernalia in her hands, needles, a plastic bag. I thought it was some kind of drug outfit. She held the contraption out to me with an importunate, guilty look in her eyes, like a dog with a forbidden bone, just like a whipped dog with something cagey, a hint of abashed ferocity in her face.

"I want us to taste each other's blood, just a little bit. You don't have to if you don't want to, but I want to drink some of yours."

"I beg your pardon?"

"I would like you to drink mine too."

"What's that supposed to mean, Gretchen?" I asked, trying to hide my fright and disgust, and not succeeding.

"Mean? Why should it mean something?" she said, her voice dead, dying, fearfully hiding back all the meaning, whatever it was, if there ever was any.

"Is that what we are now, savages?"

"I don't think savages do this."

"I doubt it, too. Who taught you?"

"We've all done it together sometimes, all my friends."

"Oh yeah? All of them, like which ones?"

"Afterwards, I'll call Gregory. And do you know what he'll do when I tell him? He'll come right over here in half an hour with everything I need, and we'll all be friends again."

Was this the gesture that he was waiting for, which might restore me to his affections? Good heavens, I couldn't keep from chuckling, demonically, in spirit with the revelations.

"A blood bond. Is that the deal?"

"What deal? It's not a deal . . . it's *for real.*"

She gave me a look so forlorn, and yet suddenly wild and bold, full of an inscrutable hunger for—well! I began thinking of those professionals at the hospital with a keen interest, to hide which thoughts I turned my back on her and stared down at the heart-shaped pool, the tennis courts, then up at the hills rising lovely with flowers and shrubs around pink-and-white high-rises, all cragged with violent purple shadows in the supreme sanity of the smoggy dawn. Out there was the lonely city, with its rugged goodness in the morning heat. Mr. Ramos's birds were softly crying. I understood her all too well. She didn't seem strange to me.

I felt fully the keen edge of her anguish. I too knew what it was like to be lonely. "The thing I can't get over is I thought you were *happy*. I should be astonished by what you've just been saying to me, but I'm more astonished at myself."

"I'm getting better," she said absurdly. She sat on the edge of the bed, and began swinging her legs like a little girl. "If you'd do as I say . . . if you'd help me. We would really be friends."

"I feel like an idiot not to have noticed you had this problem sooner. I never even noticed you using that much stuff. Strange how I thought we were happy together."

"What the hell do you know about me? We've known each other for three months. The only thing that's happened between you and me is you've come in here and alienated my friends."

"It's all too much for you, isn't it Gretchen?" I made a gesture at the window, indicating all that tacky opulence and, yes, groaning freedom, out there, laden on us all, by life itself, by the Constitution, the Bill of Rights, what have you, as I searched her eyes.

"Ye-e-s!" she moaned, and dropped her needles and tubes, and collapsed in a ball.

At the hospital it turned out she was supposed to have some insurance document of course. I wasn't going to just shove her back out the emergency room door like they wanted me to. I pulled out five hundred dollars and placed it before the receptionist. "This will have to do till later today."

"We don't take cash, sir." She looked down her nose at it, then turned up her nose knowingly and disdainfully.

"It will all be arranged. She works for a very reputable, nationally known pineapple company, with a health plan. Listen, I'm not trying to be funny. She's just eaten too much of it is all, couldn't stop this morning, pineapple can be a downer, you didn't know that, when you overdose on it. Keep this money for the moment for security and afterward use it for her personal wants, or your own, I don't care. Keep it for yourself, just check her in now. Her employer will call today, or if not him, then a friend, a follower of Charles Manson. Don't worry, she has some very strange friends in the underworld. I promise you this girl knows some vampires. I will find out your phone number and where you live, and pass that information on to some of the most unsavory—their preferred beverage is—what's your blood type? You think I'm kidding, don't you? They like to know that, just like you people here. They'll be asking me, I mean, *about you*, if you don't take her *right now!*"

Well, we're always taking out our frustrations on receptionists and other frontline employees who are only doing their job, but she suddenly stuffed the cash in an envelope and hurriedly wrote Gretchen's name on it. Tears filled my eyes as I stumbled out into the hard morning light. I had that well-known feeling of waking up in the middle of a soap opera and finding out it was real. I suppose I understood now that the happiness I had been seeking in southern California had always been a cliché, too. Does that mean it is real, that is, real people are somewhere really experiencing it as I've always suspected? At this probability, I underwent a spasm of unholy anguish or envy, considering how things had turned out for Gretchen and me, bliss having evaded me once more. I couldn't understand how I'd let myself in for the whole sad drama when all I'd ever wanted was my freedom, plus a little harmless loving. Deep down, I wondered if Julie hadn't been right, and I was paying for the wrong turn she thought I'd made (toward freedom) the night we killed the Indian.

But then again, in light of the crimes we have all committed, rapine and murder, land theft and genocides, sending whole villages up in smoke, shooting down children and squaws in cold blood, down through the ages, time and again, lately experimenting on cats and torturing chimpanzees, always for progress, all of us the least accessories to every crime there is, willfully, yesterday, and in the last five minutes, and enjoying the bloody fruits of it, how any of us imagines we might be really happy, let alone know what that happiness might be, other than raw selfishness and naked lust, the Declaration of Independence and the Bill of Rights and what we learned in school notwithstanding, I really haven't the slightest idea.

It was time to head out once more. Hit the road again and be free of all this, again, if it were only possible, Gretchen's friends, above all. The drug dealer was not exactly the nonviolent type, but I was most afraid of the lawyer, because he and his investigators were the ones most likely to be able to find me, and after that, it's lawyers we're always most afraid of, isn't it, at least the ones with ties to government agencies?

Invisible Car Dealer

In my retreat at Cloud Lake, in Washington, or Idaho, or someplace like that, down my dirt road in my cabin which I'd found with the help of the bartender at Packy's, the rhythms of country living had begun to take hold, and L.A. seemed a distant memory. I hadn't come up here specifically to enjoy myself, just to hide, but I found I loved everything, even the rain which came more often than not. It seemed to shut me in by the shores of my lake, whose grey expanse rolled away in towering mists like heavenly curtains shielding me from everything that had lately been pestering and tormenting me. The brilliancy of some mornings, by contrast, lifted my spirits sky-high. The sparkling waters before me all day, the perfumes of the water and the woods, and the evenings noisy with frogs and insects, the skies white with stars if the night chanced to stay clear, everything conspired to take me far away from myself, at least as I had recently been, to make me my real self again, with my rare sense of unhassled freedom.

On my way north to parts unknown, I'd stopped in Berkeley, never having resolved to do anything of the kind, or even admitted to myself I was doing so as I did it. I'd driven around town and tooled down Telegraph Avenue vainly pretending not to be thinking about Julie. But why else would I be doing this and what else would I be doing here? Why else would I not have headed straight north, never pausing, or northeast, to Idaho, or Canada, or wherever I am hiding out? Suddenly, to my amazement, I saw Julie on a corner of Telegraph selling flowers.

I pulled over and watched her from a short distance across the street. She hadn't been kidding, I realized, about the ways and means she had of surviving, and surviving prettily, when the chips were down. All the government grants must have fallen through, or maybe she had been fighting with her fellow minor bureaucrats apparently. On her corner she had an abundance of gorgeous blooms for sale. On the sidewalk, open for business, in front of her really opulent display, she gave an impression of ready accessibility to all, which I was afraid was not meant for me. The past months were obliterated in a twinkling, and it was as if we were back where we had left off. It was worse than that. As time shattered, I had the inappropriate feeling of being back in the first days when we'd just met and were avidly courting each other. However, this was a gross illusion, I knew, for we had chosen separate paths.

I had not been a part of her earlier life as a street person and free spirit, which she had so often spoken about, and I had become so used to thinking of her as a desk person who expressed her social concern on behalf of the needy by shuffling papers in an office, that to see her out in the open, the sun in her hair, moving about her stand with flowers in her arms, and obviously enjoying it so much, made me dizzy. Nor was hers a paltry offering, but it looked like she must have sunk all her savings in this flower business. Customers kept coming up. There was an affluence and even permanence about her stand, even though it was only on a corner and probably had to be cleared away every night.

Her smile as she handed somebody his blooms in a paper cone was something to behold. She'd been doing this long enough to have a lovely tan, maybe since I had left town, I wondered. That social concern of hers had been transformed like a grub into a butterfly. She was not gritting her teeth and tearing her hair for the sake of the poor, but scattering petals for all of God's creatures to behold, and purchase, such as God's children as are found wandering on Telegraph Avenue. She was wearing faded tight jeans and a T-shirt and not much else, and her hair in a pony tail bounced about enticingly. She was doing a brisk business among the hip middle-class people who liked mixing in and buying colorful things on the street. Her pleasure as she completed a transaction was an unaffected grace, and everything in the scene of which she was the center seemed to come together again and again before my eyes in aching flashes of sunshine and energy.

She looked free as a bird, a lot freer than I, burdened by my business problems and even on the run from them. She seemed to have found a happy perch here at curbside, one that agreed with her and brought out her grace and beauty, while I was drifting, on the lam, heading grimly where I did not know. It seemed to me that by a strange irony our roles had reversed and her liberty had waxed while by a mysterious fate mine had waned.

I watched the crowds on Telegraph, bead-sellers, stoned-out freaks, college girls, and packs of clean-cut high school kids in from the suburbs for some action. Professional people headed into the Med for a cappuccino or carried paper bags full of bread from a little bakery. I hated them one and all, whichever side of the cultural divide they were from. How I envied them their connection to Julie, no matter how circumstantial, even those who bought no flowers from her but just passed close enough to her to exchange a smile with her. A tour bus got caught in traffic and obscured my view of her. I had to wait several minutes for this idling silver bus sending up obnoxious black fumes to pass. Noses pressed to the windows, grey-faced citizens from wherever gawked at the kids on notorious Telegraph Avenue. When it finally rolled away, she was not there. The alarm and consternation this caused me to feel struck me as so insanely misplaced and downright humiliating that I just gunned the motor and took off. Out of the corner of my eye I saw her come out of a shop munching a croissant. She had never caught a glimpse of me and I wanted it to keep it that way. I could see that she was happy, and I knew that seeing me would only bring her down and ruin her day. As low as I was, it wouldn't improve my spirits either. There was nothing new to be said between us, what had separated us must only have intensified, and there was no sense putting it to the test. If I could have thought of one helpful or beautiful word to say to her, I would have walked across the street and spoken it to her.

It was astonishing I still had this amount of pain in me concerning Julie, I thought, and it seemed as strong as ever or worse. Why hand her any of it, when apparently she had moved on and was okay? I sped north, or east, to Oregon, Wyoming, or wherever I found my small cabin and Cloud Lake, which I am going to keep a little cool about, you understand. As time and distance dulled painful memories, and I began to enjoy my new surroundings in the northern forests, I found myself grateful that she was all right, and had looked so lovely and well when I caught a glimpse of her selling flowers. I even indulged the hope or dream that somehow we would be together again, life finally having taught her how much she needed me and how wrong she had been.

On some days, after lunch, I used to jump in the Jag and drive around the countryside on the lookout for old cars. It was just something enjoyable to do that seemed harmless. I didn't care if I found any or not. One rainy day I got stuck in the mud while examining a hopeless antique abandoned in a field, and the farmer on whose door I had knocked hoping for a tow offered me a beer when the job was done. Standing in the doorway of his shed where he'd parked his tractor after pulling me out, we watched the rain, drank the beer, and talked about cars, what else? He finally showed me an old moth-eaten hulk of a '57 Chrysler convertible, never dreaming for a minute I would buy it. Or did he? Maybe he took me for a fool of a city-slicker all the way, who would take it off his hands. But he could not imagine so easily as I some overpaid athlete, or actor, or Hollywood hustler, tooling down Sunset Boulevard with the top down on this baby, having shelled out twenty grand for it, once I had cherried it out, so he let me have the heap for forty-five bucks. I think economists refer to this as the "cost of incomplete knowledge." He refused to take anything for the tow, and it made me a little guilty. But such guilt is part of my job, and I bear up as I can. It is a part of that "cost" too. Had I prevailed on him to take more, it would have ruined the charm of the moment for him, when he'd ridded himself of unwanted junk, and picked up a few bucks for it, after having done me a neighborly favor. If I'd presumed to have given him more, an unpleasant element, an extra degree of consciousness might have wormed its way into what so far had been a nice, unexpected encounter, something he felt totally positive about, you know what I mean? So forty-five bucks seemed the right figure.

Then, in Packy's one day somebody told me about the Ford Victoria glass-top, and when I had acquired it I thought my luck was complete. Two was plenty, more than enough. Without realizing what I was getting into, I kept driving around on the back roads with my eye out for interesting old wrecks sitting in pastures or barnyards, high-water marks of ambition or affection from bygone days. Before I knew what had hit me, I had bought five or six. Looking back on it, I can see that was about the right number, maybe a couple of more.

These days of driving around the countryside on the lookout, with nothing much on my mind, came pretty close to happiness, if I had known it. There's a strange thing about happiness, sometimes it is not understood or even discerned, until it is over, and only looking back, one sees it for what it was, and might have been had it been maintained and prolonged, but wasn't. Because at the time, in the middle of happiness, one naturally seeks to have more of a good thing.

My troubles in Los Angeles were far away, and my enemies down there while maybe effective in the city were not the sort who could ever catch up to me far away in the countryside. None of them were intelligence agents or real gangsters, after all. But I was enjoying myself so much again, so happy to have found some engaging way to pass the time, on these treasure hunts through the fields and forests, that I didn't have the presence of mind to accurately gauge my new happy condition and to measure the good shape I was in. You need something to measure your happiness against, and it is a well-known fact that painful memories are the first to diminish, and go away even, so that you need more of them, more new miseries, to give you the grounds for ascertaining the happiness that must have been. Instead, onward you rush into fresh calamities.

No, I thought I was onto something, that I was winning again. I had my edge back and I was on a roll. I jumped out of bed in the morning ready for the day, quite unusual for me, lately. Now it's impossible to remember the pleasure of those early mornings when the limpid sunlight danced on some new set of fenders, those lazy afternoons when some miraculous great snout of the beast, front-end of a big old classic sedan, poked up at me out of the long grasses of a meadow, the feverish anticipation, the languid joy of the hunt all day, without wincing in anguish at my blindness—now that I own more than thirty cars, a few of them hopeless wrecks when viewed by the sober eye.

Invisible Car Dealer

One night, after a day of hunting, I was far from home, that is, my cabin on Cloud Lake (a true and sentimental home, had I seen this, and I was about to), with its modest adjoining wrecking yard, rather a character-giver and a landmark. Toward nine or ten o'clock, in the thickest darkness under a cloud-banked sky, at a very lonely crossroads, I stopped in a place called the Flame Bar. A flickering sign stood on the rooftop in red-orange neon letters, along with some stylized leaping flames as from a charcoal pit, or maybe the pit of Hell.

It seemed like a homey place, though, and maybe I would enjoy dinner here. I was famished, not having eaten anything since morning, and road weary. Frankly, I was beaten-down, stretched thin, could not remember what I was doing around here, in that fatigued and vulnerable condition when the normal animal spirits lag that keep us all blithely marching forward, and I had completely lost track of where I might be. Later I might have to consult a map to get home, and first I was going to have to get hold of a map, because I didn't have one and no one sells them anymore. Probably somebody in the Flame Bar would guide me home and suggest the shortest route back. I had been circling around on the back county roads, even logging roads, criss-crossing the country. It was fun not knowing where I was or where I was going, but now and then I had to stop and take stock, get something to eat, and inquire as to my whereabouts.

The place was softly lit, I observed. Then, I had to admit, it was poorly lit, it was a terrible-looking joint inside. A few drinkers slouched at the shabby tables were talking quietly, one sat hunched over nearly motionless, I suspected asleep, his head on the table, but a convivial bunch crowded the bar. Country music was playing from the juke box. Altogether the atmosphere was peaceful enough if gloomy, the furnishings were altogether unvarnished and barren, a few tattered beer posters alone decorating the bar, the tables and chairs scattered upon a litter-strewn and very dusty floor. From the outside I couldn't have told it, but inside it was the funkiest, threadbarest joint I'd been in yet up here, and it suited my mood to a T. I felt I could hide out in such a place and relax and not have to explain myself. I felt well-hidden. I would have to put on no airs. Probably I would have to be satisfied with a microwaved little bar pizza for my dinner.

Invisible Car Dealer

For a moment, after a drink, I was happy. That is, I was in that state of tired blue-sadness coupled with sudden release from it which is one funky form of happiness. Against all odds I looked forward to some pleasant exchange, something informative, even enlightening or at least entertaining happening, and every now and then glanced surreptitiously out of the corners of my eyes, not wishing to provoke anyone, but ready for a friendly moment if called upon. But nobody was at the bar with me, the small crowd who had been there at first having almost immediately departed.

Even the bartender had disappeared into the kitchen. To my delight, a mob of people suddenly came in the front door with a lot of noise, taking a while to get the last straggler caught up, and they all sat down beside and around me at the bar which was now entirely full. They were all very drunk already, and bent on staying that way, and getting worse, if at all possible. And observing all their slam-bang arrivals and fidgeting rearrangements of limbs and rear-ends on the stools, and harsh laughter and jibes at one another, I thought it quite possible something amusing would happen. Smirking inwardly, I got ready for some entertainment.

The bartender got busy fixing drinks and mostly setting up beers. The festive, feverish, slightly hysterical note brought in with the crowd livened the place up considerably, especially as it had been completely dead before they came in, and more and more quarters were dropped in the juke box as they sloshed back beers and booze. Some of the men and women were bickering in an amusing way about everything and nothing that I could make out, which passed for good fun among themselves, but suddenly threatened to turn ugly, if it didn't turn into complete nonsense first. For a moment I thought somebody was going to smack somebody and there would be a brawl, even of the male vs. female variety. What could be better! Why does somebody like me go to these bars anyway except to enjoy the proximity and intensity of crazy humanity without having to be responsible for any of it? In its habitual state of hungry, half-pleasurable torment, anguished, avid bliss, the soul of humanity, the flames that come up from the pit, can occasionally be really distracting, no matter how bad your own troubles, and even especially if they are very bad.

But before any fight could begin, which I had suspected was about to start any moment, all these people started laughing—

laughing among themselves, laughing at themselves, in a mellow aware way, at each other, at the environs of the Flame Bar, at the bartender, at the microwave which was cooking them some pizzas, they were just laughing knowingly at everything in sight. They relaxed and stopped taking whatever it was so seriously, and just calmed down. As if they had made a collective decision to do so, they were pleasant and peaceful. But now something amazing and shattering happened.

We all looked at each other. The whole crew seemed to notice me at once, for the first time, and check me out, now they were not so occupied with each other, and I in turn looked directly at them. They hadn't paid me the least attention until then. You know, no more than a minute or two had gone by since they entered. We all sort of turned toward each other, one by one, and the thing was, suddenly I was a white guy, and they were all Indians, including the bartender, none of which had been the case a moment before. The Flame Bar was a Native American tavern, and I was on their reservation.

Surprised as I was, I certainly didn't mind, but I had no idea how they felt about me, although by the blank leers on some of the guys' faces, discovering me in their favorite hang-out and watering hole was not an occasion of unalloyed joy and fellow-feeling. They all stopped talking and laughing in one accord. Had they been driving, you would have said they stopped on a dime. Being a white guy was something I was not always that conscious of, really, as I have already mentioned.

A moment before, these facts had not been established. They were not all Indians and I a white guy. If they had been Indians before they saw me, it had been in some carefree oblivious way. I don't know if it meant only that we had all been too drunk to know or care, or that this was the way in which I alone had experienced the sequence of events, and they had marked me at once, but just ignored me momentarily. I couldn't help wondering how everything could change in a flash. A political or cultural curtain suddenly had hit the floor with a crash. Did it necessarily have to? Couldn't we return to the status quo ante of innocent unknowing? No way.

I was a complete stranger to such speculations, as I believe many a paleface is at this late date, in this country, after a whole lot of history which by all rights should have made such a state of ignorance or innocence impossible. It was like, not only had the natives of our country been blind-sided, steamrolled, given the wrong name, and left for dead in the wagon trail, whether by the onrushing white hordes hell bent on land or gold, by mendacious government policy, by trigger happy cavalry, or purely by impersonal history, they had also been totally forgotten about as if they had never existed even in the sense as such pests as wolves might have been supposed to have existed and had to have been exterminated for safety's sake—*beyond* forgotten by, well, I had to admit it, such white folks just like me. Until they walked into the Flame Tavern, their own joint.

All that murder and genocide and land theft was long ago, supposedly lost in the mists of time, but events had conspired to make me aware of this history, and all our part in it, since that terrible night with Julie, and I was astonished to think that it was not going to stop. She was right, I was going to keep paying. Having come across the Flame Bar, in the mists of the present, although well aware that some parts of this territory were Indian country, it never crossed my mind and never would have that just now I myself was on their reservation, had stumbled on *their* land. This in spite of the fact that I even knew the Indian nation that lived hereabouts, the famous name of the ancient tribe. Everybody around here knew it, naturally, as much as they knew the weather or the name of their own town. (I'm not going to allude to either name though as I have my reasons for wanting to keep my tracks covered.) No, I realized, from such forgetfulness there was no going back to innocence. But my trespassing here seemed no innocent coincidence. It seemed to me darkly I had been drawn here. Something like fate or Julie's "karma" was at work.

At the same time I was certain that nobody was being completely genuine. Everybody was play-acting a bit, doing and feeling what was expected of him or her, I was sure of it. Everything had shifted in a dreamlike way, and we all seemed to be suddenly wearing hostile and suspicious masks, no longer being just what we would have liked to be, or what we had been a moment before, in our own worlds, with our private concerns, but drawn out of ourselves, forced into cynical roles. A couple of them were grinning awkwardly as though not sure what attitude to take or how hostile to be, or exactly what was called for by my obnoxious presence. So not only was it an appalling scene, but to some degree an artificial one, that is, culturally and historically conditioned, as much for them as for me.

I was sure my intuition was correct, yet it seems strange, doesn't it, because one always thinks of alienation and hostility as being the most genuine and natural emotions in the world, not the other way around, that they should have surprised and interrupted a friendly normality, such as we had been enjoying till awareness set in. In an instant, I was almost paralyzed by the wish that the unconscious conditions which a moment before had been completely valueless and happenstance might not have changed so. I certainly had no ill will, how could I? I hardly knew where I was. I wished at the end of history things were otherwise than they were for these guys, however they were. You know, I sincerely wished history could be reversed or obliterated, a futile wish indeed. Just because I was now rather uncomfortable on the bar stool and I had been looking forward to one of those microwaved little pizzas.

Most of the people, truthfully, seemed under a similar spell of hankering for a lost "normality" before we recognized each other and had to do something about it, and nobody did anything for a time, just stared over each other's shoulders at me and shuffled their feet, sipped their beers, and looked vaguely irritated and out of sorts. They resented they had to form some sort of attitude toward me and the moment and most of them looked about to forget all about it and me. They had forgotten the happy arguments and banter they had just been having with their women which had been interrupted by history and would have liked to pick them up again. A guy moved behind me and said, "What are *you* lookin for?"

"Nothing." That was the truth, surely. I had come in here for a rest from looking for cars. He might as well have memorized those lines from a movie, those stinging words were as much as etched in stone on some invisible monument around here that commemorated everybody's defeats. He was a hard-looking guy with narrowed eyes and a couple of scars on his cheeks from fights no doubt or rough work.

"Look, I just stopped in for a quiet drink. I was on the road, passing through. That's the truth. Why should I be looking for anything? I just happened in."

Invisible Car Dealer

"He just *happened in,*" he said, and looked around with a deadpan expression, and they all laughed wildly at the phrase itself apparently, the way he said it. At least they were having fun again and I realized they believed I must be "looking for something," and they laughed harder. There could be no other realistic explanation for my presence. How else had white people arrived in America in the first place? Surely they had not just *happened in,* had they! They had come over here "looking for something"—India in fact, which was why these people were called Indians, instead of their real names. It was the deplorable truth that no white person in his right mind would likely ever "happen in" here. I was proposing an absurdity over and above a plain trespass. They could never accept something like this being said to them. Anyway my presence in their inner sanctum was objectionable naturally. Awareness of all this was overpowering and cloying, the way it would influence and determine everything forever. It was all very sinister.

I felt a strong urge to clear the air with biting truths. I was on *their* side. Maybe like Julie I could say the right thing, with a good-natured laugh of my own, but not being a natural wit I was shy about it and quickly thought better of it. I could not have produced the proper face-saving and poignant nuance to carry it off, let alone sound sincere, even if I was, and was better off not trying. There was no way in the world, I knew very well how I sounded under any such stress, and they would decide I was running a game. I was a natural car salesman, I kept the ball rolling and made the deal, I didn't "speak truth." I wasn't in practice, didn't have the necessary grace, it would just sound self-serving and duplicitous. Nonetheless, being me, I gave it a shot.

"Say, in spite of everything, I mean *everything,* aren't we all *Americans* by this time, you know, of whatever background or color?" I found myself asking the crowd inappropriately, with a feeling of really clutching at a straw, or taking the bull by the horns, or floundering in the middle of a sentimental cliché with no more foundation under it than that old quicksand in Hollywood Westerns everybody was always falling into, but completely missing the boat.

I was getting off on the wrong foot completely. Why would they want to be Americans with me? I wasn't Clint Eastwood and this was definitely not Hollywood. The sad part was I really meant it. At the same time I was slyly having a hilarious and edgy joke, saying something so preposterous and dangerous that I might get myself in trouble. I mean I was trying to create some common zany new wavelength and go from there. But a wave of sentiment came over me, of a doomed universal nobility, because I meant it too, I felt that in some two beers' worth way on an empty stomach that I loved these downtrodden, castaway, marginal people in the Flame Bar in the outback, such as in my historically conditioned consciousness I conceived them in this moment. (This in no way had anything to do with who they were *in reality* obviously, as God knows them, for instance, or history will eventually redeem them.) No, I really wasn't trying to be funny or ridiculous.

I was white, but with their condition I identified completely, for it seemed to be my own by now. I was that marginal and castaway myself, and felt like I was one of them, even worse off than them, something I could never have explained to them in a million years, no matter how true it was. Still I was going to try.

"I really mean that. Look, can I buy everybody a drink?" I threw a few bills on the bar and caught the bartender's eye, who waited a moment, gauging the general opinion about this, and then proceeded to collect the bills and start pouring and setting out beers. Nobody was going to refuse a free drink, in any event, even before a scalping, why not. Nobody said no, and eventually, and soon enough, everybody drank up, too.

These guys were really amusing, cool, intelligent people definitely worth knowing, and they would never want me to know them. I recalled their roars of laughter when first coming in as they chose to gracefully defuse whatever acrimonious debate they had been having about whatever it was, and somebody's problem with a woman. The whole point of their boisterous argument was the moment they gave it up to have just plain fun. They had been in their element. But now they were stone-faced, hostile, implacable, rather serious. An overwhelming insight into the situation hit me. They were no longer capable of being amusing and funny because the moment they took notice of me, they were the *majority* here. The majority never needs to be amusing and funny and never is. The majority does not have fun. Until seeing me, they had not been the majority.

The majority may be absurd, they may *be* funny, but it needs the minority to point this out. In fact, they were the *white people* at the moment, if I may put it like that to make my point, and I was the one with no name, or the wrong name. That is, they were the normal ones in this place, with no crying need for ironic insights. I was the one needing to see all the angles, and even be amusing, because I was plain outnumbered. That's why I tried.

But you could take such thoughts only so far, since outside the Flame Bar, where they were the owners, and even the reservation, where they were "the people," was the United States, with whose peculiarities, and owners, we are familiar. This was the overriding knowledge we all had even if it took the backseat for the moment. You could never get rid of that fact. And yet, beyond the borders of the U.S., which are constantly shrinking, becoming ever more porous (walls or no walls), and steadily impinging on the white people, was the world, in which the white man comes face to face with himself and his history, no longer in the majority in need of no self-awareness. Like one of those Russian dolls ingeniously fitted one inside the next, down to the size of a pea, the white man was going to have to begin to notice, and come to terms with, where he fit in. One day, not far off, the white man would be thrown into confusion, into a hall of funhouse mirrors.

Yet again, beyond our world was . . . well, the universe. One day mankind itself would have to acquire the precious wisdom bequeathed to the minority and get the joke!

It is the minority that learns to be funny and cool, and here I was in the minority, something entirely beyond my ken and experience. I was the one who needed to be funny, really funny, not a wise guy, but charmingly so, to release the tension. With no experience and no practice at this whatsoever, being a normal white person, I was at an impasse as stark as the Rocky Mountains, the Donner Pass at that. I was just not up to it, and yet I had tried to wryly and tongue in cheek and also completely seriously allude to our being *all Americans,* as if they would either accept that seriously or savor the precious irony, either way would be okay with me. (As a salesman you know you have to keep the ball rolling however it bounces, it really doesn't matter.)

I hardly have to tell you this liberal baloney that I had imparted about being Americans (which is how it came off since nobody got either the sincere feeling or the joke) was not the coolest thing I could have said but nobody was refusing the drinks.

Invisible Car Dealer

I had the feeling one of the guys might start pounding on my head, either because they flat out objected to me or because they thought I was a sap. I wanted to tell them about Julie, who would have said something that would have relaxed everybody, who had all the right reflexes. The point is though that she would never have been quite here, in the Flame Bar, on this night, where I was, would she? All comparisons are futile, as are all regrets. But what I'd said was not completely wrong either, I noticed, as everyone seemed to ease up a notch, to shift their feet, if only out of deeper confusion, and lean on their elbows on the bar, to look at each other and smile a little, and wonder a bit what to make of it, and above all was it worth it. Probably not. What had happened to their pleasant evening? Or probably they were just enjoying the free drinks for the moment, and tired of it all. I really wasn't worth bothering about I suspected to myself hopefully.

They did not know quite how to take me. Why bother? I half hoped I was beginning to bore them. But what I'd said *was* funny, you know, and of course at some level I'd meant it to be just that. They all began to chuckle, sort of slyly at first, sardonically, then breaking into loud chortles, as though I were the funniest damn clown in the world. As if they were getting the joke? But no. It was because they thought I meant it! That's how it had gone down. I had meant it sincerely, too. I wouldn't laugh with them, I was already on the verge of being completely pathetic and vulnerable in their eyes. There was no move for me to make now. I had shot my wad. Not unless I was prepared to tell them my story down to the very last dregs. I felt it would come to that, my own history, my education as it were (which was continuing moment by moment). My fateful night with Julie coming down from the hilltop. Meanwhile they went ahead and enjoyed my drinks.

I certainly did not laugh with them, and they couldn't help noticing that, and perhaps taking me and my sentiments a little more seriously, because I was serious. But I was not right. I didn't fit in. If I wasn't cold, I wasn't warm either, didn't know how to be under the circumstances. For all they knew I had indeed come here looking for something. What other explanation was there for my being there, in the end? But what could I want here? That of course illustrates the ludicrousness of searching for explanations for everything, instead of just taking things at face value, living in the now, instead of analyzing everything—a sickness of modern culture which I was amused to see the Indians suffered from along with everyone else. When I saw Julie again, I was going to have something interesting to report to her along the lines of "what the Indians know," I was afraid. But Julie would never buy anything I had to say and would have been appalled at all my foolishness. Maybe I was never going to see Julie again anyway.

Anyway, these Indian guys and their women didn't want to hear about being "all Americans" any more than the rednecks at Packy's would have, though at least you could hardly blame these people who had been and were always excluded. I have come to the sad conclusion that about the lamest, most unpopular thing you can ever say in this country, *in any group whatsoever,* is, "We are all Americans." Nobody believes that for an instant. The *last* thing any Americans want to be is *all Americans.* They know what that means! Yes, the other guy is getting ready to slip in the knife, or if it's in already, to give it a twist, under fine sentiments. That's America, right? The carrots, potatoes, onions, and chunks of meat in that melting pot all biting each other viciously as they turn over on one another. Or I hear we are in a salad bowl now—the peppers biting the tomatoes.

"What *did* you come here for?" the leader of the bunch asked again, like genuinely curious at last, but getting weary of it.

"A drink, as a matter of fact, even dinner," I said wearily too, "as unlikely as that sounds," I couldn't help adding with a glance at the bare surroundings.

"He probably wants a big fish," said somebody.

"A what?" I said into my beer glass.

"You want a big fish? Trophy fish?"

This, ironically, was one of the things that the local whites resented about the Indians who had the treaty right to spear and gill-net gamefish in the lakes and streams in any season, that not all the fish they took went to feed their families as the Indians claimed. I had heard the rumor that there was a black market on fish, on trophy fish, especially, and come to think of it, why shouldn't there have been? If it was unpleasant to realize that the guys in Packy's were not wrong about everything, it was amusing to understand that they knew perfectly well the Indians were regular Americans like everybody else, ready to make a buck, and here was the proof.

Invisible Car Dealer

(Nothing is quite so darkly ironic, by the way, as the white man's being upset by the Indians' taking a few extra fish and manipulating, and endangering, of all things, the tourist industry!) Anyway, I didn't care about any of this, except I didn't like being mistaken for the sort of sportsman who is willing to buy a trophy fish from a poacher when he fails to catch one himself.

"I think you better buy a fish from me," the guy at my elbow said.

"No, I don't want any damn fish," I muttered, "I catch my own damn fish," and gulped down the last of my drink. Now I should have gotten straight up, having acquired the moral high ground, and vamoosed, but I couldn't move. I didn't want to move. I was very tired and almost morose. I sat there feeling foolishly depressed and insulted, and mad. I remembered standing on the night road looking down at that Indian Julie and I had run over. I remembered how that night I had thought to myself that the broken bottles and spilled wine all over him would make the cops write the case off quicker now that Julie had suggested as much and put such an idea in my mind. After several beers on an empty stomach I was getting as drunk now as he must have been then. What was I doing? Was I guilty? Trying to get my own self killed to atone? About to fall down in the road? Actually, I badly wished for one of those little pizzas like cardboard as if they were a delicacy. I was weak and hungry, and stared at the microwave behind the bar.

I was glum, starved, and feeling ornery. "Another one," I told the bartender, gently, pointing at the latest beer bottle. What I needed was something to eat. "And a pizza," I mumbled.

I felt transparent as though the Indians around me in the Flame Bar could see right through me to that unhappiest of memories and to other things as well. I was exactly the one these Indians had in their sights, exactly the right one, that average white guy who is to blame for everything and won't believe it and doesn't know it, and certainly doesn't want to hear it. I didn't hold it against them. I wasn't going to buy any fish, but not offer any more excuses either. They could see who I was, so be it. It was me all right.

But still everything good I was feeling about them and about America and her mostly aborted promise was real too. I wasn't going to deny that either. We're complex beings and I doubt we'll ever get straightened out. Not all of them appeared to be in on the party and some of them had gone back to their private conversations. I was proud of whatever was good in my drunken, cockeyed vision of things tonight, having chanced to walk in, no matter how maudlin, mischievous, and self-indulgent. It might be as close as I, at least, would ever get to goodness. I sat there at the bar clinging to a few shreds of noble feelings, as if I deserved them, wherever in the world they had come from, thinking to myself that it proved I hadn't been as bad as Julie had thought that night when we'd abandoned the dead man. Playing the fool just now proved it. Or it proved the opposite—that I was much worse even than Julie thought. It is what it is, I thought, hungry and exhausted.

Over a few murmurs, somebody said, "Who said anything about a fish? What's he talkin about a damn fish?"

I liked these guys, liked how they looked, liked how they thought, liked who they were. I was as desperate, dispossessed, and full of irony as they were even if I couldn't express it. They were handsome people, dressed in a sort of cool cowboy ranchy dusty way, lean and tough looking, with an appealing air of cheap glamorous marginality and being on the edge and ready for anything. It touched me to have arrived in their haunts. In my status of outsider, being on the run from one thing or another, alienated by circumstances beyond my control, a fugitive from justice, a butt of misunderstandings, plaything of the most measly and minor personages, the ones who were powerful, I was in fact just like they were, I was in no better shape than they, a victim of my own capricious history. And I even felt that my condition held the same despair and romance as theirs did. The inner truth was I was one of them now! However, it didn't look like that, at least to them. How could it? To them it could never be, even if it was.

Fortunately I did not try to express any of these crazy thoughts. That would have been too wonderful. They would have laughed until they fell on the floor at my insane presumption or out of pure astonishment. And they would have been all too right. Julie could have brought it off, but not me. The words came out wrong, as hers would have been apt and right. Only a gifted soul like Julie, and she was nowhere in sight. Julie could have made this particular sale. From the car dealer, they were not buying.

"You better get on your horse, buddy," said the guy behind me. I was already getting up.

Invisible Car Dealer

"Sleazy Rider!" called somebody as I went out the door.
"Bye!" came from someone else.

The open air felt good, and I drove off fast, under the allure of the wide night skies, glimpsed over the treetops, feeling strange wonderment that one plays his role in history whether he likes it or not, even the tail-end of history. But perhaps it was a beginning, a dawn, although all was blackness. Suddenly, all the fear and grief of that night Julie and I had been involved in the accident washed over me brighter, fiercer, more powerful than at the time. Everything in the way of regret and shock and sadness I should have let in back then but could not afford to came towering over my head in a ten-foot wave. I was terribly and truly sorry about that fellow we had hit in the road, his friends or family who would have missed him, if he had any. I added up my guilt, my carelessness, probably speeding down that night hill, my evasions at the time, all deplorable, regrettable and sorrowful. On top of that I felt deeply ashamed and very sorry that we Americans had driven these good people off the Great Plains into a place like the Flame Bar, who had once roamed free and powerful and carefree. It was all very sad, life was. And inevitable, as far as I can tell.

It had been beyond my abilities to articulate how we were all in this thing together, back in the Flame. I missed Julie terribly. She would have managed it. With her by my side we would have engaged those guys and their ladies some way, and still been back there cozily drinking, "good white people," Julie's effect always, even having a good time. I could have purchased a frozen pizza they would have heated in the microwave I had noticed behind the bar. Long ago I had understood she was my better half, but that of course assumed a whole to have a half of, water under the bridge. She couldn't help me now. I was starving.

At the chamber of commerce headquarters in town, the one with the giant Beaver in front of it, I had picked up some literature to read in my solitary hours, including a curious pamphlet entitled "Little Known Facts about the Indians of the Northwest." (In candor, reader, I have to admit again I might be disguising locations, as one can't be too careful, and it may have been "Midwest" or some Canadian province, or even, who knows, "Northern California.") Some of these facts in the pamphlet related to various tortures tribes used to inflict on each other, and the white man when they had the good luck to catch one. One "Fact" described in some detail their purported practice of cutting little pieces out of the victim, hundreds of bits and pieces, one after the other, that the squaws were supposed to amuse themselves with, one morsel after another (going into the pot probably) over as many days as the hapless victim could be kept alive for. This was supposed to have been the fate of a trapper named Israel McKenzie in 1852, according to the pamphlet. With death the fun stopped, since it was pointless after that. The whole tribe gathered for the action and to laugh at the victim's screams. I wondered if the chamber of commerce pamphlet was true? Did the Indians practice such exquisite tortures on each other and hapless pioneers? I would not be surprised, knowing what everyone else is capable of. Does this justify our wiping them out? Who is worse, the white man or the Indian? Is there ever an end to it, does the darkness ever lighten?

The truth is we damn near exterminated their whole race, whether some of them were torturers and deserved it or not, and I sympathized with, *empathized* with, and liked those fellows in the bar, and understood their hostility, even if it was directed at me. Maybe guys like them would never have been torturers, just average guys. They probably would though. But I was guilty as sin, not just historically, but personally, having run an Indian down myself, something I regretted with my whole heart. It occurred to me I was in the way of taking on the whole burden of history because of the single mishap that had overtaken us that night. I saw how close I had come—that after a couple of more beers I might have tried to tell them my story. Jaws would have dropped in the Flame Bar on the reservation. They might have started feeling sorry for *me*. In my headlights the primeval forest exploded around me once more, green and black, diabolical, inexorable, and deadly, reminding me of that drive down from the hills that Julie and I had taken one night not so long ago, while I barely hung onto the curves, which had ended the happy life we had had together (as I sentimentally and rosily remembered it at the moment). I was full of the sorrow and terror of that night again to add to the loneliness of this one.

Before I knew it I had blown full speed right through a little crossroads town, about one block long, which had snuck up on me in my blown-out meditative state, and happening to look back I saw a whole different species of redness on my tail, the winking light of a cop car. Deep in my cogitations on the nature of man and history, I must have been doing seventy through that village where the speed limit had probably been twenty-five. Unfortunately, the cop didn't go for my explanation that I had been trying to find a pizza joint before I died of starvation. I was so grateful not to be given a breath test that I exuded utter humility and shut up. He turned out to be a state trooper and made me follow him twenty miles to the county seat where there was a state police headquarters four stories high. There I was locked up since I didn't have the cash for the bond on me (I had shrewdly left it in the stove). To hell with it, I thought, turning to survey my solitary cell.

I was in some sort of holding cell. After all, it wasn't as if I had a lot of other plans for the rest of the night. In fact I was safe in here. I gave it up and objectively surveyed my condition, always worthwhile in case there was some chance of escape. They weren't going to shoot me in all likelihood. Not like the troops did the Indians in their stockades of yesteryear. Maybe they would feed me something. As this note sunk in, and I decided it could not be so bad, I was able to take stock of my surroundings, never expecting what I saw now. High up in a panel next to the door was a set of buttons, and a slot—with a key in it. This holding cell with its barred door was actually an elevator! If not an invitation for escape it at least afforded me opportunity of going to a "higher level"!

I laughed aloud at my own joke (always with Julie in mind). From down the hallway came the muffled buzz of booking room activity and cops jiving with each other. The elevator must have been used sometimes to transfer prisoners from floor to floor and was put to use as a temporary holding area and carelessly somebody had left the key in it for the sake of convenience. Why had they left me in it I wondered, with a key, just laziness? Apparently so. Well, where were you going to go? Up or down.

But why not, up or down? Just as the cop came back to grin at me and tell me that I couldn't make my phone call yet, I hit a button and my cell began to rise. On the next floor, another cop walked past, preoccupied. "Can I make my phone call yet?" I yelled.

"You'll just have to wait!" The off-hand pleasure he took in denying me was evident. He was so pleased with his power he didn't even notice I was in motion. I didn't care. What was the difference to me? I was starting to enjoy this. At home I was a prisoner in my cabin on Cloud Lake anyway, and it didn't ever move so nicely, except to threaten to slide down the bank in the rain straight into the lake. I pressed the top button and rose to the top floor.

This floor was darkened and deserted. I rested there. Through the bars I could see a few locked offices behind panels of black glass. As my ears adjusted to the relative silence, I heard muffled heavy breathing, and softly moaned words that sounded like somebody was being tortured at the end of the hallway. It was horrible. Police brutality it sounded like, but when a woman cried out, "God, I love it!" that theory seemed less likely. A door somewhere suddenly burst open, and light filtered up to me. There was the sound of people getting up, running steps, then somebody tripping and stumbling.

"Jesus Christ!" I recognized the sour tone of the cop who had arrested me. A woman screamed, *"Get lost!"*

After a long moment, the steps came up the hall deliberately. My captor stood in front of me, but he glanced over his shoulder with a smile, as he absently searched for the keyhole. Just at the moment when he got his key in, I hit the button and his whole ball of keys was yanked out of his hand as I descended. They clanked and grated against the edge of the elevator shaft as they bent or broke off. His shouts diminished. I reached for the key that was stuck in the control panel above my head, and the crate clanked to a halt in total darkness between floors.

I hung in space there in deep silence and blackness. The voices of scurrying cops and staff were muted as if they were at a great distance. As usual, I had against all odds created a semblance of freedom for myself, hanging in the balance, this time inside a moveable jail cell. Freedom was a pathless forest, and for the first time I wondered if I was really up to the hike. Considering the pass I had come to now, wouldn't it have been better for me just to have a regular job, a home and family, and all the trimmings, like everybody else? In other words, couldn't I have stayed with Julie? Seen it through like she said, whatever that entailed? Even stayed at the dealership with Harry? Could it have been worse than the strange and unpredictable path I was on? Maybe I would have wound up in a real jail. In case I hadn't, thought of working for Harry made me grind my teeth so hard I could feel the enamel flaking off.

A long process of liberation had begun for me and was rolling down the pike like a freight train—I would have rather gotten off. I missed Julie bitterly in the darkness of my portable cell. I even missed Gretchen. I thought of her in her hospital room, not unlike this elevator as a temporal conveyance. She, like me, was supposed to get out sometime. I prolonged my stay about forty-five minutes. Hers would be longer. Nobody was yelling at me, the cops just ignored me, and it got boring waiting in limbo. I didn't want to stay like this all night. When my cage hit the ground, no one paid me any attention for a long time. In the end the cops decided not to charge me with joy-riding in their elevator, since it would have come out that they left the keys in it I guess. I called Packy, and he got the cash out of my stove to bail me out. It seemed a paltry end after so much excitement.

Heading home to my cabin I felt a terrible sense of rootlessness overcome me. Even though I felt in my soul most like a red man by now, I could never be one of them. But I no longer felt like a "white" either, events had seen to that. That was saying something, because not long ago, I was as white as Wonder bread. To have stopped at Packy's bar with him right now would have had me thinking that I really belonged back at the Flame tavern, and that could never be the case. I headed straight home to my cabin. I had become a quintessential outsider. For some time I had been having glimpses that too much freedom was a lonely jungle. Now I realized it could be a zoo.

Invisible Car Dealer

After that, on my drives around the countryside I saw Indians everywhere that I (a Midwesterner as I have mentioned, as my general excuse, although the truth is I might be from some other part of the country) had not noticed before. It was Indian territory. On the way into town, next to the Chamber of Commerce Tourist Bureau with its giant plastic beaver with white buck teeth that looked like a piece of Disneyland broken off from the mainland and floated up here, there was an Indian curio shop that featured a totem pole in its front yard. The totem pole was full-size, but was dwarfed by that beaver, so you get an idea. But the totem pole was not cheap or phony, but very handsomely carved with its frightening and ugly masks one on top of the other. It was the real McCoy, maybe. It put the beaver to shame next to it in front of the Bureau where tourists went to get maps, brochures, and camping permits. There was a genuine spirit in that totem pole, unlike the giant beaver. At least it had an effect on me, both disturbing and hopeful, each time I passed it. Some days I went there just to look at it. I exchanged glances with the presences embodied in it.

What if there *were* a whole other reality, which they were tuned into, and maybe still are, which is still there as always, as Julie claimed, only invisible? What if by pretending a totem pole like this was just a tourist attraction, we were kidding ourselves, like children playing with a live bomb? We just couldn't see the fuse because it led into another dimension, maybe the future, where the match would be lit. What if the winning of the West had been all a vain delusion, and Destiny was Manifest on some unheard-of level where unbeknownst to us we were heading toward our ruin? What if we hadn't stolen their land after all, and all that they had said about God really owning the land, making it unstealable, was the truth, and they were just lying low and biding their time? What if under the eternal heavens we palefaces with our skyscrapers and high-tech gadgets are nothing but demented squatters, whom God will kick out by and by? These thoughts troubled me, and yet uplifted me too, as I communed with the spirits of the totem pole.

I knew how Julie would have admired that totem pole, which, along with every Indian I saw, in the end only reminded me of her, and it was hard to go two hours without seeing an Indian up in these parts unless you kept your nose in your glass in Packy's all day. That way for sure you wouldn't see any Indians. Not that they weren't allowed in Packy's. In this modern era of civil rights laws, the extremely grudging attitude of tolerance with which the rednecks greet all who are not like themselves, aware that they may be fined or even taken to jail if they don't, is alive and well under the Constitution in every corner of the land, and if an Indian had come into Packy's and sat down, he would have been served, in an atmosphere of the most profound, wild-eyed, poisonous tolerance, even more entertaining in its way than what had happened to me in the Flame Bar.

A wonderful, seething social comedy is under way in the land. But no self-respecting Indian would have wanted to drink in Packy's, for heaven's sake. They had better things to do. Or I would hope so. None would have been caught dead in Packy's. Dead! My God, time hung heavy on me so that sometimes I found myself worrying if by some Indian clairvoyance, smoke signals or something, the Native Americans around me here knew my past, my terrible secret. They looked at me that way sometimes. Yet the effect of my stop on the reservation that night had been to lighten me just a little bit of a certain burden, the sort that is cast off as your secret slowly but surely comes to light by its peculiar fate.

The old cars multiplied in ragged rows behind my cabin at Cloud Lake, and the Indians on the roads and out my windows grew more numerous each time I looked. I felt my past somehow catching up to me, but this inkling of a climax approaching was accompanied not only with dread and fear, but hope of release and a change for the better. Might it actually be that there is such a thing as too much freedom? This paradoxical notion continued to be glimpsed on the outposts of my mind like a fugitive from justice. In school when they taught us about our heritage, I had certainly never heard such a possibility mentioned. It would have been considered un-American. Even now I can't think of such a thing without feeling confused and surprised, even guilty. Who could ever get enough of freedom? One conceives of freedom as an unqualified blessing always. There were no eight o'clock wake-up calls from prospective car buyers up here. No buyers coming to call at all hours to keep me on my toes. No Mr. Ramos's bird recordings going off like clockwork, it was the real thing up here, bird cries day and night till you didn't hear it any more. Might as well be no birds when it's all birds. I lay in bed listening to the bird frenzy, their signifying, rapacious cries. Surely freedom's not an end in itself? It's a glimpse of something better, I've come to that conclusion. What we are tasting is the first flavor of freedom, but there will be others, which will justify and explain what has passed before. We'll have to earn it. Some yet unheard of refinement in the way of, or beyond, freedom. Anyway, to have thought otherwise would have been too bitter. Things begin to look profoundly different when the vacation refuses to come to an end. That totem pole, when I happened to pass it, whispered to me of other realities.

One evening I was drinking in Packy's, just watching the dice game at the bar (after my cars I didn't need to gamble), half-listening to the usual gossip and local scandals, accounts of guys' mishaps with women and wives, and their accidents, diseases and car troubles, their fish stories and hunting tales, complaints against the lumber mill owners, and the Department of Conservation or what have you in the way of all government, the Indians, arguments over why we had failed to turn Vietnam into a parking lot, and the rest of what passed for conversation in the place. Outside it was raining hard, and there was the steady drone of the rushing, falling water, and the lyric plaints coming from the juke box, and the muffled crashes of the bowling game, in the general din of talk in the full-up place. Packy's was outside the spiffed-up touristy area of Main Street, around the corner from it, but not so far away that it didn't get plenty of tourist trade from people who wanted to go to a "real" place, much to their disappointment soon enough I would hope. This afternoon there had been a storm and the bar was filled with fishermen who hadn't been able to fish, resort owners seeking relief from their complaining clientele, and loggers and millmen and others soaked to the skin. It was a warm evening, and there was a clammy, boisterous, even irritable atmosphere, which it was taking mucho gallons of beer and spirits to half mellow out.

Startling me out of my personal fog, a stranger at my elbow said, "You the guy at Cloud Lake with all the cars, aint you?"

He was drunk like everybody else. I assumed I was in for either a ribbing or a pitch. But instead, "There was a drowning almost in front of your place this afternoon, you know that?" He glanced at me to see if he was repeating common knowledge, then seeing my surprise, his face took on, not just the bluff-solemn lines with which people speak of death, but a hint of an inappropriate look of satisfaction. "The Indians are down there diving for him bare-ass."

Indians? Did they get paid for it? I had at once assumed it was a tourist story, some fisherman out there in a poncho like a tent and heavy boots and leaden tackle in his pockets, who'd gone down like a sinker.

"One less spearfisher," he smirked.

I always thought of myself as regrettably hard-boiled, but the mean casual callousness of guys like this always amazed me.

"He was drunk," he went on. "What else? You may get a dead Injun wash up by your pier in the morning, ha ha."

It made my hair stand on end. The currents would inexorably push the body my way. What was going on? Things were closing in on me! I got a horrible glimpse of something uncanny, before recognizing the ridiculousness of my drift. But, crazy as it sounded, why were dead Indians following me around, so to speak? The guy sitting on the next stool who had informed me never would have imagined the effect of his gossip on me. Where had I been this afternoon? I was trying to remember. My short-term memory was getting poor. One thing led to another. Every day, every hour was the same. I hadn't been around my cabin all day, so I'd missed the excitement.

Invisible Car Dealer

I was in a mood to question everything, all the events and the decisions regarding them going back a long way that had brought me to such unhealthy, un-Thoreau-like solitude in these woods. Julie had probably been right when she said it would haunt me. I went home to survey my estate. All my cars were there, sunk a few inches into the mud. Seeing them safe and sound as usual only gave me a new pang. There were so many. I had barely looked at them in a while, let alone counted them. They even seemed to have multiplied—like the weeds that were growing among, around, and even into them. A few of them I didn't remember at all. Hardly strangers to the elements when I'd purchased them, they disintegrated day by day in the rains that alternated with the bright sunshine that only cooked and rotted them more. Chrome trim and sections of rusty tailpipe dribbled onto the ground, old rubber fittings and seals cracked and fell off, and sagging upholstery and the musty remnants of top-liners decomposed before my eyes.

The storm had lulled but gusts of wind driving the few drops sideways suggested it would start again. Cloud Lake was black and shingled and smelled fresh. The sky was heavy with clouds that glowed dully, letting through little starlight. There was a drowning victim at the bottom of my lake tonight, a fly in my ointment, a bad olive in my martini, a nuclear bomb in my day. When you live close to the water like that, no matter if it's a fair-sized lake, or the Pacific Ocean, it's all your territory, islands, bays, holes, deeps, reefs, no telling what all down there, what odds and ends, what submerged history, it's all in your own back yard and may wash up. It seemed memory and Cloud Lake were one and the same black water.

The violent gusts brought such a bracing watery freshness to make you feel something new was being born. In the dim waves lashed by jeweled reeds a fish turned over in the shallows. Going inside my cabin to wait would have been real terror. I felt my spirit being drawn down toward the shore. I couldn't keep from going out on the short pier with a flashlight and poking around. Down by the south point there was a cluster of lights and I guessed it was the searchers. I saw it in the weeds in my cold beam of light, glossy rumpled streak of brown-blue glistening piled grained clay, floating log, mill stray, mound of muck turned up by the waves and catching my light which shook in my hand so I couldn't keep it trained on this—blue wound in my eye—I jumped off the pier into thigh-deep water and pushed through the grasses to the horror meant for me, black hair, brown skin, jean jacket, the Indian. Anguished in drowning waves, from the place where true fear comes, I stuck the flashlight into my pocket and dragged the sodden corpse by its arms onto shore, where I devoted to it vain attentions misplaced from a night road many months before, operations ineffectual not only because I didn't know the first thing about what I was doing and was half wild but because this guy really had been dead a while, drowned hours ago, though Julie probably still had doubts about the other. I stopped just short of clamping my mouth to his rubbery one in a mawkish act, and stood up alive to an electric connection between me and the leaden clouds above, the black water at my feet.

I must have been a crazy sight, dripping water. Packy's eyes bugged out. I told him and he called the cops. At the bar the guy who had warned me of what lay in store for me tonight was still cranking up the beers, a glimmer in his eyes.

The sheriff, a fire truck and paramedics, the whole weird crew played around my shore for two hours. Little did they know I was on the verge of turning myself in. Finally they took the corpse away. The rain began again in earnest. I lay in the darkness on my bunk, unable to enjoy the usually pleasant sensations of being well sheltered in a storm. I was still in wet clothes. I felt sheltered from nothing, and thought I deserved no better. A torrent of rain assaulted the rooftop, and a cold dankness clawed at the edges of my covers. In the steadily increasing downpour it seemed to me a climax was portended. Anyway the place seemed about to break up and float away.

I thought to myself that the next day I would drive to Berkeley, find Julie, and have a long talk with her, insist that she listen to me, and come back up here with me. Maybe the second Indian absolved me of the first, somehow, I fantasized. A strange notion. I wasn't sure I could explain it to her and soon enough couldn't understand it myself since in reality I was feeling worse and worse every minute. Surely she would see my panic and pity me. I wished so badly she were beside me in the bed on this miserable night, it brought tears to my eyes. I could feel her missing presence to the tips of my fingers, to say the least. I had the sneaking feeling she might have been right about something, if only that I needed her and should have listened to her.

The rain's insistent drumming hiss was like an injured creature's seeking for its home. There was an urgency in the clammy cabin, the black atmosphere, a heaviness circling relentlessly to bleak fulfillment, a balance that kept coming down. A pounding on the cabin door, solemn, importunate, made me sit bolt upright holding on to the edges of the mattress like the gunwales of a rocking boat. My heart set off like a buoy tilting in the waves, ding-dong, ding-dong. Who in God's name could be knocking on my door in this rain? What else could go wrong tonight? It was surely no farmer with a car to sell. The sheriff again? Some red tape to do with the body? The cops who had begun to suspect something finally?

Half asleep, I had the crazy dream image of an emissary from a judge, if not the Judge himself in black and flowing robes, holding a lamp into my face. Realistically, I wondered if it might be a messenger from the drug dealer Gregory, then, more realistically, a subpoena from the lawyer. The knocking came, rhythmic, robotic, like a ghost's in a horror movie. When I cracked the door, there was an Indian holding the hand of a small child, whose teeth were silently chattering. I became aware of the soles of my bare feet burning on the cold linoleum floor. All my fear seemed centered there, and I violently sneezed. Maybe there was nothing to be afraid of, for they were as timid and about as mysterious as a pair of wet squirrels, having taken two steps through the doorway, huddled just inside it, dripping pools on the floor.

I brewed a pot of coffee, and the kid slurped his hungrily through blue lips, but the man didn't touch his. Only the merest words passed between us, as I couldn't bring myself to ask him what they were doing around here, even to cover my nervousness, and he didn't offer any explanation for asking shelter with me. The storm seemed answer enough for everything. He gestured to the heavens, or at least the roof of my cabin, and we both smiled.

The downpour was the center of our attention. We sat grinning under its weight, and listening for any signs of a let-up. There was only the whir of sheets of water, and we might have been all dead, for all the human noise we made, once the kid had finished his coffee. I studied the two of them, in jeans and sodden faded flannel shirts, their wet hair in their eyes, faces alternately lit up with sheepish grins and set in the impassive way of the patient, rural American poor. Slowly a kind of peace came to me.

The man finally said, "My brother had an accident today on the water, don't come home. Drowned, people say, right here. When the searchers give up for the night, I couldn't stand to leave him alone. I thought we could wait the rain out under a tree, but she was coming down good. The boy began to get cold. The cops pointed to your cabin before. We didn't come right away. Thought the rain might stop. When she started up again, I thought we better come over."

He smiled at me, turned his head slightly to left and right, so he seemed to be peeping at me warmly out of the corners of his eyes, as though by now we shared something which he didn't want to presume on too much, however. I returned his gaze only a second, as we shared something all right, life's terrible mystery. I noticed his long black hair down his back and his brown eyes sparkling good-naturedly though sadly, and I became extremely aware of his Indianness. It sent through me a flame of sadness and remorse.

He reached into his satchel on the floor and pulled out a green bottle. He meant us to have a drink together, and I got two glasses, but he made a shy sign toward the child, and I saw he wanted the kid to drink too, so I got another. He poured only a little into the kid's glass, who was about eight years old, but he wanted to include him. It was touching, whatever was going on. The wine was real cheap stuff, but warmed me like a benediction, and I wished Julie could have seen me. Still, my knees were trembling, just bouncing up and down.

Outside the rain had stopped and dawn begun to break. It felt like a morning of mornings, when angels would descend to heal me or demons to rip my guts out. With thanks for the shelter, the man and child slipped away modestly, but not before walking to the shoreline with that bottle of wine, pouring a little onto the ground, into the lapping waves, as he cried out something, and threw back his head to gaze at the sky.

At this, I finally found the strength to do the decent thing and went after him to tell him the body had been taken away by the fire department. It came pouring out of me awkwardly and obscenely like water from the mouth of a drowned man. He gave me the blankest stare and said, "I know." Then he said, "Did you see it happen?"

"No!"

"You saw it, didn't you," he said with a sad smile.

"Heavens no, I was drinking beer in Packy's! Or I was when I first heard of it. I don't know where I was."

"You had to, right in front of your place. I don't say it's your fault or nothin for not saving him. Nobody probably could." He eyed me, his eyes like probing knives, guided by, but not really intending to produce, pain.

"Listen, I wasn't around, I'm telling you." I wished I had been, so I could tell him something useful to him about his brother's end. "I really don't know anything, other than it had to be an accident."

"I figure you saw it," he said with a rueful, but nonaccusing, glance as they walked away. "I know you couldn't do much about it, who could in this weather? It was his time. He couldn't swim. You maybe thought all Indians are good swimmers."

"No, no . . . I wasn't here."

I was of course telling the truth, but I felt I was lying. He was not hostile or blaming me, but he assumed we shared some knowledge, as it were, which he must think I had my reasons for not admitting to. Suddenly tormented in a way by my past as I had never been before, the man's grief and helplessness gripped me, and I thought we shared something inconsolable.

As they drifted away into the mist, he said, slightly smiling back over his shoulder, humbly, knowing, "How else would you know where the body was? It's not your fault. He couldn't swim."

How else! It was a good question. How had it happened so? Life suddenly had the most deplorable depths, like unexplored parts of a lake one had thought oneself familiar with. In my own heart I felt what would be missing now from the hearts of the man and his boy, a friend, a brother, like vast areas of the hunting grounds blown up by the cavalry, squaws, children, great wise chiefs and all. With a reality and vividness I had resisted up to now I imagined the someone, or someones, who would have missed the drunken stumblebum Julie and I had run over that night, who would have been expecting him to come home. Or maybe he had lived alone. Maybe it had been days before somebody had missed him, an area of their world decimated by napalm while their attention was elsewhere. I thought of the guys in Packy's Bar who discounted it all, were ignorant of it, even laughed at it, spat on all this pain. Their callous attitude, which had always struck me as normal if curious, at worst depressing, suddenly made me boiling mad. Did they think all Indians were good swimmers? Would it have ever occurred to them in a thousand years to wonder about how the entire red race almost had been wiped out for their present comfort? Yes, and they applauded it heartily. How in the name of the last shred of sanity I was holding onto had the body washed up on my shore? It was past terrifying. I was being singled out for it.

I felt the stoic grief of my visitors. They expected no help, nothing, never again. I understood the harsh plight of the red man. The instant understanding of U.S. history I had acquired the night of the accident in order to slip the noose myself turned inside out and I experienced the real if casual loss of my visitors, nothing that would make the papers. A set of righteous ideas regarding history I had been holding onto in my own self-defense slipped away, and in their place a real insight into the black heart of genocide.

Later that morning I did an unimaginable thing. I called up Gregory, the drug dealer, just to hear a familiar voice, and see if things had cooled down in L.A. The nature of the wall I was up against in the city revealed itself, like the crack of doom, a peal of thunder. Through Gregory's stoned blatherings I got a good idea of the heat lingering for me down in L.A. I could not go back. Unless I wanted to risk my freedom. He didn't mention drinking any blood, that was the only bright side. Several warrants had been issued for me as a consequence of the lawyer's efforts. He told me the consumers' rights advocate had reported me to half a dozen state agencies, and I was wanted for dealing cars without a car lot and willfully hiding defects in various Rembrandts, for selling cars without putting up some unbelievable bond with some unfathomable state department, for not selling "acres of cars" but yet a few too many square feet of them without certain paperwork and guarantees stating they were not rose gardens, above all for selling them without streamers, plastic pennants, and whirling lights. Guilty, guilty. I finally had to admit to myself I was in a jam worse than the night Julie and I had hit the Indian. Gretchen was still in the hospital too, and things had taken a turn for the worse. She had sunk into real madness, and her ex-lover biologist had got it into his head I was the cause of all her problems. He had come up with the delusion that I had supplied her with an overdose of an unheard-of designer drug the chemical composition of which had to be discovered before her successful treatment could begin. He was trying to reverse engineer it from a blood sample. Gregory screeched out all the implications including blood sugars, blood libels, blood rituals, and the dismemberment of cats. He also claimed that I had burnt up his Corvette (he must have torched it for the insurance), that I owed money to some gangster friends of his, and that there was a contract on my life. The fact that I had done my best to get Gretchen off drugs was not believed or credited. The hours I had put in finding antiques for those ungrateful assholes were forgotten. The problem was there was a grain of truth in one or two of their bizarre car stories which lent credence to the silliest of them.

I put down the phone on Packy's bar and stared out the open door into the iron-colored drizzle which was coming down softly but steadily as usual. I ordered a fresh drink, and as I began to sip it, my eye fell on the Olympia Beer clock behind the bar. (Or perhaps it was another brand of beer.) I had lost all sense of time after a couple of months up here, and to my amazement I saw it was 10:30 a.m. So now I was drinking in the mid-morning. Disgusted and disoriented, I stumbled out the door and began to walk through the light rain. With no purpose in mind, I ambled down Main Street, and off onto a dirt road into the woods, letting the cool rain, which constantly crossed and re-crossed the line between mist and shower, clear my senses and wash me into a clean sobriety. I was drenched to the skin but it was a mild day, and the walk warmed me. I felt like I was in a bath, a heavenly bath. Occasionally the sun glowed barely through the clouds, casting an eerie bronze light. The effect when it did was of waking up to a strange new dawn each time, and it was not that pleasant. The sights afforded by this little town struck me as painfully meager and barren. The storefronts and facades of the two-story Main Street buildings were peeling and dilapidated, except for the block-long stretch boutique-ized for the tourists. The place was no more than a sleepy village, and I was the idiot. The monotonous forest went on forever.

I found myself well out at the edge of town. Occasionally a logging truck or a big RV or camper careened by, throwing a stream of grit and moisture like BBs at me. After the last cabin, there was a densely wooded stretch when I was closed off and alone with my thoughts. Walking along the shoulder between the weeds and the forest, I indulged the illusion of being hidden, lost, and protected. Then a vast clearing opened and I stared at the lumber mills or paper mills, whatever they were. Logs the size of telegraph poles lay like cordwood in monstrous stacks as tall as the pyramids of the Aztecs hundreds of feet at the base and rising into the sky so high the topmost timbers looked like matchsticks. It was an awesome vision. Never had I seen a log pile like that one. In all my travels about this territory, I must never have driven by here somehow.

A party of Indians passed me by with somber faces. They stared past me with not even muted curiosity or dull recognition. In a flash of paranoia I thought they had found me out, discovered me, and knew me, but were not at all impressed by what was troubling me. In the rain, surrounded by these dark faces, staring at the colossal piles of logs that disappeared into the clouds, with the poor little town behind me which was nothing but a collection of bait shops and taverns and sad Indian gift stores, I asked myself what I was going to do around here even for one more day, even one more hour.

The party of Indians was about two hundred yards behind me by now, and over my shoulder I watched them disappear, probably just around a curve in the road, but seemingly straight into the forest, as if they were headed home. The way they walked, they seemed to know where they were going and what they were doing, no strangers around here, even if they were the defeated. They had someplace to go to, no matter how futile or stark, unlike car-happy me.

I experienced the sensation of unknowing witnessing that we sometimes have—perhaps you have had sometimes—in a crowd of strangers, at once intimate and foreign, of an intricate life profound and commonplace, going off somewhere about which we suddenly feel a wistful, unaccountable interest, but cannot follow, life relentless, unsearchable, endless, familiar. Worlds upon worlds, within worlds, without end, worlds colliding too, as the Europeans' world did upon the red man's. A whole tapestry of life sheared off, going into the forest, the trail worn by a thousand generations of feet, broken off abruptly, replaced by others, at gunpoint. At the moment of impact that night in the forest, when Julie and I had unwittingly written the last page in somebody's history book, who had been affected, who had been not come home to, who remembered him, whose plans had changed? Then I thought it was all happening to *me,* and I understood with wonder and horror that I was becoming the victim, who had never wanted to be.

The party of Indians had vanished and I was staring behind me at the empty road. Maybe they were desperate but I doubted it; that was not how I had perceived their measured gait and stolid faces. I was me, I was the desperate one by now. I contrasted my unease and lostness with something mutely adapted and sure-footed in them, as if in spite of the whites' victory and their defeat in history, they did know something I did not. It occurred to me that despite appearances they were not only survivors, but maybe secret masters of something. I wouldn't have gone so far as to say Julie was right (probably it would have taken a gun to my own head for that). Never mind Julie, the intimation came to me that they *did* know something. Their poise and quiet grace suggested it to me. They knew how to take a stand, if only an inner one, and not be completely destroyed. I wished I could have followed them into the forest and left my problems behind. Whether their adaptation as I saw it owed its power to the views or practices of their ancient culture or simply to their present state of having nothing left to lose I did not know, but to whatever degree it was the latter, I was on the verge of catching up with them. It seemed to me the tables were turned and they nobly walked on solid ground, and I was one of the hunted, and haunted.

Invisible Car Dealer

It was time to put on the brakes and stop buying old cars, and to start fixing them up and get a return on my investment. One morning I locked my cabin, jumped in the Jag, and headed south (or west) for Richmond, CA. Nothing like getting back to business and down to work to resolve all kinds of problems, money problems, legal problems, woman problems, even "Indian troubles." The thing was I had drifted along enjoying my dreamlike anonymity and spending money in a half-drunken daze so long I was pretty broke. When I'd pulled out that morning, after Jack G. and I'd chopped up the guilty Alfa, I'd promised him some work. In L.A., I had often thought of Jack and what I might do for him eventually, and on the road and later in Washington State at Cloud Lake (or someplace like that), I had found plenty of time to worry about him. I'd planned to bring him work, but this hadn't happened yet, because I had been hiding out in a somewhat paranoid frame of mind and letting one day run into the next. Now I suddenly needed him, and I had plenty of work for him.

　　The shoe was on the other foot. I needed him to help me with my herd of wrecks up at Cloud Lake. It made me feel cheap, looking him up again only when I was desperate. But I knew he would understand. He must have understood the score at once, and it shows what kind of man he was that he never hinted at any such thing, far from it. All he thought of was to get going, to get our partnership off the ground as we'd always known we would. He was all enthusiasm and never referred to the time I'd been away, or acted any way except glad as hell to see me. I thought I could imagine some other feelings he had to be holding inside, and what a good sport he was about it. I told myself I'd make him understand, make it up to him. But there was nothing to understand, and nothing to make up, as far as Jack was concerned. That was the beautiful thing about Jack, a quality which I suppose must have been created or at least honed in the war. No, there was nothing to explain. You can imagine my feelings. I thought of him as my brother.

I was so glad to find him still working at Dahomey's Wrecking Yard, where I'd last seen him, and where he'd been working since getting canned at the dealership for coming in late too often and mouthing off at both Harry and the service manager one time too many. I was greatly relieved that he hadn't gone to work again for Harmless Harry at Harry's new place, which had been my fear. I thought I was just barely equal to dealing with Dahomey, and couldn't have matched wits with Harry. I certainly did not want to run into Harry just now. We needed a yard to work out of, and a tow truck with which to start bringing the cars down, and I was banking on Dahomey's getting involved and letting us use one of his several wreckers. But for talking to Dahomey I would need Jack's help too. Dahomey loved Jack just as much as he barely tolerated the sight of me.

When I saw Jack's blue Porsche parked in front of the cavernous wrecking yard as I drove up after my long haul from Cloud Lake, my heart lifted, at the same time it kind of sank, as I say, with its load of guilt, to rise at last knowing Jack's quality of man. I was just glad I was about to see him again, a true friend. But I felt like there would be nobody like Jack to help me get back on my feet again after the beating I'd been taking, and it would be good for Jack's wallet too, I'd make sure of that. When I saw Jack's Porsche, all calculations ceased and high spirits prevailed. Jack always had a pretty car, and he kept his cars clean and polished. He was unlike most mechanics in that. It was because he was a race car driver, that was his real love. He considered working for Dahomey or Harry or whomever as a mere phase he was putting up with. I got out and stood in the shadow of the tall corrugated metal fence around the wrecker's yard drawing in the delightful dusty, greasy air. My cars could sink in Cloud Lake, if only Jack was glad to see me. Suddenly everything seemed the same again, nothing was changed at all. It had only been six months or so. Walking past his car, I knew that under the front seat would be his VC dagger, and I saw dangling from the Porsche's rearview mirror his big gold peace symbol.

The mouth of the yard was blocked by a couple of battered flatbed trucks and a towering red crane, from whose cable hung a big greasy V-8 engine. Beyond them, it was like being back in rampant nature again at my lake, but to the nth degree—the hugeness of the outfit, the dense overgrowth of half-crushed machines, the raw red paths of mud through generations of invention and design, vividness of the clay under the tangled layers upon layers of smashed chassis, the beating silence, the greatness of arrested motion in every direction as far as the eye could see— all seeming to be returning to the jungle or the very earth. My cabin had been but a miniature! I smiled. It was a shot of adrenalin, being in the grand museum, like coming home, but I was unexpectedly accosted by memories of the last time I was here, cutting up the Alfa. What was the matter with me? That was all forgotten. I had a good opportunity, a favor to offer these guys. The crazy profligacy of destroyed machines was a more or less organized business, of all things, and had its eye to its cash flow, to which I might contribute.

There was stuff in here Dahomey had forgotten about, had never realized was here to begin with. In fact, Dahomey was a rich man. Yes, something monstrous was being tamed here, no less than the traffic jams of the West Coast. It brought peace to the heart, with all the more strange force, the signs of fresh violence everywhere. A lot of these cars had wound up here after terrible accidents, multicar collisions. The rest had rolled at last to a complete stop. Nothing moved, yet transformations raged in these hills, barely under control, which the average citizen cardriver was happy never to see. It was "Bump City" (a sign in one corner proclaimed), place of rest, the well-earned reduction of civilization.

Dahomey's little shack and office in one corner of the mighty yard was like a homestead on the virgin prairie, not a soul nor another structure in sight, just the rolling hills and plains strewn with dead metal carcasses and small motors, his big square-

103

Invisible Car Dealer

muzzled puppy of a breed casually and completely vicious panting listlessly in front of it, keeping to a sliver of shade. Like the Grecian columns of an old antebellum plantation house, scorched black by time, all that was left standing (Dahomey having slit old master's throat quietly, without fanfare, burned the big house, but kept the slave quarters out of a fine sense of irony), half a dozen precarious pillars of old tires rose twenty feet high or more, adorning nothing at all. The tires were unsettling to observe, off-kilter, leaning ominously, lethal-looking towers that might fall on you if you got too close. What made it so odd was that there seemed no reason for such an arrangement of tires, nothing utilitarian, and about as decorative as loaded shotguns. Appurtenances reflecting Dahomey's rudimentary or exotic esthetics, nothing more, they were so preposterously high you couldn't get a tire you might want unless you knocked the whole thing down or resorted to the crane. It took a conscious act of courage to go near them and approach the office, past the killer dog, over the punishing ruts of muck and clay you had to traverse to arrive at this welcoming committee, every uneven foot of ground booby-trapped with jagged iron anti-tank devices.

Only the voracious appetite of modern society for discount auto parts could have ever provided Dahomey a single customer. There's an inevitable air of cavalier decadence about any wrecker's headquarters and landscapes, but the indifference of Dahomey's suggested less a natural corruption or a business running on automatic pilot than the effects of a curse. The wretched inheritor of a lost culture, Dahomey keeping a barely remembered faith against an ancient backdrop of chrome cliffs rising over gleaming lakes of black oil, the foothills of carnage extended as far as the eye could see, and here and there bare-chested greasy dudes picked at the mounds of junk like survivors of an incomprehensible catastrophe or priests of a defunct religion. I could imagine Dahomey Dismantler Comp. (another battered sign on the fence) existed at all due to secret contracts for dumping toxic wastes, or that at any rate he was bound to receive lucrative offers.

The master himself of this estate I admired as much as it was possible to admire a haughty and overbearing man. Not only was he a self-made man who had been raised on the streets of the East Oakland ghetto by heroin addicts (as he had told me once in a fit of twisted pride), who had rescued himself from life's wrecking ball by dint of his prodigious energies and some inscrutable faith, now he tried to help others like himself, and his workmen tended to be ex-cons, rehabilitated junkies, and guys with strange resumes such as Jack, or Gladstone the Nigerian, whose acquaintance I was just about to make, who because of visa restrictions must have been well-nigh unemployable elsewhere. Such was Dahomey's loyalty to his own painful origins (addicted in his junkie mother's womb, his heavyweight credentials), he exuded far from good will, but the almost malice of redeeming necessity, that was probably all that could drive his eccentric workmen and reclaim the ex-cons, and Dahomey was at least a millionaire by now.

I was looking forward to greeting him, though I knew very well immediately to be scalded by his manner. Dahomey radiated heat never warmth, and even his workmen kept their distance unless business demanded otherwise. The man was as big as a furnace, too, which raged in all seasons. Well, one couldn't speak of liking such a man. You got out of his way, until the need was as pressing as mine was. He was nowhere around that I could see, nor Jack either. The yard wore a sleepy and deserted air, but it did that even when moderately busy, it was so vast. No doubt they were out there somewhere prizing maimed bodies with crowbars. To have peeked into the office, I would have had to pass that dog. Maybe they were in there but I didn't dare. I'd have to wait for them to come out. I like dogs but this one was a trained killer which was kept hungry. It was growling at me and baring its teeth even at a distance. I was sure it could smell my desperate predicament. I would have had to be light-hearted or even more desperate than I was—for some taillight or whatever—to have confronted that inadequately leashed animal which was all set to embarrass me with a display of ill will if it didn't rip my flesh. My heart full of lyrical hopes, plans for business, anticipation of seeing my old friends—for that wolf all this complex inner life came across as plain fear.

There was nothing but to wander down the aisles of cars in hopes of seeing someone. Rising high and almost disappearing in the sun, the long arm of the crane cradled in its hook, about chest-high to me, the V-8 engine trailing wires and hoses, dribbling black oil onto the ground, like a still warm heart ripped from a body. As I walked past, I gave it a shove, and behind me it swung gently in the air back and forth, creaking. Over the oil-soaked clay I picked my way among stray transmissions, leaf springs, rear-ends, wheel rims, and all the assorted iron bits and mangled trim that clog every inch of space in such a yard like rotten twigs and fallen leaves on the forest floor, mingling with bits of tooth and bone of mythical beasts in dry streambeds choked with grass, little unheard-of treasures. It had its dark charm. General Motors shaded detroitly into Ford, American cars blended cross-culturally into Japanese, families' cars, teenagers', lovers', picnickers', movie-goers', shoppers', lost California dreamers' and drifters' horribly dented chariots, lovely as poems they had been, disappearing in the common fate and utilitarian interment. Once these stilled crates had sped along happy as top-40 tunes.

Now and again, I crossed paths with one of the workers or keepers of the place at his funereal tasks, skinny starved-looking dudes with their jeans hanging low on their hips, bare chests streaked with unmentionable fluids, silver hammers, blackened picks, and arcane clenching devices in their hands, eyes blankly staring past me as they made their rounds, lost in unimaginable reflections. I tried to speak to them, ask them if they'd seen Jack around anywhere, but their monosyllabic responses were always negative, if they answered at all. Aint seen nobody. Don't have that part. Boss aint here. Come back tomorrow. I knew the game and kept walking. For all they knew I was the Man.

Once I had been fond of this place, which had always had a comforting aura of all that is familiar and self-evident for me beyond question. Thin wails of motors, of winches, came from the distance. Hollow voices, impossible to make out, echoed over the slagheap. It seemed to me that this was not Dahomey's good old reclaiming enterprise at all, that fear had realized itself, and my miniature auto graveyard at Cloud Lake had exploded with the logic of nightmare, that I was lost in a labyrinth of wreckage, that the world had turned into one giant soulless junkyard beyond reclamation which I could not get away from. The place looked like it was one short step of disappearing back into the raw ores and minerals from which it had once been winnowed. Everything was earth-colored, red and black, collapsing, and about to take me with it. The corrugated metal walls of the yard were about to crumple—

not from all the junk they encased, but under the weight of everything they negated, something very blue, the sky itself, which I was keenly aware of, the waters of the Pacific Ocean out there someplace about to burst through the smoking metal, that invisible Pacific Ocean that was not very far from here, which many Californians, at least in places like Richmond, rarely if ever see, unless they cross the Bay Bridge, which many never do, although it's under their noses. I know these inner-city Californians too. A hallucinatory wall of cleansing blue hovered in the air over our heads with the tenderness of a pendant teardrop and the power of a tidal wave, as if everything and Dahomey's lost and desperate workmen and above all my own soul would suddenly be washed clean, and all these broken ruined jalopies would fly to heaven.

I heard voices. Through the nearest wall of cars, intimate, so nearby, from the next aisle of the store, so to speak, past the canned goods, I happily recognized Jack's belligerent, disbelieving, put-upon tones, which he had for the world that did not come up to his standard, answered by the impudent accents of a stranger, a foreigner by the impeccable English he was speaking. I looked up and down for a way through the vertical banks of cars, car bodies stacked on crushed car bodies, without a chink between them. There was no daylight between the variously dismembered frames and chassis, and whichever way I peered, only more automotive components protruded at me. I stopped still to listen.

"I won eight hundred dollars, Gladstone, whatever you say, that's what I won. It's more than you ever won," Jack was bragging rather childishly. So, he'd been to Reno, or perhaps even Vegas, lately. That could be a bad or a good sign.

"Yes, because I'm wise enough and don't gamble," retorted this Gladstone in a very superior way, which made my teeth clench, because I could just imagine how it would annoy Jack.

"That's your problem, Gladstone, that's why you'll always be a bolt-turner all your life, back in—in—"

"Nigeria."

"Yeah, some outfit like that."

"Outfit! Would you call California an *outfit?* Nigeria is much bigger, and maybe wealthier even than California!"

"Is that so. I doubt that. Matter of fact, I don't gamble either. I have a system."

"Yes? That's good for you then."

"I'll let you in on it, Gladstone. Next time you go to Vegas. Only you, I wouldn't tell just anybody."

The fellow named Gladstone said no more, but laughed long and rather richly, and sighed at foolishness which it was beyond him to admonish any further. Clearly the tourist industry in Nevada had met its match in Gladstone, maybe Nigerians in general, I didn't know, never having known any Nigerians. But from what I had heard of Nigerians, it would be in the class of selling snow to Eskimos, or bullshitting the bullshitters. It was very strange hearing this guy holding out an edge over Jack, though, whom I always thought of having the edge on everybody. There was an interlude in which only the clanking of tools against resistant metal could be heard, and the two of them grunting, Jack swearing softly. I took a few steps searching for a path to where they stood, but there seemed to be no way through, at least for the next hundred feet or so in either direction.

"Don't say I never tried to help you or nothin, Glad," said Jack still thoughtfully admiring his "system" or bent on tormenting Gladstone for his amusement.

"Look out! Don't sever that hose. They want the hose with it. See here, let me do it."

The greasy clicks of one of the wrenches ceased. Jack must have stood back. He didn't object if the other guy thought he could do the job better. Of course it was pure laziness, but not entirely. Jack was not lacking in confidence and was always ready to regard the next man and give ground to him. He began to whistle a serene and loping tune. He was happy! I laughed aloud.

"Who's laughing over there?" Jack shouted.

"Who snickers?" echoed Gladstone between tugs of his wrench. But I felt like playing with them, so didn't reply. After a while, they went back to talking.

"You don't mean to tell me, Glad, you never been to Vegas, an you been in the States, what, three, four years?"

"Not if I've been here forty years."

"Oh no, you can't go home to your country an tell your friends you never went to Vegas! Would you go to Paris an not take in the Notre Dame?"

"What do you know about Paris?"

"Oh, you'd be surprised. You wouldn't go to Indo-China and not take in the temples of Angkor Wat. Would I go to Africa an not look at the lions?"

"There are no lions."

"No lions! Get out!"

"It's a myth perpetrated on your TV screens."

"Well, damn, Sam!"

"If you went to Africa, they would find some lions for you, I'm sure, don't worry, Jack."

"Hurry up an get that hose off, man. You gonna take all day for that damn hose, they have to put on a new hose anyway, they can't use that old one."

"They want the hose, and the clamp, not broken. You Americans, always in a hurry, too impatient to do good work, always throwing away something because it is easier to do so."

Jack began to whistle again. It was fine with him.

"Always restless," exclaimed Gladstone through his teeth.

"Get the wreck on the road. You do this for fun, guy?"

"A job has a soul. Did you ever think of that? A soul. A span, a lifespan, you could say, you can't squeeze it. When I go to my country, I will have a big shop, I will be a big man. I'll have two or three pretty wives. I know what value is."

"Hey, that aint half bad."

"Because I do the job right."

"You'll always be a bolt-turner, Glad, if you don't speed up."

"What are you going to be, the President?"

"I won eight hundred bucks last weekend, in an hour."

"Maybe next week you will lose it again, and more."

"You really ought to see Vegas, Glad, talk about some hot babes!"

"No, I won't see the high-rollers there, nor the gutter-dogs either."

"Ya oughta see the people playin the slots, man, like devotees in church lightin candles."

"Shut up, I'm religious."

"No offense. I was winning my loot, man, an they're feedin me free drinks, each one brought on a tray by this beautiful chick. An afterwards I had a big steak dinner on *them*, you dig. An a whore on each knee."

Invisible Car Dealer

"You slept with whores?"

"No, no, no, I didn't sleep with nobody! I'm married," said Jack anxiously. I heard the note of anguished sincerity in his voice. He never would have played around on that lovely wife of his in a million years. What a trusting love for him she had anyway, to let him go to Vegas probably with some crazy pal of his from Nam.

"Ya know," said Jack, wistfully, "I was in the casino, checkin out the flesh, an ya know, I thought I saw my wife. 'My Lord, what if she snuck up here an *she* was playin around!' I shot through the crowd lookin for her, before I came to my senses."

Gladstone did not comment on this sudden pathetic confession. It brought up a memory. It was when a cousin of mine, Geoff, who was touring the country with a rock and roll band he was the drummer in, had decided to stop in California. Maybe his band was peaking, or more likely Hollywood was the allure. Anyway, when he managed to get himself in a tight spot, he called me and I got him a job at the dealership. Harmless Harry had hired him immediately. It was not a great job. "Straight commission," meaning he got no salary unless he actually sold a car. Harry had no problem taking on guys—at no salary. As Geoff was already crazy enough to quit his band to get in the movies, it was nothing to agree to a job with no salary unless he sold a car. He assumed he would sell lots of cars, or some anyway, and then he found out Harry's commissions were on a sliding scale—downward, as you succeeded. Everybody got cheated by Harry no matter how low your expectations—Harry found a way to get lower. Hard to imagine worse than Hollywood—until you met Harmless Harry.

So Geoff took his drumsticks and took care of himself and got a side job playing the drums again, in a band in a strip joint in Hayward, an amazing warehouse, a three-ring circus, in each ring naked girls shaking it to the music and cavorting in rare postures. It wasn't much of a setting for Geoff's talent but at least he got paid. I sat there imagining the drums being Harmless Harry's bald head. Once Jack came along with me. We enjoyed my cousin's virtuosic drumming chops. You know, it's always surprising to find out a family member is very talented at something. All of a sudden to my surprise Jack jumped up from the table and ran out of the club. When he came back, he was trembling. He allowed that he'd

thought he had seen his wife. "Your wife!" I exclaimed. The idea
was insane. "What would she be doing *here?*"

"I know, I know," he mumbled, embarrassed, "but maybe
she was trailing me, checkin up." He left for home soon after. That
was when I'd realized how wildly in love the two of them were. Jack
was that guilty at being in the joint at all. My cousin had a slighty
different take when he asked where Jack had gone. "Out *here?* His
wife? *Oh-oh."* But he didn't know Jack, or his wife.

Abruptly I heard heavy steps clumping up the oil-sodden
clay on their side of the wall of car frames. Rather, I *felt* the
footsteps resonate through the ground, rippling toward them, and
me, like an earthquake.

"*Pah!*" exclaimed Gladstone, and there came a sucking pop
of neoprene hose off a metal nipple that had been melted to it by
age. Then I heard Dahomey, their boss, say, "Gimme that wrench!
You guys take forever. Been to mechanic school."

He was on Jack's side of the "does a job have a soul?"
debate.

"Get you some fresh cat in Vegas, Jackie?"

"What!"

"Ya mean you went clear to Vegas didn't get you no fresh
cat, Jack?" asked Dahomey again.

Jack did not reply.

Gladstone said, "The job is concluded."

"Huh!" said Dahomey, who went back toward the front
with whatever component they had prized off for him. Jack and
Gladstone followed slowly after, and I trod along next to them
invisibly in my aisle.

Somewhere a mile or two away, the sirens of fire engines
began to wail, and grew piercingly insistent, before turning a
corner and beginning to fade.

"Someone is roasting his house, ha ha!" cried Gladstone
gleefully.

"Jesus," said Jack.

I laughed out loud at the Nigerian's bleak witticism.

"Who the hell's laughin over there?" Jack shouted.

I yelled back, "Guess!"

There was a long and pregnant pause, while we walked to
the end of the row, a long walk, and popped clean as babies from

the tube into each other's view. Jack's face lit up, slowly and surely, seeing me. He was glad to see me! We gripped hands and forearms and looked into each other's eyes with the light of loyalty, and fresh hope in its infancy, born anew. Gladstone kept walking in a self-contained way. He seemed a very likable and modest sort of man to me. Maybe he didn't take to it that I had been listening in on their conversation, but it probably wasn't that, we had never spoken to each other. His version of how "a job has a soul" excited my admiration for the man's abilities, and I was eager to involve him in my plans too, if I could. The more the merrier.

"So-o-o, Slick!" That was his nickname for me. "Hey! What we gonna *do!*"

Our old war cry! Jack pounded me on the back exuberantly, almost making me stumble. I felt at home again, wonderfully. I'd been a long way down. My spirits rose to immeasurable heights realizing he was glad to see me and did not count the past six months against me and that he was the same Jack I knew and was in pretty much the same space I had left him apparently. As we came up to the front, by Dahomey's office, Jack bought us a couple of Pepsis from the machine, that mean dog fawning at him, wagging its tail. Even the overtoppling towers of tires seemed more secure with Jack beside them.

We sat in my car with the doors open, kicked back, drank the Pepsis, and soon were talking nonstop in a thoughtless way about the good times we were going to have and the money we were going to make when we went out on our own—just as we always had. I implied that time was now, and he was not slow on the uptake and began to listen carefully. I told Jack my whole story, the relevant parts of it anyway, and spelled out the promising situation we were in. Just as I had hoped, and known he would be, he was all for it. He was ready to roll, and start towing my wrecks in, if he could borrow the tow truck. That involved Dahomey, something we passed over nimbly. I had the feeling of time obliterated in a flash in the crucible of friendship, while we made plans, calculated the bucks, talked all kinds of stuff, just like the old days, only this time the project might be really under way. I can hardly express the extraordinary goodness of this interlude, especially as compared to what I easily perceived as the badness of my recent months, as we lounged in my car like the best of our days. And yet the resources I had amassed in my time away in the wilderness, namely, several dozen extremely desirable auto classics, once they were cherried out and restored to mint or even quasi-mint condition, would make up the basis upon which new fruitful developments would unfold, and so I made up my mind once again that my recent adventures had not been all bad by any means, but perhaps better understood as trying and difficult.

We were feeling so good in each other's company that it proved the old observation that only to lose something, or nearly lose it, and you at once recognize anew its value, and we must have exuded so much pleasure and good will toward each other that our vibes radiated into the whole yard and touched everybody, so that no one approached, even Dahomey didn't dare to bother us, Gladstone disappeared, no customers appeared at the gate, and no business arose to interrupt us.

I hadn't felt relaxed and whole and pleasant like this for a long time, sitting there in the dust and greasy sunshine with Jack, rubbing shoulders, glad for what we represented to each other, always had, congratulating ourselves on our new plans, etc. Jack saw things my way entirely, so much I almost gasped and gulped for air, so paranoid and constrained a life had I been leading in my hideout at Cloud Lake. Now a few customers walked in and out past us, to and from the office, with drive shafts, alternators, brake drums in their hands, hopeful offerings to the automotive gods. A flatbed truck rolled up and parked in the entrance next to the others. On its bed were three fresh car wrecks. But Dahomey did not appear and the driver waited in the cab. Jack told me his news. Harry had opened his new place just as he'd told me he would, and predictably he'd offered Jack a job, but at no better wages than he was making from Dahomey. The pitch was Harry's car lot had class the wrecking yard didn't.

"Told him what I thought of that! No, said I'd think about it, ha ha. Said I'd call him."

That's right, I agreed, imagine anything resembling class associated with Harry! If there was one point on which the usually sharp Harmless Harry was sorely deluded it was that colored streamers and flattering lighting in the showroom amounted to class. Don't give anything away to Harry, I admonished Jack. I told him how much he had ripped me off for on my final check. It wasn't even the considerable sum of money, it was that the old man thought he could just get away with it, in other words, that he had class and his boys never would except if they worked for him. Just the mention of Harry's name started cold fear in me, irrationally. It was like the old days, but the shoe was on the other foot now. I had a great scheme, the last thing Harry would have credited, but it all depended on whether Dahomey tumbled for it, and that depended on how Jack broached it to him, and the truth was I felt doubtful of that conservative man of the world, Dahomey.

Somehow Julie's name came up. I guess I asked about her then. Vaguely Jack said something about his wife's having kept in touch with her, then having lost track of her lately. "You gonna go see her?" he said point-blank, surprising me, as if he were saying something too obvious to be mistaken for good advice.

I don't know why it should have surprised me, as Jack as well as his wife had always liked Julie. I had never told Jack about the Indian, at least not yet, but maybe Julie had said something to Jack's wife, I wondered. No, that was out of the question. She had said it would die with her. But he understood as much as that there had been trouble between us, and that it had been somehow part of or the cause of my leaving town. He stared at me hard and quizzically. For an instant it really was as if she and I could have picked up right where we had been before. It was what I wanted most. My heart took a dive, my mind went blank. But Jack was thinking of other things, his curious stare dissolved, and he changed the subject back to our cars and the next hurdle.

"Have a chat with Dahomey," he said confidentially.

"Me?" I gulped.

"Yeah, I'll back you up."

"Maybe you. He likes you. You know him so much better."

"The more reason you should bring it up. He's got his own problems."

So that was my next chore. I didn't entirely follow his reasoning. I kept hoping Dahomey would walk by the car. But it could wait. Sitting there in the car like old times with Jack was pure heaven and splendor. We were rich together, in command, full of insight. We smoked, bullshitted, and enjoyed ourselves. I told him a few tales of dealing cars on the road, and he traded me some more local news, including alluding to some hard times the wrecker's business was experiencing because the economy was better and people were buying new, or better, cars. But now the good life would begin, working together again, only this time on our own deal as we had always planned, a small fortune to split between us when we got the antique cars fixed up. We speculated about it as though the heavy work had already been done and the dough was already rolling in.

"A 58 Cadillac Eldorado! A 54 Ford Victoria with the glass top! A 62 Impala! A Buick Roadmaster! A 56 Volvo 444—the one that still had the split windshield!"

"Hey, I'm ready to go get em," said Jack.

"In L.A., movie people and so forth love those classic cars when they're cherried out. There's a strong demand."

"Those were golden cars," Jack chimed in reverently. All judgment suspended in such sentiment, I believed life had never tasted so good. Swamped by golden sunlight down the air laden with wholesome-smelling oils and emissions, our old dreams of making a lot of money begged to be turned into reality.

"I guess I better go talk to the boss," I said.

Instead of bursting into enthusiastic flame, my confidence began to evaporate at once like gasoline spilled in the raw sunshine at mere thought of approaching Jack's boss. But I couldn't beg Jack to do it, his own confidence might have slipped if he saw mine waver. I got out of the car, and pitched the empty Pepsi can so it ricocheted off the tin fence and into a refuse bin, the accuracy of my shot as well as the adamant clatter reassuring as I walked into the yard, Jack right behind me. Such assurance was no more than skin deep, I knew full well. Gladstone the Nigerian was working on the engine that was hanging on the hook of the crane. He didn't glance up. Jack lingered to observe him. Everyone's position was false.

I am not well liked, it's a gift I don't have, to be liked. Confidence in a car I can inspire, but the more I do, the less I am liked for it, even when it is a beaut. Even white people don't like me, my own sort. There was no way Dahomey liked me. Jack and Julie are about the only people I can think of, at least recently, I mean without going back to my mother, who have liked me. And look where they are now, or where I am I mean.

I paused a moment to perfect my attitude before walking coolly into Dahomey's office. But it was out of my control. I remembered that early morning, the silver dawn's shadows pierced by the blue flames of the cutting torches and showers of red hot sparks as we dismembered the front end of the Alfa roadster. I had been in a terrible hurry that morning to get the damaged front end chopped up before the owner of the yard showed up to take an interest in what we were doing. I had no idea what story Jack had told him about the remnants of that wrecked car, but assumed it was a good one, and that Dahomey had never conceivably connected me to it, or learned what kind of hot water I had been in at that time. You never knew though. Dahomey was not the sort to miss a trick in his own yard, and instead of mentally putting a last glistening drop of oil on my sales pitch, and lining up my ducks in a row to knock off for Dahomey's benefit, I found myself exerting maximum self-control to keep my imagination from weirdly taking off and flying awkwardly around my brain like a flock of greasy pigeons or crows descending to the pavement to pick at the carcass of evil memory. As usual Dahomey might know a lot more than one might wish. The dog exploded in a fury at my knee, and I leapt across the threshold.

Inside there were five or six customers lingering in various attitudes of resignation, boredom, and itchy impatience. The ones whom the interminable wait for some car part had finally afflicted with intolerable desolation were slouched in a couple of the mangy chairs in the corners with their eyes shut. The impatient and anxious ones who still thought this place was some kind of a store or rational business leaned on the battered wooden counters, shifting from one elbow to another, chafing at the fact that their transportation and very way of life depended on whatever kind of fortune their searches encountered in this mysterious joint, and trying to peer into the back room as though the proprietor kept his pumps and gearboxes and so on in there, and not in the obviously almost limitless storage space like the Gobi desert piled with skeletons outside.

One of the customers who did understand that the part he was after lay out their like a needle in a haystack stood in the doorway with eyes glazed from staring forever into the dusty distance where some workman must have disappeared long ago on his way to picking the desired member from a decaying cadaver. The worried way this customer's eyes peered, the workman had been gone a long time, and might still be wandering, lost in the sands, never to come back. Thinking of Jack and Gladstone back there philosophizing and bullshitting and letting the job take its sweet time, as if it had a soul, or a lifespan, or whatever Gladstone had said, I knew that this customer in the doorway had the score just about right, and I pushed past him gently like a soul brother. The impatient ones at the counter glanced around at me with undisguised hostility, jealously guarding their positions. They eyed me up and down to be sure I understood the order, and that they were first and I was last. Parts catalogs, greasy manuals, starter motors, brake drums, taillight lenses, pieces of steering mechanisms littered the counters and lay on the floor underfoot, a few items tagged for pickup.

Right in the center of the counter was a great piston disconnected from its rod, turned upside down, out of some exotic huge truck engine, making an ashtray, into which a big half-smoked cigar had been thrust, its smoking redolence proof that Dahomey had just been here. The piston reminded me of one of those wastebaskets or hassocks that used to be made from the feet of elephants by white-hunters in Africa.

Hanging from the ceiling above our heads like sausages in a butcher's shop were all sorts of hubcaps, wheel covers, silver grilles, headlight frames, and other assorted chrome trim, so you had to watch yourself and occasionally duck if you moved about the office. One of the impatient customers, with a groan of dismay, raced to the doorway to check and see if anyone might be coming or not, causing the pendant chrome items to whirl in the created breeze and gently chime one against the next. He took one long desultory look in all directions, craning his neck, and strode back to the counter so as not to lose his place. Not being careful, his head struck a hubcap, which swung on its wire, clanging against another, then another.

At last voices were heard from in back, and Dahomey and two of his workmen came in with their arms full of alternators, power window mechanisms, and motor mounts, which they deposited on the counter in a jumble and set about checking against others which lay there. The customers joined in eagerly, mumbling encouragement and some of them taking up items of interest and eyeballing them too. They all tried to hide their anticipation and leaping hearts with stony faces and gruff manners, but when it became clear that they had a fit, and that their long wait hadn't been in vain and was over, one after another they let out whoops of joy and gave each other victory grins. Dahomey, who had come through for them in the end, who had given no sign of noticing I was not one of them, either, or even seeing me, or if he had, of recognizing me, joined in the celebration beaming kindly over the crowd some of whom wanted to shake his hand. Instead he reached for their cash. He capped the moment by telling a creaky joke, which the excellent spirits the customers suddenly found themselves in allowed them to indulge him in.

"Hey," boomed Dahomey waving his cigar, "these Japanese car executives tell the designers, you know, 'Say, can't you fellows come up with a product that don't last so damn long? These here cars you been makin been lastin too damn long, ya understan? How bout one that last just in time for next year, that wear out in bout nine months!' Designers say, '*Dat-soon?*'"

It was a very bad joke even when brand new, downright embarrassing and ridiculously out of date when Japanese motors had outstripped their American counterparts, oddly touching for that reason, patriotic, you could say. Everybody laughed in a mood of indulgence, relief, and success, and incredible, irrational patriotism, even the customer seated in one of the raggedy chairs in the corner who had appeared to be asleep with his hand over his eyes, except when he was groaning. The customers at the counter handed over wads of green cash to Dahomey, who rang it into his cash register and scribbled receipts, and they left with their hard rubber motor mounts, steering gear, and electric motors.

Suddenly business picked up in a flurry, and workmen began pouring in the front and the back, and customers were mobbing the place and standing outside by the dog who was sniffing trouserlegs joyfully, smelling paying clientele. He knew the difference between paying customers and me, almost wagging his tail off. Transmissions and drive shafts were being examined in the dust outside like wild creatures recently bagged, the faces of brake rotors squinted into like magic mirrors. I spent the interval admiring some of the handsome art work around the place. Particularly impressive was a poster of a redhead, pink and proud as a Titian, sprawled over a bright red Snap-On toolchest, her ass projecting like one of those wonderful '30s hood ornaments. The wittiest though was the calendar provided by the Perfect Circle Piston Rings Co. on which the current beauty pulled one of the glittering engine rings from her panties, while with the other hand she worked a shiny piston under her slightly elevated thigh. The backrooms of garages and junkyards tend to be museums of such art treasures and rare works by unknown masters.

Behind me Dahomey cleared his throat, and said, "Don't drop your bolt." I gave a comradely laugh, I hoped, and turned around in time to see him disappear behind the counter on his way to his back office, in spite of all the action out front. This was a clear signal to me to follow I realized. At least we had started the proceedings on a raucous note. But after a minimal exchange of pleasantries, before I had said one word about my plan or mentioned that Jack was all for it, Dahomey interrupted whatever I was pattering on about with a wave of one big hand and grimly looking down at the greasy stack of papers on his desk which he began to shuffle, "All right, cool, what's my angle?" he muttered in a bored way, not looking up.

Angle on what? I hadn't said anything specific as yet about the program. That was Dahomey all right, always way ahead of you, and I was much too nervous. It was just that everything depended on his response. I wasted no time rejoining, "Dahomey, how would you like to make an extra five grand this year, for doing nothing?"

Though he still didn't look up, I saw a knowing sneer appear on his broad mouth. "That's my cut, huh?" he said, in a tone which seemed to suggest I had deprecated his intelligence, which on no account had I done. "I want that up front as a down payment."

"Hey, that aint money? Dahomey, if I could give you that up front I wouldn't be standing here in the first place, would I?" Five grand was a lot of money for doing nothing but allowing some rebuilding to happen in a corner of his yard, oh and loaning the tow truck, and providing the connections for cheap parts, etc., well, in short, Dahomey's involvement was essential and he knew it, otherwise what was I doing here indeed? But I was too broke to give him anything right now, of course. I didn't have it.

"I don't like to know my cut before I know what's being *cut up*," he said menacingly. *Cut up?* He suddenly looked up straight into my eyes giving me a knowing up-from-under stare from under his glowering brow which plunged me into anguished wondering if he had found out about the Alfa, and the Indian, after all? I swallowed hard and began to talk fast. Had Jack unintentionally let something slip? Did Dahomey imagine he had something on me? That did not bode well for my potential profits. Well, that was farfetched, but a depressing suspicion told me he might not play along. He seemed uninterested basically. I started reciting my list of cars to rebuild along with the price tags we would put on them when they were restored (marked down somewhat or else he would demand a fortune). As a matter of fact, he seemed not to be listening. Far from holding any cards in a game with me, his mind was elsewhere.

"Nice suit," said Dahomey, having risen suddenly, and fingering the material of my lapel. To suggest I was astonished, even offended by his overbearing and intimate manner, would be a mild understatement. More like mystified. Standing before me, he eyed me up and down like a tailor. He himself was wearing greasy rags, prerogative of the powerful and wealthy. He could have bought a hundred suits like mine with what he had in his petty cash drawer. Over his features had dropped a glittering interest and objectivity, in exactly what I couldn't possibly guess, as he examined my attire, but hiding something cagey I felt sure. What the hell was this sartorial satire about? I was too surprised to react. Dahomey was given to acting in the most surprising ways, I knew well. He had become completely absorbed in my suit, shirt, and finally, eyeing me from top to bottom, pulling up my trouserleg, my socks, and shoes. He was looking at me just like a friend who was about to offer good advice about matching colors or something. He stared at my boot.

"Damn white boys!" he exclaimed. "Look sharp at the top— well you need a haircut, guy—but you forgot about your shoes, man! Dress from top to bottom, don't you, when you oughta start at the bottom an work up. It's the shoes what counts and makes the man! White boys! Look at your boots, man. They look like they aint had nary shine on em since ya bought em. Feet should look smart! Feet is the basic foundation, aint they? You dig? C'mere!"

It was true enough, my boots always were scruffy and unpolished, I never did pay any attention to my shoes. Because I didn't care to. Anyway what business was it of his? I almost told him as much, but held my tongue. I was more than ever afraid of him, and at a disadvantage, since I needed him. So I had to stand there and take it, whatever he thought he was doing. I wanted to finish describing my car restoration project to him, but that would have been impossible now, because he wasn't listening. I was completely flustered and off balance, I wanted to return the conversation to my purposes, as he yanked me by the arm.

"How you sell cars, feet lookin like that? You got the world wrong way up, boy. Can't inspire no confidence in *them* boots."

Well, his point was well taken, no doubt. I finally understood his meaning, and got his drift, but the question was why he had chosen this time, or any time for that matter, to give me such advice. But perhaps if we were going to be partners, he wanted me looking my best. After all, if his money was to be tied in with mine.

Dahomey waved me to the side of his desk where there was a battered folding chair, and when I didn't move right away he grabbed me and pushed me onto it. What now? He drew up his own chair and reached under his desk, came out with a can of polish and rags and brushes, grabbed my foot between his big hard knees, almost twisting it off, and set to work shining my boot! Crying out modestly that I didn't want him to do this, I feebly tried to retrieve my leg but in vain. I had no choice but to let the work progress to its gleaming conclusion. One foot, then the other. When he was all done ten minutes later, I surely had a fine looking pair of feet, I would have been the first to admit it.

"There now! That's better," muttered Dahomey, applying a last few rat-a-tat-tats with his quick rag. I could hardly open my mouth and agree. What was I supposed to do, tell him what a good job he'd done, that I thought my shoes looked great, thank you very much? I was so embarrassed and nonplussed, naturally I began to laugh out of tension, but he didn't notice. Instead, he just smiled at me, beamed at me and at the boots. When we both got up, he gave me a big one-arm bear hug—of affection it seemed, if I didn't know better. But at this moment he radiated a kind of goodwill, for me, I could hardly believe.

"So, *Slick!*" he sent me on my way, using Jack's affectionate nickname for me. "Have a good *day* now!"

His sentiment seemed genuine. I've always thought he was a giant of an enigmatic character in many ways. He had confidence to spare, so he could be eccentric. No hard feelings, he didn't go for my plan, but personally (probably because I was Jack's friend) he had nothing special against me. That was the attitude he had taken, the craziest generous inspiration. As to whether he might like me, there was no question that he didn't.

The next instant, as he strode outside, with me after him, he had completely forgotten me, my hapless project, and my shiny boots. He bent over beside Gladstone, and examined the engine Gladstone was rebuilding. Then he began talking to a new customer who had showed up starry eyed, and issuing orders to a couple of his men. In my disappointment, my heart had descended so low, it was almost in my shiny boots. I felt like something unfathomable had passed between us, a kind of spiritual sleight of hand. What a way to get rid of a guy! He bore me no ill will, wished me the best, and had demonstrated this in the most shocking fashion. But as for my plans, he wanted no part of them. Well, it worked, because in spite of rejection, I couldn't help liking the man, as always.

As usual I could not begrudge him, I was won over by his sheer bulk and the compulsive energy he radiated. You had to be on the side of what seemed a natural force even as it overran you. He looked twice as big and strong as he strode around his yard tending to business, while I seemed to have diminished to about the size and insignificance of a shock absorber.

His complacent good-natured joke or whatever it was, or perhaps even an open-handed attempt at improving my appearance in case I was going to try selling my scheme to somebody else, touched me, moved me, but did nothing for my prospects. Had he hostiley dispensed with my sales pitch, and deplored my entreaties coldly, which would have been more expectable, my dejection might have been of more normal shape. But having lifted me up on a wave of good spirits to the height of a chair in a shoeshine palace, as it were, the drop was precipitous, and even calamitous, to my spirits.

He was roaming back and forth, talking to the one customer who was still waiting, yelling at the top of his lungs to a mechanic fifty yards away, as if his yard were twenty times as busy as it was. Right now it was barren and empty. Dahomey, his neck bulging, his eyes red, had business problems of his own, Jack had suggested. In one swipe of his rag he had summarily rejected me and, all with amazing good grace, given me a lesson in grooming. It was an extremely unhappy development, after all my courageous talk with Jack a few minutes ago. My own faith in the immediate future was shattered even if my shoes were spiffy. I couldn't figure my next move, and stood there stupidly not moving.

A new presence made itself felt in the yard. I became aware of him by the others' heads turning curiously. The only thing I could see at first was the top of a wide-brimmed tan hat approaching at a fast clip, and the free arm of the guy who was wearing it beating at a furious pace. I noticed his black loafers were well-shined, with little tassles. The brim of his hat was turned down and he stared at the ground as he came as if not wanting to trip on the stray drive-shaft, or he was studying the effect he would make looking up suddenly to confront somebody face to face. Dahomey would have approved of his shoes, if little else.

There was something a little too brisk and aggressive in the newcomer's approach. In his other hand that was not pumping as he strode toward us was a new-looking leather briefcase. When he came near, the stranger, who might have been admiring the shine on his loafers and swinging his head back and forth in time to an inner music, suddenly squared his shoulders and gazed hotly into the eyes of the first man he'd overtaken, Jack, who had turned to look back over his shoulder with bland wariness. He thrust the briefcase he'd been swinging straight into Jack's face.

"Hey, brother, check this nice case. Real leather."

Jack's brow knitted. "What's in it?"

"In it! Nothin in it, man! The case itself, brand new! Don't want nothin be in a new case like this'n. Make a man look awful right, Jim! Twenty bucks, I'm a prackly give it to ya. Genuine leather, Jack!"

"How you know my name?" asked Jack with a straight face.

"I don't know you, mister!"

Jack found that amusing. With a wink at me, he went to grab the guy by the collar of his nylon sportshirt, who was too quick for him and ducked beneath his grasp. Jack's hand brushed the wide hat changing its angle on the guy's head to almost sideways, who now made for Gladstone.

He thrust out the briefcase again, and began to stroke its leathern panels. When Gladstone made to turn aside, he clutched at the Nigerian's arm.

"Look at this quality case, brother man, worth eighty-fi' dollar if it worth a penny. Twenty dollar, dude—for *you!*"

Gladstone raised his eyebrows and widened his eyes. With marked disdain, he gingerly retrieved his arm from the other's grasp, and walked around to the other side of the V-8 engine.

"Fifteen dollar, fella, shee-it!" shouted the intruder. He pushed his wide-brimmed hat to the back of his head, his eyes glittering, perhaps under an influence. Gladstone gazed down his nose at him creating an effect of great distance, but with alarm in his look, as if at the force of his own feeling that was welling up, keeping the pendant engine between him and the intruder.

"Ten dollar!" screamed the thief to all who would hear.

Gladstone laughed lightly, regaining his composure.

"No way you caint buy this case for no ten dollar!"

"Wanna bet?" grinned Jack.

Gladstone fell back to tinkering with the engine, and the thief returned to Jack's side, who at least was willing to talk to him. "Listen, if you don't want the case, I also got a 'lectric lawn mower you can have for twenty-fi' bucks."

Gladstone laughed loudly and ruefully, bending his head over his task as if sorely embarrassed. Jack yelled, "What am I sposeta *mow!*" He advanced on the thief, who backed away, but farther into the yard, toward Gladstone again. Gladstone pursed his lips and whirled his wrenches.

In a suddenly maddened voice, Jack cried, "You see somethin aroun here I'm sposeta *mow*, motherfucker, besides your ass?"

"How I know what you got, dude, to mow? Thirty bucks for the case an the mower together!"

Jack lurched after him once more. Chased back by Jack, sent on yet farther by Gladstone's cold demeanor, he ran straight into the embrace of Dahomey, who took the thief up under his great arm like a naughty child, and as he toted him to the gate, hands and feet and brief case flailing, scolded him, "Don't you be study my yard, motherfucker, you be dogmeat!" This was no metaphor for it was no surprise that the dog had been snarling and whining and straining at his chain all this time, the strength of which the thief had gauged with a professional eye, now and then.

Dahomey's immense biceps stretching the sleeve of his black T-shirt, his huge haunches swelling his pants to bursting, the bulges at the base of his neck rippling like a triple collar of iron rings, straining forward suddenly on the balls of his feet (his own workboots were very scratched and caked with clay), he heaved the thief into the air out the front gate, and dusted off his palms once, smack! In the street outside the gate, the thief on his knees clamored up on his knuckles, picked himself up, searched about for the briefcase, and looked back disdainfully if not hatefully, but only for a moment, before resuming his business rounds.

"Here I got a whole fortune of cars up in Washington!" remonstrated Jack to Dahomey as he passed by. "I got a hundred thousand dollars' worth a precious antiques to restore an money to be made, an a junkie here wants to sell me a lawn mower!" He addressed Dahomey as if he were to blame in particular for the lawn mower. "Did you hear this man's plans?" he asked, meaning me. But Dahomey just looked at him like he was raving.

Dahomey went into his shack, as he passed through the door the tires threatening to fall, from the very weight of his footfalls. Jarred by his passing, they seemed to totter and barely hang in the heavy air. Maybe it was just my imagination, a play of the heat waves. Nothing was collapsing but my plans. Jack and I sat in the front seat of my Jag again.

"Gladstone," said Jack, "is named after some English dude. Dahomey is American, but he named himself African. These black dudes got some name problems." He lit a cigarette and blew smoke exasperatedly.

"I couldn't talk to him," I said.

"I think I could tell that somehow."

"I don't know what he has against me exactly, but it wasn't the moment."

"Know what ya mean," said Jack gloomily.

"I didn't want to waste it if it wasn't the moment. You try to talk to him. All he needs to do is loan us a little corner in here and use of a truck. It's our main hope. He's got this big place here. Funny, you'd think he'd think big too. Look at this." I kicked up one foot. "He shined my shoes."

"He what?"

"Shined em."

Jack's mouth fell open slightly. "What?"

"That's right."

Jack scratched his head, and gave me a look. "I'll talk to him tomorrow," he said vaguely. "He listens to me."

"I bought all those cars. You got to see em."

"I'll go up. I'll drive up there this weekend. Take the wife on a little vacation. Maybe we should talk to Harry."

"No Harry!"

Jack stared at me.

"I'd rather see them rot."

"What happened to your head?" asked Jack, pointing solicitously to a bruise that still lingered from the trouble I'd had in the cops' elevator when I finally landed. At this moment there was a sharp rapping on the side glass right behind Jack's own head, who started violently. It was the thief again, grinning at us ingratiatingly and tomfoolishly.

"Five bucks!" He waved the case. I couldn't help admiring his sales persistence.

Reaching inside his mechanic's coveralls as he leapt out, Jack dug his .38 under the thief's heart, who thrust out his arms, brief case swinging.

"Hey, I aint done nothin!"

"I'll blow you a new asshole, asshole," grumbled Jack.

"Hey, now! Hey, now!" The thief backed away, turned and ran, a funny, horribly pathetic figure.

If Dahomey had gotten my number somehow with that shoe-shining business, the thief with his hot briefcase and lawn mower had gotten under Jack's skin. Unaccountably, we were both low and out of sorts when a moment before we had been as high and glorious as eagles in the sky. Why a guy selling a stolen lawn mower should have rankled Jack so was beyond me, and for his part the idea that Dahomey had been shining my shoes was too bizarre for him to countenance. There was nothing more for us to say to each other just now, and it was time to part, but we agreed we'd meet again soon.

I gave Jack the extra key to my cabin, and he repeated that he'd take his wife for the weekend. I knew as soon as he saw the cars he'd know what a goldmine we had there. But you needed money to dig for gold. We needed what the old prospectors called a grubstake. I looked Jack in the eye and swore I would raise some funds somehow in Los Angeles, although I was hardly in a mood to head back down there by now.

There was no way I was driving back up to Cloud Lake empty-handed. Where I was going I really did not know, unless it was to L.A. Where else—but to do what? To see if I could interest Gregory who wanted to drink my blood, the lawyer who had a warrant out on me, or a cat-torturing biologist in a hot prospect? It was either them, or it was Harmless Harry, I supposed, thinking of everyone I knew who had money, as if grimly to torture myself with the inauspicious faces of my inner social circle. In other words, how I felt leaving Jack that day, even as I tooled away in my Jag needing gas, it was like having your back to a sheer cliff while you stared down into the abyss at your feet.

One more small incident occurred as I was leaving to unsettle me with a consciousness of my uncertainty and lack of grip on things. I took off into the empty street without looking, since there was little traffic around this industrial sector of which Dahomey's yard was the main attraction, just customers of his slowing down to park or leaving with their haul of car parts. But at this moment a gang of boys blaring ear-splittingly loud rap music tooled past in their jalopy and I had committed the egregious discourtesy of cutting them off. Seeing them coming hard at me out of the corner of my eye I hit the brakes and we both came to a trembling stop in each other's annoyed gaze and they poured out and surrounded me. They were all bare-chested with black bandanas around their heads like pirates. They rocked the Jag and I got out but instead of confronting them as they expected, I beat a hasty retreat back into the wrecking yard.

Into the yard they trooped right after me bent on mayhem, but at this moment for some reason Dahomey himself had been walking toward his front gate and instead of my ass to beat on they faced the man himself, who quickly satisfied himself as to what had just happened and began to speak to them soothing and affectionate admonitions and remonstrances. As he cooed to them, he reached out a big hand and began to stroke their leader's bare chest, round and round. He patted the leader's rib cage and neckbone and caressed his naked breast in this fashion over and over as the horse whisperer would have a wild race horse. It was just like the trainer's knowing hand soothing a frightened and angry bucking colt. Whatever happened at this primeval moment, their spirits all drooped, they saw reason, and they all calmed down, and left the yard. So did I, immediately and without another word to Jack or the master of the yard, embarrassed by having inadvertently caused the commotion, but grateful my ass was still intact. I was oddly clear-headed for a minute or two, enough time to realize I really was on my way back to Los Angeles now, and no delay.

Invisible Car Dealer

Julie and I once threw a party together. Well, it was her party, but a lot of my acquaintances from the Pontiac dealer came to it, and Jack and his wife. It was her idea, and she gave me my marching orders. Invite them all, she said. It never would have occurred to me, some of those sharks I sold cars with. Julie was sick of Berkeley parties where everyone knew each other, everyone was hip and holy, and the only game was hipper-holier-than-thou. She wanted a big, unpredictable party where people were wildly different from one another, the more the merrier, some working-class types was great. She was flush at that time. A couple of government grants had come in for her charges in the deprived sector, and her cash flow was up. The fact that the government had given her some money always made her optimistic about life in general. She would have invited the world to her party if she could have.

One amusing thing, with Julie's whole crowd there, the only genuine illegal aliens who came were my guests, a couple of mechanics from Argentina who'd been working at the dealership. (You thought the dealer would have only certified mechanics working on that new car of yours, didn't you, not some guys who barely spoke English and whose main qualification was they knew how to turn a bolt on the oil pan?) The crazy thing was, they were political refugees, so they claimed, when they quickly ascertained the score at Julie's party, and got drunk enough, refugees from the regime of the generals, which was still in power down there, in those days. Of all things, the mechanics turned out to be socialistas or Peronistas or something or other. They were the life of the party. I wouldn't have dreamed such a thing. As usual Julie had a certain genius when it came to people. She even made me invite Harmless Harry, that consummate people lover. I almost didn't do it, but in the end I always acquiesced to Julie, whose instincts in every social matter were far better than my own.

If I'd ever noticed the Argentines before, I'd just assumed that some Spanish guys who hadn't exactly been to General Motors school was only natural, given the owner's and Harmless Harry's cost-cutting policies. They had temporary visas which they kept getting extended with the help of the Rotary Club or Chamber of Commerce, and by now I was sure had overstayed them. Had she known that, it would have made Julie ecstatic. Suddenly they were instant celebrities at Julie's party, something no one could have expected, least of all themselves. When I invited Jack, I told him to invite everybody, so actually Jack had invited them. I insisted on inviting Harry myself, partly because I was trying to stay in his good graces in those days, and partly because the irony of Harmless Harry at a party of Julie's in Berkeley was just too good to be missed.

The whole legal-action committee was at the party naturally. In her business Julie knew all sorts of lawyers, far more than was healthy. All of them were left-wing types obviously, the kind who want to force everybody to wear seat-belts practically in bed, and who made their hard currency defending notorious narcotics dealers like Gregory in L.A., after having served their apprenticeships prosecuting them. Half-stoned, what with the girls staring on, the lawyers vied to see who would represent the handsome Argentines against the immigration authorities, the increasingly drunken Argentines who to their amazement finding themselves the center of attention, began to act like it was their due. At first, the Peronistas had been quiet and humble, courteous in a winning Latin way if not timid, and unsure where they were. But before the evening was well under way, they were raging drunk, calling these lawyers from the Berkeley Hills by their first names, no longer deigning to speak to the ones who had been nice to them at first, and insisting on free representation, guzzling more and more booze, grabbing for the joints as they passed, and coming on with all the girls.

Julie relished it. Ah, she had a sense of humor, but the fact remained that those Latin lovers needed help, although they no longer could remember it. And there were lots of people here who wanted to help. Situations like these were as good as gold in Julie's eyes, and I knew by the looks she gave me that I had capital with her for days, for something I would not have dreamed of doing, inviting a bunch of illegal mechanics of Harry's—and even Harry himself. In other respects, too, the chemistry of our party came off admirably. I heard more self-righteous argumentation about things like nuclear power and auto emissions and the environment, and the meanings of the war in Vietnam, than I had since my college days. Some of the guys from the dealership, with a little beer and pot in them, became absolute talking fools on these subjects, and I never would have known they had it in them. They argued as if these issues actually meant something to them, just as people do at parties, and tomorrow they wouldn't remember a thing about it. Some of them, having found a good-looking Berkeley chick to talk to, were listening raptly as the merits of the ecology movement were ticked off for them, these guys for whom the gas-powered combustion engine was the gold standard.

Jack had it made at a party like this one, where he was sure to find people to tell his Vietnam stories to. This was the post–Vietnam War era when liberals and ex-peaceniks had begun to discover that they respected the soldiers who had fought the war, since they had suffered too, and were victims too, etc. Their patronizing airs went right by Jack though, since the last thing he considered himself was any victim, not in the war anyway, only when he came home to the "world," and to hear him tell it he hadn't suffered a drop—at least not till he had come back to the States. It had been all downhill since then, with the sole and notable exception of having met and married his lovely wife. The Vietnam experience had been *fun,* that was *his* word, and it was "the world" with its rules and regulations and prescribed daily rituals of get-ahead politicking and ass-kissing and being on time for work that was the bane of his existence, not any memories or flashbacks of wartime which in fact was all that kept him going. He didn't intend to be a mechanic all his life either, he reminded me from time to time. I didn't care what he did or was as long as he remained Jack, which I figured he would. He wanted to race cars again, he said. He wanted somebody to stake him to this life in the race car scene. In fact, owing to lateness and inattention, shortly he did lose his job with at least its partial range of benefits at the dealer, and wound up at Dahomey's wrecking yard in the boonies, which he preferred.

Vietnam had been sort of a garden of Eden to him, coming back to "the world" his equivalent of the Fall. He hadn't forgotten that these people listening to his stories at Julie's were the same people who had spat on him and his friends and called them baby-killers, but he was beyond holding any sort of grudge about that, since he was a real warrior and genuinely expected nothing better from do-gooders and the civilian population in general. Also, they *were* listening to his stories. He expected them to be horrified by war, and probably he dressed up his stories to provoke such a reaction. He enjoyed playing that macho role to the hilt, and their revulsion was partly what confirmed him in his glorified self-image. He liked being disapproved of up to a point. Not everyone was capable of derring-do and violence. He knew that not far beneath the dismay, as well as the sympathy, in his audience, was some fear and even awe of him. In some sad way, he lived and died for moments and parties like these, when his tales were on. So I had to be grateful to Julie for inviting him and his wife, which she would have never missed doing. He was having a grand time.

He was not wrong about expecting an audience at such a party, for as fascinated by the Argentine mechanics as Julie's friends were, the presence of a bad Vietnam vet who was telling how it really had been had them walking on tiptoe, on eggshells, around him, and crowding in to listen to his tales. And before long they were won over, because Jack was as innocent and good-natured as his tales were sometimes shocking. He himself had no doubts about who the good guys and bad guys were in his stories, and soon it was impossible for his listeners to doubt either, at least for the duration of the spell he cast. Their politics were the exact opposite of his but they made him out to be the kind of vet they loved and pitied. Jack with his boyish good looks and eager way with words was very soon no adversary of yours, even if you were the most unreconstructed anti-war protestor around. He was the kind of tousle-haired kid who made you remember that the Vietnam War was all of our war, and that it was us they had fought it for, even if you had been against it, even if you were in jail for opposing it (I respected people who would go the limit like that, if Jack didn't). The only ones who weren't paying Jack any attention tonight were the guys from the dealer, who knew him a little too well already, or were jealous of him, and sick of his stories and what they mistook for bragging.

As for myself, I had always understood that the Vietnam war had been planned and carried out by our leaders for the purpose of ridding the planet of Indians once and for all, something that is common knowledge by now, but I knew at the time, so the issues (which never concerned Jack) being indisputable could be set aside, certainly when it came to my friend Jack, never clouding my view of him when he was telling his tales. Always I could see his beauty, as well as his self-indulgence, for what they were. I had heard all his stories by now, and could enjoy his pleasure in them just as well from a distance (I was at the other side of the room) where I could just see his lips moving.

A fresh beer in his hand, and a certain look in his eye, he was drawn up to his full height, his face flushed and animated. A quick glance Jack took caused my eyes to travel to the opposite corner of the room, where I saw his wife watching him through the crowd with a benign smile. The force of love in that smile of hers, which was certainly not maternal, or even admiring, and I don't think she even noticed his fans, was not amused, or jealous, but just expressive of plain simple, trusting love and affection, came to me so powerfully, that I felt the urge to go and chat with her. At this moment Jack had looked over to exchange a glance with her.

Jack's wife was a sexy nurse who worked at some hospital, with a good-natured intelligent way about her, such that you always knew he was going to be okay. I had met Jack's wife once or twice, but never had a chance to talk with her much, and as she was standing there alone, I thought to myself that now was the time to get more of the flavor of her. But just as I took a step toward her, Julie approached her and beat me to it, and the two of them began to talk with such a nice light of mutual esteem in their faces, that I hesitated. It amazed me a little, since Julie had dozens of people more important to her to attend to.

Invisible Car Dealer

Obviously the two women liked each other instinctively, and this pleased me, because I figured Jack was as loyal a pal as I was ever likely to have, and I took it as a sign of good things to come that the two women were attracted to each other. In the instant, I understood that this was just what Julie had in mind, too, and I pictured the four of us going on dates together, taking trips to the country, going on a fishing trip, cross-country skiing, I saw us drinking brandy by a big stone fireplace, I saw us laughing in two little boats side by side on a river while one of the girls hysterically pulled a silver fish over the side. I imagined us having all kinds of fun multiplied by our having it together, and it was a rare and warm vision, particularly for somebody like me, since I've always been more than a bit of a loner, and so has Jack for that matter. And to think such good times and happiness might have been.

There's always a price to be paid, isn't there? This was the real price I paid to the last dime, for my freedom, more than my friends in and of themselves even, but all of us potentially together, those double-dates and picnics and fishing trips we never did take, Julie and I and Jack and his wife, whom I never did get to know much. Julie was right that I would pay, and keep paying, and so I have. Well, everything costs something, why should freedom, the highest value of them all, be any different? Far from it.

When Jack had somebody to listen to his stories, his taciturn shyness vanished and he was almost as free again as he had been during the war. I let Julie and his wife chat and get to know each other better, and drifted over to hang with him, though I thought I'd heard all his tales. With his audience of girls, his beer in one hand and a glowing unfiltered Camel cigarette in the fingers of the other, his memories before him as if it were only yesterday, his stories making him a natural raconteur rather than the other way around, he was pretty near in heaven. He was telling about when they'd thrown the VC out of the helicopter, that one. Never mind, it was self-defense, and even Jane Fonda would have been rooting for Jack all the way. It is a common enough story by now, such a tactic, under the duress and shocking circumstances, but that night it was still disturbing, even for me strangely.

I'm not sure I can catch again Jack's voice, to try to describe the raptness in it. It escapes me in the recollection for some reason. I guess I'm afraid of a close miss—worse than a mile.

It's a dicey business to write about a friend. Never having been in a war, let alone that infamous one, I found the scenes of his tales marvelous, like out of the movies, but I suppose that was exactly the way it was. That's how they sell tickets to the movies, they make them like reality, as much as they dare or think advantageous to. The reality of a war escapes the most imaginative and ambitious film maker.

Somehow there was always rock music blaring. They had a tape deck or something in the chopper apparently. They did have their own sound track, in Jack's stories. It was almost a point of honor that they were always all stoned out of their minds on Thai weed laced with opium, if not acid, more likely, on their missions. This time they had taken fire going in, and the machine gunner had been hit and the floor of the chopper was slippery with blood. They were short-handed the machine gunner. Some of the wounded they'd picked up were bleeding. The wind had suddenly switched around on them, and tear gas they had laid down as an aid or precaution going in had blown back in their faces, and they were all weeping and vomiting. They had a load of wounded and prisoners. The marines "who didn't know which side of the log to shit on" hadn't adequately tied up one of the VC prisoners they'd picked up, and suddenly the little fellow slipped his bonds and, oh well, I can't describe this, I'll just try to remember it and let Jack talk, he was having such a good time.

"He was quick—want to know how quick? When he stood up, he had my .45 in his hand! And he'd been tied up one second before. He was smiling, I mean he was smiling in my face. I went for this Chinese dagger I carried in my boot, that I took off another VC one time, but I never had a chance. He sticks my .45 right in my nose, and as he pulls the trigger, he grabs this gold chain around my neck I was wearing, with a big gold peace symbol on it, I loved it. We always wore some bad jewelry, man, I wish you could a seen how bad we looked, headbands, earrings, war-paint, long hair, I mean you think some a these freaks around Berkeley look bad, my hair was down to here . . ."

Jack glancing across the room saw something that caused him to pause in his narrative.

"I'd like to go into work one time looking like we did in Nam, man, ha ha ha," he muttered aside.

Invisible Car Dealer

Harmless Harry, our chief, was seated on the small love-couch with a pleasant-looking woman about half his age, who would have yet appeared matronly to most of us in the room. Harry and his companion, sipping wine and looking content, and rather superior, as if they had just pulled something off together in the way of a boondoggle, huddled at the other end of the room, beyond hearing, Harry in his tailored suit still too big for him, with his false teeth, his red hairpiece, beaming over, no, smirking at, the room full of the dealership's employees and Julie's pot-smoking liberals, as if beyond whatever amusing ironies might be apparent to any of the rest of us, there was a joke here that only an old shark like him could truly relish, the real joke, as it were. Harry was very pleased with himself as always, and full of guile, as always, his smile for all the world like that VC's in the chopper who was trying to steal Jack's gold chain and peace symbol, who had stripped Jack of his .45 and just pulled the trigger.

For Jack at this moment, Harry was only another old remf (rear-echelon motherfucker). Jack would have fragged Harry's outhouse in a heartbeat. At a practical level he was scared of him, but hardly while he was telling one of his stories, not at this moment, and never in the way I was anyway. Maybe it took a salesman to know a salesman, but Harry always inspired in me a special fear. His humid breath in my face as he smilingly gave me the most commonplace order on the showroom floor was a fume of hell, unveiling a dropping glimpse of the pit, of unemployment if nothing else. I hated to think of all the people he had conned or halfway conned or shaded the truth on in his long career. It gave his grin its cob-smoked flavor. Though Jack had faced death, and meted it out too, in the war, he was pure and sweet as a lamb when compared with something like Harry. Harry would buy and sell ten Jacks before breakfast, and throw in all the Chinese daggers, .45s, and gold peace symbols you wanted.

It made me turn back to my friend, who was contemplating Harmless Harry with an expression as if something had gone down the wrong way with his last sip of beer and come up again. Jack's audience, which had swelled to nine or ten, waited with bated breath for him to conclude his tale and end the suspense, which was tempered somewhat by his standing warm and breathing before them. The VC had hold of his gold chain and peace symbol with one hand and in his other hand Jack's .45. He pulled the trigger. I too at this moment wanted to listen to the rest of his war tale, with a lump of pure affection in my throat. This sort of thing was what the Vietnam vets had gone through on behalf of the rest of us Americans, whether we liked it or approved of it or not, or had heard the story a hundred times. Swooping into a battle with guns and Jimi Hendrix blazing, rescuing the wounded, picking up VC prisoners, taking off again in a whirlwind, smoke and havoc, hail of bullets, always new bodies needed for this work, they could look any way they pleased, dress any way they cared, paint their faces, smoke anything they wanted, drop LSD every night and every day, the officers couldn't do a damned thing about it. Jack left off contemplating Harry and came again to himself, and was back in his world.

"I remember it like slow motion. 'Bye, American! Peace, buddy!' He's smiling like slyly at me! Pulls the trigger. Click! I always kept the round one hole back. That was just a precaution I took. Safety first. That was all I needed, you can believe that shit. That VC wasn't smiling no more, you should've seen that smile drop a thousand miles. Up we go! Took us up to about a thousand feet, he's clutching at us with every finger and his bare toes. Heave-ho! Watch him go! Well tough shit. Tried to kill me. But I would've forgave him and not done it if he hadn't a tried to take my *peace symbol,* man."

With that, the girls who had been leaning closer and closer with horror stood limply back, imagining the free-flight probably. One of them suddenly grabbed Jack in a hard embrace. "You poor guy!" she cried. She didn't seem to want to let go as she ground her breasts against his chest. Quick as Jack had once dispatched that VC, Jack's wife was separating the girl from his neck. "That's enough," she muttered firmly. Julie followed behind, and for an instant the atmosphere had been charged with another kind of violence.

Trying to smooth things over, I don't know what, just her confused response to the moment, Julie said something atrocious and unforgiveable. "Is it sad for you to remember? I mean, like your friends who didn't make it back?" she burst out nervously.

She asked Jack this out of some misguided impulse of taking his wife's interest, I guess. It was very ill-timed and really un-Julie-like. She was cooler than that. But Julie had not been close enough to hear much of the story, and she had never been in a war either.

Still it annoyed me no end. She didn't know what she was saying. She was trying to be sympathetic. But it was too abrupt, and sickly sweet. I glanced at her angrily, and she looked back at me just as stubbornly. Did she have to bring the guy down, just when he was sailing with glory? Jack was not from her world in Berkeley. I wondered if Jack would find it offensive. However my worst fear was confirmed when he took her question quite sincerely, and his expression became overcast, inward, and solemn. He appreciated the attention and the interest. He took her meaning point blank, not missing a beat. He *did* have his sadness, and turned sentimental.

"Yeah, the friends who didn't come home. Yeah. What were we fighting for, if not the good life? But they didn't make it back to have any good life. Where's the good life for them now? They're all forgotten now, already. Some of em were never remembered to be forgotten," he said quietly.

"I know," said Julie with bright feeling. She squeezed Jack not as the girl had done, but just like Jack's wife had, for a moment, who gave her a small smile. She laid her cheek on his shoulder for a heartbeat. Jack seemed to glance down at her through the mist of his memories with approval as though she'd understood something. A pall had come over us all, and it seemed to me Julie was wholly to blame, but that wasn't quite right. It was the other side of Jack's glory, inevitably.

"The good life aint all it's cracked up to be, anyway," he said. "Maybe they're better off. They have the pure glory. You know the saddest moment of all? Not the saddest, I mean, but for me anyway, the worst, the dumbest, speaking of fucked-up memories! It wasn't in Nam in the jungle either. It was back here in the States on the motherland. At Norfolk, when we came home. Plane landed—an nothin! You know what I'm sayin? Didn' see nothin! Didn' hear nothin! What was I waitin for? A band and speeches? Swear to God! A brass band, or somethin, a fucking welcoming committee, I don't know what all I had in mind, but when it wasn't there, when there was *nothin at all*, it was *terrible*. Isn't that the stupidest, saddest, fuckedupedest thing you ever heard? My heart was beatin with joy to be home, an nothin but empty tarmac! The silence was more than the worst rocket explosion in your ears. You know, I wanted to cry then, not for myself. I couldn't look the other guys in the eye after that. We hoofed it fast for the barracks, wherever the hell we were goin, nobody said nothin, lookin around, lookin down, anywhere but at each other. We didn't know where to go or what to do with ourselves. We wanted to hide! Nobody to give us directions. You know, all those guys had some image like that in their minds too. That is the sorry truth. How it was going to be when we touched down. It was pathetic. I think for a second we were all sorry to be home. We wished it wasn't over. Nobody to even meet us an tell us where we should go on base! Just abandoned. We had to go and ask them. Then it was like, who the fuck are you guys anyway, we'll see if you're on the list. But there was this one guy. Yeah, we had a one-man welcome, this photographer. I remember thinking to myself, well, at least we got one reporter or something, Christ! There he was walking backwards in front of us, snapping his shots. Everybody held himself up tall when he shoved his camera their way. I thought it might be somebody from the *Stars and Stripes* or some newspaper or whatever shit. You can't believe the difference that one dude with his little camera made. The buddies we left in the mud that aint ever havin the good life? At least they didn't have to endure that shit. Everything goin through my brain at that moment, all kinds a shit, I could've killed somebody, it was so bad. But at least there was this one reporter or photographer. We were some ragged motherfuckers. But for a minute there everybody felt almost okay again, or at least able to hide how bad they felt, you know? Because of that guy. The next day that photographer showed up again. You know what? 'Want to buy a picture of yourself comin home? Ten bucks.'"

Jack chuckled dryly, ambiguously. It was certainly sad, I guess, as life always is when the parade has passed by, or in Jack's case when the parade had been omitted altogether. Julie's eyes threatened to fill with tears, God bless her. Jack's wife's face was squinched up with a peculiar forbearance, as if she were on a familiar slope. Yet I was sure Jack hadn't meant it like it had sounded. His droll chuckle showed it. He was laughing at himself and hadn't meant to thrust us all into this morbid sadness Julie loved so much, had he? I knew how he really thought that photographer business was rather funny, damned funny in a black way. I had heard that one before. I was tempted to laugh, but of course held back. But then he laughed loudly himself, hard and long! He had put himself in a good mood again. That startled everybody. We all sobered up fast. He threw open his mouth and had a good strong laugh. This party had done so much for Julie and me, I hated to ruin what was between us, and it felt so good to hear Jack's brash laugh.

Somehow, later, I found myself at Harmless Harry's elbow. He was a little tipsy, and bragging to his girlfriend, telling her what a master salesman he was, and how at one time or another in his life he had sold everything under the sun. I could easily believe it, and it was sort of interesting to hear that he had not always been in the car business. There was something hypnotizing about Harry's rap at all times to me, at the same time I found him repulsive. He had an air of gloating, as if what he was proud of was not just that the people had paid him too much for whatever it was he had sold them, but how he had conned them into buying something that they had never needed in the first place or even remotely wanted or thought of. I have never conceived of sales in such a way, so I guess from Harry's point of view I had light-years to catch up. I've always thought of it as a service, a goodness even, linking up people to the objects of their heart's desire or at least their needs. Anyway his smug air was as always, but I had never been in a social setting with him before, or heard him being so expansive. Harry was telling his girlfriend about the days when he'd been a Christmas tree salesman with the biggest Christmas tree lot in northern California. Boy, that was funny, and I could hardly believe my ears, Harry and Christmas trees. He was telling her all about the ins and outs of that business, and how he used to go up in the woods to buy his trees for practically nothing and sell them for a small fortune in the city. Then he and his pals would follow people home, and if the people left their trees outside overnight to keep fresher, he'd steal the trees back! What a joke that was, to hear Harry tell his girl about it, downright merry!

It was eerie. It made me wonder for a moment what a Christmas tree *was*, you know? One that Harry had ripped you off for, anyway. Harry was telling his companion how he used to don a red coat and white wig and beard and play Father Christmas on the tree lot. He was getting a good laugh out of remembering that! My Lord, that tinny cackle of his for a ho ho ho. Yet there was something else. It was his description of the green woods, where he went to get his trees. If the thought of Harry mixed up in Christmas made the holiday seem weird (weirder than it always is in sunny California), the vision of him in the woods, hunting his trees, strangely softened my image of Harry. There's life on earth to celebrate too, isn't there? That's Christmas, cornering the good stuff for your friends and family, by hook or by crook. I pictured Harry as a younger man, up in the forest overseeing his purchases of evergreens. Everything just in the course of business, hustling in the thick green woods. The pine woods touched even Harry with something fresh and wholesome, as if greed weren't all bad. What was it made the world go round anyway? I guess I was feeling that expansive at this moment, that I could even forgive Harry.

Toward the end, I was standing with Jack as the party progressed to that desultory state which promised it would soon be over. Just like the war had once wound down, happily or unhappily, messily. Jack's wife was busily helping Julie do some preliminary straightening up after the night's successful mayhem. Julie was in a great mood—the job had been done! Jack's wife looked like she had been having a fine time, too. Jack and I were having a last beer.

"Aint she beautiful?" said Jack gloomily, looking across at his wife. "Sometimes I wonder what she's doin hooked up with a loser I like me."

"Cut it out, will you? If you keep up with your memories like you do, there's going to be nothing left of you. The women will pick you clean. You'll be nothing but skin and bones like that old piece of parchment over there, Harry. Look at him flapping his gums at his girlfriend. Jesus, I wonder what they do together. Do you know he used to sell *Christmas trees?* Hey, we got *business* to take care of, boy!"

That made him grin. The thing was, no matter how Jack complained, and how he wished the war was still on, at the same time he had quite a good attitude and was always ready to feel better, and get on with it. He was easy to cheer up. Talk of the next project always did it. We had a project on our minds in those days. We were going to open our own car shop together.

Invisible Car Dealer

When he got on this kick of talking about himself as some kind of a loser with his good days behind him in the war it was something of a put-on, anyway. It wasn't only that he wanted reassurance, but he thought to reassure others. Secretly, Jack thought a whole lot of himself, as we all do of ourselves of course, it's human nature. But Jack was wildly complacent deep down, and was sure Lady Luck would smile on him a smile that was going to leave everybody in the shade. So he looked down on everybody, and could barely conceal it, so much so that he tried to disguise himself. The only thing greater than his fear of failure was his soaring self-regard, and his certainty of being marked out by fate for incredible fortune. If he wasn't absolutely convinced he'd been a war hero, he was sure he was going to make it big in civilian life, somehow, some way, only he didn't know how. He hid that under his skepticism about the "world." His expectation of himself was so large, naturally it made him uneasy, since he didn't have the least plan. Sometimes I wonder, did Vietnam create a generation's insecurities, or was it only the ultimate symbol of them? Our hopes were so high at that juncture of our history, as Jack's were then too. Well, I wasn't in it, and don't care to speculate glibly on the deeper dimensions of it, since there's no shortage of people who do. But it must have been a glorious if misguided and tragic war. I say it must have been, because deep down I know my generation, and down deep where it counted, it was as courageous and idealistic a generation as there ever has been, if mixed up.

After my exile at Cloud Lake, all I wanted was to find Jack again, and I sure wasn't thinking about his minor failings. I always knew I'd run into Jack again. Not just that he had the car skills that I'd need sooner or later. But he was that rare thing, a friend. And like attracts like, and different as we might have been, well let's just say that somewhere along the line we'd both pierced the veil. The irony, I suppose, if you wanted to look at it that way, was that he had had his glimpse of a rarer, purer life in a war which was generally considered to be some sort of smirch on America's honor, whether because we were in the wrong, if you are on that side, or because we didn't go all the way and win, whatever that would have taken, or meant, had it been possible. The old truth about guys in a war only fighting for each other and for themselves was true for Jack. Nothing could have been less to the point than the meaning and purpose of such a war, but his buddies he remembered. War was just that—eternal war, fun for guys like Jack if they survived it. All that counted or was worth mentioning was how you took it. For this insight which he expressed unconsciously I loved him as much as anything, because it showed who he was and how he would act under any circumstances. In my own line, I held to similar ideas. If I had not escaped the car lot yet, the Pontiac dealership, and Harmless Harry, at the time of Julie's party, I knew someday I would, and now I have. After all, I could well imagine the twisted sort of smiles of certain people if I had ever tried to explain to them the sublime allure, visionary solitude, high satisfactions, and soaring freedom of the life of a free-lance car dealer.

In the end, we were philosophical desperadoes of a similar stripe. That morning when I had the bloodied Alfa to chop up for the smelter, he had never said a thing, but risen to the occasion uncomplainingly at three in the morning, just pitched in and rescued me, without question. He'd loved it, though he didn't let on that either. I saw in Jack innocence and integrity that had been tested in the war. The astonishing thing to me, that I loved, was that here was someone who had been a part of appalling things, maybe even crimes, who knows, who'd come out unsullied, unaffected by it all, and most especially, in view of the ambiguity with which that war afflicts our national conscience, not guilty of anything!

The truth was, I think it had always flattered me the way he had chosen to hang around me, look to me for advice, and always take his breaks and lunches with me when we both worked for Harmless Harry, particularly since, though I was a couple of years older than he, I had been a college boy, and he a soldier. Since I was a salesman and he was a mechanic, although I had made my start as a mechanic too, in spite of my education, I think he looked on me as having a skill or a way of relating to the world that he lacked, and somewhat envied, some kind of sophistication or savvy, the ability to make connections, salesmanship, in a word, which he believed would have made life much more tolerable and rewarding for him "in the world." It was at the bottom of his nostalgia for his war days that back then no such social skills had been called for. It was deeds not politics in the days when he'd flown the choppers. Deep in our friendship was the unstated recognition that we were both outsiders in our different ways, only I had the ability that Jack did not to persuade the world otherwise, if only for long enough to make the sale. If I regarded the manners and bonhomie I could switch on at will as something of a well-intentioned game, Jack paid me the compliment of taking them as a grace.

I admired his genuineness and ingenuousness, his love of a risk, his mechanic's and pilot's and race driver's skills and handiness! and most of all what I sensed was his unswerving loyalty. The nicknames we had for each other told it all. He called me "Slick," and I called him "Blue." That was as in "true-blue," like on Harry's business cards: "And we are true-blue." It was an in-joke, a twisted one. But Jack really was true-blue. We had seen those old cards of Harry's and had a laugh together about them. Jack was perfectly well aware of what the cynical world made of such military virtues he prized as open-heartedness and the tendency to come through with both barrels, but he wore his character on his sleeve anyhow.

I don't know how that nickname for me could have gotten started with him, "Slick." Personally, I felt it acknowledged and thus somehow covered the trace of irrational guilt I always felt as far as Jack was concerned. Even when I was making him money, I always felt I was leading him astray some way, something in me acting as a pure hook for something he was not always conscious of, namely his hope of that lucky combination, which he projected onto me. Okay, "Slick," I thought, with a twinge. Reliance on others for what should come from within is the root of all evil. Jack suffered from a bit of that.

"What we gonna *do*, man?" he had asked that night as the party wound down.

"Get out of the dealership, man. We're gonna have our own shop!"

We always talked like this. That was our dream then. I don't remember when or how it had been hatched. It's the romantic dream of many young men, to have their own car shop, one of those ready-made dreams that are in the air for the dreaming, and the practical doing, since the country will obviously never run out of cars to repair, whether they run on gasoline, solar power, electric batteries, or the pure light. Jack was leaving the arrangements to me. He would be the service manager and I would be sales manager, even if we had no employees, and no cars to sell. I was sure we were going to do it, too, and I would have loved it, until that night coming down the hill with Julie. I felt I'd let Jack down, even though I'd had no choice. I imagined that secretly he felt that way, and that he understood as well. It put our plans on hold, and even made our friendship seem very hazy and unsure, as much as our dream had been. I wondered why we had never made a stab at it while we'd had the chance. Jack had been counting on it so much he hadn't minded at all when his cocky attitude had gotten him in trouble with Harry and he'd been fired. When the morning came when he helped me cut up my hot car, my dented Alfa, at Dahomey's yard, he never mentioned our dream at all. But it made our dream that much more intense when I came back.

After that day of my return from Cloud Lake when Dahomey had treated me to a shoeshine, and a thief had tried to sell Jack a lawn mower, a note of reservation had come into his voice when we said goodbye once again, a faraway look was in his eye. He was going to go up and check out my cars, *our* cars I impressed upon him, at Cloud Lake, but he was no longer gung-ho, I could tell. I was no longer quite myself as I had been an hour earlier either. Something had slipped and changed, although what it was precisely would have been hard to say. Simply lack of funds, as it often is, I guess, at least partly. "Money, honey, if you want to get along with me," as the song goes, the everlasting refrain.

That went for both of us. For me, specifically, it was leaving town again, no sooner than I had come back, with no useful destination in mind, other than L.A. Things change, whether you want them to or not, especially when you don't want them to. We had never gone out on our own to have our own car shop together, but the cars I had up there for us to work on together and make a mint with were even better. Only it was a question of water, water everywhere and not a drop to drink. We were weary of our dream. And Dahomey was having none of it.

The river had flowed on, and was flowing on rapidly, and we didn't stand in the same relation to it or to each other anymore, even if we were back on the same spot of shore together. Dahomey wasn't going for our plan, and that meant I could not get parts on credit or a wrecker to bring the cars in with. In fact my whole scheme had depended on the goodwill of Dahomey, I realized with stunning dismay.

Invisible Car Dealer

The master had stood there primitively caressing the naked chest of the gang leader who had followed me into the yard the way a trainer calms down a furious pony. Even if Dahomey had refused my schemes, he had saved my ass from a kicking probably. The way it felt to me was the fickle fates were in disarray and blowing up a thunderhead on the horizon. Dahomey was the weatherman. The last thing I saw as I drove away from Dahomey Dismantler Corp. in the corner of my eye glinting through the windshield of Jack's Porsche was his gold chain and big gold peace symbol dangling from the rearview mirror.

Invisible Car Dealer

I was driving aimlessly in rush hour L.A. traffic, at dusk, through rose-orange smog, which for the first time in my life struck me as sinister stuff. I had been fond of smog in the past, my own hazardous element. I hardly knew which freeway I was getting on, or getting off, I switched from one to another just for the hell of it. Millennia of toasted fossil history were taking the form of gigantic leather-winged reptiles in the hollows above the city. I caught a glimpse of what I thought were the lights of the Dodgers ballpark in the distance. It would be nice to stop and see a game. Or maybe it was where they used to play, the Coliseum, where they played college football now. Perhaps it was the Christians versus the Lions tonight. I needed a destination, for if you didn't have one, some particular little goal a few blocks ahead, you'd never make it through traffic like this, they'd find your bleached skeleton by the roadside, if not a fossil in the asphalt. I awaited inspiration in the form of bitter necessity. Around me when the lights changed the traffic lurched forward like a herd of dinosaurs through matted grasses into the coal forests that eventually had been turned into gasoline. A further transformation lay in wait just ahead, in a hundred million years or so. It was a sort of a destination.

In the lane to the right of me just ahead a couple of Spanish kids drove a hot rod which rocked back and forth on its jacked-up springs and blew out clouds of goldblack smoke. They were playing loud music with a vengeance, yelling out the window to friends, and actually enjoying all this stop and go. The engine of the Jag was rolling badly, not running smooth at all. The Jag was like a big cat caught in a pit in a lava flow two or three million years ago. It was all the stop-and-go traffic, which had fouled the spark plugs, and I thought one chamber had begun to miss. It's just when despair takes over in the soul that the outside world boils over too. Banks of roses, lilacs, and jacaranda grew in the gardens irrigated with water precious as oil around the bungalows on the streets with the Spanish names through which these motorists were fleeing. Some of them, at least, must have goals, and I wondered what they were, and envied them for it. In the distance, behind tinted windows the office towers on the skyline were full of specialists in finance tracking the economy on phosphorescent screens. I had the impression of a rivulet of oil mixing in my sweat dripping down my brow. A gusher went off—bonanza! in the old Western movies while they tried to cap the new well they'd discovered back of the homestead, having struck it rich against all odds, the black gold oil pouring down on their faces and bathing them in wealth and happiness. (Such a scene would be incomprehensible in a movie today, or a cause for dismay, as our goals have changed.) On this snarled drive I became conscious of a sea-change that had been taking place in me. I felt like I was under water, under an oil rig in the deep ocean, trying to fix some gear or pump, before it exploded. I knew now that I was no longer an unqualified fan of the internal combustion engine. It was disturbing and disorienting on top of the fact I had no goal. What it's going to take, Paul Bunyan, as he had once dealt with the forests, re-born as Dahomey, to crush and smelt up all these machines. I would have rather been an Indian in the forest, going down a sacred and forgotten path. Little did I know I was about to get my wish.

Anyway, the problem was I didn't have a clue how I was going to raise money down here, which was my mission, and I was just driving around idly and gasping for a breath of air. You have to have money to make money, so I'd done just what at Cloud Lake I'd feared I would do, put myself in an impossible hole. What was I going to do next, call up Gregory the drug dealer or the environmental advocate and see if they had any loose change they wanted to launder through some cars? Some such vague idea had been enough to get me down here again, I had to admit to myself incredulously, but now that I was here, it suddenly occurred to me like a sack of coal hitting me in the face how misguided it was. I had actually considered calling the drug dealer and the lawyer to see if they wanted to back me! In other words, a completely insane and dangerous notion had fueled my brain the whole way down here which I had not consciously admitted to myself and had no intention of acting on. This had been my half-conscious, half-baked "goal." I had to admit that I had just fooled myself, as maybe I'd been fooling myself at Cloud Lake month after month buying all the cars, and that I did not have any realistic let alone palatable goal at all.

About to fall asleep behind the wheel, bone-weary, and very dejected, I checked into a motel and lay on the bed looking at the ceiling hoping to wake up the next day with a fresh mind. But I was so wired and depressed and goalless I couldn't even close my eyes let alone fall asleep. The only way I would have slept is if I had kept driving until I had swerved to curbside unconscious and fallen asleep in the car, if I hadn't crashed into something. Instead, checking into a motel room had focused all my worries into a burning point on the ceiling I couldn't take my eyes off of. I felt like the Indians must have, I thought, alone, bereft, hunted, friendless, barely left alive and cast off by modern society. I was bitter and I understood the Native Americans' plight as never before, and wished I could do something for them, but I could hardly help myself. Of course no actual Native Americans would have wanted to associate themselves with the state I was in! I almost turned on the TV, I was that desperate—desperate to distraction, but I knew that wouldn't do. Some inane show would make me jump out the window in utter despair and I was on the ground floor. I was hurting so bad already I was simply unwilling to torture myself further by watching TV even if it could have gotten my mind off things. There was a Bible next to the TV. I suddenly thought I might be in need of it.

I put my face in my hands, and prayed to God for some help, and a goal. I thought of that man I had accidentally killed for a long hideous moment and I regarded myself as being in worse shape than he had been on that road that night, dead or alive. I wondered what I was about to get run over by very soon. Then I picked up the Bible. How kind it was of them to put these Bibles in the rooms of motels for characters like me who had come to the end of their wits and needed them.

At the same time I picked it up, I could not believe I was actually picking up a motel room Bible, you know. It was such an uncharacteristic gesture, it must have been somebody else doing it, not me. I had often seen such Bibles in motel rooms, next to the TV, or usually in a drawer. Never had it remotely occurred to me that I might have a need of one myself. I can't say I had ever really and truly noticed such Bibles in motel rooms before, except I knew that I had out of the corner of my eye, for I recalled the faint distaste I had always felt seeing one. It had always been like, man, who would ever sink so low they would need to read a Bible in a motel room? To tell the truth, it had always been an even more foreign object to me than that. I had noticed the Gideon's Bible less than the ashtray.

Now I began to read, and was soon instilled with a desire to return to the absolute straight and narrow, and a hunch that I must go back to square one. I saw I had been on the wrong track for a long time, I felt this to my bones. But for how long had I been, and where could a new starting point be? What could this mean, in practical terms, for me? I seemed to glimpse something in a golden mist, as if I were standing on a cliff in the dawn watching the sun begin to rise, but there was nothing out there to stand on or leap to. The pages of the Bible were like leaves of a map to another world I really doubted even existed. No way would I have entertained the thought that there could be some firm place to stand in the Bible, let alone a goal, had not my present position *in this world* become untenable, unreal, unstable, and nonexistent. That is, I was exactly in the place and state of mind of many of the characters in the old stories in the Bible, when all else had failed and they were in a sore pass and had to wrestle with an angel or otherwise turn back toward God.

I recognized this, I mean, I had gone to Sunday School as a child, somewhere or other in my soul I was a Christian, what else, but I had also been to college, and succumbed to every other bad influence in our greedy, godless, hellbent society, and been *educated out of* any serious tendency to being Christian, in other words, it had been impressed upon me that life was always a dirty catch-as-catch-can rat-faced affair, the economy was directed by a beneficent invisible very sleazy and greedy hand, but not God's hand surely, one ought to live for today and only save up enough hard coin for tomorrow, no more, happiness came through chemicals and new inventions that delivered entertainment to you, and God was in bad taste. You might see truth under the microscope but never in pages of scripture, anyway, and if you had a problem it was up to you to solve it, it was not going to be *revealed* to you. I knew all that. I was a perfectly modern man. I thought to myself that it showed what I had come to that I had picked up a Bible!

So I turned a few pages dismally in a numbed and hopeless state as I read aimlessly and without comprehension here and there, until I came upon these verses, in Job.

Wherefore do the wicked live, become old, yea, are mighty in power? . . .

Their houses are safe from fear, neither is the rod of God upon them. . . .

Their bull gendereth and faileth not; . . .

They take the timbrel and harp, and rejoice at the sound of the organ. . . .

They spend their days in wealth, and in a moment go down to the grave. . . .

Therefore they say unto God, Depart from us; for we desire not the knowledge of thy ways.

As this passage fitted me to a T, or used to fit me like that, or even worse, accurately described my highest aspirations, to be in the blessed state of wealth, fat, rich, prosperous, secure, and happy, and very wicked, as so described, not troubled by the Lord or having the faintest impulse to pick up a Bible, playing the timbrel and the juke box, watching my bull gender and my cars move from place to place, saying to God, *Depart!* Please, don't bug me! I saw as in a desperate bolt of heavenly light that I was lost, all was lost, "in a moment" I would "go down to the grave," and there was no hope unless God helped me find my bearings once more. So I muttered to God a half-baked prayer to help me find some backer for my cars at Cloud Lake.

How about that! I said to God to help me sell some cars! Ha ha! I was not so far gone I could not laugh in evil irony at my condition. At the same time, I knew that whereas I very well knew how to say to God, *Depart!* I had no idea how to really pray and

151

beckon God to come near and help me. What was more, I was quite certain somebody like me deserved no help, and what was even more, nobody I had ever known, with the possible exception of Julie, deserved any such help. We had all murdered the Indians, let's face it once and for all. If I was wicked, I was surrounded by the wicked, far worse than me, as they were forgetful not regretful. I was one of the guilty pack but my problem was I just could not keep up with the general wickedness. I was bush league wicked. The wickedness as I saw it was pervasive and at everyone's door, and if you ever let go for a moment (as the Bible suggested you had to do), you would be swallowed up and eaten alive, wolfed down, bones and all. You would be a meal for the Harmless Harry's of this world. He'd pick his teeth of you.

The wickedness went far back. My people, the wicked, had been killing off Indians of all sorts and making hay off their bones for centuries, and my problem was just that I had had the misfortune of accidentally killing one myself, personally and while not in uniform, my life had been changed by it. As a person we are always to blame, while as a mob we are not. In our country you had to kill thousands to be safe. If you killed only one, you would be punished or driven mad and into exile. As a group, or a pack, it's all gravy and glory. And so I had had to flee for my life, and my freedom, as a result of which I had been sinking steadily in the ranks of the wicked, in their houses, where is not "the rod of God upon them." But damned if I knew how to pray right either. I just didn't remember how, or think I deserved to know how. Still, I gave it a shot.

After I had shut the Bible, almost angrily I may say too, as I thought what was being asked of me was too much, and left the motel room, I got into my car, and began to drive around again, as no matter how tired I was of driving, I got my best thoughts behind the wheel sometimes. I needed some thoughts. I'm not sure what impasse of the soul I had reached in the motel room, but I seemed suddenly slightly cheered up, as if what I had read had sufficed to show me that I was not *that* bad off yet. I wasn't quite ready with Job to give it *all* up that way, in hopes things would swing my way again, you know. I didn't see anything but Bible-thumping hypocrisy in that direction (in my case, I mean, not Job's obviously), and I am not a hypocrite I hope. But maybe God had just barely heard by little confused and humble petition. I was tooling around in my car again anyway and had gotten a second wind.

Maybe it was just being back on the road again after even a brief interlude. Instantly my thoughts went back in the other direction in a wholesale stampede. Suddenly I just wanted to get back in the swim again, and I was sure I would and could. I wanted only mine, as a card-carrying member of the American wicked. With all the murder, robbery, rapine, and wholesale mayhem that had been going down around here for centuries, I was sure my little slice of it really could not be denied me, in the end. Why on earth should it be? There was plenty to go around. I had a hankering to play my timbrel and gender my bull. It wasn't that I didn't believe very well what it said in the Bible, I just wanted to make some hay. You know what I mean. I just couldn't abide it to let the wicked in their houses laugh at me, shut out of the good life, with the very Indians. Oh, I know the wicked very well, I know their thoughts, and it outraged me.

After a while I happened to pass the garage of a mechanic I remembered I knew slightly. It was amazing I had passed this way in my aimless wandering, but there it was. Without meaning to I had strayed not far from my old penthouse, complete with Mr. Ramos's birds, had I wanted to go hear them and think of Gretchen wretched and desperate in the grainy dawn. I was on familiar ground and this seemed to me a sign that I had found the right track again, had picked up the scent on the trail, perhaps because of my interlude in the motel room with a motel Bible, although it could just as well have meant the exact opposite, that I was the wrong way again, on the wrong path. I knew that. I was desperate for the least hint that I had some goal or plan.

I parked and got out and walked straight toward the door of the car shop with a feeling of felicity, as of a fate finding me again. I used to send this mechanic prospective buyers who had no mechanic but wanted one to check out the car of mine they were thinking of buying. I pulled in and shot the breeze with him for a while. But as we talked, I became more and more aware that in his opinion, we had together pulled the wool over a few people's eyes, and what was worse, he was rather proud of it too, or at least found it funny. But I had never asked him not to go over those cars with a fine-tooth comb. I didn't want to wrangle with people about brake pads or tires and whatnot, and if something was wrong with the car I'd knock down the price. Or I'd have him fix it, which I'd thought was righteous enough angle for him. I'd certainly never in my own mind been mixed up in anything with him, although I did gratefully recognize that he would know a Rembrandt when he saw one and not like some ill-tempered jealous guys point out a little flake of rust on the rocker. I became incensed and ill at ease.

Yet standing around with the guy, I wondered at the old days which I had taken to thinking of as heaven. Right now what I needed was some of that real heaven that was within me that I had just been reading about in the Gideon Bible. I remembered how car problems in triplicate with Gretchen's friends had sent me into not only hiding but damn near retirement, and I had to admit to myself that perhaps a seed of corruption had snuck in. I had come to take things a little too free and easy was what it was. This mechanic was a case in point, to hear him laugh about our "old days." I had never conceived of them in that way and I resented it.

I didn't tell him about my cars up north and how I'd overextended myself, because this guy was the sort who would have needed little excuse to begin enjoying himself at my expense. I just let on I'd been into other things for a while but would be interested in getting into a project if he got wind of any. I had no idea what he'd make of that, I was just putting it out there, because who knows what tomorrow will bring, but it was clear to me just how low I'd sunk. To my surprise he did seem to make something of it, whatever it was, at once. He reacted enthusiastically. This inspired me to mention I had a couple of classic jewels needed restoring if he was interested. Yes, he was, where were they? When I admitted on the Canadian border or someplace like that, the look on his face let me know how bad a shape I was in indeed. He thought I had never left L.A.

Sullen gloom and tawdry distaste I have never known as on this night, nor did I seem able to find bottom. Now I was proposing to go into business with a guy whom I casually despised and it was apparently the best I could do. I seemed really to be freighted down with crimes from my past that I had scarcely been aware of. I knew of no better explanation than this sort of Biblical one. Julie would have been able to explain it in her own way, bad karma, throwing in an Indian or two, rightly so.

Invisible Car Dealer

The guy had a customer, a girl who had cracked up her car and was in money trouble as well, he suddenly intimated to me. She was so hard up she might part with the damaged car, which was new, for a song. Depending on the extent of the damage we might make a steal and fix it up for very little. He hadn't seen it yet. He suggested that I go by her place and take a look. If the deal looked good, I should front the money. Of course I must be "ruthless" with her—his word. (Just how ruthless he would have had no idea, since I was completely broke, I had no money, and had not walked into his shop with the least idea of anything, only to see what would happen. So as far as acquiring her car was concerned, or any car, I would have had to knock her on the head and make off with it, since if she wanted a hundred dollars for it, I could barely manage that.) With a lewd grin, he indulged a suggestive metaphor for his plan for her that made me cringe. It was hopeless unless I admitted to him he would have to front the money too.

Terror and sadness engulfed me, as I started on my lonely, pointless, and sordid mission. I wondered why I was bothering, but fate seemed to have marked me out for this, I was helpless, and almost unconscious. I had gone to look over many cars in my career but none could have afflicted me like this mission. On the way, I became aware I was passing the apartment complex where I had once lived with Gretchen, and I couldn't help taking a long glance at it. I hoped she was better. But I doubted it. By the time I found the girl's home, a small Spanish-style bungalow stuck on a hill in West Hollywood, which didn't look half-bad, I was feeling so strung-out, I didn't know what I was doing.

The mechanic had called her, and told her I was coming, but I couldn't remember what he supposedly would have said to her. I had been listening, and not listening, when he had dialed her number, my ears tuned to outer space, to the empty sky, like one of those radars the scientists are using to search for intelligent life not found locally. Of course he had assumed I had some cash to lay on her, so he'd probably given her the impression I'd pay her on the spot for her car if I liked it, and then he'd tow it in tomorrow. He remembered me as someone with ready money.

But my few dollars were not going to be remotely enough. Why was I making this drive? I asked the stars. I wondered what sad words would flow between us, while I fine-tuned the deal in the void. I would end up insulting and frightening her if I suggested she could sell it to me on credit.

I was not prepared for what sat in her driveway. It was only barely recognizable as an automobile, having been front-ended and rear-ended in a multiple collision. The hood had slid under some other vehicle and looked like the bill of a platypus which had been beaten to death with a tire iron. This was in the total loss category, not even close. Why wasn't it in a wrecking yard already? This was Dahomey's meat not mine. It was hard to believe the girl herself, who was walking out of her house to greet me, her arms clasped over her breast and a strange squint in her eye, wasn't a DOA herself, if she'd been in this. No frame man in the city would look twice at this baby, even the seats looked bent. Dahomey might have given her two hundred dollars for it, counting on finding a few motors and accessories intact. Here and there some patches of gleaming paint on parts of the body that had not buckled testified that it really had been a late model.

My sadness and lostness opened out to include the girl, who was approaching hesitantly, in shadow, with a slight limp, a wave of dark hair rising above her forehead, cascading down over a black eye, but my overwhelming emotion was relief, that I was not going to have to charm and con her after all, for I could not have charmed and conned my way out of a paper bag by now. I did not want this wreck! No more would be required of me than a few kindly meant words for her well-being. Nor was I going to have to do business with that rip-off artist acquaintance, nor would the girl either. We were both winners in that regard, little knowing it. I thought I would warn her about him, that would be my good deed for the day. She wouldn't have imagined it just now, but I looked at her and knew we'd both been spared.

Street lamps were few and far between in these hills and only a few stars twinkled dimly in the atmosphere piled with volcanic ash. As the girl came close and emerged from her own silhouette, I could make out her features in the amber glow coming from the windows of her bungalow. She must have been pretty before the accident. One eye poked out in a black-and-blue swelling like the eight-ball on a pool table, and she had a big bandage on her forehead, which I had mistaken for a wave of hair. She was wearing only slippers and a robe, which was why she had her arms tight across her chest modestly. One ankle was in a cast, which she swung out before her awkwardly.

"Hi. How're ya doing? You're from Mike, right? I didn't even own it long enough to get it insured," she lamented in a slurred voice, smiling gruesomely between thickened lips. "I only made one payment."

I didn't reply how I was doing and didn't ask her how she was doing. "I'm sorry, you'll just have to call the wrecker," I said quickly. She gulped back her emotion because no doubt she'd been getting irrational hopes up because of that Mike.

"Mike's the best mechanic I ever knew. He said he could put a new front end on it."

I refrained from asking her who was going to put a new rear end and both sides and the top on it. There was nothing to say, but to draw a deep sigh.

"I was hoping to get a few thousand for it," she said.

Oh God! I felt so bad for her. Hope springs eternal, and that's not always good. I was familiar with that myself.

"Well, I guess I'm just dead," she said.

"Well, thank heaven you're *not* dead," I said, looking at her wrecked car. "You made it through okay, that's all that counts." I put my hand up in farewell, or self-defense.

Her robe fell open slightly, showing the tops of her breasts, their moist luster with blue bruises stung through the gloom like distant moons, ones that had been landed on. Softly they prompted me, those hurt orbs, like mute signals of a far-off, unintelligible life. I felt her unknown existence in constellation with my own. I too wanted a new foothold in so-called normal existence as much as she did. Our respective moods held the same horror. I wanted to reach out and take her hand, a friend, but did not. To have done so would have buried me in erotic terror. I was desperate but not completely out of my wits. The grisly remains of her car shone in crazy fragments beside us in the drive, like a cubist painting by Picasso on a bad LSD trip, a girl's mangled dream dissected and laid bare in its pathetic insufficiency. She had no insurance. She'd made one payment. I pulled out a hundred bucks, almost my last, and handed it to her.

"I don't know how much more Mike will give you tomorrow, but here's a down payment."

"What?" She pulled her garment tight about her neck and stared at the cash in my hand. "That's not enough!"

"Yeah, yeah, Mike will take care of you tomorrow. Just take it. It won't help but it won't hurt you."

"I don't know."

"No, it's not for the car," I assured her. I forced her to take it, and took a few running steps, I could think of nothing else to say.

She didn't know what to make of that her look said. What Mike would make of it tomorrow when she called him and he saw the totaled car was rather amusing to contemplate. It would be one of those little mysteries along with my disappearance. I no longer felt entirely strange thankfully, but into the emptiness had been thrown a small token, a gesture, from which I myself drew a flicker of warmth.

"I shouldn't take this. I think the dealer will give me more!" she lamented as I drove away hurriedly. I took my hands off the wheel and held them up together Gandhi-like, in peace, something I'd learned in Berkeley, and rolled away.

Now I really was almost broke and soon would not be able to afford another day in the motel, and when the gas in the tank of my car ran out, would not be able to drive any farther. Then would come a reckoning. I was hopeful about that, as it was in the Bible when people had their backs to the wall that sustenance came. If nothing else I always had believed in the power of necessity to come up with a solution. All the same after a few minutes I became annoyed with myself when I began to suspect that I was slightly cheered up by that cheapest of human reactions to another's troubles, the feeling that there at least had been somebody worse off than I was, whom I could pity or help, and that my gift to her might have revealed nothing but an abyss of foolishness, considering the state of my finances. Superior to a poor creature who was all broken up, whose beauty slight as it had been would be marred, whose new and uninsured car was rubble, which she'd have to go on paying off for the next five years. The car company wouldn't care about her troubles. They had their own, and she'd have to make every payment, regardless if the car was a cubist painting now, while her body slowly healed. I wished her sure healing. The pain in the world was astonishing. Who could ever contemplate it or make sense of it? Or want to.

Invisible Car Dealer

After driving around for a while more, the memory of that injured girl with her crumpled car acquired a kind of dignity. I did feel better off, humbled and uplifted, to have witnessed or touched what she'd been through, and had had the good fortune to have given her a hundred bucks. A numb sort of gratitude for I knew not what faintly reached me like the dim starlight through the smoggy sky. She seemed to stand for all the travail in the world and our mute bearing of it. I mean just the commonness and triviality of her everyday but substantial, pain. I thought she would bear up. I reevaluated my impulsive charity once again, and approved it after all. I had done something. But as I motored on into downtown Hollywood, a cold premonition told me my descent had only begun, and that if I had meant that hundred bucks to bring me luck, it was a bribe the gods would deem insufficient. As when lightning strikes, a dim landscape opened momentarily through the labyrinthine city, an evil path I knew I would have to follow till it turned, till it started to go up again, if it ever did. I considered what a cockeyed conceit my onetime idea of freedom had been. I was bounding around like a billiard ball. I was behind that fabled and notorious eight-ball.

Perhaps my old cars would rust at Cloud Lake, monuments to my folly. What a laugh those farmers would have when they drove by, how they'd shake their heads at the memory of the crazy tourist who'd bought them, or perhaps at the vagaries of human nature itself. It was amazing to have turned into an anecdote! Could I of all people have suckered myself in such a fashion? So palpable was my sensation of a strange fate which had taken over my life like an alien force, that if I had run across a band of drunken Indians as I made my way back through the funky glittering streets and foothills of Hollywood, I would have experienced none of my usual fear, but recognizing them at once as brothers, embraced them and offered them some firewater to drink together, and plumbed their tragic story to its root as we stood at the bar. There are plenty of Indians around Hollywood, too, did you know that? Drawn by the same allure which attracts all the other lost uprooted drifters from around the country. We were brothers in pain now. But their loss of culture and tradition fits the lost among them especially well for a vapid and degraded existence in Tinsel Town, whereas I was a tourist and could have used a map even if I used to live here. I found myself driving past that famous corner, filthy and

159

illuminated, at Hollywood and Vine. I spotted a few mangy Indian junkies on the street, and there would be more in the dives around here. Some of them made money though, because their leatherwork and jade jewelry were very popular among the TV and movie set, and so the Indians could do better selling curios here than in the country where they had to depend on real tourists showing up. Some were used as cheap extras in the Western movies also I knew. The only difference was that when they made a little money, or when they didn't make it, they turned to cocaine here instead of cheap whiskey.

The ugly Hollywood streets, so visibly littered with broken dreams, and even more pitiable, barely intact false ones hanging on another day before being crushed, sang to me a siren song, and I was almost tempted to stop in one of the crumby bars for a drink, or five, with the human flotsam and jetsam that surged on these sidewalks lusting after the next high. Here Indians, whites, blacks, Latinos, Asians, Americans all, the kind with no goal (like me), rubbed elbows in a purgatory where dreams had turned to nightmares and really nobody could tell the difference anymore or thought it profitable to try. Boy, Julie ought to move her shop down here, if she really wanted to help. The street people and down-and-outers up in Berkeley were a wholesome lot compared to their Hollywood counterparts. A junkie or pothead on Telegraph Avenue was still likely to eat his granola for breakfast, if he could get any, if somebody gave him breakfast, but in a dive at Hollywood and Vine where they had given up all illusion except their hope of being in the movies, they would shoot cocaine for breakfast cut with ground glass. At a stoplight on a corner a black transvestite who looked like she'd been run over by a truck was getting up off the ground and posturing like a starlet. An Indian whore wearing a sequined vest and cowboy boots stumbled against my fender as she pulled up her shirt to show her breasts and tried to solicit me. If possible, she was even uglier and more harrowing than the starlet. Here was a human cargo worthy of the salvation ship all right, more like a ship of the damned flying skull and crossbones. Here was a crucifixion without a soul. This was the dropping off point, the transfer spot, of the slave ships of damned souls. Battered bodies walked around uninhabited, all that remained. Julie would never run out of work here. Hollywood and Vine.

Invisible Car Dealer

Dear Julie, she seemed an angel vision, a memory of paradise tonight. But there were limits to her understanding. Julie had the milk of human kindness, but the gall of despair was what the people on these streets had a taste for, they were no longer interested in milk of any description. Perhaps it didn't avail much to understand too well if one's intention was to help, and maybe this was the reason why I had never particularly desired to help humanity. I had drunk of that bitterness too by now, and it filled my mouth, so much that I really did think of stopping in one of these little dens of iniquity on the street and drowning my sorrows in juke box song, some bourbon, and the evil laughter of soulmates. What I would have given for Julie's breast to lay my head on tonight. Her remembered silhouette beyond the tawdry neon scenery seemed to lead me forward out of the twinkling morass. I wondered when and if I would ever find her again.

My heart swooned. I hit the accelerator, intending to get back to the motel, the Gideon Bible, and a good night's sleep after which I might have a clear head on a new morning, even if I was still more broke. I shuddered to think how close to the edge of the abyss I had lately steered, how I was skirting its cold lip now, and had had a glimpse into its depths (at Hollywood and Vine) vouchsafed only to those who were being made ready for the heady plunge themselves.

There was a shadow-side of freedom, as there was an underworld in human fate, and into this barren land my spirit had taken first faltering steps. There was hidden at the bottom of a cheerless cliff a huge stone kettle boiling red yet cold as ice, the very hell our ancestors quite accurately had insisted on, and into it I might trip and fall, where souls struggled up futiley like insects against the sloping sides, washed back again by the hot lava like ants in a bucket. I saw it!

The strangest thing at first, while crossing this bleak nightmarescape upon which my inward as well as outward glance had deathly fallen, was to realize that at a red light someone had drawn up beside me in the next lane, and was honking and waving at me. I didn't even look over, assuming it was some sort of a mistake, somebody wanted me to buy drugs, or a whore wanted my attention, or the devil himself wanted his last payment. Some fool wanting to tell me one of my tires was low or something. But as the person persisted in driving down the street in tandem with me, I finally scrutinized him out of the corner of my eye and saw it was somebody I faintly recognized. More than that, the Mercedes he was driving I definitely recognized as a car I had sold once, apparently to the guy behind its wheel. My hair stood up on my neck. I thought I was about to get shot.

But then I calmed down, for I realized at least it was none of that infamous trio whom I knew were out to get me. In fact, I remembered it was somebody who had always been pleased with his purchase, which had been a nice one. This was one of my very nice cars I had sold somebody and I almost sobbed out loud to realize it. The guy must want to thank me and pour out his gratitude. This was a great relief to me just now, and I smiled back at him. He shouted some cheerful greetings and seemed extremely pleased to see me, but it didn't stop me feeling uneasy. I knew what these happy meetings could lead to.

I waved back tentatively, and mouthed the words, "How's it running?" Just being polite. I couldn't have cared less, and didn't want to know. For me right now personally it was running much too rough for me to have any sympathy left over for car owners I once knew, even the good ones. So I shot ahead. But he came even with me again at the next light. He began motioning me to pull over. I saw I had no choice but to do so, or else try to outrun the guy, which would have looked awfully foolish, and for which I had no stomach at the moment, why fight it, if he wanted to talk to me about something, or even thank me (something I had begun to doubt). I had a clear conscience as far as that Mercedes was concerned and it was obviously still running a year or so later. So we both parked at the curb.

I shook hands with him suspiciously, while he sang his Benz's praises for a half a minute, breaking off when he saw he was boring me, and taking up a story about a rattle in the undercarriage of the car which was driving him crazy. He insisted he wasn't blaming me for it but perhaps I could help, since I knew the car. It was such a trivial matter that I barely could keep my attention on what he was saying, when I remembered the poor bruised girl I had just left with her totaled car in her driveway. I recognized in this character that moronic state of pathological self-centered obsession which passes for normality in so many car owners, and will engulf you in madness too if you don't watch out. With all the problems in the world, he wanted me to consider his rattle. However, the truth is you can be in perfect health, but if your little toe hurts you're miserable, and your automobile may spin like a Teutonic top but if it has a rattle, it may drive you around the Benz. So, not entirely without humor or sympathy, I was willing to go the distance with him a rattle or two, having nothing better to do really at this moment. So I tried to listen and keep a straight face.

Actually just the intensity of his concern, which he expressed in a whining, exasperated voice, finally got me hooked. I saw the only way I was going to get rid of him was if I helped him, and it wasn't like I had any pressing appointments or anything. I was half-dead myself and didn't have any margin to deal with him more creatively but to say, "Okay," and start thinking about it dully. A rattle like that can make a special appeal if it is in your line, and I never minded having a go at solving those little mechanical mysteries. I had been a fair mechanic in my day. In fact, when I diagnosed or fixed a car I always got a real kick out of it. A tiny rattle can be one of the most evasive and enigmatic symptoms, however, and harder to solve than a major problem, as many car owners know, and their mechanics know even better.

So I locked my Jag and got in the back seat of his Mercedes and had him drive while I cracked open the rear doors one at a time and stuck my head out to listen. We didn't have any lift to put the car up in the air on and have a real look, so this was the only way. After a few blocks and several stops and starts it appeared to me that a bushing in the suspension someplace had worn out leaving bare metal clanking, and I reported my findings to him.

"Holy shit, what am I supposed to do about that?"

I didn't catch his drift, and just looked at him blankly. Really I was in a sort of state, I was on the edge, and felt like with a good push I'd fall right over, and probably yank him along with me, and I hoped he wouldn't go on like this much longer.

"Don't you have a mechanic," I whispered, "or something?"

"But the rest of the car is great. The engine doesn't use a drop of oil, and I haven't even had a flat tire. I haven't even had the brakes worked on!"

"I'm pleased to hear that."

"I love the car, but that rattle, man!"

He wanted me to do something about the rattle. All the good qualities of the car he took for granted, traced to something exemplary or deserving in his own character, or even mine, he wished to imply good naturedly. But he was supposed to have a *perfect* car and that rattle could not be anything of his. The rattle was *mine*. He grinned slyly at me from just under his pseudo-perplexed look, and I saw how this guy must manipulate people to do things for him, a real entitled prick. I was too tired.

"It isn't so much a rattle. That's the wrong word anyway. It's more of a clunk." I stalled for time. I even wanted to help. But I didn't think I could. I wanted only to get away.

"Yeah, yeah."

"So, if you've taken it to the garage and told them a rattle, no wonder they didn't get it. When you take it in, be sure to say *clunk* not rattle. Tell em I said it was a bushing."

"Where is it coming from exactly?" he asked, seeing where I was trying to escape and heading me off.

"The left rear, I think."

"You sure?"

"No, I'm not. Noises telegraph around under a car."

"Well, I have to be sure, man."

"You do? Okay, you listen!"

I grabbed the keys and we repeated the experiment, except that he sat in back, but he didn't stick his head out where he could have actually heard something, but tried to figure out where the noise was coming from while he just sat behind me on the plush seat like a prince. I got the impression he was enjoying being driven around and paid a lot of attention to. I wondered if I wasn't a worse idiot than he was for going along with him. An appalling, lurid despondency washed over me worse than anything before that after everything and with the demons that were harrying me, breathing fire down my neck, I was monkeying around with this, and letting myself be pushed around.

"You're right! Damned if it's possible to tell where it's coming from!" He leaned over the front seat happily and agreeably. I wanted to grab the tire iron and thrash him. I told him I had done all I could for him, and wished him goodbye.

"You haven't done a damn thing. I don't know any more about that rattle or clunk than I did before. You sold me this car, you know, and you guaranteed it was perfect. That's why I paid you exactly what you asked. I didn't bargain you down a lousy nickel!"

"It's a bushing."

"What's that?"

"A bushing on the left, in the rear suspension. That's my expert diagnosis, and it's free. Now really, you have to take it from there. Be serious. I could be wrong, too. I'm not a German mechanic. I'm not Henry Ford. Or Adolph Volkswagen. I have to be going now. As much as I'd like to help more."

"How much is it going to cost me?"

"I don't know. Not a real major deal, don't worry. A small thing. Look, we're out here on the street, you know, nothing can be done tonight."

"That rattle was there the day you sold it to me, it's just gotten worse."

"Listen," I had an inspiration, an intense wish, an amusing vision, "the only way we're going to know exactly where this clunk is and exactly what it is and how much it's going to cost is if you get in the trunk and listen for it while I drive around the block and you tell me what you think, you know, then you'll know exactly where it is, and I can give you an estimate." Where this thought had come from I did not know, but it was a funny one. I was so exasperated, I was only being wise with him, slyly telling him where to get off, but for a moment there, so disgusted, my vision was of him dead in the trunk of his car which would be parked in an alley or at the airport.

"You're kidding me."

Of course I was kidding him. But after a second or two I went on, "No, that way if our impressions agree, you know, then we'll know. In the trunk you are right over it and can tell. The trouble with you, you won't stick your head out the door by the wheels while I drive."

"Yeah, a rock might jump up and hit me in the head."

"Well, you can't tell anything just riding in the back seat. A rock can't hit you in the trunk. You don't seem to want to believe my opinion of it, so you have to hear it up close yourself, then you can agree or disagree. Nothing will jump up and hit you in the trunk. You'll be safe."

I just wanted to bring things to a head somehow and get rid of the guy, one way or another.

"Are you nuts? No way I'm riding in the trunk, pal."

"Well, in that case, I have to be going."

"You want me to ride in the trunk? I'm going to hear something? Ha ha! You are a comedian. Then we'll know, huh?"

"Listen, if you will ride back there and tell me exactly what you hear, and we can get this over with, so you'll be satisfied and let me go on my way, I'll tell you what, I'll take the car and fix it right now. I mean if we know, you know, exactly what this is, I will pay for it, okay? Just to get you out of my hair. I'll have it fixed tonight. You know Mike's place? Or what I'll do, it's late—I'll give you the bread. Just to be done with this."

Of course I had no bread.

"You will, hey? You really will?"

I could see him looking at me like he liked that part about me paying for the whole thing. I know his kind very well. I saw that he was a demon from hell, my demon from hell, just the one sent to finally drive me into the pit of self-loathing, maybe insanity, but that unexpectedly I had his number. I saw that he might get into the trunk. He was that greedy. He was a con-man himself, and there was a slim chance he could be conned. But it never occurred to me he would get in the trunk, I had no real desire for him to do so, and I was only trying to escape his clutches. All I had really been doing was trying to embarrass or irritate him enough with my insulting patter that he'd blow up and threaten to sue me and that would be the end of it and this stupid scene would be over. But I suddenly thought to myself he might be going to climb in the trunk, and what then?

"I don't think I can ride in the trunk," he said, but eyeing it now as I stuck in the key and opened it.

"Look, you keep it nice and clean. One spin around the block, and see if you don't agree with my diagnosis. Get this over. Then we'll know exactly what it is, when *you* hear it, and if I can fix it easily, I mean if we're absolutely sure, we'll just find somebody, and go ahead and have it taken care of. Or if it's too late tonight, I'll give you the money."

After another second, he climbed in. I couldn't believe it. I had no idea where all this could be leading and wished he would just drive away not climb in his own trunk, but there he was, he had climbed in. I stared down at him wonderingly for a moment.

Invisible Car Dealer

"Do you know how sad and ridiculous it is really, compared to half-starved Native American children without decent schools out on the reservation," I remarked in a low voice to him as I slammed the trunk lid down on him. "We have our little problems, you and me, and we make so much of them, while meanwhile we have killed almost all the Indians and pushed the remnants of them onto barren reservations and look down our noses at them and think of them as savages to this day. That's what we have done, the white man. Haven't we? They don't even have a job. Who are the savages, anyway, when you stop to think of it? For God's sake."

I felt the horrible truth of my words and the strangeness of belonging to a civilization that was founded upon the total destruction of another and all its people. I felt the misery and terror of the processes of history that we all find so normal and not worth a moment's reflection. He had stared up at me with an obtuse and frightened look in his eye vanishing in an instant beneath the trunk lid with a firm clunk indeed, and I got behind the wheel, and turned on the radio to cover any squawks that might be coming from him. I found a hard rock station, and turned up the volume. There began a dull knocking from the rear of the car, no clunk or rattle, he must have objected to rock music.

It made me so angry, that he had cried so much about nothing, with all the pain that's in the world. He was rich enough to own this beautiful Mercedes and he wanted to come over like he had a problem. After that poor lovely girl with her black eyes and pancaked car, and hopeless Indian children on the reservation whose ancestors and whole way of life have been run off the road. Other people were on the planet to solve *his* problems, that was the only use they were. He believed that so firmly that he had finally gotten in his own trunk.

I drove off in no particular direction, mulling things over, trying to think clearly. I felt rather triumphant, exulting in a small way, like an Indian warrior who had taken a hapless paleface captive and was going home with him tied across a pony to show him off around the campfire, roast him slow. Maybe I could ransom this guy? Nothing serious, just what his wife might have lying around in cash, plus what she could draw from the ATM. She had to have heard of the rattle that was driving him crazy. It had turned out to be the transmission and he needed two thousand. It would

167

be helpful to get him to talk to her. Pull up at that pay phone in front of the convenience store just ahead, place the receiver by the trunk lock, tell him to shout. Then off to the cash station. First though, soften him up a little more.

I couldn't hear him back there because the rock music was reaching a jagged crescendo and I had it turned up very high. I hated the music too. I would have hated to go through adolescence again, that dark isolation chamber, reverberating with haunting rock screams and cryptic signals from a half-blind youth culture, over a shifting bog of loneliness, rage, and sex. In short, a foretaste of the rest of one's life, apparently—this music. The insane howl in the rock music was more than justified, and made me want to shed a tear of pity for the poor kids for whom it articulated something, but it was not near insane or howl enough for me right now.

I was now feeling far worse about the guy's rattle. The moment I turned the music off, as I couldn't take it a second more, in the trunk he began to hammer away and to howl loudly himself. Maybe he had been howling and I couldn't hear it. What was the matter with him? He was supposed to pound or yell only when it clunked. What could his problem be? His steady banging was completely meaningless, and got us no nearer the solution. After a quarter of an hour of this he must have realized we couldn't possibly be going just around the block.

My name hadn't appeared on the registration of this car he had bought from me, which I had turned over so fast the previous owner's name had still been on it. He'd recognized me, but I was willing to bet he had never even bothered to memorize my license plate. He was far too self-centered and full of his own little problems to have checked things out to that extent. People wandered around the jungle in the unconscious belief that everything had been cunningly designed to go their way. And when it didn't they were beside themselves.

I've never sold a car as a flying carpet, the fountain of youth, or the sure ticket to picking up girls. God forbid. They aren't made in paradise, only Deutschland, or Detroit. No more complaints from anybody not prepared to go on foot! Is it just Californians, or all Americans, or everybody everywhere, who believe that the sun should shine on them always, that it should swing in the heavens to keep track of them personally, that nothing should rattle? Even in this age, even in America, the individual can't avoid all difficulty, no matter what it says in the Bill of Rights. I veered over the curb a couple of times, and for a moment his pounding stopped. Then it began again, though more tentatively. I hit another curb, and another, twenty or thirty times in a row. After that came a pleasing calm from in back and all around. Here I was in a terrible jam, the worst predicament I'd been in in a long time, my whole life coming apart at the seams and dead broke, and driving around recklessly bouncing a guy in the trunk. But it was a comfort.

Ahead, the lights of a tavern showered their illusion of happiness into the street, and I swerved over. I had been needing a drink for hours, and even the illusion would do. I thought about asking my friend to join me, but a wonderful peace now exuded from the trunk. Inside the lounge it was cozy and hidden. A woman was playing popular tunes on a dim piano, and a subdued, poor but tasteful atmosphere prevailed. It seemed to me there was something good-natured and sane about the people in here, consoling themselves with their nightly measure of illusions, knowing that a little of such a thing is good for you, and what's more there weren't too many people. A number of booths were empty and dark, and I found myself a seat in one of them, and drank a couple of bourbons rapidly.

The sparse crowd was over middle-aged and average looking, and the tunes being played were well-worn and mellow. Actually, it seemed impossible that anyone could be entertained by such muzak no matter how drunk they were, even if it was played by a real woman, who was probably forced to play such stuff by some horrible circumstance. It was a pathetic, threadbare, plastic place which radiated a tawdry and lunatic wonder. What did it all mean? It was intensely eerie, somnolent, and bizarre.

Unnerved by normality I guess, but having regained a certain perspective on things, with the bourbons, I left the lounge, but when I got back to the car parked at the curb, a woman with a shopping bag was standing beside it in a state of alarm.

"This your car?" she asked me, as I started to get into it.

"No, I'm going to steal it. Of course it's mine. That's why I'm getting in it. Well, as a matter of fact, it belongs to an acquaintance. What's it to you?"

"Somebody's in the trunk, that's what! He said he was fixing it or something, and the guy—you, I guess—drove away with him! I was just walking along, and I heard this voice coming from in there!" She pointed at the trunk as you would at some horror, holding out her whole arm, as if to push it away, while at the same time backing away. "I'm going to call the cops!" she cried.

I smiled at her suddenly good-humoredly, and gave her a big wink. Making friendly calming gestures, at the same time cocking my head as if to indicate some hidden audience, and turning to grin at the almost empty street, I walked up to her, and for some reason she stood still for this. Probably she'd had a hunch what it was all along. "You're a good sport!" I suddenly shouted, grinning for all I was worth, and gazing straight across the street at the one car on that side, a van that was parked there, I waved, and mugged at the van, and looked at her candidly and knowingly.

"Ever seen America's Funniest Videos?"

"Candid Camera?"

"Yeah! No, the other show."

"I knew it!" She covered her face, and looked from the van to the trunk of my car, all her suspicion dissolving in a wave of recognition. Everyone in L.A. wants to be on TV or in the movies, and supposes that one day they will be, assumes it, takes it for granted, if unconsciously. Most of the cops you see on the streets are actually being filmed for some show if you take a closer look, speaking of calling the cops. Movie and TV sets everywhere, so it's hard to tell what's real anymore. So apparently she really believed she was on Candid Camera, or America's Videos, apparently so.

"You're going to receive two free passes to Jay Leno, and you can choose between a dinette set and a new carpet for your living room. Okay boys, take care of this lady!" I called loudly to the van. "They'll be right over," I assured her, and while she pushed at her hair, before her suspicions came back, I jumped in the car and sped away. I watched her eyes in the rear view mirror, and they remained on the van. But it was time to call it a night and I hurried back toward the intersection where I'd left my Jag. The amazing thing was not a peep had come from the trunk while I'd been talking to her. He was listening to us. But as we drove, he began to make an unholy grinding racket again. It seemed like he'd found the tire iron and was trying to pry the lid open with it. Didn't he stop to

170

think he was going to have more repair expense when he was through doing that? Horrible grating and kicking noises became very annoying. The idea of forcing him to give me all the money he had on him at least began to compel me again in a rage. It would serve the greedy fool right. I'd go back and give most of it to that girl with the crashed car and receive another of her deerlike glances.

Suddenly, an amazing noise began right under the dash, something shaking badly, vibrating like a dentist's drill. It was the rattle! This was what the guy had been complaining about. No wonder he had considered my explanation about a clunk in a lower bushing inadequate! What in the hell? It seemed like a panel was coming loose. Nobody could live with that going on in their car for five minutes. I felt bad, and terribly sympathetic to the guy whom I had misjudged, at least slightly, in regard to the genuineness of his rattle. I was overcome by furtive guilt, and in memory I seemed to hear all the people who had ever complained to me about rattles and strange noises now join together in a chorus of lament. It was an unearthly drone of mechanical rattling and human woe, as if a hundred cars were flying apart and a hundred tragic owners were gnashing their teeth and beseeching me.

By good luck, I happened upon a railroad crossing, in a bad state of repair, with huge chunks of asphalt missing from the bed between the rails, and it felt so good when I hit it, that I turned around and went over it again, and then made another U-turn and accelerated over it several more times, again and again, each time the car flying up and down on its springs like an accordion, after which the sweetest silence came to my ears. The people had all stopped moaning, and in the trunk the guy had desisted scraping and prying with the tool, and that unbelievable dentist-drill rattle had completely stopped too. I never heard that bushing clunk again either. All was nice and quiet as a pair of bare feet.

Now came the problem of releasing this motorist, who must have been regretting having made me pull over as he had. Maybe he'd learned his lesson by now, about burdening others with his problems. I sincerely doubted it, but that was no reason not to anticipate his imminent liberation warmly. I wouldn't imprison a dog, not for long. I pictured it almost as a resurrection, two eyes gleaming at me from the dark hole, then a pair of hands reaching over the metal lip, freedom grasped like the prize that it was. You could almost hope the experience might prove a gift to the guy in the long run, after it had sunk in some day, and he would learn his lesson, but I could see the white knuckles of those hands squeezing the edge, the eyes from the deep glinting like a caged animal's, and I had a hunch he was not going to be in a really great mood immediately, the benefits would dawn on him only later.

I really didn't need to be a witness to his return from the underworld, I decided, I had my own darkness to deal with, and I had the certain feeling I was still descending. But somebody had to let him out. I spotted a black kid loitering on the corner a block ahead, and drove up to him.

"Want to make ten bucks in the next sixty seconds?"

"Yeah," he said in a voice so soft and reluctant it was almost a whisper. His eyes fixed on me, deep pools of suspicion, with a ripple on them, wild gust of hope.

"Okay, take these keys, I'm getting my car over there, and when you see me give the signal, just open the trunk of this car."

"Wha' for? That all?"

But at this moment the guy in the trunk let out a really magnificent blood-curdling yell, and the kid bolted.

"Fergit you!" He slapped the air waving me away.

"Hey!" I jumped out of the car and ran after him, fluttering the green ten-spot in the air. "Look, don't you want it?" I really couldn't offer him more. The actual sight of the money had its predictable effect, and he stopped and stared back at it, remaining on the balls of his tattered high-top sneakers. Twin forces of fear and desire fought for his soul.

I had prepaid my motel room according to local custom and so that would leave me enough for a breakfast special, a tank of gas, maybe one more night and one phone call. Prisoners got that much, and by this time I really viewed myself as a prisoner of fate. With the kid shivering at my heels, I returned to the Mercedes and stuck the key in the trunk lock. I pointed to it.

"Don't move till I give you the nod!" I said severely. "Then unlock it and run like hell. I'll give you the ten as I drive by." He rocked on his feet, hesitating. He was a game one though.

When I got to my own car, he was still there, studying me intently, as he shifted from foot to foot, ready to make it. I waved at him to go over right to the trunk of the Mercedes, and he did with wild fear in his eyes. Then I drove straight at him, and as I accelerated past, I stabbed the air with my forefinger, and I saw him twist the key. The trunk lid flew open, I handed him the ten like a baton as I went by, and he took off like a junior Olympian out of the blocks. I shot past into the green gloom of the city.

The pleasurable effects of this insipid episode stayed with me for a little while, but not for long. I changed freeways a few times and sped through twilit neighborhoods. In my loneliness, as I drove aimlessly, I began thinking about Julie, naturally, whom I couldn't get by a day without missing. My heart hauled a thousand itchy images of her out of memory, and sent them to my brain, which hardly knew if it was being tickled or tortured. Visions of Julie, pure and sordid, racked my protesting soul. She represented all that I had lost, I guess, and all that I wished to return to, in my roundabout way. I felt like a Cherokee chief, who had signed a peace treaty with the Great White Father, only to realize it was not worth the parchment it was written on, and all my land was going to be torn out from under me anyway, and I would be marched away at gunpoint. I'd made my own fateful bargain, and it was a hopeless feeling. Well, they'd have to catch me first. I'd die fighting!

Dreaming fearfully in this way as I drove, I soon realized that I was in a strange part of the white man's town, which I didn't think I had ever seen before. Well, there are a lot of parts of L.A., and they are all strange and many are rich. This was a nice part, elegant part, maybe Pasadena, maybe not, very white-on-white. Before I knew it, I was completely turned around. And now I was about to have an even more unaccountable adventure with an even odder—and yet so typical—car owner—owner indeed of the *white car.* But of that in a moment, after a mechanical breakdown and a descent into a new and even weirder landscape of nightmare with which, reader, if you are an urban dweller, you may have made acquaintance also, on the worst night of your life.

Invisible Car Dealer

The pleasure of release from an irate insane car buyer was so sublime that for some time I lost my senses and winged it in a wild meditation. I savored my freedom from my pursuer and all my pursuers however short-lived and confused it might be. But it couldn't last in the face of an implacable overpowering enemy, invisible just beyond the hills though he be yet. I was outnumbered and outgunned. My back was against the cliffs and the cavalry approached. It seemed I had been driving through the wilderness of the city for many nights, forever. My hands were welded to the wheel. My legs were fried in gear grease and my feet had burned stuck to the floorboards. When I got out next time, I'd have to lift one leg then the other to the ground like a crash victim's. But I couldn't conceive of getting out. No balm in Hollywood. As I have said, by now I was long gone from Hollywood, and in another part of L.A. "civilization." I wanted to drive forever and never stop driving. I was a renegade Indian fleeing to Canada (or Mexico).

I was deep under that road hypnosis whose overwhelming character is reluctance to pause for anything, before stopping for good at one's final abysmal destination, and I didn't have one, neither a destination nor a goal, except my motel whose address I'd forgotten. I had reached the state of fatigue which sees the things that normal consciousness filters out as irrelevant, the charred remains lying clumped along the curbs. I smelled something peculiar, too. Something was going wrong with the car, and I had sensed it since I had hit town. The engine was no longer bucking and missing as it had been earlier, but I knew this was the calm before the storm. When the motor did freeze and give out shortly, it was no surprise, but that didn't make it any less gravely worrisome and disappointing. Unable to put one rational thought in line with the next, disturbed by fervid wishes for Julie, soul and body, lost in the city, aching and burning from head to toe, still a little drunk from the bourbons I'd enjoyed with the crew from America's Funniest Videos, I pressed the clutch and coasted to the curb. No longer protected by the bubble-cockpit of my car, but I must venture out into the poisonous atmosphere, on foot, through alien terrain with no trace of intelligent life, even distant, to guide me.

With a jagged pang like a head-on collision, I remembered how Julie had once invited me to join a community of just two. Julie was hundreds of miles away at the wrong end of the state, and if we'd ever had a chance, I'd blown it long ago. In a chorus of anguish and desire, my instincts sang out into nowhere like a vacant lot full of grasshoppers on a moonsoaked night. But there seemed to be no moon tonight, no stars, this dark night. That didn't discourage the grasshoppers aloose in my insides. There were no streetlamps in these parts either, no sidewalks, no pedestrians, other than me. It was that nice part of town with the big houses well separated by wide driveways to hold all the expensive cars. In the livid silence which ensued after the dead Jaguar coasted to the curb, the singing of the grasshoppers abruptly ceased. I had no food and no water, no arrows and no gun. I was not prepared to set out on a hike across the city, but I locked up the car and proceeded to do just that. There was nothing else to do. I must set out alone. I feared waking up in the car here tomorrow, with the rude sun stabbing glass fragments of indecipherable guilt into my eyes. I seemed to have made a wrong turn someplace back there, maybe several years earlier.

If only I kept walking, some plan might come to me, I hoped, although where such idiotic optimism kept coming from I might have wondered. I was in the trance of the all but doomed, and there was nothing but to keep marching, and sometimes that is all there is, as you know. The Native Americans have known this for a while. I believed all my gods had failed me, and freedom had not proved the self-evident glory it had been cracked up to be. The more powerful can come down from the hills or across the ocean in tall ships and wipe you out at any moment. Now I was like a man turned out in a desert who knows nothing but to walk deeper into the black sands, following his mirage. (But there was still a chance it was an ideal, and not a mirage.)

A couple of coughs, and the noble Jag had gone to the side of the road. I was so sentimentally connected to that car, it really was as if somebody had died. Worse than that, you are familiar with the gritty despair that comes over you when your favorite car breaks down on a dark night just when you need it most. One's own despair of the failure of a mindless machine is the worst of all because so pointless and futile. What a pass to have come to, wrapped up in a gadget. But that was only my irritation talking because the automobile is a daemon, as I was soon to be reminded.

The automobile is our essential tool and now I would confront city life barehanded, on foot. There being no sidewalks in this affluent sector whose planners had assumed every homeowner would own three, four cars, my kind of people of course, I placed one foot ahead of the other down the asphalt of a side street on the wrong side of paradise. One giant step backward for a man. I felt like I was walking backward. I was looking at the world recede away from me. It got darker and darker. The lights were going out all over the city. As I walked I seemed to cast a weird tremulous shadow far ahead of me (or behind me if I was indeed going in reverse, which it felt like), throwing everything I approached into a pure and devouring blackness. Once or twice I stumbled and, holding my hands out to save me, barely caught my balance. My feeling with every step was I might fall into a hole I couldn't see. Far from having been an expert on liberty, with its intricate system of checks and balances, and its price of eternal vigilance, I wondered if I had ever had a clue as to its real meanings or mechanisms, but hadn't always been operating on blind impulse.

The only thing more painful than continuing on this impossible ramble whose purpose when last glimpsed had been only to locate my motel room with its dubious comforts (and Bible!) would have been to stop, surrender, and sleep under a rose bush. The devils would have feasted on me uncontrollably, in the morning nothing left but a few rags and bones. But I was sorely tempted to lie down on the ground and perish. Each step was more than I could bear. Not to have taken it risked the unthinkable collapse! Left, right, left, right. Freedom was a tattered banner on a dim battlefield. I became the prey of a new fiendish notion, that not only should I stop right now and lie down against one of the trees that ornamented this neighborhood and wait for help or die, but could I have stopped myself but a few moments before, all would have been well. That is, if I had stopped at a gas station for some directions, I might have gotten back to the motel before the fuel pump had gone out. Or if only I had not driven out to see that girl's crushed car, which had cast a pall over me and changed my luck for the worse. Or if I had stayed in San Francisco to encourage Jack and persuade Dahomey little by little. Or if I had never made my fateful visit to Cloud Lake and bought all the cars I would have something in my bank account.

If I had smiled at Gretchen that sunny day in the lobby and kept on going. If I had stayed in Berkeley as Julie had wanted me to and protested my innocence in regard to that Indian who had strayed across my path on another dark night. I would have wound up in jail—in a jail constructed by the very hypocrites and unconscious mass murderers who had left one lone victim alive to fall in front of my car! But at least I would have had three hots and a cot, as they say. Aghast, I wondered if I was so low I could almost wish to still be working for Harmless Harry.

Had I not pushed my leg through the arc of the last step I had just completed on this spectral suburban street, I would not have to put my foot down one more time along a route which led nowhere, each faltering step a terrifying descent on a deadly downward spiral. Finally, I rued the day I was born.

But lamentably, I was born, I was lost in Los Angeles, the hardest place this side of the Sahara desert to have been lost and out of money in, Julie was at the other end of California, British cars were notoriously finicky, etc., etc., endless proofs of mortal birth, and I had just taken one more shaky stride, this time really tripping on something, and crashing arm first up to my shoulder into somebody's thick hedge, dense, oily, green, and full of thorns like a pit of fanged snakes, which all struck at once, drawing blood.

With horror I gingerly retrieved my arm with its torn sleeve from the hedge, and dozens of little prickmarks oozing red.

Invisible Car Dealer

The darkness hung in streaming clumps from the limbs of the trees and the eaves of the houses. It spurted from my eyes and ears, and clung in the air, before slowly sinking as dozens of tiny African sky-divers summoned by Dahomey from the heart of Africa on a secret mission to save my soul swarmed earthward, whose little black chutes like Japanese flowers were opening before my eyes with a heartening flapping sound, held up gently by the weight of the air before descending around my ankles, where I could feel them trying to redeem my footfalls before it was too late.

"Stop! In the name of Love," I heard a brown-skinned girl sing, the Supremes I believe. But Julie was far away, and there was no stopping, I thought.

Intensely aware of my feet in this way, being lifted in their progress by the tiny African paratroopers, I remembered how shiny my shoes were, and thought fondly of crazy Dahomey, the cause of this, whom I really should have stayed and tried harder to talk to. How could I have mistaken that act of his as anything but an impetuous gesture of friendship, laced with unavoidable ironies, as it must have been? I had missed one opportunity after another. But unaccountably a rescue squad had showed up from the green hills of Africa, as if I deserved it.

The tiny parachutists from the Congo dragged at my pantscuffs and did all they could to deflect my steps, in which direction it was not clear to me. I couldn't really tell if they were trying to stop me, change my direction, or rather were drawing me on, which I actually believed they were. I tried to relax and give in to their guidance. Whatever it was, I was sure that the paratrooper battalion had been sent to help. I was overcome with gratitude. Their presence around my ankles became one of those nagging yet indecipherable moral urges which finally bedevil one into making a move, any move, just to be rid of the impulse, even if it's the wrong move, better than no move.

I leapt ahead, my legs amazingly kicking out in an odd dance they had never practiced. Once all the minuscule parachuters had landed, the darkness kept flowing down remorselessly, the blood of the massacred spilling from broken hearts endlessly on the Plains before dawn. Suddenly, to my wonder, I was dancing the ghost dance. The tiny freedom-fighters who were holding onto my cuffs changed into ceremonial anklets with rattles once worn by

Invisible Car Dealer

Native Americans. This really was too much, but I realized I had come to a condition close to that of the truly downtrodden of this earth, those defeated by technologically superior powers backed up by efficient monotheistic religions, the wretched whose old prayers and rituals no longer availed, for the time being anyway, and thus might as well be given a try when every last other thing had failed. So I danced—I danced along on an impulse—the ghost dance—and dreamed of lost worlds. Now I knew I myself was lost beyond finding, yet at the same time a feeling of strength and doomed nobility entered my veins. I might well dance the ghost dance along with the brave wretched of this earth, for I was in the same boat as they were. Surely some vision would appear?

I had turned a corner onto a main drag, and I was dancing past used car dealers, furniture dealers, laundromats, flower shops, antique shops, taverns, a motley of stores and enterprises, useful enterprises all, but all closed for the night. Cars were whizzing by, late night people, drunk and weaving badly in their lanes, breaking the speed limit. *Wha! Wha! Wha!* The gusts the cars stirred up whipped me harshly. It is appalling to be hoofing along a main artery in L.A. late in the pitiless night with the cars spitting stones at your shins after your own ride has broken down. Everyone who sees you covers you in their contempt, glad in their hearts that it's not they who are in such a fix, sure it could not possibly be they, no way. Obviously you are a thief, a drifter, homeless, or some other worthless character, probably an Indian. Perhaps you have had the bad taste to run out of gas or have a flat tire, and are not a member of AAA. Probably you do not even own a car, not even a broken one, you are of that finally doomed and damned class of persons—a pedestrian. (This particular thought troubled me obscenely.) It is inconceivable to them that someone like you on foot, even dancing it seems, has ever owned a car in your life. You are a homeless waif and not worth spit. Because you are on foot! In a suburb with no sidewalks, not one!

But suddenly on this main drag sidewalks had appeared, not altogether a good feeling, like finding the steps to the hangman's platform. Still the cars came on, too close for comfort. Inside their cozy glass bubbles the comfortable half-drunk people in their automobiles tooling irresponsibly forward shut you out, and kill you over and over again in their minds as they cover you in grit and dust. So much for Christian charity. Realistically, I know, it's impossible to stop and offer somebody a lift when you are traveling a hundred feet a second in a machine wrapped around you like a steel skin, a coat of mail. Before a chivalrous impulse has a chance to take hold in your mind, in the unlikely case it should try to do so, you are two hundred yards down the road, and there's no use braking, too much inertia and momentum. Plus, why stop for a rascal who will probably rob and kill you.

I know how it is. I didn't hold it against them. Cars have re-created the wide open spaces between people once common on the frontier. Every solitary car a little homestead on the lonely prairie, encircled by hostile Indians. *But I was the Indian now,* the man on the outside, the passed-by, the enemy, the foot traffic, the defeated and endlessly undeserving, a walker, indeed a dancer. Through their tinted windows I saw the smug faces of the people as they caught sight of me just for an instant, and eagerly at once let the sight of me go, unwholesome, unholy, beyond the pale, not all of the faces white by any means in this neighborhood either, distant and deadly for all that. An Indian is an Indian. None of them ever entertained for a moment the possibility that I had a compelling personal history, that I was a human being deserving of mercy and trust the same as they, and for all they knew capable of a smugness as thick as their own, that a few minutes ago I had been riding around in a Jaguar far more fashionable than that square tin can they called a car, that I had cars by the dozen, rare Americans, minor glories of our national genius, a fortune locked up in old cars at Cloud Lake. All they saw was a downtrodden footsore Indian dancing away past closed storefronts and never imagined the sacred soul, the helpful practices and lost lore.

I promised God that if any of these people passing by stopped for me and gave me a ride to my motel, I would get their address and write them a check for five thousand dollars and send it to them the moment I got back on my feet again. I walked along curious to see if this experiment in telepathy or prayer might work. But it didn't. This was not God's fault, but that of the all too complacent people in those cars who weren't listening. By the same token, I had suffered so much at their hands by this time, that I would have been justified in laying a trap for one of them in the road and forcing them to stop, killing them, and stealing their car. I imagined a pile of burning tires one sees on the news. It occurred to me that if I were to go through with such a plan, at the last moment before the ambush was ready, a Samaritan might pull over by a special grace, and in that case I would never have harmed a hair on his or her head. Even though the trap had been laid, and a moment later I could have forced them to stop, I would send them that check anyway.

In the middle of these considerations, the most godawful metallic crashing I had ever heard in my life started up back up the road. I almost jumped through a plate-glass window in alarm. The gnashing, grinding racket grew louder and louder. Something like a herd of murderous knights on a crusade against heathen Moslems or Indians was bearing down on me from behind, hundreds of them in a posse, all clanking their chain mail and banging their poleaxes against their shields, urging on their armor-plated horses, and chanting in chorus for my blood.

I hurried on as fast as my feet would take me, afraid to look back. But the caravan kept gaining on me. At the last moment, wondering which way to leap, I finally glanced over my shoulder, and it was worse than I thought. A monstrous yellow machine, bigger than a tank, tall as a house, with flashing lights and dizzily spinning brushes, was overtaking me and about to run me over. I slipped into a doorway and watched it go by, a long conveyor belt with a scoop on the end of it sucking up charred timbers, old mattresses, piles of burned leaves and car parts and other decaying refuse piled along the streetside, while the whirling brushes scoured the curb. The driver was invisible high above, where he looked out through a little turret. Anything smaller than a parked car was sucked up instantly. The operator could probably barely see the ground. Somebody like me would have gone down the gullet like an olive.

No doubt the problem of waste had reached such proportions in the city, dying and broken creatures and their artifacts littering the streets everywhere and accumulating dangerously, giant cleaning devices like this were the order of the day. But it looked like an outfit designed by Rube Goldberg under orders from Hitler. I had barely escaped with my skin, and lingered thoughtfully in my doorway, watching it rampage up the street. Just off this commercial thoroughfare, running back up to the brown hills, were the opulent mansions of the citizenry, the "saved," whose taxes paid for these devices and procedures.

Suddenly, at the next corner I spied the makings of a tragedy in the huddled form of a bum sleeping under his tattered coat at the curbside. I hadn't imagined I still had it in me to run so fast, and only arrived at the corner about twenty feet ahead of the street-cleaner. I gave the bum a couple of kicks and yelled at him to move, but he only moaned and swore in his drunken slumber and curled up more tightly in a fetal position. I managed to haul him out of the path of the oncoming brushes at the last second. His coat had slipped from him, and a paper sack of his possessions as well as the cardboard bed he had been sleeping on I had no chance to retrieve before they disappeared down the throat of the monster, but the guy could have been wire-brushed to death, or wound up buried in a landfill. The street-cleaner ground away all trace of the bum's rest, but at least he was still here, in this doorway of a shuttered restaurant I'd dragged him into, where in the morning he would feel pain anew, all his usual pain, never knowing how lucky he was to feel pain. I breathed a sigh of relief, or even achievement.

A great deal of low anxiety had been brushed out of me, spiritual refuse, by the broom of raw fear. I relished a fragile peace as I walked along, as the din of the sweeping machine diminished ahead of me. How different things looked all at once, having escaped a ludicrous fate. I had my two legs to walk on, I owned an expensive car which after repairs would be as good as new, and I was a long way from being a poor, half-dead bum, too. For a blessed moment I could barely remember what I had been so worked up about these past hours and days. Who cared about any of that, especially those damned cars of mine? They had been rotting before I ever saw them, let them rot some more. None of it was worth worrying about!

Somehow just like that, all worry and despondency had flown from me. If I was an Indian, I was the kind who has regained his fierce pride. The street eventually turned residential again, or inadvertently I turned a corner, and the more spacious and high class wound the sidewalkless street before my feet, and I ambled along enjoying the soft night, filled with the lovely pungencies of all the spiky greenery, banks of exotic flowering bushes and trees, overlaid by the reassuring aroma of petrochemicals, which no longer irritated my membranes, but only added subtle hints of possibility and redemption, once again.

Here I'd been suffering and crying in my beer, but life would go on, even if I'd made a thousand mistakes. A sweet sorrowful composure overtook me. I had even regained some sense of direction, and when the main boulevard swung off to the left, I must have kept heading straight through the residential streets, sensing a shortcut to my motel bed, so I imagined. Or maybe space had curved. Anyway I was suddenly in a terribly affluent sector of society, although I'd not gone through a gate. These people were so rich and confident, they eschewed the gates. And the streets were clean. They had invented these incredible machines that appeared to be equipped to scoop up boulders fallen from the hills if it came to that. They were ready for every contingency. Those brushes were wonderful the way they had eaten up everything in their path. But they weren't needed in prosperous streets like these.

I ambled on with up-from-under confidence I didn't care to examine, as much as I had been through. My new mood lay fresh and delicate on me as the petals of a rose. I couldn't have any more explained how it had come over me than all the scientists in the world could explain the existence of a rose. It was more proof, however, that barring prejudicial circumstances, such as being run over by a street-cleaning device, pierced by the arrows of hostile Indians, or the bullets of posses of vigilantes and crusaders out hunting them or oneself, one's attitude counts for a lot.

On the next corner was a white car with a handwritten FOR SALE BY OWNER sign in its rear window. How interesting, unlikely and appealing, on such a street. I think an hour earlier I might have missed it altogether or walked to the other side of the street with my eyes averted to get away from it, but now I bent closer for an inspection. The car was not in the driveway but at curbside so as to gain attention. In this neighborhood it was the only vehicle at the curb. Some of my interest in life and even buying cars again returned to me like a ray of sanity from heaven. But of course I had no money, so it had the safety of a fantasy, which is what it felt and looked like, really. I felt free to indulge.

The white car gleamed as though cream from the Milky Way had spilled down over it. Maybe it was an American, maybe a British, Italian, Swedish, or even a spanking Japanese beauty, does it matter? All that matters is my freedom, so I won't say. The car was a Mona Lisa, as we say in the trade. She had that smile, and I couldn't stop myself from rubbing my cheek against one of the passenger windows. You know, I was half delirious.

"I'd given up on you!" cried a hearty voice, coming up behind me and giving me a start. "You're an hour late!"

I leapt back embarrassed, afraid of being misunderstood and arrested, but there was something indulgent and approving about the tone of that voice of somebody who had caught me in a fond act with his car, so I straightened up slowly so as not to make myself appear weak or hypocritical by trying to dissemble my obvious attraction. I even let the wishful reverie linger on my face, since I sensed I was in a situation where normal cunning would do me no good, and actually I felt strangely at ease, why I couldn't imagine.

Maybe he hadn't noticed me caressing his car, or he was glad to excuse it, he must have thought a lot of his car, or else . . . I studied him and waited for him to speak again and reveal himself. He was wearing white duck pants, white loafers (highly polished, which would have been sure to gain Dahomey's approval) with no socks, a blue and white pullover, and he was smoking a small cigar which perfumed the air with a no-nonsense, good-guy pungency. He was about sixty, with a cheerful, lined face, and silver hair cropped close yet styled elegantly. He looked like a character in a movie, but then almost everybody in L.A. takes care to present that appearance, and many of them have been in the movies. One is always crossing paths with minor actors, and I was about to ask him if I didn't recognize him from some film, with yachts in it, just to break a thin surface of tension which had started to form, when he said, "You are Nick's friend, aren't you?"

Which Nick would that be? Of course, how would I be supposed to know some friend of his named Nick, but just the same it was a strange night and stranger things have happened. I racked my brain, but the only Nick I could come up with at this awkward moment was St. Nick. From the point of view of the man in white in front of me, there were a lot of commonplace facts which explained everything, but I didn't have such facts. It was as good as anything to surmise that Santa Claus had a finger in it. There was that Christmassy feel in the air, when gifts are given impulsively (or compulsively) and just for the fun of it. Parenthetically, I never could believe in modern Californians of the well-to-do variety with their swimming pools, palm trees, sports clothes and sports cars, gadgets, bank accounts, and sunshine celebrating Christmas. It seemed a new pagan holiday should have been invented. I felt a new one was on its way, or was already here but we had failed to recognize it so stealthily had it taken over the old one, and maybe this was it. Perhaps the newfangled Christmas was today. But I thought best to keep my mouth shut on any of this, and I held my peace and just smiled agreeably.

"You're lucky I didn't go to bed. Well, you going to drive it around the block?" He took a step toward me, smiling, proffering me the keys. There are no "blocks" in such a neighborhood, he was just using the good-natured lingo to put me at ease.

"Oh, I don't really need to," I mumbled, uneasy at the pace at which things were developing. For an instant I felt all my weariness. I wondered if this Santa Claus was Harmless Harry, in his disguise on the Christmas tree lot. Don't look a gift horse in the mouth and all that, and yet something about his insistence started to irritate me. I wasn't asking for any of this.

"Of course not. But I'd rather you took it on a short drive at least, you know. You understand."

I understood. I found the keys in my hand. I glanced from them to the distinguished-looking guy who was sucking on his cigar with a shrewd friendly look in his eyes. He hoped it was shrewd. He was so close the smoke of his cigar was a cloud around my head through which I could not see. His face was a clouded blur. The guy was expecting me to buy the car and he wanted things to be on the up and up if I drove it around the block first. Good luck. It brought a lump of pity to my throat. Maybe Nick's friend had been looking for exactly this make and model, had heard all about it, and since we were supposed to have had a mutual friend in Nick and all that, assurances must have been given. He wanted me to test-drive the car, though, since it was the gentlemanly thing to insist on, as it would be for me to take him up on it so that we were all square. I did not think this was a good idea myself, but the words to explain this without giving offense escaped me.

"Well, go on. I'm beat. I've got to get up in the morning. I'll be in the house. Here!" He walked forward smiling with what I instantly even at a distance through the smoke from long experience recognized as the title to the car in his hand. The registration as well! The cherished pink slip. Everything had already been arranged and assurances given among friends. All the rest was a formality, after which we would exchange a pleasantry. He opened the passenger door and thrust the papers into the glove compartment. "It's already signed. Drive around. You'll love it. It's a dream. When you come back, we'll have a beer."

The feeling I had as I got into the white car was that I had been presented with a passport to a foreign country not the registration for a car. It seemed like a dream all right. I started to drive around the block, but there were no blocks, just snakelike streets writhing around one another in a developer's idea of charm or probably because of the hillside we were on there had once been no other way to lay out any streets but in loops and turns. Didn't the guy know I might get lost right away? Within a few minutes I had no idea where I was and could not remember the direction I had come from. It made me angry and almost despondent again. With each turn I had spiraled farther away, remarking to myself at the smooth suspension and nice tight steering. The car drove like a dream, okay, a bad dream—for the guy back there.

I was driving in this car, it might as well have been mine. It was mine. I was being positively asked just to take it, to steal it. I had the pink slip. I didn't know whether to laugh or cry. What if I got into serious trouble? What if he called the cops when I didn't come back and give him a check? Why had this temptation been placed before me? I might be able to get a good hour out of town before he brought himself to call the cops.

It was a beautiful car. At a breathtakingly low price of say fifteen thousand dollars, I could sell it within the hour, within the next five minutes, if it took that long, though it would be better to sell it in another part of the state or in another state. Suddenly I could barely recognize myself in the circumstances. But that wasn't anything new, I barely recognized myself lately anyway. I began to feel beguilingly comfortable. I saw I was just going to do it.

On the way out of town, I called Mike and left a sad story about my broken Jag. Maybe it would explain my behavior with the girl. I could only give him an approximate notion where it was, but Mike would find it. It might be a while before I got back, but he would have the car for security. I'd call again and send something if parts were going to be expensive.

The thought came to me again and again, what if I had been an Indian, would the man in white with the silver hair (St. Nick himself maybe, if not Mephistopheles) have been so eager to hand over the keys to me then? No, he wouldn't have. Damn sure not. Suppose I were a Native American, with dark skin. Indians had not heard of Santa Claus before the missions. You didn't hand over the keys to a fine automobile for a test drive to a remnant of the band you had recently slaughtered. My pale skin had deceived him, as I was a half-breed. Less than an hour ago I had been dancing the ghost dance, along a forlorn and forbidden (by the missionaries) path, one of the damned of the earth, and in my heart as I drove I was still dancing.

Invisible Car Dealer

America once belonged to the Indians, although they claim otherwise. They have this story about the land belonging to the Great Spirit and how in their culture the land never was owned by anyone. But we whites have to believe it all certainly did belong to them, because if not, how could we have stolen it from them? And how would we own it now, if we hadn't stolen it from them? If it belonged to God or to the Indians' ancestors, as they like to pretend, by what stretch of the imagination could we have ripped it off and possess it presently? Could we have stolen it from God or ghosts or spirits? No, logically, we have to reject any of that smoke they are blowing. Their arrows are all gone, and their warpath is done with, about all they can do to us now is make us feel bad and uncertain about things, with help from the likes of Julie.

Anyway, that is the white man's point of view. I was trying to keep in mind how the white man understood things because I felt I was on the verge of forgetting. It had been some time since I had thought of myself as a white man. I wasn't sure what I was becoming, but the amnesia and arrogance characteristic of white folks were a thing of the past as far as I was concerned. At the same time I couldn't afford to lose touch completely with the blasé and entitled state of mind of the master race any more than I could dispense with the maps of their cities. When in Rome do as the Romans do. I didn't want to tip my hand and offend someone. I might make a bad mistake.

Invisible Car Dealer

So, back to the Indians then. The tribes fought against tribes, surely, and expanded, or lost, their hunting grounds and territories. I know that from a pamphlet I read given out at the Welcome Center. That's all the white man did, too. Stole it from them fair and square, as Packy said. Meanwhile it is absolutely essential that we stole their land from them. Or *our own* ghosts and gods did it, as we're told at Thanksgiving. Think about it. "Manifest Destiny" is no more than a puff of wind momentarily scattering things if there was never anybody out there to roll over and our ownership of the country is not a historical and legal fact based on good old-fashioned murder and grand larceny. Just think if it were ever proved the Indians are right, that nobody can own the place, and that we don't own it, since it had never had owners whom we could have taken it from! Talk about consternation and mayhem. The white man might not be able to recover from an insight like that. How about your neighbor, with his little farm, and your cousin with his suburban spread, or you yourself with your little parcel, *what if what you think you have you do not have because it is unownable?*

One has only to read a few accounts of the old American trappers and mountain men and pioneers to recall a way of life back in those days unsurpassed in freedom, wholeness, excitement, and beauty. They had their eye on the real estate. That was when life was worth living, even if the show was based on wholesale robbery, especially if it was, that made the game all the more fun and gallant. They were playing for all the marbles. Ask Custer. Either that, or at once one finds oneself in a world of horror and pity. There are times when it is unacceptable, cowardly, and blameworthy not to steal, as during most of this country's history, or baseball season. No, no. They know where the ball is hidden, the Indians do.

We stole it all right. (I was thinking as a white man, since Indians would view that as an absurdity and impossibility.) But I had switched sides. I was a renegade. However I retained all consciousnesses. I knew what my own people had been up to, and I was ashamed and sorry for it. I was going to get some back. I was going on the warpath, in my own way. The white car was going to be my tomahawk and scalping knife. Black blood was spilling down the tailgates of trucks, and splattering over the hood of my car and windshield, as I headed north again, drove all night, back to San Francisco, where the white car was a stranger, if I made it that far without being caught. Those poor people, the Indians, were just deprived of everything they'd had for centuries by the rest of us for no good reason I've ever heard of except our mere convenience and pleasure. There's no sounder view of our national origins than Packy's cheerful one. Okay, fine. Black blood lapped the shoulders of the highway and streaked the windshield, and I was going to spill a little more, in the name of love—of love of all the world's losers, even that girl back in Hollywood, "friend" of Mike's.

I was in an evil state of mind. I drove all night. Nobody stopped me. I did make it. I checked into what struck me as a very obscure motel off the highway and had breakfast at an admirably generic joint like a Denny's. Before I slept, I drove to Dahomey's wrecking yard. It was about eight. Jack's Porsche was parked in front. Jack got to work early under normal circumstances. So my guess was things were going on about normally with him, I was glad to see. Things had changed with me, for the better. I figured to have some capital to start our car restoration project very shortly. To say I was in a different space from just days ago when I last saw him would have been a wild understatement. I was in a mood to light a fire under these guys now, for their own sakes. I felt burning up with a strange sacred anger.

I intended to shake up Jack's life and make him some money as I had always promised I would. The sky was the limit, as I saw it, with the white car. Life looked very different with the white car in tow. We'd have the cash to get all my Cloud Lake cars rolling and then the real money would be coming in. Even Dahomey's dog no longer struck fear into me. It bared its teeth at me but did not get up. It quieted down right away. Anyway I was well aware of its exact parameters of freedom on its chain and slipped in the door of the shack past its fangs none the worse but for a few drops of saliva on my still shiny boots. The beast only gave a tentative growl back in its throat for appearances' sake, not sure it even recognized me since a different sort of vibes must have greeted its various sensory organs as I strode confidently past.

Jack was in Dahomey's office curled up in a chair reading a book in *The Executioner* series, one of Jack's means of escape from his problems. If he had been happy at his job, or had any sort of project going of his own, he would have already been at work at it. It was a little early in the morning for him to be reading. It was how he liked to end his day sometimes. He read during his breaks. This early he was already reading avidly about Mack Bolan, ex–jungle assassin from Vietnam, who had spurned a raft of commissions and promotions, preferring his solitary mission through the mountains and rice paddies in pursuit of high-ranking enemy officers to squeeze off, and squads of VC jungle-fighters to engage in hand to hand combat. But upon completion of his years of service, Mack Bolan had wished nothing more than to return to a peaceful civilian life full of all the regular recreations and innocent American amusements, a house and family behind a picket fence, a Corvette, or well, maybe a Maserati in the garage (nice cars were his understandable weakness) and nobody could have deserved such a pleasant life more than such a war hero. But while he had been away in service to his country in Vietnam, his father, a small businessman, had been forced by dire circumstances to take out a loan from gangster loan sharks, and having repaid it in full, had been murdered anyway for having unknowingly offended a crime boss in some way, maybe he should have tipped somebody too, and after him Mack's mother and the rest of the family (the author of this series never believed in doing any sort of a half job to whet the reader's taste for vengeance), all killed to forestall retaliation by any normal American family members, not to be confused with the mob "family." A normal family would get the message in no uncertain terms and if any of them happened still to be alive would be paralyzed with fear. The crooks were unaware that one brother was away at war, or if aware they thought he was a sucker for being a "hero." The Mafia had little idea and had not reckoned with Mack Bolan, however, who, having had this unspeakable war de-clared upon him by the author of these books, returned to his trade of being an assassin, and a new war, this time back in the States, a holy war this time, as the Sicilians met their fates in countless, delicious variation, as Mack Bolan called on his cohorts from the jungle, who were reunited on their new mission to dole out high-tech death to the crooked villains in scores of paperbacks, as the series rolled on and on.

Jack did not look up from his book at first, he was so deeply engrossed, or desirous of shutting out reality. He assumed I was some sort of customer. When he finally did, he was very surprised to see me back so soon, and his face slowly lit up. He dropped his book, and displayed his earnest winning smile. But some shadow remained. He was really glad to see me, but having caught him off guard and into his book, I could see right away something was troubling him. Otherwise why was he reading Mack Bolan at eight in the morning? Now what could it possibly be?

Jack was the decentest guy I've ever known, loyal and ready to show it. He may have been a young vet from Nam, but I swear he was a soldier from the old school. He made his expression confident, though he was depressed as hell, I realized quickly. He seemed to be in a completely different mood from two days before, that is, it had gotten worse. Or maybe not. I wondered if it could have been that, low as I had been then, I hadn't taken it all in. I had been so desperate myself, I hadn't been too observant, other than to painfully register Dahomey's resistance to my plans and sales pitch. I now remembered how irrationally irritable Jack had been when that thief had tried to sell him a lawn mower, and how he had disagreed endlessly with Gladstone about the meaning of "a job."

Once we exchanged our greetings and salutations, Jack listened to my new plans politely, even eagerly, once more. They seemed to stir some hope in him. He soon caught the new enthusiasm in my voice and reacted about as I had imagined and hoped he would. I mentioned I had "a nice car" I was selling and would soon have "maybe fifteen grand" with which to start working on our cars. (This was a slight exaggeration because I meant to sell it even further under its true price point so as to move it quickly, if that's what it took, but it was certainly worth far more than fifteen grand, and it would sell fast.)

But suddenly Jack lost interest and cast his glance around the place forlornly. A darkness crossed his face and he stopped listening to me completely. I could see he didn't believe a single word I was saying! It was just that like his hero, Mack Bolan, Jack had been meant for something so much better. He almost looked like his own family had been bumped off. The truth was he was in a state of profound annoyance and frustration with his life, I could see, and this struck me so forcefully it made me unsteady on my feet and I had to prop myself against one of the stools at Dahomey's counter.

"Damn guy is impossible to figure anymore," muttered Jack, referring to Dahomey, I knew well enough. He frowned with his familiar righteous exasperation, as he did his best to suppress any responsibility for the inevitable misunderstanding that experience told me he was having with his boss, all his bosses, even a boss that basically liked him a lot like Dahomey.

"He's making a work schedule that makes no sense. I think he is gambling or something. He wants to close on Friday, wants his three-day weekend, but the other days wants to stay open till nine at night. Wants me to work twelve-hour days. Wrecking yard can't stay in business like that. You need Friday and Saturday, those are big days. I think he wants to go out of business, wants to sell out, but who will buy this joint? He don't come in till eleven o'clock some days." That was okay by me as I needed to sell my scheme exclusively to Jack, I didn't want to talk to Dahomey any more.

Having been in Vietnam, Jack was not about to get along with any boss, that is, any officer, for too long, even as crazy and colorful a man or officer as Dahomey. The thing about Jack, every now and again he would weary of any routine, the day-to-day grind, even on so loose a schedule as at the junkyard, and go into a blue funk. Our Cloud Lake project meant real work, a thorough stint of the gritty unglamorous knuckle-busting kind, probably several months, maybe a year, not the same thing as the dreaming and talking we had indulged in the other day. But it also meant real money and hard cash in the end.

I was sure the prospect of that would straighten out Jack's head in no time. As soon as I sold the white car, I would have the few bucks necessary to get us started. Then he would be okay once he saw I meant business and real work began and he saw we really had the dough to get going with. I was in no mood to listen to Jack start whining about things pointlessly right now, as he had it in him to do sometimes, how he was a loser, since he worked in a junkyard, and so on, how "it sucked to be him" and how his wife was too good for him. Actually he could be pretty pathetic when he got in the mood to be. But I meant business today. I had just wanted to alert him good times really were coming, and now I had to get out of here. But I knew I couldn't, with Jack like this.

Suddenly Dahomey's dog outside the shack could be heard growling far back in its throat, just the hint of a threat, but the vibration that it set up pervading the place, causing the chrome trim dangling from the ceiling to tremble and tinkle and the hair on my neck to stand up. The animal barked once, rather listlessly, and shifted its position. I could hear the chain ratchet out like the dry rattle of a snake. I hoped these demonstrations weren't meant for me. I thought I heard someone call out softly and hopelessly in the yard. Whoever it was had started to come into the shack but had thought better of it. Probably only a customer.

"I don't know how you manage that dog. I mean I like dogs, but Dahomey should feed it or something. In the morning if it hasn't gotten its fill ripping the hands and feet off thieves all night, it must be starving. It acts like it."

"That puppy? She eats out of my hand."

"You have nerves of steel, boy! It knows a good man!"

I had the conviction that nothing I could do, not if I brought it ten pounds of filet mignon every day for a week, would ever induce that huge puppy to have a better opinion of me. I don't know if it suspected me of having secret designs on some of its owner's rusty brake drums or greasy scraps of iron lying about. I was always afraid of losing a few body parts, or at least my pantscuffs, when I got near it. That chain it was on looked perilously thin.

But there was one thing about it I did like—it confirmed my confidence in Jack. I was grateful for the chance to express this just now. It didn't surprise me that it liked Jack, not just because he worked here every day. Jack was the cowboy, and I was the Indian, as far as that junkyard dog was concerned, and if I believed in anything I believed in that dog's nose. In spite of his war experience, his crazy fantasies, his obsessive reading of the Mack Bolan series, his inability to hold one job for long, and his sullen discontent with his place in everyday society, or maybe because of these very things as a matter of fact, Jack was far more in touch with something quintessential in the mainstream of life than I was, his visions, sensibilities, and limitations much closer to the average normal wavelength, and the dog knew that, and approved. I liked being around Jack for the same reason. I more than ever enjoyed his company this morning when I was sort of sailing uncharted waters. I was so glad to see him and my plans depended on him. I leaned back on the counter. Suddenly I was in no hurry to go.

Invisible Car Dealer

It wasn't that I didn't imagine Jack could one day go off the deep end if he kept up his pot smoking, Mack Bolan reading, and other anti-social behavior, wrangling with every boss he had, but when he did, it would be in a way that was perfectly understandable to the man in the street, down to this very dog, and probably admirable from the same point of view. It was even that quality that I found so attractive in Jack, and which I frankly valued, something rooted and real and average in spite of everything, even his maladjustments and malingerings so very normal, while I sensed in myself traces of exotic states, and half-feared I was caught in a web of fate leading me into uninhabitable dimensions, or at least causing me to be skirting the spider's web pretty close. Dahomey's dog had given me a pass this morning, but it had its eye on me just the same. After the all-night drive from L.A., a night of no sleep, I had a frantic flash or two that the white car was made of nothing but desperate hope, was a dream, might disappear on me without warning, was made out of something like snow that had drifted down from the tops of the Sierras, on the heels of St. Nick, that guy in the white sweater who had unaccountably handed me the pink slip and begged me to "drive around the block," that it would melt and be gone when I walked out of Dahomey's office, and that I was on the verge of making more horrible discoveries.

So I sat around with Jack for an hour or so, drinking coffee, and listening to a tentative exciting Vietnam reminiscence or two, offered by Jack as a telling contrast to the tedious state of things he was putting up with at Dahomey's. It was just good to be around Jack, in spite of the shape he was obviously in. But he began to say a few wistful things about Mack Bolan, as if he were not a fictional character in a book, but an exemplary character. I was gripped by alarm at that. Mack Bolan was so real to him! Now it was my turn to hide my feelings, and make confident faces, as if I were interested in "what Mack would do." I wondered if that was all Jack had been doing, really, the other morning as we sat around in my car, and this morning as I tried to convey my sense of urgency and the nearness of the realization of my plan. He was pretending to believe me but what was important to him was elsewhere. Mack Bolan was realer to him than my real antiques at Cloud Lake, which must have struck him in the same suspicious delusional light always cast on them by the locals I had bought them from.

195

Invisible Car Dealer

What would become of Jack, I wondered but did not know, for he was a true romantic, a dreamer down to his boots, no one more impractical, even though he was an ace mechanic, a loyal friend, a good husband, and no doubt had been a hell of a chopper pilot. I was so sure I would come through for us both yet! He had an ambition burning in him that was impossible because it was so formless, the war having drawn all his sense of the structure of things back upon itself, leaving the days of "this world" without driving shape as much as without guiding soul. How did he keep this from his wife? Didn't she sense his melancholy ambition and despair? Or was she just as worried about him as I was becoming? What was important to him was not really his past, but his memories, not the war, but his visions, which could never be drained of their drug-like allure by nuts-and-bolts reality. In this lay his common touch, however, what was so magnetic and compelling about him, his dreams were just the average guy's, like all the readers of the Mack Bolan series. His dreams were ultimately not that big, unlike mine, which had no proper boundaries. I was on the verge of a real success and about to make a lot of money. I should have worried about myself. He was going to be all right. He was just like half the populace, in my experience, who would like to dream of violent glory forever, but if you ever placed a real scheme for getting ahead before them, would turn up their noses as if it were too small for them. And I loved him for this as for all his qualities, and determined I would show him the way to his best interests in spite of himself. But I would not involve him in my immediate adventure with the white car. It was too dangerous. He would be better off just muddling ahead in the normal routine even if he hated it, until I had my capital together.

As Dahomey had still not come in, and no customers either, Jack began to indulge one of his favorite fantasies for striking it *really rich* (as opposed to actually rich, which was in my line), which was robbing a casino at Tahoe or Vegas. I had heard this one before. This was straight out of Mack Bolan, and the wild suicidal impracticability on the face of it of such criminal fantasies made no difference. It was the vision that counted, a matter of a sort of faith, sordid and flawed as it might be, and nothing he had any intention of doing, but it was important for him to plan it out, to show how it was *possible*. Life springs eternal in sadder weeds than that, and through slimmer cracks in the pavement. Jack was convinced that the hoods in the Nevada gambling towns would never be ready for what he and a few of his Vietnam buddies would come down on them with, shoulder-fired missiles, machine guns, and a singleness of intention born of fighting a thankless and desperate jungle war, which would overmatch anything any coldhearted businessmen or greasy thugs defending the cash vault could offer. For the moment he had become Mack Bolan and I let him talk. He was just fantasizing (for the moment).

"The point is, you can't have a surgical strike. You can't match wits with those boys, because it's their store and they know where the mines are laid. Everybody who ever tried something like that tried to be clever about it. You have to go in prepared to kill a lot of people and then do it. Not smart, just overpower em. Kill em all—all! That's what they're not prepared for. They're soft, clever nowadays, just accountants with sidearms. They know the odds, they are way more clever than you or I could ever be, and they assume you know that. They're waitin for the *smart* move. They don't expect you to come in an burn the roof off the joint, vaporize the control room, and without warning kill them *all*. To them that would be dumb, and old-fashioned. You know, in fact—*war*. They don't think in terms of actual *war*. That's just a word to them for their game. The carnage itself paralyzes em. If you're not ready to do a lot of killing, there's no way. Also you need your aircraft to get out of there to the mountains. You just park it right on the lake. You just kill em *all*, take *all* their money, an fly the hell out. The scale and audacity of the thing makes it succeed. No survivors."

I didn't say that the scale and audacity of things in Vietnam hadn't made it succeed, as I couldn't have been that heartless. I wanted him to get out of his bad mood not confirm him in it or throw him into a rage. I was tired, and needed to sleep, but had I been sprawled out in my motel bed right now, I couldn't have dropped off for being tormented by what was happening to Jack's mind apparently these days. I doubted he talked like this in front of that wife of his, about Mack Bolan and all. And at the same time it struck me as being absolutely normal, that is, that every guy on the street, you know, was capable of exactly the same spectacular fantasies, and would have applauded their being carried out, as from time to time guys really tried to do. It was sane! If somebody did pull off such a bloody caper as Jack had outlined he would instantly double his winnings with the movie rights. By money Jack meant millions of course. Not even that, but a mythical sort of money, like they had in places like the vaults of casinos, a treasure guarded by monsters, magical money, the kind with which you worked wonders. The plain old world with its funky little games like my own, but workable ones, sensible amounts of money, held no allure for Jack. He didn't understand that the real miracles occurred where you least expected them, in your own back yard, in someplace beneath your notice, like this dusty wrecker's yard, for instance, or Cloud Lake, or a winding street in L.A. I felt a chill of fear for him, and I seemed to see into the future.

I wondered if Jack's demons could ever drive him to such real adventures if they got bad enough. There really seemed a slight chance that they someday would, if I didn't help him. It was not as far-fetched as it sounded, because after all he had been trained for this sort of thing in Vietnam, and he had seen how well outrageous overwhelming violence worked there, where you just did it and got away with it, and he had been trained to do it, and been in the middle of the doing it. He had seen it done and was familiar with it. Of course he knew the risks were different if you pulled that same thing in "the world," but still he knew it could be done. He had told me a story once about somebody killing some drug dealers over there just for their stash. You could just take things from people, at least from the Vietnamese people over there, with your guns. Why not here too? One look at Jack's yellowed fingertips showed me how much pot he was smoking these days, too. He was reading those Mack Bolan books one after another. Then the clammy and much worse suspicion took hold of me that of course he was not going to rob a casino, he was going to start spending more and more of his time just smoking pot and reading Mack Bolan. A casino would be better.

Nobody had to tell me that his job around here was hanging on a thread, that was plain as day, and where did you go from here, the corner gas station? Dahomey didn't pay too well, but the job here had a certain dignity, being in a wrecking yard, which still had not slipped from Jack's grasp. It seemed to me terribly important to get Jack started restoring my Cloud Lake cars, to get some good cash flow for us both, to make the reality of the extra money in his pocket settle in. It wasn't Mack Bolan, but it was some good survival. That would help him. After a couple months we might have enough dough to open that car shop, and the real romance of that might save Jack yet. But the sad thing was that I could see that he had ceased believing in it. Just at the moment I was in a position to redeem that old dream of ours, he didn't want it any more. For some reason he didn't seem gung-ho for the project at all, as he had a couple of days ago. I hated to think so, but perhaps he had just been so surprised to see me then, it had seemed to relieve his depression for a short while, without really doing so. I stared at him, worried.

The trouble was, now that I owned the white car, all my relics up at Cloud Lake seemed no more than a side deal to me too, in truth. I couldn't remember how crucial they had seemed, how exciting their promise, even as I extolled them and my plans to Jack, and maybe he sensed this. The strange adventure or set of circumstances by which I had obtained the white car, and the night-time getaway from L.A. with all that adrenaline burned through me, had me in a state of exaltation where anything magical or unbelievable might happen, or keep happening. The ghost dance I had danced had availed and worked its spell. The strenuous endeavor of bringing all my classics down here seemed enormous, and very hard work, compared to the white car, the way it had flown to me out of the white man's hand. Maybe that's how Jack looked at it too—I mean the hard work, not the white car, of course, of which he knew nothing. I meant to keep it that way. I could imagine what his wife, or even Julie if she caught wind of it, God forbid, would think of me if I introduced Jack to the white car. I meant the white car to remain my secret.

We had a job to do. I would roll up my sleeves too when the time came. First I needed to sell the white car and with the cash we would start to work bringing down my wrecks from the Lake and restoring them. We would both be restored oiurselves by that job, not just the cars, some good hard greasy work. That was my mental promise to Jack and myself this morning. I was fading and about falling off the stool and had to get some sleep. Just as I was going out the gate, Gladstone the Nigerian brushed past me coming in to work. I greeted him, but he gave me the barest nod, which was more of a drawing up of his whole person in some inscrutable attitude. He was wearing freshly washed overalls. I glanced back at him as I was getting into my car. He had squatted down in front of the office and begun to polish his tools with a soft rag—to polish them *before* going to work in the greasy junkyard. They were already clean, as he had wiped them down after work yesterday no doubt. He would never have gone home or put away his tools without cleaning them, and now he was polishing them all over again, making sure, *before* work. Such a thing was unheard of and slightly compulsive really. It was just the ritual how he started his day.

There, I thought, was a dedicated if not efficient workman. But it was a kind of bizarre extreme of admirable behavior that would have made Jack gnash his teeth today if he saw it. It might destroy the remnant of Jack's peace of mind if he saw that sort of thing, as he must each morning. It probably added to Jack's present malaise. Once or twice I had even imagined roping Gladstone into rebuilding my old cars for sale to Hollywood stars. I knew he was a good mechanic. I wondered what he would think of my project. Not much, probably. He would have sneered down his nose. I had my hands full with Jack, anyway. I really didn't have it in me to try to speak to Gladstone this morning.

At least I hadn't spilled the beans and told Jack the whole story about the white car, I told myself with pride as I drove out of Richmond. If I got into trouble, I wouldn't have Jack's being involved on my conscience. I could never have faced his wife, not that I'd ever have to. He had never left Dahomey's office shack so as to see the white car, and I had not suggested he do so or let on a thing. I never told him how I was going on the warpath and taking some back for the downtrodden of the earth. The sorrow and the pain I had come across in my travels I was going to vindicate and punish. I had been to hell and back, I had glimpsed what the Native Americans have suffered, and I meant to strike a blow in their behalf. The only thing I worried about was, if Jack ever got wind of it, his resenting not having been included in the fun and never forgiving me for this, if he heard somehow and I never told him the story of the white car and let him join me. But on my honor I had promised myself that I would keep my mouth shut and not get him involved even to the extent of hearing about it, because although the white car had clearly been given to me by the cheerful and merciless fates, it was car theft. It was like the Indians stealing U.S. cavalry ponies, justifiable, admirable, glamorous, and wild laughs no doubt, but they shot you and hung you for it.

Before going to the motel, I stopped at the offices of the *Oakland Tribune* and then the *San Francisco Chronicle* and placed ads for the white car that would appear in the next day's editions. It was noon when I finally pulled the heavy motel curtains closed to cut out the metallic light that was coming off the asphalt parking lot and the chrome bumpers of stray midday parked cars killing my eyes, and fell into bed in a sort of a sick fatigue that came over me in spite of my careful attention to detail. The thick curtains made it quite dark and I could sleep. The motel I had chosen was well off the beaten track, and anyway there were so many stolen cars out there these days that unless I ran a red light or ran into somebody, I was not likely to be spotted. But it wasn't that so much, but my awareness how everything depended on the white car, and hinged on its weird magnetism. It needed to sell next morning, or sometime tomorrow, no later, not another day. I couldn't hang onto it. My last feeling as I drifted into oblivion was an irrational terror that when I awoke, the white car would have somehow lost its appeal.

But it was sleekly glowing in the purple twilight, when I awoke and had ordered my sensations sufficiently to get up and pull the curtains and study it for a whole minute. It was as charming as ever, and I knew I was going to have to keep the buyers away with the proverbial baseball bat, as the saying goes. Well, nothing as crude as that. (I did like thinking of baseball in the circumstances, a game in which *stealing* is not only legal but admired and well paid for. A good *base stealer* was a special sort of player, sort of rare, and looked on with interest. Maybe there'd be a ballgame on TV later to help me kill the time.) I needed to sell the white car and get on my horse, as the Indians had said to me that night in the Flame Bar, and *make tracks*. Still, the hazard and questionability of the adventure stood out starkly. Car theft, like horse rustling, was a time-honored pursuit in America, and so was lynching. The dusky parking lot seemed a weird dreamscape, and I was cutting more ties, deep mooring strings, and loneliness washed over me, cold and pure. Julie would not have stood for it for an instant. But Julie would never know.

Invisible Car Dealer

I had the whole night ahead of me to kill before the morning papers came out and buyers started calling on the phone beside my bed. So I turned on the TV and fortunately there was a baseball game on. When a guy stole second, I jumped out of bed and cheered lustily, and stood mulling it all over a long time, how normal stealing is, how essential to everything. I was yelling at the set for him to swipe third as well. After the game was over, I watched a talk show, and there was a scientist talking to Jay Leno who was saying that the odds in favor of extra-terrestrial life existing somewhere out there were a million to one, but, of course, there was that one. I mean, the *one* to this guy was the chance that we were all *alone* and how disappointing would that be? But how crazy is that? He thought the odds overwhelmingly in favor we would have company someday. Personally I would prefer to be left alone and had never imagined it like that before, and was greatly alarmed. The chances were that good? But he was all for the invaders. Of course he did not call them that, but implied they would be true friends. To hear him talk it would be unbearably lonely if we were all there was in the universe. Myself, I'm satisfied with the way things are. He explained the mathematics of how he had figured it all out, how we were surely not alone, which impressed me as being convincing and reasonable, although the more disturbing. It seemed to me that he was probably right, when you thought of all the stars out there, although the probability didn't make me ecstatic like he was. The stars out there didn't come by the millions but by far vaster numbers than millions or even trillions. So there had to be other life out there for us to meet one day, he was happy to say. I agreed, it seemed inevitable, in the nature of things. Ask the Native Americans.

I'm not sure how I would feel if the scientists started picking up their fabled radio messages from outer space that they seem to believe will come in one day inevitably and no doubt will. Partly horror, don't you know? How about you? Just the idea of it, hearing the guy talk about what advanced cultures out there would teach us, made my skin prickle and my hair stand up. Yes, they'd have some pleasant things to teach us. There was a time when people thought the world was flat, a sort of table carried on the back of a giant tortoise, and then Columbus and the other explorers reached land and met the red Indians (as they called them), and all that changed, and it was the end of a lot of our old cozy views on things. But just imagine how it changed for the Indians. Think of the things they were about to learn. Those immense beautiful cities that had been so majestic and unassailable that they had in Mexico and South America were about to be wiped off the face of the planet. A few ruins remain. Gringo tourists and anthropologists go down there to see them. Have you ever contemplated the ineffable sorrow and unimaginable horror of something like that? I mean if you were a taxpayer in or a believer in one of those cities. Yes I know, their culture involved human sacrifices to propitiate their strange gods, very objectionable by our liberal standards, and they deserved to be replaced by Catholics and Presbyterians. But to get back to our scientists and their radios, our high priests, as it were, the thing to ponder is, when contact is made, who will be the cowboys and who will be the Indians, am I right? Now that's a gamble, and the odds are not good in my estimation. I'm not totally convinced of the wisdom of contributing toward speeding up an eventuality whose outcome is uncertain at best, and quite likely unpleasant. But the taxpayers will do it. They'll pay for the rockets and radios. The scientists are on the talk shows lathering them up for the skinning. There are suckers born every minute.

Imagine those Indians, priests, chiefs, and average Joes and squaws alike, in their resplendent cities in South America, or out there growing maize and drinking mescal or eating mushrooms and whatever, on our Great Plains, so pleasantly secure in their great cycle of life, so certain about everything, in particular their strength and stability, even generously helping the Pilgrims invent Thanksgiving, when it hit them that the newcomers were not friendlies, or even if they were personally friendly, they carried smallpox. But in the end the white man was not even that personally friendly, as we know. Which is why I am trading in my whiteness presently and sharpening my ax (figuratively). If he was not morally superior, technologically and in firepower he was way advanced, and still is, of course, for the foreseeable future, so no apologies will be forthcoming for anything. The only good Indian is a dead Indian, and still is, unless he can tell you where the gold is. The Chinese are getting whiter by the minute too, even if they were never thought to be good for anything in this country but laying track and digging tunnels, but lo and behold they are joining in the horseplay. We want to make contact with "advanced" civilizations on the stars? Like our own, on that same dubious moral plane, with some embellishments and improvements probably in the way of artillery? Of course we imagine they will be enlightened, and it is said the white man on the beach was first thought to be a god. When the next hand is dealt and the world changes forever once again, how would you like to wake up as the Indian, or even the giant tortoise? I never hear the scientists speculating on that possibility.

The attitude of the little green men will be benevolent, and they'll send us a lot of friendly advice, according to the scientists who are angling for a government grant. There is just as much chance of the extraterrestrials turning out like they used to picture it in the fifties and sixties in the movies, before Hollywood was persuaded by the scientific establishment or the advertising industry that the monsters would be cuddly and friendly like ET. Much more likely the Blob or the Thing will show up on the spaceship. Hollywood used to be smarter, and realer, when they just wanted to scare you.

Then the world will be turned into a universal Indian reservation, to use an easily understandable metaphor. Even amiable powers might turn us all into slaves, for our own good, naturally. Even today Southerners (white ones) hanker after the good old slave times, when black people were well taken care of in every sense. After all, not all white men were or are evil. In fact, obviously, most white men are not evil—they are *good*, aren't they? Ask yourself, aren't they? I certainly hope so, being one. Unless you're a Black Muslim and hold that all whites are blue-eyed devils, born in the laboratory of a mad scientist, the thing is white people are just like you and me and everybody else basically, maybe an ounce more ambition probably. It may be Elijah Muhammed is right though come to think on it, who knows.

That has to be the craziest part of it from the Indians' point of view, that the white man ran over them like a fantastic out-of-control steamroller, but not out of some isolated or peculiar evil, but just because it was the *next thing* for them all to do, the white man felt like doing it and thought it was the proper and *next thing* to do, to take the land, and *could* do it, never considered *not* doing it, and did it. It was *manifestly* the thing to do, a *destiny*. Hard to argue with that. I know that part of it would gall me, if the little green men came from the stars that the scientists are so eager to make contact with, the naturalness and preternaturalness of it all, when they invaded their new colony—us. It wouldn't worry me for long though. Why resent? I'd get along somehow. Somebody would have to sell them a car if they were to get around. Harmless Harry would see the opportunity.

And what if the new religion, the views on land ownership, man's relationship with nature, etc., of the creatures from outer space happened to coincide with those of the Indians of yore and not the white man's? What if the government and the white man in general were informed that the land *really did not belong to anybody* and therefore could *not* have been stolen fair and square? Private property as our religion conceives it was an illusion? Now all would be governed by the ETs' laws. By a wonderful irony not hard to imagine, what if the far evolution of life resembles something we imagine we've left in the dust, or that has never yet actually existed on this earth of ours, but the Indians came closest to it (Julie believes that), and the ETs take all the Indians out of their reservations and put them in charge? Talk about a bunch of unhappy campers and irate taxpayers. I can hear the guys up in Packy's bitching and moaning. The scientists would have a dirty name. But Julie could say, "I told you so." She'd get a grant right away from the new ET administration.

Fortunately, I'm a car dealer, and there will always be cars, or their equivalent, to sell, so I'll squeak by. Somebody has to sell the damn things, even in space. Maybe those little like golf carts the astronauts ride around on. There's always a chance that the universe is flat, and we're coming to the edge on our golfcarts and about to roll over. The white man, especially, I would say. Not to mention the Japanese, Chinese, etc., etc., everybody else who is working too hard, getting too smart, and running too fast these days. Very close to the edge. The scientists looking for water on Mars and grants in Washington and Palo Alto. We may meet the giant tortoise soon, just as we fall off his back.

Jay Leno had some of these misgivings himself, for he finally asked the scientist, "What if the people from the stars are smarter, I mean *way smarter* than we are, you know? How will we know what they are really up to?"

Invisible Car Dealer

The scientist had an answer for that. "By then our computers will be about the size of a bug, a gnat, even an atom. The entire world's knowledge will fit on the point of a pin and it will be surgically implanted in our brains, and there is no limit to how smart we will be, so no problem. We'll be smarter than they are."

Well, that sounded hopeful, I had to admit. But an absurd idea which is hardly novel and no one wants to hear any more kept coming to me: how about turning off the giant radios and minding our own business? The TV station went off the air at 3:00 in the morning, just for an hour or two. They showed an image of the American flag for half an hour. Then a pattern of buzzing dots took over. I stumbled out the door of my room, feeling my neck for pods. Light would soon break, and a swarm of aliens in the form of car buyers would come to match wits with me. The silence just before dawn was deep, full of mysteries and surprises. The white man was about to show up on the horizon.

The first buyers who came this morning were convinced they were going to be given a present, a Christmas gift, you know, out of season, it would be like re-gifting in this case, considering the present of the car that the man in white had made to me, although the prospective buyers were doing their best to hide these precious feelings of theirs. But it was clear enough to one who knew how to read car buyers. It became clear to me that the gentleman had read a book on how to buy a used car. He had a list of items to inspect and consult about, pointless in the face of his transparent yen for the white car. It never occurred to him to ask an intelligent question like whether I was the real owner and could prove it somehow, beyond having title and the pink slip. He had gotten himself into a state of perfect gullibility and mental paralysis as a result of having studied up for this moment and gotten his ducks in a row. His wife was more forthright, though no less tiresome, gushing to me how they had been looking for *just this* car, and how pleased she was, as though to make up for her husband's tough-customer act, and to suggest I was personally the cause of all her happiness, and I should feel good because of it. Didn't it occur to her that I might be sad to part with the white car, that money wasn't everything to me?

Naturally, the price was too nice, it wasn't in my interest to price the car out of reach, on the contrary. I don't suppose his gruffness and her ebullience had something to do with the incredibly low price, especially when they had a look at it! They probably even knew the blue-book value of the car, had all the facts. They knew that $12,000 for the white car was pure robbery or a Christmas gift, so they probably just imagined they were extremely lucky and could hardly believe their luck. (I decided for the lowball as I had to keep a move on, I wanted the cash this morning no later.) So I didn't say much, I didn't need to, and it was better not to. They would sell themselves. I took the attitude I didn't care, but I did mention that I was moving away and just wanted to sell fast. That seemed to make sense, and it did the trick.

It wasn't as if I were going to take pleasure in beating these people for no reason or out of greed. I wasn't Harmless Harry. They were the descendants of our bloodthirsty and land robbing forefathers and so was I and I was going to make up for it. I was taking something back for the dispossessed and starting my own Trail of Tears.

It certainly never occurred to them that they would soon be hauled into the stationhouse for auto theft or receiving stolen property! That wasn't my idea, I couldn't help that, any more than that the beaten Indians were forced onto the poor lands of the reservations, a mere side effect. I'm sure it made me unhappy to have to skin them, and I probably despised them to the degree I despised myself. But I had my reasons, which I am trying to explain. What's more, I was dead broke and I had to do something. I was an outcast on the Great Plains of "modern life" myself.

I suddenly realized the depths of the true affinity I had developed for the white car. Had I been so tactless as to talk of my sadness at losing the white car, I'm sure they would have managed to rub it in even without meaning to. The white car was a kind of talisman and a magical object to me, by now, sort of sacred because of the crazy way I had acquired it. Its creamy beauty had worked its way into my heart and I would have felt lost without it. How could they have guessed this searing ambiguity! Naturally they imagined I would be happy if they bought it from me, but this wasn't so. The opposite was the case. I was going to be forlorn and deprived without it. Twelve thousand bucks or whatever meant nothing compared to my loss. For a moment a fancy caught me, to use that old-fashioned word, that the white car was a kind of innocence itself, the kind the Indians had before the European invasion. It was not in the white car that I had accidentally run over a Native American that night. The white car seemed a new chance to me.

On the moment I got this sort of glimpse of the state I was going to be in when they had the white car and I had their money, and I realized the advantage was not all the one way because the white car was more than just a car, as you can see yourself, I suddenly realized what a loss it would be to me, as though having been handed such a talisman by the fates, I would throw it away without ever having understood either its real nature or its real value, for a few dollars. I began to wonder if I had priced it way too low, and indeed if I should be selling it at all.

Apparently sensing my mood shifting in a big way, as car buyers are supersensitive in that way, if the advantage begins to swing the other way, they quickly asked to drive it around the block and jumped in. Just as I had last night! That made me smile in what must have looked a weird ironic way, if only they had looked back, but there are really blocks to "drive around" in San Francisco, and I didn't mind. Last night I had not asked but been asked, practically been forced, to drive the white car. As soon as they returned, they practically forced the money on me (I had insisted on cash) because they knew enough to have seen the white car ran like a dream. They must have sensed I was about to back out. I had the money in my hand before I knew it, and then an interesting idea came to me, and I saw what I had known I would do all along, without quite admitting it to myself.

Since I did not know its real meaning yet, and wished I did know, and saw I might not have time to plumb its lovely depths of mystery, if I really sold it to these people, I saw I had to go through with my half-thought-out plans of only appearing to sell it, selling it without selling it, even if it was going to be a bit distasteful to me personally.

So, as they drove off, I wasn't all that sad, because what I now had in mind was that this would not really be *sayonara* to the white car. (Don't take that as a hint of the make of the car, I might just as well have said *auf Wiedersehen,* or "See ya later," or something in Swedish, Italian, or something else.) Although I had the address of their home in the city, while I was waving good-bye to them, a cab happened to pass, and on the spur of the moment I jumped in and followed them. I guess I just couldn't bear to watch it go out of my sight at all. A few miles down the road, a frightening thing happened. It was very frightening to me, so I can imagine how it must have unsettled the new owners when a squad car suddenly turned on its siren and pulled them over. I exclaimed under my breath at the closeness of things, and the cabby glanced at me in his mirror. I told him to pull up. The cops treated them roughly, making the driver lean against the car while frisking him. The poor guy's face went beet-red. A shouted conversation ensued, after which the people had to follow the cops to the station. I threw the cabby a twenty, and we kept a discreet distance behind. At the cop station, we sat in dead silence, while he read the paper, occasionally raising his head to watch with satisfaction his meter turn over, and look back in a semi-interested way at me. After about forty minutes, the buyers of the white car came out and drove away in it. That surprised me as well as pleased me no end. The cops were not keeping the car. The cab driver and I followed them. Was a trap being set for me?

We arrived at a lovely white townhouse on a hill overlooking San Francisco Bay. They pulled the car into the driveway and proceeded straight inside. I watched all this as the cab pulled by slowly. He must have wondered what was up but being a pro he never asked. He made out not to care, as I kept feeding him money. Then I had the cab driver take me back to my motel, but as we approached I asked him just to drive on, and while he did so, I checked the street and parking lot out. Maybe some new buyers would be around, I thought, but couldn't spot any. I had the cab driver take me across the Bay to a bar in Jack London Square, and gave him the sort of tip that instills forgetfulness or at least a bit of goodwill. But there was no way to be sure, so after a quick drink I left in another cab for the airport, where I took a third cab, then a fourth, and in this manner made my way to the wrecking yard in Richmond owned by Dahomey and worked in by Jack. With the price of the white car in my pocket, less quite a bit of cab fare, scuffed shoes or no, I felt I could talk to Dahomey man to man.

Jack wasn't around. His car wasn't there. That didn't worry me, he was probably gone on business, arranging to pick up a car, or to buy or sell some piece, part, or portion of a car, for Dahomey. I was relieved that he wasn't there moping around to distract me from my business with Dahomey, who wasn't in sight either, however. The place was in the doldrums, in the siesta hour. A handful of the usual forlorn customers waited impatiently and grimly in the office, exchanging looks of blank dismay with each other, and staring at the walls and one or two tattered *Road and Track* magazines, while a workman behind the counter endlessly debated with somebody on the phone whether one section of one model car would or wouldn't match up with some fragment of another, a conversation so hellishly futile it made me tremble.

A few flies lazily noised about in the grimy windows casements, the sun beat down on the roof of the shack and drew a burning rubber smell. The dog had opened one disapproving eye as I had passed but hadn't exerted itself to growl, as if it too knew what hopeless time of day it was, lunch hour when everybody but hapless customers was out, and even the dog was off duty.

Only the Perfect Circle Piston Rings calendar girl displayed her customary charms. One glance into the office and I backed out again. I couldn't have lingered two minutes in that company of near-prostrate customers who reminded me of the sort of hardened pitiful people in an old Western movie marooned in a lost gulch railway station waiting for the one train of the week to roll in, which was going to be extremely late, with bandits on it. Something petulant and ugly about their spirit made me want to put extreme distance between myself and them, since I could never have afforded such emotions for a second. I could understand Dahomey's reaction when he often simply walked to the far end of his yard and forgot about them, which was also probably why his business was rumored to be in trouble.

I roamed into the middle of the yard. The sense of awe which the unfathomable automobile friezes like Pompeii always brought me was heightened by the afternoon sun, which emblazoned everything, leaving hardly a shadow, picking out every twisted piece of chrome.

Like an old graveyard, or some ageless rock formation, or the shores of the Pacific, in Dahomey's yard there was the peacefulness of that which was here yesterday and will be here tomorrow, for which the passing years are blinks of an eye, a vast somnolence and quietude beneath the rolling waves of traffic all around, wherein one glimpsed ancient tragedies of persons as if frozen in amber, glimmers of long-vanished violence, carwrecks like shipwrecks at the bottom of the sea, buried skeletons, forgotten dreams in the coils of metal, patterns of fate which consummated the mysteries of the individual in transport.

There was an old car seat off to one side which seemed to have fallen off a truck or been otherwise forgotten in the dust, and I flung myself down on it with the abandon of giving myself up to the fates, to that which was beyond me and had brought me here, and for a moment it brought me some comfort, as I stared at nothing but the walls on walls of eternal cars. But at once I began to think of the people to whom I'd sold the white car. I remembered how the woman had gone on so as though I had found that miraculous car, and risked all to bring it to San Francisco, just to please her. As if the white car were in the world for little her alone. When she went to the museum and saw a sketch by Da Vinci or Picasso she probably dreamed of owning that too and supposed it was in the museum just for her. What about me and my feelings on parting? The realization of all the trouble and danger I was going to have to go through to steal the car back from them filled me with annoyance. A few thousand dollars would not be enough to pay me for the sort of hot water I found myself in now. It was easy to guess that they had held nothing back in the way of a description of me when they had talked to the cops. When they glanced out the window at the white car in their driveway now, there must have seemed something sinister in its beauty. At least I meant it that way. Like everyone else they imagined themselves innocent, undeserving of any trouble, slaughterers of nations. Had they ever, for one second, fully accepted the horror that had been visited upon the red man by their bloodthirsty and rapacious forbears for the sake of *their* future?

Dahomey came up on me from behind, and I suddenly felt his presence looming over my shoulder. Seated right on the ground as I was, he towered over me like one of his unstable-looking columns of rubber tires. I got up and had no trouble meeting and holding his gaze today. Whatever he saw in my eyes was enough to make him break contact and walk straight back into his inner office, where he silently waited for me behind his desk, his drooping eyelids and drooping lower lip masking whatever feelings or suspicions he might have had. He was implacable. He was ready to talk business. There was to be no shoe-shining routine this time, even less any ambiguous display of affection.

I didn't beat around the bush explaining to him that I needed plates and a pink slip to match the white car and offering him five hundred bucks for them. After a long silence, during which he seemed to take my entire measure, he agreed in a flat voice, but demanded more money. We came to an agreement, after which he informed me that the title he had for me was an exact fit except for one detail, and I would have to have the white car painted. He tossed me the card of a paint shop of a friend of his, and eventually I did have the car painted to match the papers he sold me, although for me it remained the white car, and I had no trouble seeing the real color beneath the expedient gloss. It will always remain the white car for me, pearl without price—I say this at risk of blasphemy, for it gives an indication of the sway it held over me. Perhaps the only thing I can't explain is the mysterious and nearly fatal attraction that that car had for me until the end. Pretty and creamy white as it always was in my eyes, and eventually there were a string of buyers to prove its fascination, it was never a matter of the particular model, make, or color it happened to have been, not at all. I don't know as you would have found it so deliriously fetching as I did, but you would have dug it, I guarantee.

Invisible Car Dealer

In the dark before next dawn I was walking up a hill lined with smart white townhomes, elegant and old-fashioned. In the pale starlight they seemed to have been carved out of a ghostly marble, but I knew they were as real as real estate could be, since this was an exclusive section of town. Location, location, and I wasn't surprised at the location I found myself in, considering the charms of the white car. Perhaps it had been just the right second car for them, or for her. You could smell the view of the Bay out there, but not see it yet. I was operating on my sixth, or even seventh sense, by now. The townhouses reminded me of the bygone and well-hedged era when they'd been built more than the present, as if there were something truly permanent about good taste and reputableness. In the silver light they looked like tombstones. I had little compunction about stealing back the white car from people who lived here. Was that going to turn them into confused and illiterate Indian children on the reservation, covered with flies and watching their elders drown their sorrows in the white man's firewater? The well-off have their illusions of unassailability and unaccountability just as the poor have theirs of irredemption and vulnerability. Well, I had more sympathy with the latter.

I hadn't bothered to remember the exact house number because if the car wasn't still out on the driveway as I had last seen it, I'd have to wait for another opportunity anyhow, and go away emptyhanded this morning. It was around here somewhere. Dawn

Invisible Car Dealer

was just beginning to break, a dollop of cream in the black east. I walked up the hill squinting ahead of me for the car, like looking for a tiny pearl in sands of black glass, in the onset of a mystifying white San Francisco fog. Then out of the mists it practically rushed at me, as big as a bus for an instant. I almost bumped up against her. I reached out and held her beneath my hand, my breath raking out of my throat from the climb and fear. Looking about to see no one was watching, I gave the trunk lid a big kiss and friendly pat, while a tear came to my eye, it was so good to have found her.

No one was abroad so early on this handsome street which went up and then over a hill. We were almost at the top. Distant delivery vehicles could be heard, as well as the desultory warblings of a few starlings or sparrows or something. Actual birds, rather paltry and thin. But the real thing, not a recording. It was a long way from Mr. Ramos's lush recordings back in L.A. That hadn't exactly been poverty either, but in some class sense that nouveau riche neighborhood I had once lived in with Gretchen was about as far away from this one as the ghetto, and the people there suffering in comparison to this, suffering existentially and mysteriously like Gretchen, on account of being only mildly rich, or because they had to listen to the recordings. No, the people around here would not have gone for recordings of jungle birds in the morning, they would never have thought that very chic. As a matter of fact, I couldn't have agreed with them more. Nothing like the real thing, even if it was only a few hoarse pigeons—or the strange light and rare emotion of this moment.

I was standing a few feet from the sleepers who had bought the car from me and spent near an hour in the police station afterward. Low pale cement walls tapered uphill on either side of their drive with my car squeezed in between them. I slipped in on the driver side and turned my key in the door. I found I had now locked it and wasted a precious instant in panic until I realized they had left the car open! The comfortable are careless or maybe they had been too pissed off after that visit to the police station to care. I eased silently behind the wheel, dragging one foot out the door. The drive looked to have been cut into the hillside so the grade was rather slight, not as steep as I had hoped. I wanted to ease back out and down the hill and roll away without starting the engine for half a block.

Invisible Car Dealer

I thought I could just put it in neutral, release the emergency brake, and lean against the door frame and push the car backward to the lip of the drive, where gravity would take over. But the angle of those white walls was deceptive, the drive actually sloped slightly toward the closed garage. The gradient was too much for me. The car headed the wrong direction, and I had to pull the emergency brake on again with a disagreeable and really unbearable ratcheting sound. I was inches from the door of the garage. My heart was racing. I was kind of new to this sort of thing.

I wished Jack was with me just now. He would have been a great help, and it would have made it more companionable. Between the two of us we would have pushed the car out of this drive in two seconds. It was just something like this that would have perked Jack up and taken him out of his depression in a minute. The strange circumstances under which I'd acquired the beautiful white car came back to me and made me the dizzier to be reacquiring it. A shame I had vowed to myself not to tell Jack the story or he'd have been hooked instantly. He'd have loved it. This would have been meat to him, and potatoes, and probably a new lease on life. But I wasn't sure he could handle the moral dimension of it. I was sure his wife couldn't that he told everything to.

Moreover, it was marvels I was banking on the car to perform after this, once I had it out of this damned driveway. I wondered after all if I hadn't entered a nightmare world worse than Jack's. No, this was real, if pretty far out, and Jack's knocking-over-casino dreams were nonsense. I had promised myself that above all and come what may, I would not get Jack involved and so far I was proud of myself that I had not. I could imagine what his wife, a nurse, would think of this escapade I was presently in the thick of and smiled grimly to myself as I realized I was going to have to start the engine underneath the people's bedroom window. If I got in trouble, I thought I could handle it, because I was already in mortal trouble, and I understood what I was about. I'd come to terms with the stark truth that America is founded upon mass murder and wholesale robbery of the Native cultures and—let's call a spade a spade—*genocide*. I wasn't too worried about the moral dimension of stealing back the white car, a minor annoyance to the well-fed occupants of this townhouse if they lost it, compared to hungry children on the reservation waking up to brain trauma and permanent disability brought on by starvation and alcoholic mothers when they were in the womb. It was too bad Jack would not enjoy the extreme thrill I was experiencing just now, but none of the considerable danger either, of being alarmingly stuck in the drive of this townhouse with the sleeping owners just a few feet away beyond the black window overhead.

At this rate I was going to awaken them with all the screwing around. Time to go! The motor responded instantly as though the white car was glad to have me back. In two seconds I was headed not downhill but up for a view of the Bay since I had the engine running and had already made enough noise to wake up the whole street. The engine whined in low gear. I crested the hilltop. The wide sky was a bright pearly hue like a blank movie screen on which I could project my heart's desire.

On my walk up the hill I had glanced cautiously into every parked car. I was certain no cops were watching the car or the house, car theft was not that big a deal. But now I wondered about their leaving the car unlocked as they had. It was too easy. What if I was wrong and it had been a setup, the unlocked car a bait? In my rear view mirror there were no lights. No one was following. I was alone and free. I thought I had got away with it.

What had people in this neighborhood bought the white car for anyway? It was a nice car, but not a new car. Maybe they'd bought it for a child of theirs, and that was why it was sitting outside? An overfed, entitled, insufferable teenager probably. No, the woman would have told me that while she was telling me her life story yesterday, it was probably just to be hers, that was bad enough. I bet she had not made one donation to the reservation in her life. But now she had.

The fact was that they—and the cops—imagined the crime had already occurred. Incredibly (no doubt) to them, they had bought a stolen car. Who would have thought it hadn't happened yet, or was ongoing, and I'd steal it back all over again on top of its being a stolen car already, novelty enough? To tell the truth I laughed aloud thinking of it this way. I stopped on the hilltop to watch the silver dawn steal over the still, black Bay. Wondering how good my luck could get, I reached in the glove compartment, and there was the title, just as it had been after I had signed it over to them and they threw it in there. Well probably they had shown it to the cops while screaming irately about their fate. Well-off comfortable people like them who thought they were entitled to all the breaks or at least would never have believed something like this could happen to them could not conceive of the troubles and despair to be found in the real world below their plush hilltop.

I didn't want luck so good. But this was good. I didn't have to waste Dahomey's papers or get the white car painted yet. I still had the title in my hand and placed it back in the glovebox carefully and gratefully. They must have really been disgusted when they'd pulled up here yesterday after their run-in with the cops and just gotten out and slammed the door. The white car didn't deserve to be treated that way. Leave the title in the glove box for any passerby to take? I was appalled but it was nice. My uneasiness came back as I glided downhill toward the water. It could be a setup. Frankly, I had no experience, no idea how cops thought. I was new to crime. This was all new to me. I was pretty sure with all the crime in this city a stolen car would not rate too highly. The only thing that would save me was to follow my own script, something the cops had just as little knowledge of as I did. Apparently I had gotten away clean.

I had business to take care of. I had to find myself a new motel, then put a new ad in the paper for the white car, with a new phone number. Lights glowed suddenly in the rear view mirror, a car closing very fast—*cops?* For a few seconds I paid the whole price, the realization of what was in store for me if they caught me. The strange and intolerable truth was that I was risking my freedom. I touched my face thoughtfully and let the passing car pass straight out of my heart. I rubbed my jaw with relief and wonder and grew calm again. I found I had a gnawing appetite. I picked a breakfast joint with a big window and parked the car right in front so I could see it while I ate. The cooks and waitresses were inside but they hadn't opened up yet. I was in such wild spirits it was no problem banging on the door till they let me in.

The sun had come up and infused the fog. As I walked out of the joint picking my teeth, about to make my way to the newspaper office, a hint of danger forewarned me like a form in the mist that some detective might be reading the classifieds the next few days. I needed some different, brand new copy for the ad. It would take a poetic leap in the automotive sense, a gasoline-powered impulse at copy writing, over the heads of cops. I wrote out the copy. I made the year of the car a couple of years older, the best I could come up with. It would be a pleasant surprise for buyers that it was newer at the same price.

I left the white car well hidden at the far end of the parking lot of a convenience store and hailed a cab. I offered him ten bucks over the meter if he would sit in the back seat and pretend to be the fare while I drove his cab. I started to tell him a tale about an estranged woman that I didn't want to recognize me, which he cut off by stopping the car on a dime and giving me that patented cab driver's look, like don't bother, he'd heard everything, but he agreed without hesitation, and immediately began to play another part, making himself comfortable in the back seat as though that were where he really belonged, while I rolled up my sleeves and took the wheel. After a little while, once I had given him more money and he had dropped off the copy I gave him for the newspaper, and he returned to the back seat to ride around with me some more, he launched into a recital of his achievements as well as his tribulations as a young actor. The first time he glanced at me as he talked, I gave *him* that patented cab driver's look, right? He caught it and shut up, going red in the face, and I laughed. I wished he'd shut up for I needed to be as observant as I could be when I cruised by my old motel. As long as my last customers had been kind enough to leave the title in the glove box, I might as well try to sell the white car one more time at least from the old ad. But it wasn't long before the cabby in the back seat was telling me about his highlights on the dramatic stage, as well as his undeserved suffering as a mostly unemployed acting genius.

"Your story is one of the most moving I have heard, and I understand completely, and wish you well," I said in what I took to be a cab driver's professional sympathetic tone and glared at him.

My hunch was some buyers might show up at the motel this morning in response to the original ad in the paper, not the new one for tomorrow the cab driver (soliloquizing in the back seat) had dropped off at the paper for me. People do that, hang onto the same edition of the paper for a day or two, assuming no car is going to sell that fast. Yesterday, before selling the car to the first people who had showed up, I had answered a number of calls and given out the address of the place, telling people to come by and look at the car any time they liked, and I remembered somebody who'd said they might not get by until the following day if the car had not been sold by then. I had wished them luck. Anyway, I was right.

After a couple of passes by the place I couldn't see any cops. But that didn't mean anything. They must have been here yesterday to question people about me, after that long talk they'd had with the white car's first owners. Now it would be a matter of persuading the desk clerk to play along with me the next couple of hours. Everyone has his price and fortunately it is often quite low. I had already proved that with the actor-cab driver, who was contentedly smoking a cigarette behind me. I pulled up in front of the glass door of the motel and leaned on the horn a few times, making a spectacle of myself. Nobody was stirring. Finally I got out, and went inside pretending to be looking for a fare.

As I rapidly whispered the nature of my needs to the motel clerk with a fifty between my fingers, I was prepared for almost any response other than the one I got. While smilingly accepting my blandishment, he nodded and seemed to point with his eyes behind me. I whipped my head around, the blood rushing in my ears like a waterfall, expecting to see detectives, or worse, irate ex-car buyers, I didn't know what. But it was a couple of girls, who wanted to buy the white car, who had just walked in looking for me. I tried to dissemble my emotion. They looked like nice girls. But it hardly mattered. Car buyers in their enthusiasm do tend to overlook anything, especially precisely what they should be most curious about. I wondered about the clerk. He was awfully cool. It had happened so fast, and now I needed to make it happen even faster. I explained the whole situation to the girls, some lie or other about why the white car was not here, feeling sorry that it would be nice innocent girls this time.

I ran out the door and gave the cab driver in the back seat a meaningful look, who didn't seem to get it, just blew smoke in my face, and blandly waited till I had opened the door for him, pulled him out by the arm and pushed him back where he belonged behind the wheel. Very crossly he started the engine and made out the huge figure on his meter meant nothing to him. The girls didn't seem to notice a thing. They went to their own car and followed behind us. First we went to the convenience store, where I paid him off and said goodbye to the cab driver wishing him well in his career in the theater. Waving cheerily at the girls, as soon as the cab had pulled out I motioned them over to the white car as I walked up to it. They barely even got there but just trusted me completely and were instantly charmed by the lovely white car. In a matter of minutes, the girls and I were in the lobby of their bank, the white car parked next to theirs in the lot. They were only a pair of innocent co-eds, but they knew a beautiful car and most of all a low price as well as the next fellow. I was playing it by ear, and had no idea what would happen next, as moment succeeded moment. But it was going like clockwork.

I hadn't had time to think about it yet, but I suppose I was prepared to retrieve the car again from them in somewhat the same fashion as I had from the previous "owners" this morning. I wondered where they lived and hoped it wasn't too far away. Somehow we found ourselves sitting at an unused desk in the bank's lobby. I don't know if it was their idea, or if some officious clerk seeing us waving around a lot of cash and a car title suggested it. I disliked the idea of skinning these friendly girls. In fact I deeply hated myself for it. I was doing my best to find something I didn't like about them, but they were full of fun and anticipation, and I liked everything about them more and more. But it had to be done, and as nice as they were, the white car could not be left in their hands either, and tomorrow I'd be paying them a visit real early. Nobody had ever shot them in the freezing dawn and murdered their mothers and fathers in order to steal their land from them.

I imagined every pair of eyes in the bank was on us. The white car was getting sort of hot, probably, and it was only going to get hotter. But it was only the second time I'd sold it, I thought, and calmed down. In my confusion, I suddenly thought of something I'd overlooked. The one thing the former buyers had not forgotten in the unlocked car on the hilltop was their own set of keys, rather thoughtless of them not to have just left them in the ignition for me, and I had only my own pair left, which I would have to give these girls. In that case I would have to break into the car this time, to get it back from the girls, more time-consuming and dangerous, unless they left it unlocked too. But I couldn't count on that. In fact I was sure they would lock it up, those girls. I'd have to acquire a tool I didn't have about me to efficiently break into the car this time.

Invisible Car Dealer

It wasn't just that either. It was all those prudish eyes focused on me in the bank, irritating the hell out of me. I decided to see what I could get away with right under those eyes, in the cold gleam of the bank's fluorescent lighting, or rather the hard daylight out in the parking lot. Sitting at the table in the lobby I made a pretense of signing my name on the pink slip, which I had already done yesterday of course, and the three of us happily exchanged money and title, them carefully inspecting the paper, for what I don't know, and me counting the money, though if it had been a few bucks short I wouldn't have mentioned it. I didn't bother finishing counting it. In a minute we were standing together outside in the parking lot bantering with each other pleasantly as if about to part forever on the happiest terms and wishing each other the best.

I was holding the keys in my hand and tossing them up and down playfully, while one of them stretched out her pretty palm to me for them. It struck me that these chicks didn't even know how good a deal they had gotten on the price, not really, they were simply way too good-spirited and plain young. They just liked the car, for some reason causing a lump in my throat. They didn't realize I could have asked a lot more for it, and would have had this all been a legit sale. I would have started at ten grand higher, $22,000, or more, if I had really been in no hurry to part with it.

They didn't know. They were pure as lambs. There was nothing at all about them on which I could hang an impulse to do them an evil turn and make what was coming next any easier. It was very hard on me, I can tell you. For a second, I doubted I could go through with it, and I had to harden myself for it.

One of the girls asked me if she could give me a lift somewhere, her touching thoughtfulness really giving me a moment of the most paralyzing fellow-feeling. She was going to drive the white car, while the other one took the car they'd come in. How would I get home? At this, all was almost lost, and the white car gone forever. I was in near despair, even though the Indians had gotten skinned by the white man far worse than these two were going to be by me. I had to swallow all my compunctions fast, and they made a pretty good mouthful going down. I was still holding the keys.

Whoever had swindled the Indians and butchered the buffaloes on the Great Plains, it had not been nice co-eds like these.

Invisible Car Dealer

I made to hand them the keys for the final farewell, then as if it were an afterthought that seemed to strike me, I asked for the title back for a moment, explaining that I had forgotten to fill in the odometer reading. I showed them the box where the mileage had to be written down at the time of a transaction, and pulling out a pen, slid behind the wheel so I could properly read the figure under the speedometer. I ducked down low as if to read the numbers. Then I simply turned the key, which I had slipped into the ignition, and drove away.

It probably isn't necessary to describe the looks on their faces, which I studied for a split second (but that was enough) as I tore out of the parking lot. Funny how in moments like that people will wear identical expressions like twins. They seemed in awe, as if some incalculable recognition of something they may have once dreamed unpleasantly in a distant nightmare had impossibly hit them between the eyes. A horror from the far end of the universe was theirs to grapple with, as if The Thing had climbed out of the swamp. They were frozen in space as every drop of energy was taken up processing what was happening to them. They never moved.

I wasn't too worried as I really doubted if they had had the presence of mind to memorize the license plate number of their own new car yet, not that it mattered. All they might know was the year, model, and color of their new car, the last of which was about to change radically, along with the plates, in the next day or two. But not right away. Not today. I still had the original title, the keys, and my new ad in the paper had not come out yet with the new phone number at the coffeehouse in Berkeley where I planned to relax hoping to catch a glimpse of Julie as I awaited new buyers.

I headed straight back to my old motel, and when I got there I wasn't surprised to find yet another set of would-be buyers of the white car who had seen the first ad and were waiting for me. To make a long story short, I had sold the white car again before the evening, and only then did I call it a day. Along the way I had made a couple of extra sets of keys, which I figured to have need for, and I procured a certain tool at an auto parts store, one of those multi-purpose tools that the guy behind the counter knew quite well could be used to jimmy a car door, but he kept a stone face. The next day I sold the car again on Telegraph Ave, retrieved it once more, and finally decided it was time to change colors. Forgive me, dear reader, for not relating all the gory details of these last "sales," but you get the idea and probably have had enough by now, and they may still be looking for me.

The white car would no longer be white in a few hours, after I'd had it repainted. By now I figured the detectives must be really seriously looking for me, so it wasn't going to be enough to just change the color of the car, but I was going to have to advertise a totally different year, make, and model, too. I put the ad in the Oakland paper this time. But the ad was for the same class, quality, the same *sort* of automobile, so that when the buyers came, when it wasn't the make they were looking for, the sheer beauty of the car, the vibes which would take off where the image they had come for disappeared, so to speak, plus the deceptively low price, of course, would do the selling. I would make up some story. My wife put in the ad for the wrong car, thinking we were selling mine not hers.

I headed for the hole-in-the-wall body shop Dahomey had recommended, and breathed easily again in its gloom once the Mexicans began to tape the glass and trim in preparation for applying paint. But it was hard to stop seeing the violated faces of those people, the hopeful buyers, full of blank stupefaction. It was getting to be quite a list. I was haunted to the point of being completely overcome by their eyes wide and wondering, their pathetic expressions of acute and incomprehensible loss, and the suffering that was about to set in, which I had witnessed in the rear view mirror, or just my vivid imagination. They reminded me of the children at Wounded Knee, perhaps, having lost their parents or dying themselves, and also the faces of nurses, or even young soldiers, struck by haphazard death or absurd tragedy in a war, Jack's war, in fact, let's say, when the immensity of things was about to swallow them up, and they saw it all, just how bad and awful it really was. Jack would have been ready for it I knew, but I wasn't ready for him yet.

At moments as the Mexicans worked on their car (guiltily and with a full heart I thought of it as partly those first girls' forever now, so I say "their"), I saw what they had seen too, and their horror was mine. History is as full of such moments as they are never mentioned in the history books. Think of the Indian massacres coldly ordered by American politicians and generals we presently revere and have always built statues to, and the sheer surprise in the hearts of the Indians as they were shot dead and burned out and their wives murdered before their eyes, when they had just signed a treaty with the white man to the effect that if they ceded half their land they would be left in peace on what remained of it.

Then the soldiers had just shown up to wipe them out completely when the generals or the mayor or governor realized that actually half wouldn't do and they wanted *all* the land, with no living Indians cluttering up the place. So the peace was a short-lived one.

Think how surprised Sitting Bull and others must have been at such treachery, as he was shot dead, something new in Indians' experience, such rank duplicity, no matter how cruel Indians were to each other. (Yes, I know Indians were always marauding and stealing from each other, but since God owned the land they never pretended that they had to kill *all* of the other tribe so as to acquire it, nor did they insist on always making a big deal of signing a solemn and binding treaty pledging eternal friendship immediately before mowing down the other signatory.) Like car buyers acquiring car titles, the Indians had always hoped for the best when they signed that paper treaty, that the car would come with it, you know. This sort of thing is never in a history book, part of the reason I am including it in this one. All I had done was even the score one iota.

No doubt the simple amazement that it is happening to you in these sorts of circumstances is the overriding feeling. I don't suggest for a moment the red man is unique in being victimized in this fashion; if you go back in history no doubt the white man in his tribes in Europe bore the brunt of this behavior countless times beyond reckoning (and you don't have to go back very far either, do you? couple of months is enough), each one an occasion for disbelief and wonder. In fact, the sheer quantity of violence and laying waste (I don't mean statistics or allusions to it, but the raw overpowering real suffering of this shattering mayhem) that is never spoken of or written about in history or literature or the newspapers is rather staggering to contemplate every time you casually come across it or are struck in the face by it in real life. Then you know what is left out of books.

Invisible Car Dealer

I'm sure nothing in their lives had ever taught those girls or even the older buyers to expect anything of the kind, they had merely thought that once again life was handing them a pretty nice deal, in fact, a bargain, America being wonderful that way, and when I had driven off in the car, or picked it up later, and it turned out to be a raw deal, the pavement might as well have opened up in one of the famous West Coast earthquakes, although at the last moment by the looks on their faces in the mirror something ancient in their blood seemed to have remembered what this was all about and what was happening to them.

I was truly sorry it had to be any of them, especially the girls, and suffered considerably as I watched the Mexicans apply new paint to the white car. Before my eyes the girls' and others' faces constantly streamed, fading again and again with sorrow and finality, blotting out the activity of the team of Mexicans who were doing the rush job, the hissing of the paint going on, the sharp lacquer smells, the hellish illumination of the bake-lights. The white car had zero dents or faults and so it was simply a matter of a little sanding and repainting it. Two coats, no more, it took just the morning. I handed the boss the pink slip and pointed to the color on it. "That color," I said. I think it just said red actually.

In one part of my brain I was overcome with disgust at myself, while in another it was as if a movie were being played at fast-forward of all the suffering in the world, which was to be mine now. The mind-blowing aspect was to realize how little worth mentioning my crimes were, evil as they were, how much more pain than that was required of millions and entire populaces at every moment of time, by Nature, by governments, and inflicted by other well-wishers. All of this torture and displacement was going on all over the globe right now this instant, putting in the shade what I had just done, but since it was me that had just done it, my own shame and horror were near absolute. Although I would remember their faces for the rest of my life, the minor financial embarrassment of those girls and the others was only a drop in the sea of suffering as rolls in tidal waves across the globe always every second. Take the Middle East, if you want to, or all of U.S. history unless you are the white man.

Nevertheless every drop of pain and disappointment exists in itself and is as intense as each individual can make it. This is the most fundamental reality, and the part that is never mentioned in any of the books. Think of what we Americans required of the Indians in the way of a contribution to a good cause, for instance, and your entire apprehension of so-called reality takes a shift. Imagine the looks on the faces of those pioneer maidens when the curtain came down, and the white car rolled away.

I began to fall prey to a powerful emotion, more than guilt, a terrible longing, for what or whom I didn't know, just human companionship in any form. I felt like I was being pulled inexorably out of the human orbit by these acts of mine. I wasn't cold enough, hard-hearted enough, for this job by any means. My soul was parched by the adrenaline which had burned out of me. The anguish which poured in in return was so large it seemed to come from something like History or the Cosmos, as if unwittingly I now found myself on the wrong side of these entities, or more like it, swimming right down the middle of the maelstrom. I couldn't help looking through the eyes of the victims, something of a flaw in a criminal, nor did this sympathy in its intensity lessen the aching isolation which falls on those who are wanted by the law. I almost wondered if Julie hadn't been right, and by some wayward alchemy I had become the source of unmitigated, blameworthy evil, which by no stretch of the imagination referred to anything other than itself any more, and couldn't be cured by a thousand allusions to History, mine included.

But still I wondered why I should be bothered in this way when generations of my good countrymen had rubbed out the indigenous populations of this country like flies and never lost a night or even a wink of sleep over it, and considered it their duty to conduct wholesale national-scale land theft and mass murder. As a destiny! I wondered if this was my "destiny" too.

When I rolled out of the body shop with my new red (or blue or green or black) paint job, I couldn't deny who it was I needed to see. The hard part would be to get across to her how I was feeling without explaining just exactly why, so as not to strain her sympathies too much. My hope was that the intensity of my pain would be so plain that it would stop her curiosity, and she would understand at a glance, and blame it on that Indian, know what it was about, and the two of us could happily and blindly drown in her compassionate instinct.

Invisible Car Dealer

By the way, let's say the car was red, or blue, or green, or whatever, *before,* and now was white. Just for the sake of convention, since I'm so used to calling it the white car, even if it wasn't now (or before). But that's just it, before it wasn't, but I'm not going to change all that, and now it really was a white car, a pale ivory shadow of a machine. The Mexicans had painted it white, let's say. So for the sake of ease of narrative I will go on speaking of the white car, then, but let's just say that before it was blue, and now white. So, *voila!* the *white car.*

I didn't have a clue where to start looking for Julie. I was fairly sure by now she wouldn't be living in the same house, since she never stayed in one place for very long, and after all these months I doubted she'd still be selling flowers on Telegraph Avenue either, which she wasn't. I might end up having to scout up some of her acquaintances if I was serious about finding her, and I hated to think of having to beg information from any of those turkeys. I found myself tooling down Telegraph staring foolishly into the crowds for lack of any better idea. The flower stand was still there, but another girl was tending it. The futility of my search was equaled only by the depression that came over me staring into these hedonistic throngs who thought that parading around in the sun, getting high, selling their arts and crafts, going into the "Med" for coffee, or into a health food shop for a veggie sandwich, in general hanging out on this utterly silly street, constituted a useful day. I guess deep down by now I would have exchanged all my bitterly won insights for five minutes' worth of such indolence and guiltless pleasure as they had on Telegraph.

I had just about given up hope of finding Julie, at least very soon, and my dejection was complete, when I suddenly spotted the last person I would have expected to see around here, Jack. I even doubted it was really him, and hastily parked the car to walk back and see, but it was him all right, standing on a corner with some buddies of his, veterans probably, openly passing a joint around. Smoking grass on the street here was nothing, since by this period and at this place the weed was more or less informally decriminalized already, Berkeley quite a few years ahead of and showing more wisdom in this regard than most of the rest of the nation then or since, which might really give you cause to wonder if you stopped to ponder it, something I had no time to do.

Invisible Car Dealer

What was amazing and did make me wonder was seeing Jack around here at all, since Telegraph was not his style, and to see him in this unlikely spot was instantly to know something was wrong with him. The guys he was with must have brought him here, one glance showed they belonged. I was touched by the pathos of having spotted a friend in danger in the wilderness, and instinctively I was afraid that between his problems and my lonely isolation and criminal life, my best intentions of getting us on our feet again were about to go all astray. He seemed as shocked to see me as I had been to see him, a flicker of something, perhaps shame, crossing his face. That was the last emotion I cared to evince in as good a man as Jack, and whispered quickly, "Hey, man, I got a job for us tomorrow morning."

As soon as I'd said that, I knew all was lost, for I'd gone back on my promise to myself that I'd never involve Jack in my current adventure. The only rationalization for this abysmal weakness on my part was that what he was into on Telegraph was even worse, for I could see he was into nothing at all. Well, that was just it, anything was better than standing on the corner on Telegraph passing a joint. At the word "job" his face lit up, because the way I had said it suggested some excitement, not just boring work, but not only that, he was just a good man who preferred to have some living, a job, any kind of challenge, not like these characters he was with in their street outfits who probably liked living off the land. At this moment, even before he admitted it, I realized that he must have finally got himself canned by Dahomey.

"I got fired," he said after a silence. "Dahomey aint doing so well. Probably the way he treats his customers. He let me go, and a couple other guys. He's only keeping that African dude Gladstone and a couple ex-cons the government pays part of their wages. Some foundation pays that African's salary, so he can learn about cars and go home and teach his people, and the ex-cons are in some program Dahomey only kicks in like five bucks an hour."

It wouldn't have done to remark on his alienating his bosses almost as fast as he first charmed them, which I was overwhelmingly tempted to do, partly out of despair how I was going to stave off my severe guilt that I was going to bring him in on my crimes. I was about to blame him! How good it was I was in a position to help him, and I had just what the doctor ordered for

Jack. Bad as it was it wasn't worse than this. I asked him what he was doing on Telegraph. He grinned sheepishly, and thumbed at his buddies. "Doing our Vets outreach thing, you know."

He meant some clinic's or shrink's office around here where they met and unburdened themselves under the auspices of someone like Julie who was "outreaching."

"Outreaching a reefer you mean. You? I thought you had it together."

"Sometime you gotta admit your problems I guess," he said blankly and helplessly staring over the street.

"What are your problems, man?"

He thought about that. "The 'world' takes too much patience I guess." He eyed his friends loyally. "What the hell *you* doin on Telegraph?" He gave it back to me.

I was reluctant to admit the truth. Then I thought, what the hell, and told him, and tactfully he looked away over the street and repeated something he'd said once before. "Oh yeah, you better look her up, man. The wife kept up with her a bit, but I aint seen her in a while. You know what's good for you. "

"Well go get your head straightened out. But tomorrow we got something that'll get all the cramps out," I said to him with a sly smile.

"What is it?" he said in a low voice with his eyes riveted on mine. He visibly left his crowd then and moved closer to me morally without budging an inch. We seemed alone on the street.

Point-blank in a cold whisper into his ear I gave him a bare idea what sort of work I had in mind for us tomorrow, without saying too much, and told him the address where he should meet me first thing in the morning. As the clear impression that there would be a little danger, as well as fast money, dawned on him, his features which had been sagging firmed up, his eyes brightened, and in fact he grew stone sober, the giddy influence of the weed passed right out of him, and he looked healthy and strong again.

I was positively glad I had betrayed my promise not to involve Jack in the white car, because I could see that it was just what he needed, as I knew it would be. A flicker of doubt passed over his expression though, and he seemed to weigh something in the balance. A glance at his friends who were staring at him and passing him the joint (even to me, too) showed me the general nature of what it was, and it gave me an ironic pleasure to have been in the position of offering Jack some daring work that was far more in his line than in mine, which he was having to take a second to consider, just as he was about to "reform" and probably try to land a straight job. A desk job or menial work that would bring him down completely? Well not hardly, they were just about crying on each other's shoulders here and paralyzing themselves with understanding and compassion for one another that would get them nowhere but back here tomorrow to talk it over forever.

As for me, I was going to be a hell of a lot less lonely now that I had broken down and let Jack in on it. A rush of relief and camaraderie blew through me again and again just standing there with him, and I'd momentarily forgotten about Julie. It seemed to me there was no one else I had ever known whom I would rather have along for this ride than Jack (well, I had always known that and that hadn't been the issue). I felt it was positively the right thing to do, though, for him, as well. He needed it even more than I did. His Vietnam experiences would make him comprehend at once the maniac mission I was on. Well, that was what I had been afraid of. But it was too late now, I had done it, and he was all for it, and it was good. The thing was, with Jack, there didn't have to be a reason, no more than there had ever been a reason in Vietnam. My real reason, my secret reason, evening the score for the red man, I kept to myself.

I was beginning to feel a lot of sympathy for that intelligent creature the scientists are hunting on the dark side of the moon. I had found the Indian in my soul. By a strange logic, I had become that Indian, not the drunken one who had sought oblivion beneath my wheels, not exactly the proud spirit who fought us first in New England, then all across the Great Plains and in the swamps of Florida and south Georgia either, but the elusive remnant of the band, alive and nobly kicking still today, the sullen, angry and very brave one you read about in the paper occasionally up till now, who refuses to go under, who fights it out with Federal agents on the boundary of the reservation, stands up and takes a potshot at the ATF and survives on the fringes of society by hook or by crook, defender of the earth and sky, and all that is sacred to him, and ought to be to us, on the verge of extinction even now if the Republicans have any say in it, or apotheosis, a new career in the movies as white people's tastes evolve, anything rather than becoming a homogenized citizen and losing everything, even memory of the genocide. I put the struggling tribes who object to oilpipes run across their rivers and their reservations, and hire lawyers, and the richer tribes that own the casinos, in that spirited category, too, the masters of ceremonies at the billiards and blackjack tournaments with the cowboy hats with the jade-studded bands and the eagle feathers in them perched over their eyes. They know the score.

By the way, when I say I had become an Indian, one does not become another of whom one has little or no experience, or even one's next door neighbor. We are all strangers to each other, however. I know nothing about American Indians, having run across a few rag-tag members in the northwoods, or studied their stunningly handsome faces in museum photographs from the old West, or palavered with a few lost souls over a beer in the Flame Bar, and so forth. I know nothing of their pain, or the shape of their loss, their courage or hopes. How would I? But can't I imagine it, after all, all of us being human? Across time and space I had perceived I knew *some* of how *some* of them must have felt, forced into a marginal existence to preserve a vestige of their freedom, a flickering flame, precious above all. If this was a rank piece of totally presumptuous nonsense that Native Americans themselves would laugh their heads off at bitterly, I'm just trying honestly to explain to you how I felt, and the terror and anger of the "alien within" that unaccountably had taken hold and grown in me. Okay it's a prolonged metaphor. They are real people confronting the implications of a strange and terrible fate, they really had their way of life disrupted, and in one degree they are bereft and noble, and above all are just trying to keep it together, and I was an asshole on a rampage. But I didn't care if my conceit was laughable. I wasn't trying to persuade anybody to come along with me—except Jack—and I wasn't going to tell him about it either.

The thing I admired about Jack (as always) was how he kept it together to present that cool demeanor, glance at me coolly from behind the wheel as if there were all the time in the world, as I jumped in the seat next to him, while they were warming up the jail cell for us, and the latest buyers of the white (red) car tore after us, hands outstretched for our throats. Then after just that long second that meant so much to him, when he showed that ice-cool look, that he had it together, he pushed his foot to the metal, and drove just as hell-bent as his greeting had been stoical and even languorous when I jumped in after the "sale."

I hate to think what my face showed. I always dispensed with showmanship and seeming cool the second it was over. I was just hell-bent out of there and probably looked as wild and frantic as I felt. If it'd been him making the dash with the cash, he would have still been cool. He knew how you were supposed to look at such moments, and it was important to him. I so admired that about him, among other things. Myself, I've had no benefit of the martial experience he'd had, and I can't say I've ever regretted missing that quintessentially social experience, but I'd had no training at concealing my emotions when they were boiling, and really had no idea how you were supposed to look. My discomposure, I know I must have looked like I was about to shit, must have incited that dry look of his all the more, that small smile of his, which said so much, and which I took in good spirit, and from which I drew strength.

Manner is half of everything, as I well knew having just managed to sell somebody a make and model of car unlike the one which they had come to inspect. My ploy had been to flat out pretend I had never bothered to take a look at the advertisement as it had appeared in the paper, and that I had misunderstood them on the phone. I mean this was the car I had for sale, wasn't it pretty? My wife had made an unbelievable mistake. Then, as the white (red or blue) car was a beauty, and the price so beguilingly low, a couple thousand less than in the ad, they lingered, and decided to buy. An instant later, cash in hand, the bold grab, I felt the most acute embarrassment mixed with sorrow when I returned to myself the title right out of their hands like that, and the keys in case I had had to hand them over, until it was all but choked out of me by Jack's cold easy smile. My face probably showed everything.

It felt mighty fine and made a whole world of difference having Jack along to steal the white car back with, that comradeship and complicity, again and again. My last view of the poor people, who never seemed to stop coming, took in their eyes bulging, throats swelling, chests heaving, knees pumping, at last giving up, in wild despair, the expression on their faces speaking volumes, the misery and horror that aint in the history books. Now the looks of outrage on their faces are as hard for me to forget as they were to endure at the time. But we have all been injured badly, you know, not a one who hasn't. And I must bear up too. And so no one who isn't capable of anything. I found this out. There was a time when I couldn't have imagined myself capable of such cruel hoaxes. The aftermath of the event was to feel waves of objectless contempt, not for the victims exactly or only, which drowned out the relief and triumph, as if once primed the volcano of primitive feelings would burn down everything in sight. It was the strangest thing, since I had just robbed someone, but it seemed to me that it was I who had been violated, injured, and insulted, and I was getting my own back. Something buried in the past, all sorts of little psycho things, hell, the whole dismal weight of lonely existence itself, I understood with an inward shudder.

Think of the nearly exterminated Indians, the murdered Jews, the enslaved and tortured Africans, the battered and abused women, the persecuted-by-power and ransacked ethnic minorities around the globe, today, this moment, think of all the gall and bile that festers in the race really and for good reason, and it boggles the mind what we may eventually be in for, when they *all* throw off their chains as I, a mere suffering car dealer, have done. What if they were all to throw off their shackles right now, as I had done, instead of just talking so much about it, and mine were light by comparison, mine were just average white guy's chains and suffering. Theirs must be very, very heavy in comparison, theirs a mighty liberation when it comes. What if they were all to decide they'd had enough, *at once?*

It was a lot to study on and to bear. I who always tried to be positive had slipped into a negative personality without memory of when or why the change had begun. I wasn't even aware of any change, but seemed to have passed into this night in the most logical way without having crossed any twilight border. Had all the hours of overtime at the Pontiac dealer left me without an ounce of sympathy for the car-buying race whatsoever?

"How dare you! How dare you!" screamed the people running after us disappearing in the white car, once more.

How dared I? or we, rather, since Jack was performing the honors of the wheelman accelerating out of sight? We dared in the white car, that's how we dared, fast pale beast, my eyes glittering at the people through the rear window and seeing them till the last instant when they disappeared. And they ran like hell, losing all grasp of reality. You can't catch a speeding car on foot. But they were well aware how quickly the cops would respond, so they kept running up the street. I imagined them coming to the bitter realization that I, or we, did not exist soley to have brought the white car into their lives to please them. It must have been a hard truth to come to grips with. It must have been somewhat like how Native Americans felt when they saw the slave ships of Columbus, or the cavalry coming over the hill. Some people had shown up who did not mean well. Wow! Those white guys we showed how to make pumpkin pie! A commoner experience than we think, at any rate one that we inflicted upon whole nations of people who once roamed our country, and a few millions of Africans from Africa, too, enslaved poor people. How monstrous do you want? No, the next thing that develops and comes around the bend is not necessarily all you had been hoping for, my friend.

Their ragged cries illumined a whole realm of pain, pain which I hadn't known I had, like lightning eerily revealing a tormented landscape. As if a prisoner's chains would become truly unbearable in the last moment before freedom, when he cuts the jailer's throat, I understood what bound me to the victims as we left them in our dust, and it wasn't respect and love, which we are supposed to feel toward our neighbors as good Christians and Americans, but a harsh weight of oppression and hypocrisy that seemed to have been the really effective agent in the civic glue all along, as the denizens in Packy's Bar and the Flame Tavern very well know. I didn't know about Jack, but I rejoiced in my soul as I cracked that bond, false and brittle and dead as it had really always been, and realized with a shock that what I was doing was nothing short of finally gaining my freedom, the first of our moral virtues, and the one which I had always imagined I had kept uppermost already. This time I paid tribute to it in absolute and no uncertain terms. But what would come now?

What have we been doing this past century, in fact the whole history of America, if not getting our freedom? First the colonists, the white male land-holders, fleeing the king and tyrant, then waves of immigrants, gold seekers, the pioneers in their

Invisible Car Dealer

wagons heading for fame and fortune, happily adding to the list of Indian fighters, and next black people (for about five years in Reconstruction), then women as they acquired the vote, the poor white guys with no land get to vote at some point, and now the gays and Lesbians are no longer in hiding, but doing their thing, and more and more immigrants come over for their freedom, new ones from new places, women get the pill, black people get to sit at lunch counters, and then the Mexicans showing up to silently take over what was ripped off from them years ago, and wait at tables and pick fruit, everybody everywhere all over America expanding their freedoms, except for Indians, who still have to shoot it out to get noticed, but no, I swear it, even them, they too may eventually fire the last bullet—so why not the *car dealer?* All seeking a liberation ever more complete, freedom from despots, freedom from the church, from the state, from the man, from each other, from pestilence, from marauding Indian tribes, from insane white people, from drudgery, from prejudice, from the weather, from the Earth, from Heaven itself, from our bodies. from our minds, from drugs and chemicals (which formerly were thought to free us from our minds), freedom, yes, from normal unconscious white gringos above all—freedom, freedom and more freedom for *all* from *everything*—then even whitey himself noticing he needs more of the freedom he used to think he had the corner on, lately I have heard even he starts causing trouble wanting his big share which he thinks is getting slim—liberty *from everything* and *for anything,* a wondrous exoneration is what has characterized and epitomized us—ultimately from getting out of bed in the morning at all, freer and freer, until we all owe nothing to anyone and float like buzzards in the clouds. Even the car dealer, I repeat, it seems, will be free.

How dared we! How dared any of us so much as draw a breath, let alone enjoy our families and hearths and toys and freedom, in a society that began with the blatant running down and manslaughter of a whole race and the obliteration of all that a whole portion of humankind held dear and true (and kidnapped and enslaved a few million more of another). But it's just the same old story isn't it, until it happens to *you!* And we couldn't even get their names straight, all the names of their many nations, but call them all "Indians" because of a stupid mistake of an Italian seaman.

And even name a baseball team "the Indians," for the wrong continent. There is no end to the misery and absurdity it seems.

Not that it's anything new, but history never records such things, so it is new, for people don't remember five minutes later whom they have murdered, as long as the numbers of the dead and maimed are astronomical enough. So everything's new every day. After that, as all good Americans know deep in their hearts, who stole this country fair and square, nothing ever need be apologized for, ever again. That's freedom! Anyway the whole world knows as much, and I am not advocating anything. No apologies, certainly. And that is why we keep doing it and always will on the most massive scale possible, which is the one you don't get punished for, or even noticed. *So we don't have to remember!* And yet payment is made sometimes. I finally did come to believe that I was stealing the white car back for the Indians, you know? And the craziest part of it, you may well think, is that it was true. And yes, it *was* true. Why not? That's why I was doing it, no matter what anyone thinks.

At the end of a bloodsoaked history, I was only doing what came natural, and getting something back for the downtrodden and forgotten. We had come to the first stoplight. It had been five or six long blocks which had flashed by in an instant, completely outdistancing the latest hot pursuers, otherwise Jack might have run the light. Not that we weren't shooting glances into the rear view mirror thinking we might see them coming over the horizon behind us, closing on us in a cab or something. The light changed. Now it was time to blend in with the traffic, while making all haste ingeniously, which I left to Jack. I never commented on his driving. That would have been like suggesting a little salt and pepper to a chef at a five-star restaurant. I just left it to him no matter what was happening. He always made the right decision and the smart move.

Then I noticed something in the rear view mirror that I hadn't when I had looked into it while it had been filled with the captivating, glowing figures of the people who for a few seconds had chased us and filled the screen, their warm breaths almost down our necks. What I saw was the tops of two heads. That was a shock. I elevated myself, and saw in the mirror then it was two feminine foreheads, and at that I turned around to face Jack's wife, and Julie, looking at me, who must have slipped into the backseat of the car while I was busy with the buyers.

"You take this car right back to those poor people *this minute!* Jesus, what have you *become?*" said Julie almost choking. Rising up in outrage from her concealed position, she was now looking straight into my eyes with black indignation, and sputtering in my face in a righteous fury. How in the world could she be taking up my case again in this manner, I wondered. Where had they come from? What did she care about it? *Did* she care? I was overcome by the amazing, confusing and welcome realization that maybe she did. All I could think about was how close together we were at this moment and how good it felt to look into her eyes. I didn't hear what she said really.

"They just jumped in the car, man," Jack put in lamely, out of the corner of his mouth to me. "I don't know where they were hiding." But the truth was I didn't mind.

"I can't believe you've sunk *this* goddamn low!" said Julie, not mincing words.

I was overcome by seeing her, being in the same car with her, the white car of all things, that she cared, and I was speechless. There was something a little fishy in Jack's comment about not knowing where they were hiding.

"Jack is out of it," said Jack's wife leaning forward, speaking into his ear, in a firm voice.

"How could you bring your buddy into some evil, dangerous, low-life shit like this!" said Julie. I wanted to tell her I had never intended to, but I had.

"Hold on a minute, hold on," muttered Jack, weakly, and now I was sure it was all a setup, but of the best, well-intentioned kind, that somebody, or all three of them, had decided to try to get us back together again, and rescue me from myself, and put a stop to my crimes. This moved me terribly, even humbled me, but at the same time it irritated me. Julie's emotion was real, that was another question.

We rode in sizzling silence for a minute as Jack rededicated his efforts at the wheel. For the moment we did have to get away, after all. That was indisputable. Jack was a practical man first of all, and knew what had to be done even as we reconsidered everything, or at least they hoped! So he laid on the moves. Fear rode with us, with the hate, love, outrage, awfulness and anger. The creepy reality, and the danger, made themselves felt the more with the women in the car. I felt resentment at what she had just said, but she was right and I felt guilty about involving Jack. I'd been pining for her all this time too. I couldn't look her in the eye and tell her that she was right, that I admitted it, that I would do it, whatever she wanted me to do, because I loved her. It would have satisfied my soul, though. I was so happy to see her.

"I'm stealing a car!" Julie exclaimed suddenly and laughing wildly and almost demonically, hysterically, very unlike her style. She really meant it. "Stop this car right now and let me out!" It was very compelling. But Jack of course didn't do it. He was going to get us to our safe haven.

"I'm sorry, Julie, all I wanted was to see you again, and here you are. I'll do anything you say!" I saw the light.

"Then leave this off now. You value your freedom that much I know."

"Julie, I've missed you so much!"

"I've missed you, too," she conceded grudgingly, "until I found out you were a car thief. Let's take this car back to those people right now! Jack, turn around!"

It was all that needed to be said. I stared over the seatback at her, and she raised her eyes to mine. Another minute of this and we would make it! I would back down, and relent if not kiss her very feet, which I would like to do anyway. Tears came to Jack's wife's eyes as she stared at us. Jack, who had sped up much faster each time she cried to him to stop, seemed to slouch suddenly, almost collapse, and then he pulled himself together and concentrated on his driving, but I could sense he approved of the tack Julie and I were taking and had his hopes up. However he was not going back there to take the car back to the people because we might all be arrested. He never even considered that. He was one boy who knew what had to be done. He was heading for home fast no matter what anyone said. Good old Jack.

The mood of redemption and togetherness was intense, explosive. It seemed that fishing trip and the four of us doing things together were finally about to materialize and much more. Added in very warmly was the risk the women had taken in trying to break up the party. They would have been accomplices if something had gone wrong. But at the same time I took an implied criticism from my moral certainty that Jack had been in on this with them. It was three against one. Something about him suggested a judgment on my relationship or rather lack of it with Julie that I'd never quite known he'd felt before, and he had unconsciously revealed it, and it irritated me. Not that he was going to say anything, his hunched posture at the wheel assured. But then, as I considered it, I was humble enough not to mind if Jack secretly thought I didn't know how to treat Julie right, because I agreed with him, and nothing could be more obvious, although she had her faults too.

What's more, to accept this from Jack (that is, his mere presence at this moment, aligned with the women, because how else would they have known about it let alone hidden in the back seat) might even be enough to finish off the guilt I had always felt about him, as if I were always leading him on in business matters, such as our car shop that never materialized, and this hijacking of cars, because it would be admitting that he knew more about life than I did, which I suddenly realized he plainly did, managing to keep his marriage together through thick and thin as he did. An equality had suddenly come between us, weighted the more toward him, in fact, and liberating me.

Yep, we might all go on that fishing trip together yet, I thought in a rapture, and tables would be turned, doves of peace come home to rest, and we would be members of a wonderful community of friends which I am sure is the highest goal of freedom. I felt myself being liberated from *myself,* the highest kind of emancipation I'm sure. The fact was Julie's point of view now represented free will more than mine did, with my obsession with the white car. All my schemes collapsed of their own frenetic weight in the presence of my friends. It was time to quit while we were still winning, to say nothing of how much I needed her, and freedom from needs as we all know is insanity. I could even admit she was right, I had never denied she was right. Love allowed me to see everything in its softening redeeming light that seems to afford complete security to do so. Even if for just one fleeting moment.

"Julie, I looked for you before, and I really appreciate you looking for me. I hope to God we could try to be with each other again."

After a long silence in which she turned her head and looked out the window, she said, "I do too. But I don't know. Let's take this car back. I don't think I can stand to be in this car one more second I'm so scared! It makes me feel so vile and dirty!"

Imagine that, I thought, the white car made her feel dirty. That troubled me, I must say. I somewhat took this the wrong way. "You know what is vile and dirty, it's all the oblivious people wandering around here wondering if their teeth are white enough, or in summer if their skin is too white and not tan, whether there is going to be enough white snow for their ski trip or if there will be a white Christmas or they can get away to Jamaica and get a tan, and never give one moment of consideration that they owe it all to our forefathers who had the high criminal vision to commit genocide and ethnic cleansing of the Indian nations, to murder everybody in sight and wipe out their cultures!"

At this Julie's face certainly went a shade whiter, for she was troubled by what I said. By her own lights she knew the truth of it. I could sense that she was almost overwhelmed by the righteousness of my vision of things, could never gainsay it, and would not try again. As I glanced behind me at her sitting upright in the back seat of the white car, it was evident to me that she confronted the radical truths I and the white car presented, truths from which you must draw your own conclusions once you've seen them. You may go one direction or another after that, it doesn't matter, your feet are on the ground. But until you truly confront them and make a final judgment, you are just a vacationer on this planet, your views of no more weight than a tourist's.

By this time we had reached the garage where I kept the car in between appointments to sell it. I hit the electronic opener, and Jack drove under the door, which I closed behind us, leaving us in darkness. There were no windows in the shed.

Jack's wife in the total blackness before our eyes adjusted said, "Anyway, Jack is out of this as of right now. And if you know what's good for you, you better listen to Julie while you still have the chance." Her voice was trembling with contemptuous rage. It was as if I challenged her existence. If I went along with them, I knew she would get over it though, because she would know I had made the decision to give in, making her right.

"Those people back there might be the most recent owners of the white car, but they are not the only owners of it. So, I mean, I can't give it back. Which ones would I give it back to? It's like a chain letter," I explained, hoping to annoy her more. Jack's wife groaned loudly and lamentably.

"If people are going to be friends, let alone lovers again and soulmates, or husband and wife," I added daringly, "don't they need to listen to each other a little, and give a little bit?"

"Oh my God!" Jack's wife remonstrated bitterly. "No, you listen!" she shouted, but began laughing hysterically. "It's not my business," she apologized, chortling incredulously and manically.

I could tell she was thinking how incredibly stupid I was. And I was wondering myself. What in the world could I be saying? I didn't recognize my own voice. If I had gone as far as I could go on the warpath with the white car, and I decided so, and then there were business details to take care of, I had to take care of these myself, not explain them or put them up for a vote. How I could be insisting that anyone listen to me just now was a bit much also, I had to admit to myself. These matters were open to argument only up to a certain point. I seemed to have lost the thread of my own thoughts and I sat there in the darkness stubbornly.

"Look, are you quitting this horrible insane business for good right now?" asked Julie in a low tone. She seemed to have made her judgment.

"I want to be with you is all I want."

"You're going to get caught and go to jail this time. You have completely lost it this time. This is a crime *for real.* I mean one there's no excuse for. There's no way you can explain this to me. You have to stop this second if you want to be with me."

"Just sell it once more."

"What! You're out of your mind. Look—you have enough money. I mean there's never enough, and you're hip enough to know that. Why you haven't been caught yet, I don't know. I guess the cops are stupider idiots than you are."

"Listen, I just need to sell it once more. Maybe twice."

"Oh God. Have it your way, you always do. From what I hear you have enough. It's all over then if you don't think so."

"You always say that! 'You have enough.' If I had two cents, you'd say that was enough money, but if I told you you were never going to get another government grant, you'd jump out a window."

"Oh, boy," she moaned. "I knew it."

"Just in case your grant doesn't come through!"

"You're starting right up again, aren't you?"

She was right. The whole business had gotten sidetracked and we were all discussing nonissues. I wondered what I could be arguing about, because I did have plenty of money now, after having resold the white car all these times, more than enough to fix all my cars at Cloud Lake, way more than enough, so it wasn't that. Of course I should just quit. Now was the time. Before it really was too late. Especially to do as Julie wanted me to. Hadn't I made my statement with the white car, done what it had been sent me to do, and accomplished all that was ever going to be accomplished, since that was basically only going to be symbolic in nature and a spiritual gesture? There was no "enough" or "once more" about it.

We would all live happily ever after. Maybe Jack and I could open that car shop, or I'd go back to work at the dealer or even for Harry, whatever it took. But in another part of me I felt like arguing with her, because she was arguing with me and refused to see the practical side of things as they stood right now. Why couldn't she see things like I did just once? And there was something more, of course. I wanted her to understand.

"Look, you are into Indian culture and what they knew about life and nature and things. Think about what we did to the Indians for a minute. Every last white person in this country is doing their thing and making money and partying and having the good life on the basis of we robbed and murdered the Indians and stole their land and whole way of life from them. Our whole country is based on this heinous crime—do you think a few minor auto thefts amount to anything by comparison?"

"Oh, man, wow, Indians, oh, I know, I knew it . . . gimme a break, really. How can you do evil things to people like this?" she groaned. "*Hurt* people."

She seemed to be actually asking me, but how do you ask something like that. Anyway since she asked, I was trying to tell her. In the end I did not think she really accepted it, or that Jack or his wife saw it either. Jack had only been in on it as a great game, a dangerous diversion, a chance to show his mettle, and I doubted he ever really saw anything of what I had tried to explain to him about the Native Americans while we rode.

"Every last co-ed and hippy on the Ave is up to her elbows in blood, let alone those car buyers. Especially the hippies, okay?

Invisible Car Dealer

All our so-called highs and happiness begin with indecent acts and mass murder. Those are not innocent lambs I have stolen the white car from. Those are accessories after the fact of genocide, lynching, burning people, and unimaginable desecrations."

The white car had come to me as in a dream one night, a gift from fate when I had been as low as any drunken Indian without hope on the reservation, that is, I had accepted the fate of those dispossessed people in my heart then, I dispossessed them no longer. I had meant to dispossess a few white people was all. I sat there groping in the darkness of my mind, trying to remember how it had been with me then, how it still was, so I could explain myself further. I seemed not to be finished with it. At the same time I was overcome with memory how it had been with us, Julie and me, and how much I'd missed her, and I sought the bridge between us that I would not jump off.

"Look, I'm just going to sell it a couple of more times, okay? Then I have to get rid of it in the right way. That won't be easy. It can't just sit around or be . . . abandoned. Realistically, as a practical matter, that will take a few days. I'm doing this for the *Indians*, Julie!"

"The—! Thumbing your nose at good people, and hurting them, for no reason, except you are above it all. Because everybody is corrupt, evil and weak so stick their faces in it and go them one better because you don't have any morals at all!"

"Your Native Americans, baby, they cleared them out along with the wolves! Dispossessed them, robbed them, massacred them and exterminated them, wiped the land clean of them, as they felt called to do. Not even because they were so evil, but just because they goddam *felt* like it and could do it. Genocide, fair and square."

"Some poor girls who are buying their first car? For God's sake man, *please!*" She stifled a sob.

"*Your* Native Americans, Julie, that *know* things. Shot in their tents, in the freezing dawn, shot in the back, with no shred of dignity, chiefs and even even children. All left for dead! Burned alive. Nobody has a problem with that! Since it is our manifest destiny including those girls, I'm taking something back for *them!*"

"Oh boy . . . are you nuts," she muttered softly, but I could almost hear her involuntarily giving in to my brutal unanswerable logic in the darkness because we were at it again, and she loved it just like I did. I was suddenly turned on to her, and I knew that she was to me, in the midst of all the horror, in spite of herself.

"I told you if you didn't face up to it, it would haunt you forever, it would get to you, and boy, it *has* gotten to you!" But there was a tremor in her voice that showed I had gotten to her too.

The garage door suddenly flew upward in a clatter of steel bearings in their tracks, and we were flooded with searching daylight, like the disorienting unpleasant sunlight you emerge into after seeing a tearjerker of a matinee afternoon movie in the darkness of a theater. Jack had hit the garage door button right out of my hand. He gripped me by the forearm and gave me the driest look imaginable. "Take care, buddy. You don't know the caster from the camber."

It was the funniest thing to have said. You know, that has to do with the pitch at which the wheels are set. He was always more of a mechanic than I was. As he got out of the car, I tried to grab his hand and give him the cash, his half of the deal that had just gone down. He wouldn't take it. I was very eager for him to have it, as it was his fair share, but I wasn't desperate about it.

"You aint right!" yelled his wife and bolted from the car.

He went after his wife. I could hear their footsteps in the street, but then I heard them stop too soon, and I knew they were waiting for Julie. I reached out and took her hands and squeezed them, and she squeezed back, and we looked into each other's eyes.

"Are we going to blow it again?" I said.

"You have to stop *running*, man."

"Just give me two days, Julie." I wanted her to say yes to something I said. Actually I was ready to get rid of the car and come with her that minute. *"One* day!"

She eyed me grimly. "Not even one more minute."

I saw that it was just like that night after the Indian when she had run into her house, and that it was going to end that way again.

"I have to deal with the car properly. I can't just leave it by the side of the road like we did that poor Indian," I heard the sullen belligerence creep in my voice that seemed to belie my words.

As soon as I'd said that, I couldn't believe that I had. I could see her eyes fill with sadness and horror. "It hasn't left you alone either," I said knowing I was wrong in every way. "You might as well have come with me," I went on rubbing it in when there was nothing to rub. We had been through all this already, and there would be no reprieve.

That did it. A blank serenity or curtain of indifference passed over her features and wordlessly she pulled away her hands and ran after Jack and his wife. She didn't look back. I sat in the car, feeling mean and foolish for having brought it up again. We'd had our moment of truth, and there would not be another. She was gone, again. My friend Jack, too. I wondered if I had behaved badly in a way that was incredibly small and stupid. These people were extremely important to me, they were great people, the best people, and I loved, respected, and valued them, and they were sincerely trying to help me to do the sane thing. What a vain character I probably was, I knew. All that forlorn history I was harping about was long gone. I or nobody could ever do a thing about it. Apparently I felt the world's weight on my shoulders and was proud of it.

Sitting alone in the white car listening to their footfalls outside, then the rich thunk, thunk of the Porsche's doors as the three of them crammed inside it (where would I have sat anyway? it was a two-seater, but I guess we would have squeezed in) and slammed them, and the soft rumble of its pipes for a minute after Jack started up, while they waited there for something, me, I guess, our history together, I felt oppressed by an exploding weight on my chest as if I were leaving the earth and being crushed by gravity as I rocketed past an invisible barrier into some terrible outer twilight zone into which my truth and pride were leading me. I longed to give up my convictions and run after my friends and tell them how much I loved and needed them, but beautiful people as they were, the whole scene no longer made sense to me. It seemed somehow untruthful and even second rate. I could not return to their warmth and decency, because I had seen too clearly all the evil and horror that underpinned it, which somehow I had been doing my best in my own blundering way to erase, even if I was just compounding it, making everything worse, when common sense should have told me to just let go.

The final thing to say about the truths I had spoken to Julie and the others is that I meant every word. I think that is why they all vanished so suddenly, they knew how insane truth can be.

Invisible Car Dealer

Maybe I should have settled for one of those compromises on which the good life for people is always built, if not civilization itself. I could still leap out of the white car, race out of my garage and join them, if I knew what was good for me. They were waiting for me, those kind, cool friends. I didn't need to go ahead into nowhere. But I couldn't move a little finger against the horrible weight that was pressing me down in my seat as I seemed to head into ice-cold outer space. Nor did I want the trip to stop. My abiding impression was that I was making a ridiculous and terrible mistake letting my beautiful friends go. I felt the redoubled loneliness would cut me in two. But then I noticed it had a delicious edge to it. I missed them unbearably, yet with them gone, something light and lovely began stirring in my breast. I was glad to be rid of them, glad to be alone again. I savored the stab of the cutting knife, the soaring thrill of the onset of a new wave of freedom.

Invisible Car Dealer

From the first moment I won my freedom, or accidentally crashed into it, I've had time to think. More than enough time. Still, I've begun to have an insight into human nature, with its infatuation with the next thing, which is nothing but a towering cliff that keeps on thrusting up into the sky ahead of us as we climb, the view ever more resplendent as time goes on, about whose munificence in future we can barely speculate, full of faith though we are, a view with everything you would ever hope for, the kindest, most helpful things, those intangible nurturing things, superabundant, exciting, ever newly discovered, fruitful and grand, no Indians in sight, increase of freedom, gifts of power, secrets untold, knowledge replete, complete with a blessed forgetfulness—and the urge to jump.

     Yep, the white man, and every color of man, and woman, if they're interested, and apparently they are (that's an irony isn't it? as the white man disappears, every other tribe, and the females, who replace him, turn out to be—what else?—the white man all over again), needn't fear that there won't always be a new frontier, because that's the easiest question of all, it's only the next thing. I can attest to that. The *last* thing, that's the real, the interesting question. Only there is a certain exasperating invisibility to it that puts people off. Not that the last thing doesn't depend on the next thing. As a good American, I'm sure it does, I have faith, and have always believed that beyond the next thing is that good thing, as we all believe. Anyway, it is all rushing past me now.

After I parted from my friends, I might have sold the white car a couple more times, yes I did, who knows, maybe two or three more times, at least, I won't say. I was in the habit of it was all. By now I had plenty of money, more than enough to last somebody like me with few wants a long time. I had received my final warning that day from Julie, Jack, and Jack's wife, dear friends that they were, or had been. I was on thin ice, they were right. I couldn't drive past a squad car without severe palpitations any more.

The time came when I figured I'd better part with my darling demon of a white car before codependence reached its ultimate conclusion in mutual self-destruction. The trouble is you want an adventure like that to go on forever. I realized I had to sink the knife first, in self-defense, into my beauty's heart.

Before I did though, I drove back up to Indian country, to look somebody up, and to see if all my old wrecks were still there. They hadn't rolled into the lake yet. I spent a day or two trying to find out who the guy was who had come by my shack that night with his little boy, after his brother had been drowned. But that kind of an investigation would have taken days, time I didn't think I had. So finally I just headed for the Flame Bar. From outside I could hear it rocking tonight, and there were cars and pickups parked all over. Inside, I scanned the crowd. Nobody paid me any attention at first. I saw the guy at the bar, the main troublemaker who had picked on me that night. He recognized me too as I walked up. He was so shocked to see me his curiosity made his expression almost friendly, but his words weren't.

"Look who's back. What are you doin here again?"

I didn't waste time with conversation, but opened my briefcase full of cash on top of the bar. I asked him if he knew my cabin over by Cloud Lake with my old cars parked around it. I really didn't know if he would have ever noticed it, or if he would admit to it if he had, but to my surprise, he said, "Yeah, I seen it. Why?"

This guy was so cool that after once glance at the mounds of cash in the briefcase he did not look at it again. However several others were crowding around.

"Do any of you guys fix cars? They are all yours." From a pocket inside the case I pulled out several titles. Some of the old cars even had titles although not all of them. Some of them were too far gone to need a title anyway. I threw the titles onto the pile of cash.

"What do we want with that junk." He was assiduously not eyeing all the cash lying in the open briefcase before him.

"If you fix them up they would be worth a fortune, and here is some money for you guys to fix them up with."

His mouth dropped open then. By now several others had crowded in around us and I was surrounded.

"What are you doin here? What do you want?"

"Not buy a goddamn fish!"

"He's Fish and Game," said somebody. "This is a setup."

"There's nothin for sale here, nothin for you."

Somebody standing in the doorway exclaimed, "Hey look what he's driving! You oughta see this! Look at his ride, this white car out here!"

"I think he's FBI. It's a trap."

"Well for God's sake at least I can buy you a drink!" I laughed at the inevitable pass we found ourselves in once more. I grabbed a handful of the bills and threw them on the bar, which impressed the bartender anyway. "Drinks for everybody! For the next two days! Ha ha!" I grabbed another bunch of hundreds and gave them to the bartender. "The next week!"

"What is this anyway," said the ringleader absently and suspiciously but with a faint tremble. The bartender had the smarts not to look at the gift horse too closely and was opening beers right and left with one hand as he pocketed some of my cash with the other. But my old acquaintance stood there remembering a long and bitter history and wouldn't stop wondering about everything.

"Are you Fish and Game? We don't do nothin like that. You're in the wrong place. What the hell is this?"

"Make me a pizza," I said to the bartender and threw him a fifty. After he folded the bill neatly into his pocket, he pulled one from the freezer and put it into the microwave straightaway.

"You want to know what this is about?" I said to the guys crowding around me.

"Leave him alone!" yelled a pretty woman at my side. She wound her arms around me charmingly, and reached out one hand to shove the bartender's elbow. "Make mine a Manhattan!"

Invisible Car Dealer

A Manhattan. I couldn't help smiling bitterly at that. I glanced sharply at her to see if she was joking darkly. But she seemed innocent and serious. I doubted that the bartender had any idea what a Manhattan was. Anyway, he ignored her.

"You want to know what this is for?" I repeated more loudly as I gestured at the thousands of dollars, in fact, tens of thousands of dollars—about $40,000, although I hadn't bothered counting it. "This is for . . . you know those fucked up treaties they signed . . . all the ones they broke no sooner than they signed them, I don't even know what they made those treaties for, a figleaf I guess. I guess they made those treaties in order to have something to break, right? How would they break them if they didn't make them? There would be no progress at all. But this here . . ." I pointed at the money in a heap in the briefcase on the bar. "This here, friends . . . is . . . *reparations.* I'm only one guy and there is so much I can do . . . but this here is MY REPARATIONS!"

I leaned back with self-satisfaction at my speech. The bartender filled the glass of the young lady who had wanted a Manhattan with something. She slugged it back and now with some friends started to dance. They threw back their heads and began to sing a pop song in snatches. Whatever it was, they seemed happy. Now and again somebody came up to me and gave me a solemn handshake of approval. Money will do that! The main guys were crowding the bar and discussing the money, ignoring me benignly. I would have wished it no other way.

If you think I wanted to hang around with them now and be a blood brother, you're wrong. If recently I had conceived of my condition as "Indian," this had been to explain myself to myself, not a vain, despicable delusion. I am a white guy, I am more convinced of that every day. I was satisfied with my gesture. Anyway, I wasn't Sleazy Rider anymore. Or maybe I was, I don't know. As soon as I got my pizza, I took it with me and ate it in the car as I drove south.

I'm sure God loves and forgives our forebears, who wiped out the Indians enthusiastically and ferociously, out of greed, piety, to settle scores, to protect their families, with an eye on the next tract of land, or mostly just because they felt like doing it—that is, the bloodthirsty, lusty, "hot and cold" sinners, caught up in the thick of things—much more than the lukewarm population of today who have forgotten all about such crimes and sins, swept them under the rug, don't give such things a passing thought anymore, except to say "I wasn't there," and "that's the way it is," won't hear of helping anybody out, least of all any Indians, and have never seen an American Indian close up that they know of anyway, and certainly don't ever read one of those Bibles when they are in a motel room, and are just "getting ahead in life" "without hurting anybody." The white car had been sent me to scourge a representative sample of this lukewarm population, and I had done my best.

Eventually the day came when I went out to Richmond to see Dahomey, parked the white car in front of his wrecking yard, where she glimmered shyly like a snowball in hell, like a lamb for the slaughter. I was distraught, almost in tears. I felt crazy with mixed emotions since, although you might not have a lot of admiration for what she did mean to me, you can see how the white car meant a lot. That car was more than a friend, more than an accomplice in the shadow world I had been living in.

In spite of the urgency of my position, I was in a weird and pensive mood when I walked in looking for Dahomey. When I found him in his office, I felt so glad to see him, I couldn't help telling him so.

By the blank look he returned me, I figured he must think I was drunk, dissembling, or leading up to something, which of course I was. But it was just the mood I was in, exhausted. I had never thought of him as a friend before, and now he was like a long, lost friend. Before I knew it, I had launched into the most unlikely speech about how I admired him, how much I appreciated what he had accomplished in his life, considering his beginnings, and so forth. What did he care what I thought of him? In the middle of a sentence I suddenly realized how I must sound, or I realized I had no idea. I handed him the appropriate amount of cash, probably a little too much. He stared at me blankly like I was a form of notoriously unintelligent and distant life and, pocketing the money, walked away, saying over his shoulder, "Get busy!"

Dahomey had looked at me as though I had soiled him with my affection. This had a chastening effect, and brought me back to the day's hard reality. The world might look like a cold, vicious place to me, and I might wish to be buddies with the wrecker, as lonely as I was, after my crimes, just to show myself there was a drop of warmth left, but that didn't prove that everybody was in as bad shape as I was. Dahomey loved Jack who was a Vietnam vet but that didn't mean he would ever like me. He assumed when I expressed some liberal sentiments about life and my admiration for himself that I was trying to con him, and of course Dahomey himself was no liberal, far from it. I was almost shaking with the unacknowledged feelings and apprehensions of the moment of truth I faced. After the white car, what did I have left?

Once again the torches sparked and burned, and the white car was reduced to ragged chunks of silver. I had been learning many lessons on the shadow-side of freedom, but the last was that pushed to the limit, the mind and body that are too free begin to decompose and float into space. I had quit in the nick of time. Nothing is more tempting in the kind of adventure I'd been having than the idea of prolonging it.

Down the vast yard the black cliffs of Chevys blended in with the Buicks and the Fords, and now into these hills the bones of the white car would be laid. The dismantlers and torch-men descended on the poor body, their outfits spitting blue flame, their air tools whining, drops of molten steel flying sideways like windblown rain, shorn bolts, shreds of trim, and jigsaw puzzle pieces of red-hot metal trickling and shooting to the ground beneath their feet, the chaff of a harvest ecstasy, a winnowing I felt to the bottoms of my feet. Various useful organs were set aside for transplants later. The glass-man cut out the windshield. For some reason the pain of watching that was the worst of all, like an eyeball being removed. The doors were plucked off, dripping wings. The poor carcasse of the white car picked clean by army ants was lifted onto a flat-bed truck bound for the crusher with others, which rolled out of the yard with the solemnity of a hearse, and in the end there was nothing left but a little glitter on the ground.

This time, of course, Jack had not had a hand in the operation. Dahomey, having given his permission and directed his workmen, understanding the urgency concerning the white car, and caressing the fee I had laid in his palm, had retreated behind the counter of the office to joke with the customers and help them persevere through yet another delay.

Gladstone, the African, nearby, all his attention absorbed by the progress of some job of his own, had never even glanced up once. I don't think he had the slightest idea what the white car was or had been, or wanted to know. He was too sane and focused. If Jack and I by some chance ever had opened that car shop of ours together, I would have done my best to hire Gladstone away from Dahomey, visa or no visa. I admired his craftsmanship, for whom the immediate task was the be-all and end-all of everything for the duration, and who didn't stick his nose in where it didn't belong. A sort of rare wisdom seemed to emanate from the Nigerian.

Once it was all over, I felt a profound relief that the incriminating evidence was gone, and the car could no longer get me into trouble. At the same time, the main prop in my show was no more, and the show would no longer go on, and I was bereft and completely at loose ends. I was just standing in the big yard, not knowing where to go, or what to do next. Now that I had plenty of money, and nothing whatever I needed to do, and the last material tie having been unfastened, I faced the harrowing prospect of real freedom, total freedom.

I had to leave town, hide out, lay low, do nothing, enjoy myself, and let time pass, forever. That was my plan, but I feared being engulfed in a wave of confusion, regret, and boredom, in short *pure freedom*, once I had nothing to do and no friends to do it with. Memories of Cloud Lake were still fresh. It might be far worse. Things were sometimes. Without the white car I felt abysmally lonely and abandoned. Watching the white car cut up was like watching the lynching of a family member. It was hard to admit to myself I didn't have the white car any more, I felt at a loss, even violated and deprived. But I did feel free, suddenly whistling a happy phrase, and even dancing a step or two in the dust.

"Poof! It's invisible!" remarked Gladstone, the African, looking up, grinning, perhaps noticing my manic state, who had taken no part in the dismemberment and transformation, but who somehow at this moment pronounced the most fitting benediction.

"What did you say?" I wanted to be sure I had heard rightly such a charming, redeeming comment that seemed fraught with strange grace.

"*Invisible!*" exclaimed Gladstone, grinning jubilantly and mysteriously at me.

Invisible? Invisible suggested not altogether gone but here in some new dimension, right? He was just playing and having fun, another admirable aspect of his character. It made me hopeful somehow, out of nothing. As little as I had been around him, Gladstone had always made a happy impression on me. On the one hand he was clearly a sound and useful man or else his tenure at Dahomey's would have been cut short long ago. A solid and responsible workman, he "added value," as the catchphrase goes. He exuded sense and his judgment was conservative. Something antic and playful about the man, on the other hand, added even more to the exchange, some spice, or energy, coming out of fruitful left field, as I apprehended him. More than quick-witted, where he was coming from, Africa, there was no margin for error, life danced on the edge, was unsentimental and even cruel, but could be nice. Not knowing how else to put it to myself, I left it with his Africanness, something direct, even primitive, sly and sure. I always had liked him, and not knowing him in the least, I was moved to trust him, and hear what he said.

Invisible! I must have looked at him with dismay and fascination. The notion began to prey on me, of *invisibility*, the ultimate freedom, I suppose. I turned the idea around in my mind. In some sense you could say the white car still existed, or Gladstone had implied as much, it was just invisible. Maybe this was an African idea. I had heard they were good businessmen. If the white car was now invisible, as Gladstone had seriously jested, did that mean you could still sell it?

I did some fast thinking. Maybe you could just as well keep selling it, like a view of some famous landmark in the luminous distance, couldn't you, why not? The view would be into another world, even better. I had a hunch there were people that would appeal to, especially around San Francisco and Berkeley. The advantages were obvious. For starters, you didn't have to park it anywhere or ever have to fix it or put gas in the tank. I placed a new ad in the newspaper.

Invisible Car. Indescribable. One-owner. Phone . . .

I wondered what in the world I was doing, to tell the truth. The callers (who started calling right away) thought I was only being coy, or poetic, or something like that. Maybe it was "performance art." They were sure something was going on, and that they were onto something, and they wanted to find out what it was, and be in on the party. They were determined to find out what make of car I really alluded to, or if not, what the heck I was talking about, as if it were all going to be something special, and a happy surprise. Universally, people believe in happy surprises, and something special, or all salesmen would be out of business. There are also people with a lot of time on their hands who read the classifieds from beginning to end, apparently.

Some who called imagined it was not a car at all, but something else altogether and wondered what. In other words, it was a metaphor. That was amusing to me. I had a hunch it was completely the opposite, an *anti-metaphor*. A *real* step onto some invisible "level." At first I made the mistake of playing along for the sheer fun of it, and encouraging these callers, and one of them finally made an appointment to meet me. Oh boy, that was going to be a moment of truth. Anyway it was passing the time for me.

It's always better to play hard to get and make them chase you, thereby getting half the sales job over with before you even start, but I was just as curious as they were to find out what in the world an invisible car could be all about and didn't want to be too hard to get. I could hardly wait. I named a street corner nearby, almost at random, as good a spot as any to see nothing, although I thought I recalled some kind of garage there. I couldn't remember what was on or around that corner, but as I approached the intersection of our rendezvous a few minutes ahead of schedule, I did see a car shop named Sonny's Speed Shop nearby in the middle of the block.

Shortly, I led the party who had called there. We recognized each other at once by a sort of mystified look in the eye. I saw him as soon as he drove up and his eyes instantly found mine. We were both in a daze on the street corner. We walked fast in the doorway of Sonny's together, eager to make a discovery. I wondered if the prospective buyer's heart was beating as fast as mine. I inquired if he had brought the deposit.

"Deposit?"

"That we spoke of on the phone. The 'visible token.'"

"Token? Yeah, I remember. I didn't know what you were talking about. Ride the bus? What is this? I don't have any deposit. Let's see the car first."

Invisible Car Dealer

"See? What do you mean, see? It's not going to be easy. I mean it'll take some faith. I mean, it's *invisible*, like the ad said. Like I said to you. What's more, Speedy Sonny isn't going to get it out of storage unless you have the deposit."

"How much?"

"Five hundred. We discussed this. I told you that."

"We did? All right. I have that."

"Well let's see it."

"I've got it. It's invisible for the moment, ha ha."

"Well, let me hold it, touch it, while I tell Sonny. I won't look at it, I won't even count it. You'll be right next to me but I have to hold something. He'll want to see the color of it. There's a little too much invisibility going on already for his taste without your deposit being invisible too, okay? That may be too much for him."

"Get outa here. Where is this thing? All I can say, this car better be beautiful. All right, here!" He flashed a wad of bills at me, but didn't seem to want to let me hold any of it.

"Never mind. Come on." I led him further into the shop, past the waiting area, to a doorway through which mechanics could be seen working on and under cars on hydraulic racks. I stepped just inside like I knew what I was doing and the interested party followed grinning. A busy-looking man behind a podium-like desk talking animatedly on the phone glanced at us without interest.

"Hey, there she is!" I smiled proudly. "He's brought it out."

"Which one? Where?"

"There, behind Sonny. He brought it out already. One of a kind!"

"What in the world! I don't see anything."

"Naturally. What are you talking about? If you could see it, it wouldn't be an invisible car, would it? I keep telling you. It was in the ad. Just let me hold the money so I know you're sincere. Then you can touch it, feel it, rub your hands all over her. I'm not going anyplace. We'll walk over and you can feel it."

"Is this some kind of trick? I don't think you'd bring me over here for a complete joke but I'm starting to wonder."

"Of course not. The car is invisible. But you'll be able to feel it, put your hands on it and rub its pretty fenders . . . when I point out exactly . . . where it is."

"How do you do it, mirrors?"

256

Invisible Car Dealer

At that, the guy took a step toward the podium, trying to see in every direction around the shop, past the shop foreman standing there.

"How do you do it, like with lights?"

"Go on, if you want. Ask *him*. Sonny's got the keys."

The idea of asking the service manager where the invisible car was seemed to strike him as both reasonable and absurd at the same time, creating paralysis and possibility, so that he lurched forward and backward several times, winding up in the same spot. He gave me a searching look. "Here, you can hold a hundred," he said as if that would give him the moral right to advance, and he handed over that much of his cash. He took a few quick steps forward.

"Go ahead!" A hundred was better than nothing. This was just an experiment. As he took another couple of steps toward the foreman who was now squinting at us strangely, I took the opportunity to step backward. When he glanced over his shoulder at me, my retreat had been concealed by his own motion.

"Where?"

I pointed again and again toward a far corner of the garage and made shooing movements with my fingertips. Compelled by what misbegotten hope I can't imagine, he suddenly marched rapidly forward and began talking to the foreman, gesturing with his thumb at me.

Then he headed past the open-mouthed foreman straight to the back of the place I had pointed at, with Sonny's manager vaguely scowling after him. I took the opportunity of running out the door and raced around the corner. A hundred wasn't much, but it was an interesting beginning.

People had to be discouraged from thinking I was concealing something, trying to whet their curiosity, that sort of thing. That had been the problem, I didn't need buyers like that. So from then on, when they asked, I did my utmost to impress on them that the car really was invisible, just as advertised, they would never be able to see it, and it wasn't a symbol for something else either. My honesty took a few moments to sink in, but eventually after I had repeated myself a few times, it cooled their ardor, and they hung up with expressions of annoyance and disbelief, but none of us had to waste our time.

Invisible Car Dealer

There were others though who didn't seem to want to give up. Nothing could shake their suspicion that I was playing some cagey, fascinating game. Vaguely and circumspectly, not completing their sentences, they tried to trick and bluff information out of me. These were some of the strangest conversations I've ever had, and none of them got anywhere, and ended with soft clicks.

"What makes it come visible then? What is the secret?" They supposed it was a condition or state that could be altered, and I had to repeat, "Invisible, permanently." I renewed the ad and hung on to see what would happen. I got a few crank calls, a few maniacs, also some heavy breathers who were sure it had to have something to do with exotic unimaginable sex that they had always dreamed of. To these I couldn't help admitting that it definitely might, but when I insisted their partner would forever be invisible, they hung up without arranging a rendezvous.

Whom did I hope would call? A scientist, a guru, who would explain it all to me? Intelligent life on the line, at last? After several days, and with the conversations becoming steadily less droll, that someone I may have been waiting for finally called.

"*Why* can't it be seen?" Nobody had asked *why* before.

"Think of it this way. You have lite beer, lite desserts, skim milk, meat without fat, eggs without yolks, coffee without caffeine, fast food with no taste. The classics are made into musicals. Drugs give the kids instant wisdom. Computers save us work and deprive us of time. The zeitgeist is a certain lite-headedness. Nobody wants to be bothered, and why should they? You want a car whose ride is so lush, quiet, exquisitely engineered, and safe, you experience it only as pure possessive bliss and ownership-induced nirvana, without even the objectionable sensation of motion, don't you? Let alone the necessity of buying tires. Or you buy the invisible car and ride your bike instead like in the Saab ads. Pollutant-free for your environmentally conscious neighbors and couldn't be any safer since half the time you can't find it."

"Christ, you're a crook and insane too."

"Yeah, I'm a crook and you're a kook for still being on the phone."

"I admire your nerve, anyway. You mean you're selling, essentially, nothing? I love it. I don't believe it."

"Believe it. Nothing exactly that you can *see* anyway."

Invisible Car Dealer

"Man, you know, ha ha, you're gonna wind up in trouble, if you don't get killed first."

"Another dead Injun."

"There's something familiar about your voice."

There was something familiar about *his* voice too.

I'd had the tremulous feeling that anything might happen on some wonderful new frontier I was crossing in an *invisible car*. Then a bolt from the past and the night. Yes, there was something horribly familiar about the caller's voice, I wondered how I could have forgotten the old villain. My heart took off like an engine with a rod knock, and my veins swelled with murder. There was that leering, smiling tone in his voice, as always, as if he didn't care what traps you were laying for him, he knew all about them, he'd invented them, a man who really didn't hide his intention of eating you bones and all. It was Harmless Harry. He, of all people, had bitten, and I knew at last why I had placed the ad in the paper.

From the moment we made the appointment and I slammed down the phone, I couldn't keep still. I paced back and forth across the motel room staring at my watch. I didn't know what I was thinking, my head was burning hot but my brain was solid ice. For the first time in ages I pulled out my Beretta 9mm, and checked to see that it was fully loaded. I switched off the safety and then switched it on again. I hid the gun at first behind the microwave, then moved it behind a more accessible lamp.

"You've swindled poor girls out of their savings, you've said goodbye for the second time to your best girl and best friend, you've stared to the bottom of the abyss into which whole cultures were thrown in the name of national progress, and you can't handle an old fart with a red wig?" I told myself.

There are people you don't want to tangle with again, no matter how able you become, because they bring with them a whiff of former times, when they had your number. I was just about to duck out the door and check out of the motel when he knocked. I could tell him even in his imperative but somehow sly knock. The impulse to escape had come too late. I had given him my room number. I couldn't hide, he'd know I was in here, and be laughing at me. I felt stripped naked. It was too horribly pathetic that Harry of all people had seen that ad and smelled something. I felt ridiculous to be selling Harry an invisible car. Harry would laugh in my face at the condition I'd sunk to. I suddenly felt exactly what kind of shape I was in, and Harry would see this instantly, and call my bluff. Until now I had felt on the vertiginous edge of new knowledge, I'd felt clear as a bell, and filled with holy anticipation. Now I seemed to have come to the grubby end of a dead-end alley only to come face to face with Harmless Harry.

Still it seemed to me this confrontation was the secret and invisible reason Gladstone had cracked that joke and I had placed that classified ad. To confront Harry. Harry didn't even pretend surprise seeing me, just grinned quick and looked at me with a hint of superior disapproval like a teacher confronting a student's prank. I wondered why he'd come. It was almost midnight. His suit was rumpled, and his tie loose, and his orange hairpiece sat on his dome about as gracefully as if he were balancing a pumpkin pie there. His face was flushed, his shoulders covered with bits of dandruff or eczema. He'd had the whole day and night to let his appearance disintegrate, and it was none too choice first thing in the morning. He didn't care, he actually seemed to imagine he cut quite a figure. There was hardly anything holding Harry together but his malevolent spirit.

I tried to draw some satisfaction from the fact that he had come to see me this time, not the other way around, but the second he came in, he seemed to belong here more than I did and to command the situation. He was the sort of old wise-ass who looked totally in his element in any kind of public accommodation, hotel, restaurant, including my motel room whose generic and ersatz furnishings matched him to a T. The car dealership, an impersonal and façade-like environment if there ever was one, had always fitted him like a glove and seemed like his very artificial home-sweet-home. Salesmen in the showroom, like waiters when he went to a restaurant, hovered around him expectantly, drawn like filings to the magnet of the moneyed authority he exuded, seedy though he was in his unkempt suits, which never fit him right. He looked like he could give you a large tip or nice bonus, and never would, thus perfecting his animal magnetism. So he took over in two seconds my motel room and turned it into a sordid scene of misery and contempt, as in my old days at the dealership. He brought with him the awful dominating atmosphere of the showroom which immediately enveloped me like a poison gas.

Invisible Car Dealer

I wanted to stumble out of the room and run away. But I was held in place by his negative charm as always, and after all he was answering my ad in the paper, not the other way around. But just as always, I was waiting for him to dispense with me or tell me I had to work late. Somehow, just like always, he intended to rob me, it was the only game he played. I knew he was going to rob me, of my self-esteem first of all, and I gathered my wits as best I could, tried to plan my defense, and struggled to pull myself together.

Harry slowly hobbled over to a chair without being asked, before he'd said a word to me. It was crystal clear he thought no more of me than he ever had, invisible car or no. The way he squinted at me even made me wonder if he did remember me, or if he did, whether he attached any importance to it. A salesman of his age and everyday experience must remember thousands of people, and not many of them happy enough memories to want to keep. He collapsed into the chair with the oblivious air of somebody whose comfort came first, who might even die on the spot as a matter of fact. He licked his lips and wheezed, pulled out his checkbook and examined it in his spotted hand. Then glancing sharply at me, as if to catch me eyeing his checkbook, he grinned luridly and knowingly, and tucked his checkbook out of sight again firmly, as if to tell me he knew what was on my mind but that I wasn't likely to get a glimpse of it again.

Same old act. Same powerplay. What an old ham. But he knew how to buy a car, I guess the old rat did. As much as a shark can swim. And bite. I could feel his old blunt snout nudging me, in fact I could feel the teeth sinking in already. An invisible car would be nothing much for Harry, because he intended always to pay you with invisible money if possible.

"Harry," I said, my voice shaking, "I don't work for you any more, remember? I'm selling, you're buying this time, so don't pull your old airs on me. Because I don't care if you buy the invisible car or not, you know?"

"Hm! Don't talk to me that way, boy! I taught you that pitch. I could have met you in the lobby, neutral ground, but I thought I might as well be comfortable, since this car of yours is invisible, and I can't see it anyway, I guess, is that right? That's the big build-up. Your idea of one anyway. Okay, what is it? This better be good."

Invisible Car Dealer

He thought I had something up my sleeve, something *not* invisible to sell, just like other callers. He thought my ad was a bait and switch, like he would have done. Suddenly he just looked like a sad old man, trying to earn some extra income, maybe after a not successful night of looking for cars. Probably he had nothing else to do. It had seemed like some car type entertainment to him. I wondered what had happened to his girlfriend. She had probably been some whore. I seemed to see behind his operator's façade his sordid loneliness, and felt my terror of him drain away.

"I don't know what the game is yet, but why are you doing it? Outsiders think they're smart but they always work twice as hard. You can come back to work for me, fella, I always need good salesmen. That's why I came here. To offer you some honest work. I know you aint got anything worthwhile enough for me to see."

"That's not what you're here for."

"Maybe it is," he said, giving me his teacher's look again. "You'd be better off, you know." He always did like to pretend he was doing his boys a big favor.

"Just tell me if you want to buy the car, yes or no."

"What are we talking about? So big deal, it's invisible. It's special, a big surprise, what else is new? You think you can beat me with techniques I taught you? This is me, boy, Harmless Harry!"

"No."

"No? No what? I can't see it? You think I'm a mark or something? If I say yes I'll buy, if I promise you I'm tantalized by your ad, really interested, and promise not to tell anybody the dirty truth in case I don't buy, can I see it?"

"No."

"No? Why the ad in the paper then. Why am I here?"

"No. You remember *no*, don't you? I heard you say it enough times."

"So if I fork over a down payment, you thief?"

"It's invisible, Harry, like the ad said. You can't see it."

"So it's a big surprise. Gimme a break."

"I'm telling you everything I know about it. I can't see it either."

"Haw-haw-haw! You're trying to tease me into giving you money, and it'll be a big piece of crap. It'll be nothing, in fact. It's the oldest scam going. An interesting variation thereof I admit. Then you'll try to keep a hundred bucks for your time, for your inconvenience, you sorry hustler. How about my inconvenience?"

"No, Harry, I'm telling you it's invisible. Even if you buy it, it will still be invisible."

"What make?"

"Invisible make."

"What? If I ride in it, will it still be invisible?"

"Yes."

"Really? Can I test-drive this monster?"

"Only if you decide absolutely you'll buy beforehand no matter what, and before that, you give me what you owe me."

"I would never be listening to this guff if I didn't know you. I couldn't believe it when I heard your voice on the phone. I wondered what had happened to you. I'm glad to see you looking in good health, I mean still alive, back in town. But you lost your mind. I told you you'd come back, I knew you'd come back, and I hope we do business again sometime. You can start work tomorrow selling for me. But I think your mind is fried. You need some time off first. What've you been up to you're in sad shape like this? You're under strain, aren't you, I can see that. I thought it was some kind of smart come-on, invisible, very catchy for the kids, time is passing me by. It's goddamned loony tunes. Are you high on drugs? Don't waste *my time*. You know one thing I'm almost religious about, *my time*."

"Look, I didn't invite you. You answered an ad. I used to know you, so I'm being patient. If you aren't interested, just go, no hard feelings. Don't waste *my* time." I gave my voice the most audacious edge imaginable, and it just got away with Harry. He started laughing uproariously. It was infectious and I laughed too, hating myself for doing so. I guess he could only picture me still in his showroom doing his bidding. But I had the strangest feeling that it was he who had taken a bite. Yes, the hook had gone in! I'd felt the tug on the line. We laughed together for a time.

"Okay, I'll pay!" he crowed disdainfully. He got out his checkbook and waved it around. "How much? A hundred enough for you?" He kept laughing, the tone of his laughter changing from real mirth to a contemptuous snicker and back again, like it was the funniest joke. "It's worth it for an invisible car! In a few minutes I'm calling the guys in the white coats!"

"I don't take checks from you. I know you got the cash."

He wheezed out an expletive or two and a big sigh. "Okay, okay, a hundred bucks, I got that much." From his wad he peeled off a C-note and tendered it to me. "This is the most outrageous hocum I ever heard, and I've heard every goofball gambit in the business, my boy, but if all this is some low-life runaround, I might even take back my offer to let you sell for me again, because maybe you lost your marbles completely on the road wherever you been.

"You don't know whether you're having a good time or not, do you, Harry? But I am."

I walked to the lamp and retrieved my gun from behind it. I didn't point it at him but let it dangle from my hand, just like he had that day when I had gone by to see him on my way out of town to get my commissions. It was hard to tell with Harry but I think it impressed him a little. Evil came into his old eyes, cold as a lizard's, opening wide involuntarily seeing the gun, but instantly narrowing to slits.

"What you owe me."

"What I owe *you!* What you owe *me,* boy!" He seemed genuinely perplexed, to show you just what an incorrigible old shark he was. What I owed him? There wasn't an honest piece of cartilage in his body.

"What you *owe* me, Harry!"

"I owe *you?*"

"Harry, you cheated me on my last check, remember?"

"No, I don't remember. I remember you up and quit on me without notice and left me short-handed of salesmen and I paid you anyway. Gimme back that hundred."

"Harry, you cheated me out of most of my commissions, you remember. I had to go on the road with my clothes in a paper bag."

"Who taught you everything you know? Who made you what you are!"

That did it. I didn't have to be reminded of that.

"Yes, Harry, you certainly did have some seriously unhelpful effects on my character, I will be the first to admit. You set me the worst example of anybody in my life, and at the end you wrote me a bad check."

"You're just sitting here trying to make me give you money for nothing—give you money so I can see and get nothing! Because the car is invisible! Have you done this to other people? I have made some great deals in my time, I admit, but I don't outright cheat people and sell them *nothing*. At least they get *something*. Has anybody given you their money to see something that's invisible? Anybody called the cops on you yet? You're just a crook now. I'm a businessman but you are a thief! People like me make the economy hum. You are a fool, you are!"

"You're calling me a thief, Harry? *You* ordered the Indian massacres and took their homes without a qualm. You're the Indian agent who gave them the smallpox blankets and the shopkeeper who sold them bad firewater at a high price! You caused Wounded Knee and the Trail of Tears—so greedy old boys like you could make a killing on some land deals. Yes, you taught me everything I know, and now I am going to teach you something!"

"I—I—! The *Indians*—!? Call the cavalry! Let me outa here!" He made a move to lurch to his feet. The habitual shady expression on his face had gone to a semi-serious one of concern.

"You are here because they are gone! We're all having a big party on their graves. The whole country is based on a crime—an *invisible crime,* one that has been totally forgotten. Only I am here to remind *you* about it, Harry! To remind *you!*"

As I aimed the gun at him, he fell back in the chair. I had half expected him to call my bluff and keep going. The true intentions and possibilities of the other guy are always invisible when it comes to a gun pointed at you. I contemplated pulling the trigger, just to see what it felt like to murder Harry. I saw the hint in his eyes already of surprise, or recognition, like in old cowboy movies when the bad guy gets it, his comeuppance, that it could happen to *him.* Back on the car lot he had that pearl-handled gun he used to lay out on his desk to impress his obstreperous underlings, as he had me, but people didn't shoot *him.* But maybe they did, he must have been thinking. I used to remark that if you wanted anything out of Harry you really would have to shoot him. It never occurred to me that one day I would.

He sprawled in the tawdry cheap motel chair, hairpiece even more askew from having sat down too hard, with the look on his face. In his last second on earth, he was real and human, at least to the extent of a cliché in an old B western or detective movie. I almost felt compelled to act my part and kill him. The shot I might place in his forehead would wipe out that look (both knowing and astonished) forever, who wouldn't be writing no more bad checks and cheating his workmen, not any more.

I felt a little sadness for old Harry, as he was a child of God too, like the rest of us, all the cowboys and Indians. He *had* given me my start in California, come to think of it, such as it had been. Before I could drop the gun, he incredibly croaked, "Okay, okay, how much am I supposed to owe you?"

"Thirteen hundred. Cash. I know you have the cash on you." He was famous for carrying lots of cash which he liked to flash in front of his starved help. When he was out car hunting he was always loaded, ready to make a killing. Nothing like waving the cash in front of the nose of some desperate soul. He'd been out scouting up cars from nice middle-class people who were in a jam, playing the genteel fellow all the way, beating them every time. I'd caught him on the rebound from easy work. Thirteen hundred. He paid.

To my surprise the money didn't improve my mood but whetted my rage against him all the more. I was beside myself with the conviction that it was much more than the money. One bad memory after another concerning Harry burned through me. I was no longer driving, and my car was invisible. And so was I. I'm invisible too, like my car. So are my fingerprints, as well as my fingers, trigger finger in particular. I might as well kill him, I thought righteously, since I could get away with it, and he deserved it. I could have gone to the dealership, got their customer list, and sent out a newsletter on the end of Harry that would have been highly popular. I just decided to shoot him, since I wanted to, he was Harmless Harry, and I was invisible. I slowly raised the gun, took aim—and squeezed the trigger.

I put a finish to Harry in that motel room, even if he had sold Christmas trees in his youth and been human to that extent. Even though I had no idea where such an act would lead me, I pulled the trigger calmly, if vengefully. In the Westerns, the hero having obliterated the blight on the land at some personal risk blows the smoke from the muzzle of his gun, reholsters it, and heads into the frontier where the process of reinventing his life will be rewarding. So I hoped, too. Harry's mystified or knowing look was blasted off his face all right. His hairpiece had bounced down over his nose absorbing some of the blood. The blast had been very loud in the confined space of the motel room. Even though invisible I could make a lot of noise.

From out of nowhere fluttered a cloud of tiny colorful birds with big emerald eyes, blocking off my line of sight. They swirled around my head like an ethereal symphony I was on the verge of hearing even with the reverberating report of the gun. No larger than bumblebees, the birds' little round bodies and short wings were iridescent, giving off many happy hues. They had rather large yellow talons, for such tiny birds, and there were swarms of them, several descending upon and seizing the barrel of my gun in their claws. Although I had squeezed off the shot before they swooped down on me from heaven, the first ones just grasped the gun barrel at the last instant and managed to avert it by a half inch at best so the slug blew barely over Harry's head, but nicking his hairpiece and flipping it onto his nose.

Harry whose sight was partially blocked by his hairpiece was feeling over his body with both hands. After a pregnant moment of discovery, he exclaimed, "You missed!"

More and more tiny birds managed to take hold of the gun and pry it right out of my hand before I could get off another shot, and all of a sudden I lost all desire to shoot Harry anyway, who sat there holding himself and shaking violently. An infinite pity sprang in my heart, centering on poor old Harry and expanding forever and ever. The birds flocked here and there in a golden cloud filling the room, and soared away taking my gun with them.

Where would killing Harry have landed me? I was shaking as much as Harry. Everything had flown from my hand and I thanked God. Harry was collapsed in relief in the chair unable to move. On my way out of the motel room I picked up the Gideon Bible the way a drowning man grabs for a rope. I scooped the Book out of its drawer, where it had always lain, probably since it had been put there. The pages were so crisp and seemingly unturned. Perhaps I was the first to take it up in eager hands. Hard to believe, considering what life is like for many people, but nobody consults the ancient texts any more or can understand them, especially those who could most be helped by them. Now the Book just floats along through thin air with me, as it has done for thousands of years, with every sort of person.

Invisible Car Dealer

How is it after a career of crime, I find peace (the prosperity part at least more understandable as flowing from wickedness)? Nobody left out, it seems, not even the invisible car dealer. The Bible, as you recall, has some memorable things to say about invisibility. I have had the time to find them out and mull them over. The "eternal things that are not seen," the "evidence of things not seen"—these have come to my attention, as there is little to distract me from them anymore. *Something* had sent those tiny golden birds to tilt my gun barrel a bare half an inch up at the last moment, and save my soul.

Julie's face came before me as I headed out the motel room door into the invisible night. I glimpsed the sorrow in her eyes when she learned I had tried to shoot Harry (who had been at her party!), thereby becoming a real as well as an accidental murderer, and her consolation when she realized that the golden birds had prevented me from doing it, and it was only attempted murder.

But I don't think so. Julie must be no more than a figment of my imagination by now, and so am I myself. All in all it brings a sense of relief.

www.ingramcontent.com/pod-product-compliance
Lightning Source LLC
Chambersburg PA
CBHW050019180626
46810CB00002B/482